QUANDO

DORMO

(WHEN I SLEEP)

A NOVEL

By
EDWARD IZZI

Quando Dormo (When I Sleep)

ISBN 978-0-578-23101-3

AUTHOR'S DISCLAIMER

"Quando Dormo (When I Sleep)," is a complete work of fiction. All names, characters, businesses, places, events, references, and incidents are either the products of the author's imagination or are used in a fictitious manner to tell the story. Any references to real-life characters or events are used purely as a fictitious means of reciting a narrative, for enjoyment purposes only.

The author makes no claims of any real-life inferences or actual events other than to recite a fabricated story with a fictitious plot. Any resemblance to real persons, living or dead, or actual events is purely coincidental or used for entertainment purposes.

ABOUT THE AUTHOR

Edward Izzi is a native of Detroit, Michigan, and is a Certified Public Accountant with a successful accounting firm in suburban Chicago, Illinois. He is the father of four grown children and one all-too-grown-up granddaughter, Brianna.

He has written many poems and stories over the years, including the following fiction thrillers:

Of Bread & Wine

A Rose from The Executioner

Demons of Divine Wrath

Quando Dormo (When I Sleep)

El Camino Drive

His novels and writings are available at www.edwardizzi.com.

He currently lives in Chicago, Illinois. And like the main character of this book, he has sleep issues and battles nocturnal demons every evening.

For a beautiful man...
Amatore "Mike" DiNatale
Best friends don't come any better than this...

Quando i mostri vengono a giocare,
Quando gli occhi non possono mai chiudersi,
Possiate che gli angeli uccidono i demoni,
E mi abbracciano...**quando dormo.**

When the monsters come to play,
When one's eyes can never close,
May the angels slay the demons,
And embrace me...**when I sleep.**

Italian Proverb.

PREFACE

A Nightmare

I was sitting in a dark room, totally disoriented as if the black darkened space was rotating and turning around and around. There were loud, abrupt noises coming from each corner of the room, as if they were sounds of distress, seeping from the cracks in the walls. I got up to go towards the disturbing echoes for help, as those distressful sounds continued to get louder and louder. There was a glowing light coming from underneath the crack of the door, flickering, looking as though the adjacent room was on fire.

The intense heat was radiating from the steel door as I placed my hand over the hot doorknob. It took all my power to push that jammed entrance door open, as I was carefully trying not to burn my hands. It felt as though an intense fire was swelling from the next room, as the gray paint from the steel door began to peel. Loud noises, like screams and cries for help, became louder and louder as I walked around that open room, looking for where all the shrieking sounds were coming from. I took off my shirt as the heat in the room became intensely hot and almost unbearable. Sweat was pouring from my forehead and eyebrows, as I was having difficulty seeing around the darkened room.

The noise and the cries for help kept getting louder and louder as the screaming became more prevalent. The shrilling noises were sounding more and more like the sounds of distressed babies. I kept walking around that room as the intensity of the heat kept getting hotter and hotter. There was another door at the most distant side of the room, and now I could see that the entire building was on fire. More and more cries for help, with the distinct noises of babies crying. Not one baby, but many babies, moaning louder and louder.

When I opened the door, the flames from the fire seemed to engulf me, and I tried to avoid getting burned from the sudden combustions of intense heat and light. Looking at the other side of the room, there was a massive flame distended in the center. Men and women, dressed as doctors and nurses, were holding babies, as they were newborns, wrapped in blankets, and crying in distress.

Suddenly, I could see one of the doctors throwing the baby he was holding into the fire while the other babies continued to scream and cry louder and louder. I tried to stop the doctor from throwing that infant into the burning inferno, but he continued to laugh as more infants kept getting thrown into the fiery flames. I began to wrestle with the man dressed as a doctor, trying to pull the infant away from him. I kept hitting the doctor in the face with my right hand, trying to get him to hand me the baby he was holding. I was desperately trying to get him to give me that baby, trying to rescue it from being thrown into the blazing inferno. The man didn't flinch. It was as if he couldn't feel the pain from any of the punches I was directing at his face. He continued to wrestle the baby away, flinging it into the burning fire in the center of the room. There were suddenly more doctors, holding more crying infants in their hands. More and more babies kept getting thrown into the fire, and I kept desperately trying to stop them, urgently trying to save their lives.

I then tried to put out the fire, grabbing a blanket sitting on a nearby chair. But the fire kept getting more prominent and more extensive, as more and more babies were disappearing into the growing, hot flames. Suddenly, my clothes started to catch on fire, as I couldn't stop the children from being murdered and thrown into the blazing inferno.

I started screaming as the flames began burning the skin off my hands and arms, while the intense cries of babies became deafening. All that I could see and hear were the engulfing flames and roar of the fire. I kept screaming as loudly as I could.

The babies are burning.

CHAPTER ONE

A Bad Dream

"David? David?"

I felt someone shaking me hard.

"*THE BABIES ARE BURNING!*" I continued to scream.

"What? David! Wake up!" a familiar female voice was getting louder and louder, as I could feel someone trying feverishly to bring me back to consciousness.

I was awakened by my girlfriend, Rosa, and the dampness of a very wet pillow.

"David, are you alright?" she asked, rubbing her hand across my wet forehead.

I immediately sat up in bed, sweat pouring from my face and chest. I felt both of my hands as if a burning hot sensation instigated an incredible amount of pain. There was a burning feeling coming from each side as if they were on fire. I immediately got up and went into the bathroom, turning on the light. I quickly turned on the water faucet, letting the cold-water rush across both of my hands. They felt as though I had been burned, as a painful sensation was coming from them. As I shut off the water, I looked at my fingers.

There were welt marks on my hands and fingers as if I had burned them in my sleep.

"David? You were yelling and screaming. Are you okay?" Rosa kept calling my name.

"Yes," I slowly answered, wrapping a towel around both of my hands, trying to subside the burning sensation.

"Are you alright? This is the second night you've had these nightmares. You were screaming in your sleep."

"I'm sorry," I apologized, looking over at the clock, glowing its red light from my nightstand. It was only 3:37 am.

"Go back to sleep, honey," as I smiled and kissed her on her forehead. I knew Rosa had to get up early to be at the hospital.

I quickly walked into the kitchen, with my hands still covered with the towel, and I managed to put them under the ice dispenser on the refrigerator door. Several ice cubes brought immediate relief to both of my hands, and I continued to cradle the freezing cubes of ice.

Still holding the towel in my hands wrapped with ice, I walked over toward the balcony window. It was a warm summer evening in June, as I managed to open the sliding door and stepped onto the veranda, still holding the towel in my hands. I stood over the railing of the balcony, staring at the Lakeshore Drive traffic bustling twenty floors below.

My luxury condominium on North Lakeshore Drive Avenue faced the open, dark vastness of Lake Michigan, and there were only a few flickering lights from the DuSable Harbor. The blackened sky served as a darkened backdrop for the bright illumination of all the stars dancing across the heavens. The star constellations up above were terrific, as I was quickly able to pick out the Big Dipper from the rest of the shining stars in the sky. I momentarily found a peaceful solace in staring out towards the Great Lake that early morning hour, as if to bring me peace from the violent nightmare that I had just experienced.

I had a nasty sleeping disorder, and it was getting worse. I've had trouble sleeping most of my life, but my nocturnal rest issues were now becoming uncontrollable. I was having a difficult time sleeping, and it was getting to the point where I needed professional help.

As an obstetrician at Chicago-Western Medical Center, my days were usually long and intense, generally starting at six in the morning and lasting well after seven or eight in the evening. I needed to be well-rested. I needed to get every bit of my sleep to get through my daily, stressful schedule. I had taken sleeping pills and other over the counter drugs to help my sleeping condition in the past, but to no avail. I was indeed having trouble falling asleep, and when I was sleeping, I had these intense, disturbing nightmares.

It was too early to get up, knowing that I had to be at the hospital to do patient rounds at six o'clock in the morning. But I was afraid to go back to sleep. I was just freaking out. I couldn't understand how my nightmares of babies screaming and hot burning fire had caused burning welts to appear on both of my hands and fingers.

The babies are burning. I continued to say it to myself over and over.

I couldn't forget that phrase that had shaken me to my core and awakened me from that dreadful nightmare.

It was so bizarre. I continued to look down below on Lakeshore Drive while still holding the ice cubes in my hands. I then suddenly heard the faint sounds of sirens and the honking of loud horns. I noticed several fire trucks and ambulances with their red lights and sirens, near the corner of Lakeshore and Randolph Streets, at one of the adjacent structures down below.

One of the buildings was on fire.

CHAPTER TWO
Chicago Fire House Engine No. One

The firehouse on 419 South Wells Street was somewhat quiet on that hot summer evening, as the firefighters of Chicago Fire Department Engine No. 1 were fast asleep that warm summer night. The air conditioning was on low, and the firehouse's ventilation was rather stuffy, as the kitchen odors of refried beans, tamales, and pork fajitas were still lingering in the air. Two of the firemen were still awake, laying on separate couches watching the 'Late Night Show with Jimmy Fallon,' as they couldn't seem to get comfortable enough within the dense summer air to sleep on their cots.

Battalion Chief Commander Terrance Janko was asleep on his cot that evening and was ultimately out. In the middle of his seventy-two-hour shift, he looked forward to going back to his bungalow in Portage Park. It had been a stressful few days, with fire drills, auto accidents, and various paramedic calls in and around the Chicago Loop, the area district for their firehouse. There had been a multi-car accident on the Kennedy Expressway earlier that day, with several burn injuries, which had to be rushed to the trauma and burn centers at Chicago-Western Medical Center.

Janko was a handsome, stocky Chicago firefighter whose large and muscular six-foot frame was almost intimidating at first glance. But his warm, extroverted personality and ease in disarming his fellow firefighters made him a popular choice when he was selected to head up Chicago's Engine No. 1 over a year ago. He was a twenty-year veteran of the Chicago Fire Department. Although he was very popular, Terrance's management style had a hard nose, no-nonsense philosophy when dealing with his firefighters. He sometimes found it necessary to run his firehouse with an iron fist. Although he knew all of his firemen and paramedics very well, he always tried to stay above his subordinate's drama and problems.

Terry was married to his wife, Gina, for almost fifteen years, and they were raising two small boys at home. Although he enjoyed being with his family, his job as a Battalion Chief Commander was extremely time consuming and forced him to spend extended periods away from his family. There were always personnel and management issues to deal with that expended a tremendous amount of his time and mental energy.

On that evening, Chief Janko was suffering from one of his intense migraine headaches. There was a growing rift between his captain, Stuart Durham, and several of his lieutenants regarding some equipment maintenance policies within the firehouse that the Chief was trying to understand. The Chief hoped that getting some immediate rest would alleviate his migraine, and some of the stress he was feeling was from all the firehouse drama that was going around within his staff.

At exactly 3:37 am, the fire alarm sounded, and the blaring intercom noise went on, indicating a three-alarm fire at 400 East Randolph Street. All the firemen jumped out of their cots and threw on their firefighting gear, with the two fire trucks and two paramedic ambulances proceeding to the fire's location. Within a few minutes, the firemen that arrived at the scene were able to assess the situation.

The Affiliated Center for Women's Health and Family Planning on the Randolph Street location's bottom floor was intensely burning. Fierce flames of fire and broken glass had become an intense blazing inferno. Commander Janko became extremely concerned when he arrived at the scene. He was aware that the small medical out-patient center had a twelve-bed capacity that allowed many patients to spend the night resting and recuperating from their gynecological procedures rather than being sent over to the hospital. It was operated by a small group of doctors and nursing staff, and several of them worked the night shift or were on call for any medical problems that may arise.

The Battalion Chief's first concern was that there were no people inside. That fear became a reality when two of his firefighters broke into the blazing inferno.

"Go in there and assess the situation," he instructed two of his men.

Upon entering the building, there were screaming sounds of trapped people inside. Two of them were patients and disoriented from all the smoke inhalation. They were having trouble finding the emergency exit door.

Captain Stuart Durham, who was second in command at Engine No. 1, radioed for additional men to assist him and the other firefighters in carrying out two of the patients safely out of the burning structure.

"Is there anyone else in there?" he asked one of the young women who were still conscious enough to respond.

"There are a doctor and two or three nurses still inside," the young patient replied.

At that moment, Commander Janko instructed two more men, Firemen Jim Sweenor and Mike Palazzola, to go back inside to find more survivors. The outpatient medical facility layout indicated that the doctors and nursing staff-maintained offices in the building's very rear. The back portion of the office was completely ablaze.

"Go back in there! We need to know that everyone is out!" Janko fearfully declared, as the other firefighters were hooked up to the fire hydrants and began shooting water on the blazing fire. Other firefighters went around the structure and tried to enter the facility from the rear entrance but to no avail. The fire had spread throughout the medical facility, as the liquid oxygen tanks had previously exploded and were feeding the blaze.

It became apparent that one medical doctor and two nurses were still inside the burning building, and unfortunately, unable to escape. After three hours of dousing the fiery inferno with intense streams of water, three severely burned bodies were recovered from the scene. They were barely alive when the firefighters could recover them and remove them from the blazing fire. They were quickly loaded into the 'bus' and transported to nearby Northwestern Memorial Hospital. Within an hour of their arrival, the victims had died from their third-degree burn injuries.

It became clear later how that fire had erupted. The liquid oxygen tanks had somehow ignited in the rear of the building, which caused an intense explosion and light inside. The family planning facility victims didn't have a chance, as the fierce flames had surrounded them. Smoke inhalation made it impossible for them to escape the burning structure as there was no doubt that, due to the heightened security involved in keeping those liquid oxygen tanks segregated from the rest of the clinic, this tragic fire had been caused by arson. There was evidence upon inspection that the oxygen room had been broken into and compromised, causing the liquid element to ignite and explode upon contact with the accelerant.

Commander Janko continued to supervise the extinguishment of the building's intense inferno on East Randolph Street. Soon, several Chicago P.D. squad cars from District Sixteen had arrived, along with the news trucks from Channel Eight and Channel Three, which were parked nearby.

"What do you think?" Detective Tommy Morton from the Chicago Police Department Sixteenth District asked the Battalion Commander.

"I just can't figure out how the hell those liquid oxygen tanks ignited. They were safeguarded and well protected in that fireproof room in the back of that office. They shouldn't have exploded and caused this kind of fire damage," Janko tried to explain.

"Think this could be arson? Who would want to start a fire here?" Morton ignorantly asked.

"Are you kidding," the Commander looked at Detective Morton, shaking his head.

"Somebody has it out for abortion clinics," the Battalion Chief speculated.

The three victims of the clinic fire were Alyssa Coleman, 29 years old, an African American nurse at the facility; Theresa Biela, 48 years old, a white Caucasian who was a nursing supervisor; and Dr. Mikhail Petrovitch, a white Caucasian, 39- years-old, who was the obstetrician on staff and who was on call that evening. All three medical staff members were required to spend the evening there and take care of the two patients who had late-term abortions performed the day before.

As the morning progressed and additional arson investigators arrived at the scene, it had become evident that the liquid oxygen tanks exploded in a location where they weren't supposed to be. This led to the theory that someone had purposely started the fire by moving the liquid oxygen tanks and igniting them where they would cause the most damage. Their subsequent explosion and their specific location accentuated the blazing inferno, and the three clinical medical staff members didn't have any chance of escaping.

Based on how the fire had started, it was a miracle that the two patients had escaped with only very minor injuries and smoke inhalation. This was because the patient beds were located in the front of the building, while the intentional explosion occurred in the rear of the clinic where the medical staff was stationed.

News reporters from Channel Eight and Channel Three were there interviewing Chief Janko, while the Chicago P.D. detectives were busy taking pictures and assessing the damage. Randolph and Lakeshore Drives' whole intersection was blocked off, as the morning rush hour traffic was diverted off to Washington and Michigan Avenues.

The morning news programs and newspapers were quick to headline the tragedy:

Abortion Clinic Fire Claims Three Victims

It was almost ten o'clock that morning when Commander Janko finally arrived back at the firehouse's office. He had been up since three-thirty that morning, and his exhausted body was still pumping adrenalin. Janko was nervous, anxious, and on edge. He took off his fireman's gear and sat behind his desk, rubbing his temples. He felt one of his famous migraine headaches coming on. The Chief pulled out his right-hand desk drawer to make sure that his trusty bottle of Tylenol was standing at attention and ready to serve.

There was a loud knock on his door.

"Come in," he directed his firehouse captain, Stuart Durham, to sit down at one of his two black leather chairs situated in front of his wooden oak desk.

"How are you feeling, Chief?" Durham asked as he was finally sitting down to enjoy his first cup of coffee.

"I feel a headache coming on," the Commander predicted.

19

"I get it. Nothing like staying up all night trying to put out a three-alarm fire," Durham answered, in between loud slurps of his black coffee.

"What are your thoughts?" the Captain inquired.

Janko looked perplexed, as he was too mentally exhausted at that moment to render an answer.

"We'll have to see what the arson investigators come up with. By all accounts, those liquid oxygen tanks were not where they belong and should have never exploded," the Commander observed.

"Okay, Chief. But how did someone get into that secured area and start that fire? That clinic was personally inspected by our firehouse three months ago. The only way those tanks would have become an accelerant in that blaze is if someone willfully unlocked those tanks and started that fire themselves."

They both looked at each other.

"Are you saying that the fire was started purposely by someone there at the clinic?"

"Well, that's how it looks. There was no forced entry that I could see. But there was a tremendous amount of damage at the rear of the clinic so that one couldn't say for sure," Durham observed, continuing to enjoy his coffee loudly.

"Well, let's see what the investigators say. I just feel so bad about those victims," the Chief verbalized. He had been informed by radio on his way back to the firehouse that the three fire victims had died from their injuries.

"Well...keep me posted, Chief," as Durham got up from his chair and started to make his way back to the firehouse kitchen. Captain Durham made no secret for his penchant for strong, black coffee and openly assaulted the Bunn coffee maker regularly.

Commander Janko looked out of his office's sectioned window, observing South Wells Street's morning traffic. He continued to think about that clinic fire and how out of place such a tragic accident could have occurred near the Gold Coast section of Lakeshore Drive. He only shook his head in silence and said few quick prayers to himself. He prayed for the three burn victims of that fire that tragically died that morning.

He prayed for their families and hoped that they would eventually heal from such a tragic fire occurring in that clinic on Randolph Street.

But most of all, he prayed that it wasn't arson.

CHAPTER THREE
Detective Romanowski

The Chicago Police Station District Eighteen was rather busy that Tuesday morning, as Detective Dennis Romanowski was preoccupied with shuffling papers and finishing some police reports from the previous day. It had been a hectic few days, and he was waist-deep with homicides and drug busts that he was investigating. It was only the middle of June, and he had twenty-two unsolved homicides and two dozen drug busts to investigate and file reports. The violent incidents within his district continued to keep coming.

Welcome to summer in Chicago, he thought to himself. All the gangbangers, drug-dealers, and wise-guy wanna-bees were all out of hibernation and on the streets in full force that early summer. The detective continued to shake his head. It was only 10:30 in the morning, and he already felt his migraine headache coming on. As he was about to get up and walk over to the cafeteria to refill his cup of black coffee, his desk phone loudly rang.

"Detective Romanowski," he eagerly answered.

"Morning, Denny," the familiar voice on the other end of the line brought a smile onto the detective's face.

"Terry...what's the good word?"

The voice of Battalion Chief Commander Terrance Janko from the Chicago Firehouse Engine No. One was a familiar one. The police detective and the firehouse battalion chief commander were life-long best friends, with a friendship that went way back to the third grade at St. Veronica's Catholic School in Logan Square. The two, forty-one-year-old men had both joined their respective Chicago departments back in 1995, and both had the pleasure of serving the City of Chicago faithfully within their respective districts.

22

They had worked together on several criminal arson cases in the past. Because of their shared childhood and similar backgrounds, they had more than enough in common to continue their close, personal friendship.

Denny Romanowski and Terry Janko spent almost every Friday evening doing shots at Diamond Lil's Bar and Grill on North Milwaukee Avenue in Wicker Park. Besides growing up on Kimball and Armitage Avenues and graduating from St. Patrick's High School on Belmont Avenue, they were both the first-generation offspring of Polish immigrants.

When they called one another on their desk telephones during the day, it was usually to find out what time the other's shift would be finished to plan to meet at their favorite watering hole. Since knowing each other while in high school, they both had a refined taste for imported vodka, for which the two of them enthusiastically shared at Diamond Lil's every Friday night after their shifts. They were the best men at each other's weddings and baptized each other's firstborn. The only reason why Denny Romanowski decided to go into the police academy instead of being a fireman along with his best friend was that he had an intense, horrible fear of fires.

When Dennis was only six years old, he barely escaped a kitchen fire at his grandmother's house, which took both of his grandparents' lives. The horror of that night as a young boy has always haunted him to this day and has caused him many sleepless nights. Romanowski has often refused to assist any Chicago firehouse on any fire-related crime, making an exception only for his best friend and his firehouse.

"Is it Friday already? Are we drinking tonight?" The detective jokingly asked.

"I wish," the battalion commander answered. "Did you hear about that three-alarm fire at that abortion clinic we had this morning on Randolph Street?"

"I heard," Denny replied. "We sent a few of our squads over there to help out. I heard there were some casualties."

There was a ten-second silence on the phone.

"Terry? Are you there?" the detective asked.

"Yeah...I'm here. Yes...there were some casualties. A doctor and two nurses died in that fire this morning over at Northwestern. I gotta tell ya, Denny...this one has me spooked. Big time. Do you have a few minutes to stop by? I've got some stuff I need to talk about."

The veteran Chicago police detective could tell by the sound of his voice that his fireman pallie was not himself. He sounded a bit off-kilter, which was unusual for his best friend.

"Okay, buddy. I'll be right over."

It took almost twenty minutes for Detective Romanowski to travel through the late morning traffic from his North Larrabee police district to South Wells Street's firehouse. As he pulled up in front of the firehouse, Captain Stuart Durham welcomed him to the station.

"What's up, Denny?" Captain Durham knew the District Eighteen detective very well, as he was a frequent guest of their Friday night taste-testing activities.

"Where's your boss?" Denny jokingly asked.

"In his office, overdosing on Tylenol."

"Thanks."

The Chicago police detective was very familiar with Engine No. One Firehouse. He made his way to the battalion commander's office, exchanging warm greetings with several firefighters along the way.

The two best friends locked eyes as Romanowski entered his office.

"Hey," he only said, as he hugged his best friend.

Battalion Commander Janko initially didn't say a word, as the Eighteenth District detective made himself comfortable in one of the two comfortable leather chairs placed in front of the firehouse chief's desk.

"So...are we starting early today?" Denny eagerly asked.

'Chief Terry', still silent, pulled out two ceramic coffee cups from his credenza drawer, along with a bottle of Stolichnaya Vodka that the fire chief kept hidden in his private stash. This forbidden, concealed bottle was only for special guests. As Terry poured the two fingers of vodka into each coffee cup, Denny noticed his right-hand shaking.

"Wow," Denny observed. "This fire has you spooked."

The two men locked eyes again, and Denny could read his best friend's mind. Having known each other for over thirty-five years allowed them the luxury of having x-ray vision. The two understood each other's silent thoughts, and the detective didn't like the vibes he was getting.

"Cheers," Denny said before consuming the contents of his ceramic coffee cup.

"Salute," Terry replied, using only one of the few Italian words he knew.

The two of them sat there silently for several moments, as the two servants of the City of Chicago were breaking Code of Ethics Rule No. 17: Drinking alcoholic beverages while on duty or in uniform is strictly forbidden.

Terry finished his coffee cup's contents, knowing that the two Tylenol aspirin he had taken earlier would mix well with his late morning beverage.

"So, what's up, babe?" Denny eagerly asked.

"This clinic fire was an act of arson, Denny. I'll bet my paycheck on it," Chief Terry slowly said, expressing his morning fears.

"How so?" The Chicago P.D. detective was pretending to be ignorant.

"Those liquid oxygen tanks are required to be locked up and in a separate, insulated chamber in the back of that clinic. We inspected that clinic three months ago, and those tanks and their storage method passed our inspection. Those liquid oxygen tanks had exploded and were unlocked, far away from their chamber of storage," Chief Terry explained.

"Somebody had to know about those secured liquid oxygen tanks, and somebody had to unlock those tanks and to start that fire. I doubt that the victims or the patients in that clinic would have purposely ignited those liquid oxygen tanks."

The battalion commander was looking outside of his glass-windowed office, making sure no one else was observing their conversation.

"And this is telling you what? That an arsonist is out there, breaking in and unlocking liquid oxygen tanks in clinics, which by the way are especially locked and keyed, and then randomly setting them on fire?" Detective Romanowski was questioning his best friend's logic.

"How do you know this wasn't an accident? How do you know one of the nurses had taken out those tanks for a specific medical procedure and somehow ignited the fire? You don't know that this was an act of arson for sure," the detective answered, mentally wishing his best friend would pour him another shot of Stolichnaya Vodka.

"That's highly unusual, Denny. Most medical clinics are very careful in handling those liquid oxygen tanks, and that clinic on Randolph Street was no different. And besides, what procedure would they need to perform at three-thirty in the morning?"

The detective and the commander looked at each other, perplexed that this early morning fire on Randolph Street clinic was anything other than an act of arson.

"What are the arson investigators saying?" Denny asked.

"Nothing yet. They were just arriving as we were putting out that fire this morning."

"Well, it's too early to draw any conclusions right now. We can't assume anything until the arson investigators can make certain of the definite cause of this fire."

Chief Terry continued to shake his head.

"This was an abortion clinic, Denny."

"So?"

"You're not getting it, Dennis. This was a high-volume abortion clinic. I read some news articles on social media a few months ago about New York City. Several acts of arson on abortion clinics have been taking place...clinics are doing partial-birth and full-term abortions. They passed the same abortion law in Albany as they passed in Springfield, allowing for the same kinds of abortions," the firehouse commander explained.

Detective Romanowski sat there, shaking his head.

"And you're thinking some pro-life, fanatical whack-job is out there, lighting up abortion clinics?"

Chief Janko silently looked at his best friend, knowing that the detective didn't want to believe his theory.

"Just because that happened in New York doesn't mean it's going to happen here."

"I wouldn't take that bet, Dennis. I'm telling you, this clinic fire was anything but an accident."

Detective Romanowski quietly smiled, figuring that his pallies hypothesis was, for the most part, only a presumption and incredibly flawed.

"Terry, let's wait for the arson investigators to do their job. For now, you need to get some rest. I can tell you've been up most of the night," the detective observed, noticing the battalion commander's deep blue eyes were very red and blood-shot.

The detective slowly rose from the commander's comfortable, black leather chair and gave his best friend a departing hug.

"Let me know if you're up for drinks at Lil's later," Denny suggested, knowing that the chances of Terry's wife, Gina granting him a hall pass to go out for drinks after his seventy-two-hour shift that evening were very low.

"Don't hold your breath," Terry said, smiling. "Thanks for coming over."

"Thanks for not dragging me over to that fire scene," the detective appreciatively remarked. "I thought for sure you were going to drag me over to that burnt-down clinic."

The firehouse commander knew of his best friend's distinctive fears of fires and horrific, morbid fire scenes. As the Chicago Police detective sped off in his Crown Victoria squad car, the fire chief tried to put his worst fears to rest. Maybe he was just too tired to reason about anything at that moment logically. Perhaps he was just overreacting when he realized that those oxygen tanks had exploded at a location within the clinic where they weren't supposed to be, he thought. A cold chill started to go up to his spine. But maybe, just like New York City, there was an abortion clinic arsonist out there.

Deep down in his stomach, Chief Terry Janko feared that this burnt down abortion clinic wouldn't be the last.

CHAPTER FOUR

Chicago-Western Medical Center

I had arrived rather early that morning at five-thirty for my morning rounds at Chicago-Western Medical Center that day. I had difficulty maneuvering my way around the blocked off traffic on Randolph and Lakeshore Drives, and I was thankful that I had left my house early that morning. There were still EMS trucks and Chicago Fire Department Truck Engines blocking Randolph Street. I couldn't tell what exactly was going on or which building was on fire. I could see several Chicago P.D squad cars double-parked on Randolph and Michigan Avenues, with news crews from all the local television stations parked nearby.

Although the burning sensation had subsided quite a bit since keeping them wrapped with ice cubes, my hands were still in pain. I continued to hold the plastic bags filled with ice in my hands while trying to maneuver my Mercedes 450 SL in traffic. I was cautiously using my knees and my elbows to steer my vehicle around the heavy traffic carefully. As I arrived at work, I immediately brought my very minor burn injuries to one of the nurses on staff on the hospital's seventh floor.

"What happened to your hands, David?" Nurse Linda Ciccone inquired as she began applying burn ointment onto both of my hands and fingers.

"I burned them on the stove this morning," I lied, knowing that she would never believe the truth.

"What was for breakfast," she kiddingly asked.

"Jimmy Dean...I never thought cooking breakfast sausage would be so hazardous," I joked. I was trying to make up a believable story so that Nurse Linda wouldn't become suspicious.

She only smiled at me while applying more burn ointment and then wrapping my hands up with gauze.

Linda and I were always good friends and often talked, as we both enjoyed our now very present platonic relationship. We made small talk that morning about each other's weekend activities and our personal lives. She knew that I had a steady girlfriend, Rosa, an intensive care nurse, whom I've been dating a little less than a year.

Linda was an attractive, shapely brunette in her middle forties who was already on her third marriage. I had been married twice before, so we had our horrific divorce experiences and legal bills that we mutually shared. We were also Italian. We often enjoyed our light-hearted but heated discussions about whether tomato sauce is called 'sauce' or 'gravy,' as she insisted on always calling it the latter.

Linda and I had some history. In between her marriages, we had an intense relationship a few years ago. I was just getting out of my second marriage while she was aggressively searching for a third husband.

One night, we went to a play at the Cadillac Theater to see "Dirty Dancing," after an Italian dinner at Il Porcino and late-night drinks after the performance at Redhead's Piano Bar. She ended up spending the night at my house afterward, and I have to say, the sex was incredible. We ended up going together for several months, and we enjoyed a great relationship. But soon I discovered that she wanted a wedding ring on her finger. The thought of my ringing her third set of wedding bells scared the living shit out of me, and I desperately tried to let her down gently.

She didn't talk to me for several months until I approached her in the cafeteria one day, and we had a long talk. I heard that she had found a new candidate to marry her and be her third spouse. I congratulated her on her new marriage, and we put our differences behind us. We've become good friends since.

"It's too bad about that abortion clinic fire," she casually mentioned, as the blaring television sets from the nearby waiting room was announcing the tragic news.

I looked at her for a second, initially not understanding what she was referring to. Then I began listening to the full news reports while she finished wrapping up and taping my hands. I suddenly realized that the intense fire on Randolph Street was coming from the Affiliated Family Planning Clinic located there. I tried to listen to the news reports' details, only understanding that the fiery inferno produced severe casualties. That burning family clinic was within a block of my home, and I wondered if my intense 'burning inferno' nightmare had something to do with that vigorous, tragic fire.

"You're not performing any deliveries today, I hope," she mentioned as she finished treating my very minor burn injuries.

"Not today. That's why we have you, nurses," I proudly laughed, trying very hard to finish all of this nominal first aid stuff and get on with my busy day.

"We're always here to help disabled doctors, even the ones that are confused about what to put on their pasta," she smiled, although I could tell there was a small amount of suspicion coming from the corner of her mouth.

I thanked her and walked over to the television in our Obstetrics and Gynecology Department's patient waiting room on the seventh floor. I stood there for several minutes, trying to absorb all the information coming from that early morning newscast.

I suddenly felt a cold chill come down my spine when I heard that all three fire victims had died at Northwestern Hospital from that fire. I soon realized that the clinic on fire that morning was the family planning center or the 'abortion' clinic on Randolph

Street adjacent to my home. I continued to stand there in front of the television while Channel Eight Eyewitness News was broadcasting the details of that fire and their interviews with the Chicago Fire Department. I thought for a moment, looking at my scorched hands, wondering if there was a connection.

I realized that one of the victims who had died, Dr. Mikhail Petrovitch, was an obstetrician that I had personally known for many years.

He was a younger man in his late thirties, a foreign-educated physician from Croatia, who had done very well in the medical field of family planning. I had crossed paths with him several times in medical seminars and symposiums sponsored by Chicago-Western Medical Center over the last several years. Petrovitch made no secret of his pro-choice views and saw the new State of Illinois law passage as a means of increasing business and boosting the bottom line of the various family planning clinics in which he was affiliated. He was very much a pro-choice proponent and performed over 800 abortions a year at that Randolph Street clinic alone.

We had both gotten into several intense discussions over the years and especially had a very heated debate at the last health symposium that we had both attended a few months ago. We had the pleasure of sitting together for lunch at the Trump International Hotel on North Wabash, where our medical seminar and symposium was being held.

Dr. Petrovitch, in my opinion, was a 'blow-hard.' He was a partner in a few family planning clinics in and around the Chicagoland area. He was practically bragging about the number of 'procedures' that he performed every week. He had a staff of several nurses within each family planning clinic that performed the actual procedures, as he supervised each operation. At an average cost of approximately $1,500 a piece, he bragged about the millions of gross sales dollars that each clinic was bringing in on an annual basis and how well they were all financially doing.

Petrovitch's logic on that day was that, as a doctor, 'you're not going to reverse the wave of public opinion and the state laws that supported abortions, so you might as well cash in and profit from them.'

I found his logic and personality very offensive that day, especially after realizing that one of his clinics was within walking distance from my home on Lakeshore Drive.

Due to the recent new passage of the Reproductive Health Act (RHA), repealing the state's Partial-Birth Abortion Ban Act, and the Illinois Abortion Act of 1975, business at his clinic was booming. I knew Dr. Petrovitch did not have the same sleep issues I was having. He had no problem performing the late-term and partial-birth abortion procedures on fully developed, eight or nine-month-old fetuses in that clinic. Pregnant women from all over the country were arriving every day at that clinic on Randolph Street, coming from other states and areas of the country where abortions and especially late-term abortions are banned.

As an obstetrician at Chicago-Western Medical Center, I had verbally made no secret of my personal views regarding the performance of abortions. I had made it very clear to everyone on Chicago-Western Medical Center's Board of Directors and the hospital administration regarding my personal feelings.

I was devoutly pro-life, and I didn't perform abortions. Period.

If a patient came to me and requested an abortion, I would either try to counsel them out of their decision or require the patient to find another doctor. Since being a staff physician at Chicago-Western Medical Center, the hospital administrators and medical staff have tolerated my pro-life views, and so far, haven't pressured me to do otherwise.

That is until this RHA Act was just recently passed in Springfield. Repealing the partial-birth abortion bans and the abortion act now lessens restrictions on abortions later in pregnancy and removes criminal penalties on physicians who perform them. Suddenly, all the public hospitals in Illinois are being pressured to perform late-term abortion procedures due to the increased patient demand from all of those coming in from other states. I was now fearful that I was working in a ruthless, pro-choice environment.

Not because I was a Catholic, as the Lord knows that I was no model Christian. And not because I came from a very religious upbringing, going to parochial schools while growing up. And I was certainly not some 'holy roller,' trying to instill my religious views on others and making them question their basic morals and principles about what was morally right and wrong. Certainly not for any of those stated reasons.

But because an abortion, especially a late-term abortion, in my mind, was just plain wrong. In my personal opinion, abortion was always murder. In today's society, everyone is entitled to their own opinion, especially after the emergence of the current "Me-Too" Movements. To those within the community who are pro-choice, I have always respected their opinions, never trying to judgmentally or forcefully convert them or their viewpoints.

But in my personal opinion, within my conscience, an abortion, especially a full-term one on any baby, was murder. Plain and simple.

Having delivered thousands of newborn babies during my twenty-five-year career as an obstetrics physician at Chicago-Western, the best part of my job was delivering precious infant children. I loved nothing

34

more than to bring in the blessings and joys of a beautiful newborn child into this beautiful world.

I began to walk away from that patient waiting room, trying to tune out the horrific details of that abortion clinic fire. I didn't want to dwell on the details of that fire and how specifically that tragedy could be related to my burnt hands and that terrible nightmare I had experienced the night before.

I began thinking and reinforcing my pro-life views in my head. I had more than my share of discussions with other doctors within the hospital regarding my pro-life beliefs. I was advised many times by other physicians to perhaps, find another medical specialty.

If you like children so much, go into pediatrics, my peers and colleagues often advised me.

But I enjoyed being a 'baby-doctor.' And I was not about to medically terminate anything with a heartbeat. However, I also knew that with the recent passage of this new RHA law, I was fearful that the City of Chicago, with all its nationally renowned public teaching hospitals, was now going to become the abortion capital of the Midwest.

And I didn't like it.

CHAPTER FIVE

Rosa Hudson

The taxicab driver was maneuvering around the city traffic in the Chicago Loop as Rosa Hudson was desperately trying to get to work on time for her seven o'clock shift. She was an intensive care nurse at Chicago-Western Medical Center on Harrison and Ashland Avenues, and the traffic around the intersection was arduous. It was sunny and warm outside, and the morning temperature was already in the 70's that early June morning. Rosa was desperately trying to put her eyeshadow and makeup on, trying to keep her hand steady with the back and forth motions of the jittering taxicab. The taxi windows were all open, and it was a beautiful summer morning, as the rushing, fresh urban air was somberly awakening the hospital nurse.

"Let me out here," she exclaimed to the cab driver, as she handed him a ten-dollar bill and jumped off the Ashland and Jackson Avenue intersection. The nurse decided to run to work in her nursing outfit, and she was glad that she was wearing her Nike running shoes, which she always worked in.

Rosa was furious that morning. She had spent the night at her boyfriend's house the night before, and due to his intermittent sleeping habits, she was not able to get a good night's sleep. Rosa was up part of the evening, then overslept and didn't hear her cell phone alarm go off. The intensive care nurse, unfortunately, was awakened almost an hour late at 6:45 am. She had to throw on her uniform and barely had time to brush her teeth before catching the taxicab downstairs in front of his condominium building on North Lakeshore Drive.

"You're late again, Rosa," her nursing supervisor Laurie Plati said, as she arrived on the eleventh floor of

Chicago-Western Medical Center almost a half-hour late.

"I'm sorry, Laurie. Dr. Fazio had another nightmare again," she complained, as she rested her purse on her workstation and tried to settle in.

The nursing supervisor of the intensive care unit laughed. "Just because you're sleeping with one of the doctors doesn't mean you're exempt from punctuality," the nursing supervisor flatly observed, with her tongue in cheek.

"I'm sorry," Rosa said again. She had a good relationship with her nursing unit supervisor, and she knew that her boss appreciated her incredible nursing skills.

"I think you and that sexy baby doctor of yours are making way too much 'Whoopi,'" Nurse Plati joked, taking a loud slurp of her morning coffee.

"I wish," Rosa said as she walked over to the coffee pot, expecting the dark, black caffeine to work miracles.

Rosa got settled into her workstation and logged onto her computer. She reviewed the floor patients' charts in the intensive care unit that morning, reviewing their medication dispensaries and any special notes from their doctors. Several doctors had already made their morning rounds and asked about her whereabouts, as she oversaw several patients who had a difficult time sleeping, just like she did.

She was almost an hour into her shift when she grasped her cell phone in her spare moments and sent a nasty text to her baby doctor boyfriend:

This shit has got to stop.

There was no response that the whole morning from David, like Rosa's temper continued to boil. It wasn't until 12:30 pm, and she was on her lunch break at the hospital cafeteria downstairs, where she met Dr. Fazio. They had a usual place and time that they usually met at the hospital cafeteria at a table next to a large picture window, facing the open garden outside. When the weather was beautiful, the two met and ate their lunches outdoors, enjoying the fresh air and each other during their brief break time together. On that day, although the weather was perfect, it was not such a day.

Rosa went through the cafeteria line, got her usual chicken Caesar salad and Diet Coke, and saw David sitting at their typical table next to the window.

David stood up and greeted his girlfriend with a kiss on her cheek.

"Hey, honey."

"Thanks for responding to my text message this morning," she sarcastically replied, sitting down at the table and applying her oil and vinegar dressing on her salad.

Rosa was a petite, blue-eyed shapely brunette with a beautiful, model-like figure. At thirty-seven years old and at one hundred fifteen pounds, she looked like a sexy Jennifer Lawrence and prided herself on being able to still fit into her size five blue-jeans. She ran on the lakefront at five o'clock almost every morning, doing her usual five-mile route. The nurse lived in a small townhouse on West Dakin Street in the Irving Park neighborhood and was always able to safely work on time. Her workplace attendance problems began when she spent the night at her boyfriend's Lake Shore Drive condominium.

David looked bewildered and had no idea what she was talking about.

"I'm sorry, honey. I've had three deliveries this morning, including a C-section, and I've barely had time to go to the bathroom, let alone answer my texts," he patiently explained.

Rosa look perturbed as she sat down and began eating her lunch, while David sat there, finishing his grilled chicken sandwich. They both knew what all of this was about. They both knew that his abnormal sleep patterns and intense, violent nightmares were beginning to toll on their relationship. The two of them had been dating for over eleven months and hadn't encountered any real problems in their amicable relationship until she started spending nights at his condo.

Their romantic bond had come to the point where they could only spend the nights together when Rosa was not required to go to work the next morning. She had only spent the night at David's home the night before because they had a late-night dinner at Dei Primavera, a quaint Italian restaurant on North State Street. Rosa had way too much to drink to go home from David's house after dinner.

In all honesty, the late-night sex with David was always phenomenal. But his sleepless nights and his recurrent traumatic nightmares were beginning to take a physical toll on her.

They both ate their lunches in silence for several long minutes until Rosa began to speak:

"David, when are you going to get some help? You can't keep living like this. You're an insomniac who can barely sleep, and when you do sleep, you have these terrible, traumatic nightmares."

David only quietly sat there, nodding his head. He had heard this many times before.

"I know," he only said.

"You say 'I know,' but nothing changes. You've promised me before that you would seek some help. David, honey…you need your sleep."

David sat there, finishing his sandwich when he began to wipe his hands with his napkin. At that point, Rosa noticed the burn welts on his hands.

"David, what happened to your hands?" as she asked to see them.

"Oh, it's nothing, Rosa. I must have touched the stove in the middle of the night."

"Really?" Rosa looked doubtful, suspicious, and concerned, all at the same time. She grasped his hands and continued to hold them, caressing them and observing the significant burn marks on his hands.

"How were you able to work today?" she asked.

"That was easy. I was barking out orders to the nurses all day," he laughed. "But seriously, my hands don't hurt anymore. Nurse Linda applied some burn ointment and some aloe vera on them this morning," he tried to lie, wanting desperately to change the subject.

Rosa looked at him while still caressing his hands.

"I was late to work again this morning, thanks to you. It's a good thing that I have an understanding supervisor who knows what a psycho insomniac you are," she started to joke.

"She almost always knows that when I'm late in the morning, it's because I've spent the night at your house the night before," Rosa explained.

David smiled and nodded his head. He started to become very lethargic and began wishing he could get up and get a triple-shot of espresso from the Starbucks coffee bar in the hospital's reception area. He was starting to feel very tired and wished he could put his legs up somewhere and take a ten-minute 'power nap.'

This was David Fazio's usual routine. Every time he had a rough, sleepless, nightmare-ridden evening, he usually had to go into his office at mid-day. He would often lock his door, close the lights, shut off his desk and cell phones. He would then begin to take a 'power nap,' which usually consisted of ten minutes of solid, uninterrupted rest. His eyes were starting to feel very tired, and at that moment, he could barely keep them open.

Rosa was still caressing his hands, periodically kissing them while she watched David struggle to keep his eyes open.

"You're getting sleepy now, aren't you? You can barely keep your eyes open," Rosa observed.

"Yes," David replied.

"Do you have time to go to your office and take a quick nap?"

"I wish I could. I have another patient scheduled at one-thirty. I won't be finished until 7:00 pm," the exhausted, sleep-deprived doctor said.

At that moment, they both decided to finish their lunch hour and walk over to the Starbucks coffee kiosk located in the reception area of the hospital. They both ordered strong double espressos, with Dr. Fazio pulling out a twenty-dollar bill. They then sat down together at a nearby leather couch located within the Chicago-Western Medical Center's massive reception area.

"David?" Rosa lovingly suggested, "Let me find you a sleep doctor. I have a few names you can call here at the hospital."

"I have a recommendation that Dr. Worrell gave me a few weeks ago. I will make an appointment, baby, I promise," David lied.

Dr. Calvin Worrell was the head of the obstetrics department of Chicago-Western Medical Center, and David had a good working relationship with his department Chief of Staff. He had asked him several times to recommend a medical colleague who focused and specialized in severe sleep disorders. But unfortunately, Dr. Worrell had still not gotten back to him.

They both sat there, finishing their espressos and discussing their upcoming weekend plans. David was waiting for the miraculous effects of the double espresso to kick in so that he could go on with his day. As they both stood up to say good-bye and return to their jobs, Rosa kissed him. It was a long, sensual wet kiss, as nearby strangers began to take notice of the couple, romantically making out in the middle of the hospital's reception area.

"Should we get a room?" David joked.

"I'm sure we can find an open patient room somewhere," Rosa kiddingly responded.

She gave him several long, wet kisses before pushing away from his strong embrace and returning to her job on the eleventh floor.

"Call me later," she instructed David as they both said good-bye. Rosa then quickly walked towards the elevator.

Dr. Fazio looked at his watch while consuming the last drop of his Starbucks espresso. He still had twenty minutes before having to return to the obstetrics floor of the hospital. David then sat back down on the leather couch in the reception area and closed his eyes, trying to recuperate some of the sleep he had lost the night before.

As he began to rest, he thought about the neighborhood abortion clinic that had burned down on Randolph Street earlier that morning. He reflected on Dr. Mikhail Petrovitch and the unfortunate casualties of that intense fire. As much as he disliked Dr. Petrovitch and the numerous abortions he performed at that clinic, he certainly didn't deserve to die. He was desperately trying to relax his mind, attempting to put all of that out of his head. David then remembered that gory, violent phrase from the nightmare he had experienced the night before, that vehement mantra that had kept him up most of the evening.

The babies are burning, he repeated to himself again and again, as he finally...closed his eyes.

CHAPTER SIX
Meeting with Dr. Worrell

"Dr. Fazio? Dr. Fazio?"

"Huh? What?"

I was abruptly awakened by a very young, beautiful receptionist from the main floor of Chicago-Western Medical Center's reception area. I had utterly dozed off on the couch, and nurses from the hospital's obstetrics floor were paging me via loudspeaker. I looked at my watch and noticed that it was 2:20 pm. I was late for my next patient appointment.

"I'm sorry to wake you," the young receptionist said. "They're looking for you upstairs in the maternity ward."

The attractive young receptionist was probably no older than twenty-one years old. She was a gorgeous young blonde whom I had seen working at the reception desk several times before. She must have known who I was, as she politely awakened me from my intense 'power nap.'

"Oh...I'm sorry," I said, rubbing my eyes to make sure I was in the right place and the right time and that I wasn't having another one of my intense dreams.

"Thank you, Bridget," as I was reading her name on her name tag. "Please call them upstairs and let them know that I'm on my way up."

"No problem, Doctor."

I walked over to the elevator and made my way up to the maternity ward of the hospital. I knew that I had to rush over to my office on the west end of the hospital and begin seeing patients in my office as well.

It was a busy afternoon, and I was grateful for the forty-minute 'power nap' that I could take downstairs on the couch. I had seen the various patients that afternoon varied from pregnant women in their second and third trimesters to several patients

43

recovering from a hysterectomy and tubal ligation surgeries. I was happy to see seven o'clock come around, as my mental gas tank was on empty.

As I walked back to my office and sat at my desk, there was a message from the Chief of Staff of the Obstetrics Department, Dr. Calvin Worrell, waiting for me. He had called late that afternoon and requested a return phone call.

I slumped down on my office chair, hoping that no one else would interrupt me as I dialed his office number.

"Hello?" he responded after going through his receptionist.

"Dr. Cal? This is David Fazio, returning your call."

"Dr. Fazio...thank you for returning my call this evening. I was hoping I would talk to you before the end of the day."

Dr. Calvin Worrell was an obstetrician and gynecologist in his late sixties, who had been affiliated with the Chicago-Western Medical Group for over forty years. He was a soft-spoken, well-liked gentlemen who pretty much managed his medical and nursing staff with a 'hands-off' approach. There were several other obstetricians on our team here at the hospital. As long as we saw and took care of our hospital patients without any problems or incidents, we pretty much didn't hear from him. We had our weekly 'round table' department meetings to review and discuss all the problem medical cases that we were assigned to, but mostly, I never saw or heard from him outside of our weekly case reviews.

We exchanged pleasantries for a few moments. Being an avid Chicago Cubs fan, we discussed some of the teams' baseball statistics and Anthony Rizzo's recent home runs over the last several games.

"Dr. Fazio...I was wondering if you were available for lunch tomorrow? Dr. Caminiti and I would like to have lunch and discuss a few things with you."

Dr. Ronald Caminiti was the OB-GYN department's associate director, so he must have felt that this meeting was necessary.

"Sure...where at and what time?"

"There's that new Italian place on Kinzie Ave...Ristorante Lo Scoglio. Let's meet there tomorrow...say...around 12:30?"

"Okay...I'll be there. Anything that I should be concerned about?" I decided to pry, perhaps getting him to tip his cards a little before the meeting.

"Oh, no, Doctor...just a few departmental policy changes we would like to review with you."

A few departmental policy changes.

That phrase automatically made my neck hairs stand up on end. Having a meeting with the head of the department regarding policy changes made me extremely suspicious. I knew what this meeting was about. I had to think about how I would respond and what my 'defense' plan was going to be.

I went home that evening and changed out of my suit and tie. I then stood in front of the microwave in my underwear while warming up some pasta leftovers from the weekend. My days were always long, starting from six in the morning until seven or eight o'clock every night, six days a week, including on-call hours. My seventy-plus hour work weeks, with all its pressures, made my $315,000 a year salary seem like a minimum wage.

I had just celebrated my fiftieth birthday last month and was starting to take inventory of my life. Although I considered myself an established and well-respected hospital physician at Chicago-Western Medical Center, there were so many things that were personally missing in my life.

My private life was in shambles. I had been married and divorced twice to two narcissistic women who would probably pay an enormous bounty to see my lifeless body face down on Ashland Avenue. They were both stormy marriages and later, contentious divorces that thankfully produced no children. But the large alimony settlements and over $250,000 in legal fees had recently put me in a precarious financial position that left me in a tremendous amount of debt. My last divorce was settled almost four years ago with my ex-wife, Francine.

We had been married for twelve years, and she was a personal injury attorney with a large Chicago Loop law firm. There is no doubt in my mind that she saw me coming down the road. When our marriage finally broke down, she hired one of her divorce law firm colleagues to shake me down for over half a million dollars in alimony settlements that have left me financially reeling. According to the judge, the fact that she was a controlling alcoholic with a borderline personality disorder was not a good enough reason to have a few girlfriends on the side. She had me labeled as a narcissistic 'liar' and 'cheater,' who could not maintain an honest, monogamous relationship with anyone.

At that point in my life, she was probably right. I was very unsettled emotionally and had been serial dating since my divorce. I had been involved in many recent romantic flings, never lasting more than one or two months, before currently settling down with my latest girlfriend, Rosa.

We had been dating for almost a year now, and Rosa was a great girl. I had powerful feelings for her. But my sleep disorder issues had been getting worse over the last few years. It had been taking a steady, burdensome toll on both of us. She had also been verbalizing her desire to get married and have children eventually. I had mentioned to her several times before that getting married again wasn't on my radar and was a potential situation that I was very much opposed to.

The last thing I needed in my life was to get married again. At the ripe old age of fifty, I had realized that I was a great baby doctor and a better human being, but a lousy husband. And after two disastrous marriages, I was not about to try that out again in my life. I was beginning to believe that I was destined to be alone. Other than having a revolving front door of girls coming in and out of my life to keep me company when I wasn't working, I was probably better off being by myself than experience another destructive relationship or marriage with the wrong person.

I made a late-night phone call to Rosa after wolfing down my warmed-up dinner, chatting on the phone until almost eleven o'clock. I then laid down on the couch with the sliding door to my high-rise veranda wide open, watching late-night reruns of "Bluebloods" until intermittently dozing off. The Lake Michigan summer breeze felt refreshing as I laid on my sectional leather couch, almost naked wearing only my underwear, watching the flickering lights of the boats off the Gold Coast harbor. I got up to take a few melatonin pills at about twelve-thirty, which helped me get a few hours of sound sleep.

I woke up in my car that morning. I couldn't remember how or why I was sitting in the front seat of my Mercedes in the parking garage of my condo building. I was wearing a pair of white shorts, and my black tee shirt was on inside out.

I didn't remember getting up. I didn't recall getting dressed and going out. I didn't remember going anywhere. This was a bad habit that occurred inconsistently in my life. Sometimes it would happen often. Sometimes, there would be long periods when it wouldn't happen at all. The only pattern that I could put together was when there was more stress in my life; I tended to wake up in strange, unusual places more frequently.

I was a chronic sleepwalker.

I've recalled waking up in some bizarre places, especially during my last divorce, which I attributed to stress. I once woke up in front of an all-night adult theater, which I didn't recall getting up and going. I realized that I had walked several blocks without a jacket or coat, and the only reason I wasn't inside was I didn't have my wallet to pay the admission.

My sleepwalking was a severe condition of my severe sleep deficiencies, and I had been having aberrant sleep problems most of my adult life. It was like I lived a second life in my sleep. I would wake up in a park, in an all-night grocery store, even in front of a church once. But I never recalled how I got there and never waked up while performing these strange acts.

I had tried seeking help several times, without any real results. One therapist suggested that I start sleeping while wearing a straight-jacket or locking myself into a room where I couldn't escape. It was a sleeping condition that I couldn't control, which was often related to whatever stress I was experiencing in my life.

I returned to my condominium upstairs that morning. I packed a backpack with my shoes and clothing and rode my bike to the hospital early that morning. I usually tried to take my bicycle to work two or three times a week when the weather permitted, as it was often the only active exercise that I was able to get in with my intense working schedule. I showered and dressed at my office and was on the floor doing patient rounds by 6:15 am.

It was just after 12:30 pm when I arrived at the Ristorante Lo Scoglio on Kinzie Street. I decided to

'Uber' it, and the ten-minute ride to River North was uneventful and without traffic.

The beige chairs and modern décor of the upscale restaurant blended nicely with the ambiance and the casual atmosphere of Chicago's River North neighborhood. Ristorante Lo Scoglio was a trendy, contemporary nightspot for those wishing to enjoy its top-shelf martinis and food menu, along with its classy, elegant dining room design.

The beautiful young hostess brought me over to the other two gentlemen who had a table next to the picture window, where they could observe all the foot traffic on Kinzie Avenue.

"Dr. Fazio," as they both stood up and simultaneously exclaimed. The two of them looked overanxious to see me, which, of course, made me very suspicious. The waiter came around, and we put in our drink orders, deciding on an 'Arnold Palmer', which was iced tea and lemonade, while the two of them started their afternoons early with lime margaritas on the rocks.

The three of us sat there and exchanged pleasantries, talking about the Chicago Cubs and the upcoming Chicago Bears football season, which got us through the ordering of our entrée's. I decided on a light, veal marsala entrée', while the two of them chose to load their bellies up with a heavy, baked rigatoni and lasagna. They were probably going to take the rest of the afternoon off after lunch, I thought to myself.

Dr. Worrell then casually handed me a business card. It was for a sleep doctor specialist whom I had asked him to refer me to a few weeks ago.

"Give Dr. Callahan a call. She runs the sleep center here at Chicago-Western. She's excellent," he proclaimed.

They continued to make small talk at the table, almost as though they were afraid to encounter the real reason why they had decided to take me out for lunch. I then became impatient and decided to bring up the subject.

"So, Doctors...what department policy changes are we here to discuss today?" I eagerly asked.

"Well, Dr. Fazio," Dr. Worrell began, "You are aware of the new abortion laws that have just been passed in Springfield. Due to the recent new passage of the Reproductive Health Act and the repealing the state's Partial-Birth Abortion Ban Act, our hospital is under intense pressure to perform more state and federally funded abortions."

I sat there and silently nodded my head. *I knew these bastards were going to bring this subject up with me sooner or later.*

"We are all aware of your pro-life stance, Dr. Fazio. But our department is now required to perform these partial and full-term abortions. Before, we could discern and respect our doctor's personal and moral stands regarding their performing abortions on patients. We know that we cannot force or pressure you to perform abortions at our hospital. But now, if we want to continue to be a state-funded public hospital, we have no choice but to comply with this new Illinois law requirement."

I only sat there, sipping on my Arnold Palmer, wishing that we weren't having this unfortunate conversation.

There was a full minute of silence, and the two department heads sat there, trying to study my reaction.

These two bastards both knew of my very public pro-life stance on abortion. It was as if they were expecting me to either suddenly start performing

50

abortions or submit my resignation and work at a Christian, pro-life hospital.

At that moment, our entrées arrived just in time to break up the tension at the table, and we began eating our meals. I observed them devouring those big, fat, heavy pasta dishes for lunch, figuring that I would have to order them a wheel barrel rather than a taxicab when we left afterward.

The three of us continued to be cordial, making more small talk about the restaurant's ambiance and how fantastic the food was. When the waiter came back, I decided to order a scotch on the rocks.

I just figured the hell with it. If I was going to get fired for not complying with their new pro-choice abortion policies, I was going to make sure that I got liquored up on their dime.

"So," Dr. Worrell said again, knowing that I was trying very hard not to give them a reaction to their new pro-choice policy ultimatum.

"What are your thoughts, Doctor?"

I looked at both men and took a long swallow of my top-shelf scotch whiskey, twirling the ice cubes in my crystal drink tumbler.

"I'm sorry, gentlemen, but I can't help you. You understand my pro-life position. I'm not going to change that because we have a reckless governor and several state representatives who have no conscience or respect for life," I replied, taking another long sip from my drink.

"I imagine, Dr. Worrell, there are going to be numerous pro-life obstetricians working for publicly funded hospitals in Illinois who are going to be placed in the same position that you are both putting me in," I answered, as I took one more sip from my drink.

Then I went for their throats.

"It's going to be interesting to see how many work-place lawsuits are going to be filed against these public hospitals. Especially those in Chicago, by pro-life doctors like myself who are being forced by their hospital employers to perform medical procedures against their will and religious beliefs."

The two of them sat there, with their jaws open. They must have figured out that I had taken a Mickey-Mouse remedial law course on employee relations and religious discrimination in the workplace.

"Dr. Fazio, please don't misunderstand us. We are not forcing you personally to go against your personal, religious beliefs. We are only explaining to you that the State of Illinois is pressuring us to comply with these new abortion measures. Without our doctors performing these late-term abortions, our hospital will be forced to hire midwives and physician assistants to be available on our staff to do them. This will be a detriment to our salary budgets and ability to keep our physicians gainfully employed."

I called the waiter over and ordered another whiskey-on-the-rocks.

"Makers Mark, three fingers, please."

"Right away, sir."

Dr. Caminiti glared at me, knowing that I was enjoying a double cocktail lunch on his dime.

"I'm not sure how that is my problem," I replied.

"Look, David, you're one of the best baby doctors that we have here at this hospital. I've seen you perform C-section births on distressed infants better than any other obstetrician that we have here at Chicago-Western. You've saved hundreds of infant lives, distressed mothers in delivery, and premature infants who are now alive and well, thanks to your incredible abilities and knowledge as a physician," Dr. Caminiti said.

I smiled. "Thank you, Doctor."

"We are not forcing you to do anything contrary to your beliefs, Dr. Fazio. We are only asking you to reconsider your position on this matter, considering the pressure that will be put on our hospital," Worrell remarked.

"But the direction of health and infant care is, unfortunately, going against your very adamant, pro-life beliefs. And we certainly don't want to lose you to another hospital," the department head continued to explain.

"That would be a shame, wouldn't it?" I casually said. "Just imagine the employee lawsuits that Chicago-Western Medical would be confronted with. Not to mention all of the publicity..." I sarcastically suggested.

I then decided to play some hardball.

"By the way, did I ever tell you that I'm very close, personal friends with Chaz Rizzo? We went to high school together. You both know him, right? He's the Channel Eight Eyewitness News reporter who did those big splash news stories on the Chicago Mafia, the Chicago Archdiocese, and those pedophile priest murders going around last summer."

I figured that name-dropping my high school buddy in the news media would let them know how serious I was about not going down without a fight.

The two doctors only sat there in a trance.

"I'm sure he would be interested in doing a hospital morality story like this one. That will grab the public's attention, wouldn't you both agree?"

More silence at the table.

"Imagine the headlines...*Chicago-Western Baby Doc Fired for Not Performing Abortions*..." I was twirling the ice cubes of my almost finished scotch.

"Not very good public relations for the hospital. Just imagine, gentlemen, all the negative publicity, the boycotts from the Christian right-wingers, the pro-life Catholics, the media press releases, and the pro-life statements from the Chicago Archdiocese," I smiled.

"Who knows, maybe Father Pfleger might come over here too, conduct a sit-in and do a pro-life march in front of the hospital. Now I'm sure that would probably make the national news, don't you think?"

They were both extremely quiet, paying extreme attention to my every word.

"You guys are going to have your hands full," I remarked, taking the last gulp of my amazingly smooth drink. By this time, they were both staring at me like I was some outer space alien from another planet.

"You know, David...you can go to work at a Catholic hospital somewhere else in Chicago. You don't have to stay here. You know this, correct?" Dr. Worrell remarked.

"Yes, Cal, you're right. I can go to work for a Catholic hospital. Or change specialties. Or if staying in this sickening, over-taxed State of Illinois gets on my nerves, I can even move and go to another religious hospital in another state. Or work for a small private practice. Or, better yet, hang out my shingle and go out on my own," I argued.

"But here's the problem, Doctors..." I explained.

"I like it here. I like my medical staff. I like the nurses that work for me. I like the medical conditions and the state-of-art treatments that we offer to our patients. I like my OB-GYN department, and I like my fellow doctors," I loudly affirmed.

"But most of all, I like getting up on a beautiful summer day and pedaling my fucking bicycle to work in the morning."

"There is no need to be nasty, Doctor..." Caminiti reprimanded.

"No, Dr. Caminiti," I corrected him.

"I'm not nasty. I'm only reiterating the facts. This hospital has employed me for the last twenty-five years. I've done my internship and residency here," My voice started going up several decibels, as other restaurant customers were beginning to stare at us while I was making my loud, pro-life statements.

"I am and will always be a 'Baby Doctor.' I've delivered thousands and thousands of babies here," I loudly stated.

"And I like it here. And I'm not going to let some monstrous pro-choice fucking governor, or any of his brutal abortion laws, push me out of a job that I truly enjoy. A job which I do better than anyone else, I might add, for a hospital where I relish my employment."

There were several moments of silence as Caminiti and Worrell sat there, speechless.

"Well, gentleman, this lunch has been amazing. Thank you again for the meal and the top-shelf booze. I truly enjoyed it."

I rose from the table and politely nodded my head at them both without offering to shake their hands. I then walked out of the restaurant and grabbed the first taxicab back to the hospital.

I was angry, offended, and extremely aggravated. I was also a little buzzed from all the scotch whiskey. But I also felt bold and fearless. No matter what they were going to try to pressure me into doing, I was not about to go away without a fight. I was a pro-life baby doctor, and I was not about to be pulled to the left into being some monstrous abortionist.

Little did I realize how far to the right I was willing to go to fight for those pro-life views?

CHAPTER SEVEN
Unwanted Baby

It was a scorching Friday afternoon in July, as the emergency room of Chicago-Western Medical Center was quickly filling up with variant patients. Most of them were suffering from minor food sickness and heat stroke from the Taste of Chicago Music and Food Feast currently going on in Grant Park.

The annual city event was a popular, five-day festival of endless food and food stands, beverage tents, and several free concerts by various, well-known acts in the Petrillo Music Shell. It is attended by millions of people and is a popular event within the City of Chicago. The temperature outside was 98 degrees off the lakefront, with temperatures above 102 degrees inland and a heat index of almost 110 degrees.

The hospital's air-conditioned room temperature was significantly cooler in the wing of the emergency room, and parts of the hospital were available as a cooling center for the homeless. Many of those victims were predominately African American, living outdoors in and around the city on that day. The Chicago P.D. had been bringing in many victims sleeping in the nearby viaducts of Lower Wacker Drive and other underground passageways in and around the West Loop. The 'cooling center' was already filled for those homeless sufferers, making sure that none of them experienced a heat stroke from the intensely hot weather.

Dr. Fazio had just finished eating his lunch alone in the hospital cafeteria on the fourth floor. He was waiting for his girlfriend, Rosa, to have lunch with him, but she could not break away that Friday afternoon. A medical emergency had occurred with one of the ICU patients, which immediately dominated Rosa's time, and she couldn't leave. As he was leaving the cafeteria, he heard his name paged over the loudspeaker.

"Dr. Fazio, line 17 please...Dr. Fazio, line 17."

He walked over to answer one of the emergency landlines.

"Dr. Fazio? This is Dr. Robert Langmeyer. I'm one of the attending residents over in the emergency room. We have an emergency delivery here that we need your help with, please."

"Okay, I'll be right there."

Dr. Fazio immediately rushed over to the elevator, then quickly walked to the hospital's eastern wing where the emergency room was located. Within five minutes, Dr. Fazio had located the attending resident who had paged him earlier.

As he walked into one of the curtained-off areas of the emergency room, there was a patient, probably in her thirties, experiencing labor pains.

"What seems to be the problem, Doctor?" Fazio asked the young resident.

"We have a patient who looks to be having intense labor pains. She seems to be suffering from heatstroke and has gone into labor. She is almost full-term at eight months but looks as though she is ready to deliver now immediately. We did an ultra-sound on her, and the baby's heart rate is normal."

"Okay... it looks like we're going to have a premature baby being delivered here. Let's get her wheeled up to maternity and get this baby delivered." Dr. Fazio replied.

"Well, Dr. Fazio...that seems to be the problem," the resident said. He then motioned Dr. Fazio outside of the curtained off area to speak to the baby doctor alone in private.

"Dr. Fazio...she wants to terminate the pregnancy. We did an ultrasound, and it looks as though the fetus has severe cranial deformities."

Dr. Fazio just stood there, silent.

"Looking at the position of the fetus, natural delivery is not an option, as it will put the mother's life at risk. She has formally requested that we abort the pregnancy."

Dr. Fazio walked over to the patient, laying down on the gurney in intense pain. Her name was Zoraida Hernandez, and she was a 39-year-old Latino woman. He reviewed her charts and was told by one of the Spanish speaking nurses that the patient was a single mother with three other children at home. She was on welfare and lived in one of the more impoverished neighborhoods on the south side. She spoke and understood very little English.

The baby doctor performed an ultra-sound and examined the pre-mature fetus in the mother's womb. The fetus appeared to have craniosynostosis, a congenital deformity of the infant skull that occurs when the fibrous joints between the bones of the head (called cranial sutures) close prematurely. Due to this closure, the baby develops an abnormally shaped skull because the bones do generally not expand with the brain's growth. The condition is usually apparent in infancy as abnormal, but the characteristic head shape and, in some patients, unusual facial features. In some cases, the growth of the skull is restricted enough to cause increased pressure in the head. It can lead to headaches, visual problems, or developmental delays as the infant develops.

Dr. Fazio determined that although the baby's skull was severely deformed, he did not feel that the baby's deformities couldn't be corrected with surgery later after birth. Because of the over-sized head of the fetus and its position, the safest delivery for this baby would be to perform a Cesarean section.

"¿Cómo te sientes?" Dr. Fazio asked the patient in Spanish how she was feeling. The veteran obstetrician was moderately fluent in Spanish after spending many years working in Chicago's near West Side.

"No quiero a este bebé," the patient said repeatedly, reiterating her desire to abort the fetus.

"No puedo realizar un aborto por ti. Un nacimiento natural pondrá tu vida en riesgo. Mi única solución para ti es tener el parto de la cesárea para este bebé," the doctor explained, telling her that the safest means in saving her life would be allow them to perform a Cesarean section and allow the baby to be born.

"No! No! No!" the patient loudly protested. It was as though she would rather lose her life than to have the birth of this deformed infant.

"She doesn't want the C-section, Doctor," Estelle Matarano, an older maternity nurse, explained.

"I know. I heard her," Dr. Fazio frustratingly replied. "She would rather die in this bed than deliver this baby."

The nurses and the doctor looked at each other in the curtained cubicle of the hospital's emergency room. They were all speechless, without any direction as to what to do regarding this distressing delivery. They were not about to let this woman die while trying to give birth naturally to this infant. Seeing that she didn't want a C-section, the only other solution was to inject the abortive solution into the mother's womb, killing the fetus before it was born. Then perform a surgical abortion, removing the fetus's lifeless remains in sections and pieces from the mother's uterus.

Knowing that the previous state laws would have forbidden any doctor from doing a partial-birth abortion, he would have been allowed to safely deliver the deformed baby by C-section, being that the mother's life was otherwise in danger. But with the new RHA laws in Illinois, the other method now available in saving the mother's life was to perform a surgical partial-birth abortion, which is that she insisted on aborting the baby.

Dr. David Fazio, at that moment, made a bold decision.

"Prep her up for surgery. We are going to do a C-section."

"But Doctor, she doesn't want..." Nurse Estelle protested.

"You heard me! We need to save this mother's life, even if it means saving the life of this child as well."

Dr. Langmeyer and Nurse Matarano looked at each other, both knowing that they had no choice but to follow the orders of the lead obstetrician currently on duty. Neither was in a position to go over the head of Dr. Fazio, as he continuously insisted on prepping the patient for Cesarean section surgery.

Although the patient was verbally protesting, the anesthesiologist was called in and administered the anesthesia by putting the oxygen mask over her face, immediately knocking her out cold. Dr. Fazio then prepped himself along with the two other nurses for the surgical operation. The emergency C-section was then directly performed on Ms. Hernandez by cutting open her womb horizontally. Within eight minutes, her deformed infant child was safely delivered.

The infant had a severe cranial deformity. Its eyes were extremely sunken in, with one eye looking as though it was fused and had not fully developed. The infant's weight was four pounds, six ounces, and was sixteen inches long. The baby's head was hugely enlarged, looking to be almost twice as large as the rest of the infant's body. The baby was breathing and had a good cry as the premature baby was immediately put into the intensive care incubator. When the mother had awakened from the anesthesia, she went into mild shock. Ms. Hernandez began to loudly scream and cry, her shrilling voice carrying loudly throughout the adjacent hospital room. She continued to protest in Spanish, knowing that the child which she wished to have aborted had been safely delivered in order to save her life loudly.

She refused to look at her newborn infant baby as she was wheeled into recovery after the surgery. As Dr. Fazio exited the operation room, Nurse Estelle approached the baby doctor.

"You do realize that you're going to have a problem with what just happened," she exclaimed, as Dr. Fazio removed his surgical garb and blood-soaked gloves.

Dr. Fazio looked at her without saying a word at first. He knew that both she and Dr. Langmeyer had been exclusive witnesses to what had just happened on that hot summer afternoon at Chicago-Western Medical Center's emergency room.

"So, you think we should have let both of them die because she didn't want to deliver a deformed baby?" the doctor asked the maternity nurse.

"I didn't say that, Doctor. I only said that you're going to have a problem," she replied. They looked at each other silently for about ten seconds.

Dr. Langmeyer was nearby and was overhearing their conversation. He had assisted Dr. Fazio in that C-section delivery. He then boldly walked over to the two of them.

"You should have performed the abortion, Dr. Fazio, rather than allowing that extremely deformed infant to be born. You would have still saved the mother's life," he judgmentally said in a loud, condescending voice.

Dr. Fazio angrily glared at the young emergency room resident. He was fuming. He looked as though he was ready to lunge at the immature, arrogant doctor and make him permanently deformed. The baby doctor then approached the resident within centimeters of his personal space. David Fazio's eyes started to bulge with anger. Langmeyer, who was much shorter and probably forty pounds lighter than Fazio, immediately knew that he had pissed off the veteran baby doctor.

Fazio then suddenly grabbed the young doctor by his white lab coat and quickly shoved him up hard against the wall.

"Listen, asshole...when you're all grown up and ready to play God, you fucking let me know."

Fazio had him pinned up against the wall and looked as though he was ready to violently assault him and send him directly to the emergency room himself. Two of the other nurses ran up to separate them as Dr. Langmeyer ran out of that room. He looked as though he was running away with a long tail between his legs.

Dr. Fazio straightened himself up and took a deep breath when Nurse Estelle approached him again.

"For what it's worth," she quietly said, "I support you, Dr. Fazio. You made the right decision," and she gave Dr. Fazio a firm, emotional hug. They both cried on each other's shoulders for about ten seconds.

"I'm sure the hospital administrators will say otherwise," he replied, wiping his eyes. They then both left the surgical room and walked silently over to the elevator together on the other side of the sixth floor. Although they had followed their moral conscience, they were both visibly shaken.

They both knew there would be 'hell to pay' for that deformed infant's delivery.

CHAPTER EIGHT
Jeanne Callahan

The line of people at Starbucks was almost to the door as Dr. Jeanne Callahan arrived for her usual morning cappuccino, for which she preferred grande, with an extra shot of espresso. It was a beautiful Friday summer morning in the West Loop of Chicago, as the temperature was starting to climb to 78 degrees without the heat index. She was still a little tired from the night before and was a bit groggy. She needed her extra shot of caffeine and was hoping this fresh cup of cappuccino was going to do her some good.

The pretty, 48-year-old physician had just gotten off the CTA train on Ashland Avenue and entered the Starbucks coffee shop before going to her office at Chicago-Western Medical Center. She lived in a luxury home in Wilmette and took public transportation every morning to her hospital office. Dr. Callahan was a neurologist and was department head of the sleep center at Chicago-Western that specialized in severe sleep disorders. Her patients ranged from those having sleep apnea and needing a prescription for a CPAP machine to those insomniac patients who have severe difficulties falling and staying asleep.

Although neurologists specialize in treating diseases and disorders of the brain, spinal cord, and nervous systems, her office specializes in insomnia and sleep disorder issues that were very much related to neurological matters affecting the patient. Dr. Callahan and her staff have recently discovered that there were conscious similarities between patients suffering from intense sleep disorders and severe neurological issues affecting the patient's nerves and brain.

Jeanne grabbed her coffee that morning and walked the half block to the hospital over to her office on Paulina Street. She was a beautiful, smart, well-educated brunette who received her medical degree from the Stritch School of Medicine at Loyola University. She had done her internship and residencies in neurology afterward at the University of Chicago Hospital in Hyde Park. Dr. Callahan received a fellowship at Chicago-Western Medical Center and a grant recently to do additional studies on sleep issues and somnambulism or sleepwalking.

Sleepwalking is a behavior in which an individual appears to wake up during the night and walk or do other activities without any memory of having engaged in the actions. Sleepwalking tends to occur within an hour or two of falling asleep and may last on average between 5 and 15 minutes or longer, depending on the severity of the condition. Dr. Callahan had treated several hundred cases of sleepwalking, and as a result, was considered one of the best physicians in the Midwest for treatment of this strange sleeping disorder.

"Good morning, Doctor," greeted her administrative assistant as she walked into her office at 710 South Paulina Street.

"Good morning, Vanessa. Any messages?" she inquired as it was almost nine o'clock in the morning.

"I put them on your desk."

"Thank you...Thank God it's Friday, huh Vanessa?" she smiled as she walked to the last office on the right.

"TGIF, Doctor," Vanessa happily replied.

Dr. Callahan was a single parent, having been divorced for the last ten years. Her estranged attorney ex-husband, John Riordan, took off with his young legal secretary to live in New York City, leaving her to raise their two young sons by herself.

She was in a perfect mood that morning. Both of her sons were home from college for the summer, and she had modified her working office hours to spend more time with them hopefully.

Her oldest son, Paul, who had just turned 21, was entering his senior year at Indiana University and was doing a summer internship at a law firm for one of her lawyer-friends downtown in the Loop. He planned to go to law school after he graduated. Her younger son, Michael, 19, had just finished his freshman year at Michigan State University. He had a mild interest in accounting and finance but was mostly interested in sorority girls and partying with his Sigma Phi Epsilon fraternity brothers. He was home for the summer and without a job, realizing that such an activity would inconvenience his excessive sleeping and summer partying schedule. Her younger son was taking his time on declaring his major since he was pursuing his probable five-year college degree on his mother's dime.

As a single parent, Dr. Callahan tried to spend as much time as she could with her young adult boys. In prior years, she had prided herself on taking her sons on exotic summer vacations to Paris, Rome, and Barcelona or on a luxury cruise to some Caribbean island destinations. But this summer, neither of her boys had any desire to vacation with their boring, physician mother. With one working full time and the other partying with his buddies all summer, it looked as though she would be spending most of the summer alone, despite her good intentions.

Dr. Callahan sat at her desk for the next hour, consuming her Starbucks coffee and returning a few of her phone call messages. At 10:05 am, Vanessa buzzed her on her desk phone.

"Dr. Callahan, your ten o'clock appointment is here to see you."

She had almost forgotten that she had a full day of appointments on that Friday. She looked at her appointment schedule on her computer—someone named David Fazio, M.D., a fellow physician here at the hospital.

"This is odd," she casually mentioned to Vanessa. "Why would a doctor on staff have an appointment here to see me?"

"This was a referral from Dr. Worrell, Head of Obstetrics," her administrative assistant replied.

Dr. Jeanne Callahan groaned out loud. She figured this probably had something to do with some hospital policy changes, as it was rare that a physician on staff would make an appointment.

She rose from her desk and walked out to her waiting room. Sitting at one of the black leather chairs was a handsome, salt and pepper haired doctor wearing a white lab coat, blueprinted shirt, and a striped tie.

He was well dressed and was sitting up in his chair, looking almost impatient to see her immediately. He looked familiar, as she had remembered seeing him around the hospital before.

"Good morning, Doctor," as he casually rose from the waiting room chair to greet her, his right hand extended. "I'm David Fazio."

"Good morning, Doctor," she returned the formal greeting. "It's not often that we get a baby doctor here to see us," Dr. Jeanne smiled.

"I got your name from our department head, Dr. Worrell. He highly recommended you," Dr. Fazio mentioned.

He had requested a referral from him a few weeks ago and asked him again this past week after some prodding from his girlfriend. Dr. Worrell spoke very highly of her.

"How nice of him," as the two of them walked into her spacious office on the right.

"May I offer you something?"

"No thanks, Dr. Callahan. I've had several cups of coffee already. I see you have the same addiction I have," Fazio smiled, observing her Starbucks coffee on her desk.

"I should think about buying some stock in Starbucks. Between the coffee shop on Ashland Avenue and the kiosk downstairs, I'm constantly consuming cappuccinos," she politely observed.

"Well...thank you for seeing me, Doctor."

"You can call me Jeanne...let's forget the formalities."

"Okay...David works for me too."

"No one calls you, Dave?"

"The last one who called me Dave received a black eye in the fifth grade."

They both laughed, as she was mildly amused at the likable charm of this handsome, Ray Liotta look-a-like.

"How long have you been here at Chicago-Western," Jeanne inquired, taking another sip of her now cold cappuccino.

"Going on twenty-five years. Yourself?"

"I was at U of C in Hyde Park before coming here a little over twenty years ago. I've seen you around the hospital before," she said, realizing that his salt and pepper good looks were now unforgettable.

There seemed to be immediate chemistry between the two doctors, as they both spent the first fifteen minutes of their appointment exchanging pleasantries and personal information about each other and their own lives. She immediately reminded him of the actress Natalie Wood, with her short dark hair, alluring brown eyes, and bubbly smile. Although he quickly realized that she was probably in her late forties, she didn't look old enough to have college-age children.

"Well, now..." Jeanne finally said, now nervously finishing her cold Starbucks.

"What can I do for you, David?"

Dr. David Fazio hesitated, as he had never discussed his intense sleeping issues professionally with anyone else before.

"I have terrible sleeping issues," he started.

"Most of my patients do," she smiled.

"I've been an insomniac most of my life. But now it is getting worse. My nightmares are becoming more and more realistic, and I suspect that I probably sleepwalk on occasion. One morning several days ago, I woke up from an intense nightmare with burning welts on my hands, as if I had touched the stove or hot surface of some kind," David explained.

"How long have you had these nightmares?"

"Probably most of my adult life. But now, they are getting more intense. The burns on my hands the other morning scared the hell out of me. I have no idea how I had managed to burn my hands in my sleep," the baby doctor described.

"Has anyone ever observed your sleepwalking?" she inquired.

"No, not really. Because I am usually up and down most of the evening when I sleep, my partners have never taken notice of my sleepwalking."

"So, your significant others have never mentioned anything about your sleepwalking," she asked, figuring he was probably involved in a current relationship.

"No. But my sleeping issues have become a big problem in my past and current relationships."

"I see. How long do you sleep?"

"No more than three of four hours at a time. When I take a sleeping pill, I can usually get a few more hours," Fazio explained.

"Other than the burned hands, have you ever noticed any other injuries when you've awakened in the morning?"

"Yes. I've had some unexplained cuts and bruises in the past. But my burned hands the other morning spooked me."

"I can imagine," Dr. Jeanne observed.

A few silent moments as the sleep doctor took notes while Dr. Fazio explained his sleep disorder.

"Do you remember your dreams?"

"Sometimes."

"Do you recall the dream or nightmare you were having when you woke up with burned hands?"

"Yes," Dr. Fazio hesitated.

A few silent moments as Dr. Callahan was taking notes.

"What was the nightmare about?" she asked.

Dr. Fazio vacillated, embarrassed to discuss the vivid details of his last, terrible nightmare.

"Burning babies," he simply said.

"What?"

"Burning babies. I had a nightmare last Monday night about burning babies. I dreamed I was in a clinic, and the attending doctors there were throwing newborn babies into a scorching fire."

Dr. Callahan was surprised, realizing that this obstetrician had intense dreams that concerned his medical profession.

"Why do you think you're having these dreams?

Dr. Fazio hesitated to answer the question at first, only shaking his head. He rubbed his forehead with his hands, feeling an intense headache starting to come on.

"I don't know, Jeanne. Maybe because I don't do abortions? I'm not sure."

Dr. Callahan looked at her new patient intensely.

"So...you're a pro-life doctor?"

"Yes."

The two of them sat there in silence as Jeanne Callahan started to put together all the pieces of Fazio's nocturnal sleeping habits. She continued to write down notes in his file, making some personal observations on her new patient's demeanor and his explanation of his sleeping disorder.

Suddenly, Dr. Fazio's cell phone went off. He was being paged by the obstetrics ward for one of his patients, who was about to deliver.

"I'm sorry, Jeanne, I will need to come back here and finish our appointment. I have a patient who needs me right now."

"Of course," Jeanne politely responded. "We will have to do a sleep study on you here at the hospital. You will need to come in here and spend the night while we hook you up to an EKG machine and a heart rate monitor to observe your vitals and sleeping patterns."

"I sort of figured you would need to do that, Doctor."

"Come back here and make an appointment for that sleep study, David. Bring your pajamas and your teddy bear," she jokingly added.

"Yes, I will," Dr. Fazio replied, although he was not enthusiastic about being hooked up to some EKG machines and some monitors while he was sleeping.

They both rose from their chairs and shook hands as Dr. Callahan escorted Dr. Fazio out of her office, and he immediately exited the sleep center. Callahan then walked back to her office and wrote down a few more notes in Fazio's file.

She suddenly remembered something and decided to look up the information on her computer. In Chicago, an abortion clinic had burned down several days ago, she recalled, with a doctor and two nurses who had recently been killed. She read up on the details of that massive, three-alarm fire and realized a shocking, dreadful similarity as she looked at her calendar:

The recent fire at that abortion clinic was on the same night as Fazio's horrible nightmare.

CHAPTER NINE
An Innocent Passage

The maternity ward of Chicago-Western Medical Center was bustling on that early Saturday morning in July. Over thirty newborn babies were born during the last twenty-four hours, with several of them being born prematurely and placed in the neonatal intensive care unit (NICU) on the seventh floor. It was barely four o'clock in the morning, as the maternity nurses were busy bringing the newborn infants back and forth to their mothers for their early morning feedings.

One child was sleeping soundly in the incubator, which had been born less than twenty-four hours ago. The baby was profoundly deformed and occasionally had difficulty breathing, with its deformed head much larger than the rest of its body. The identification on the baby's incubator was labeled 'Baby Boy Hernandez.' Although the baby had awakened several times to be formula fed by one of the maternity nurses during the previous day, it continued to have labored breathing while it slept.

The maternal mother had refused even to acknowledge and care for the baby and also declined to see it, as it laid there in the infant incubator, struggling to breathe. One of the nurses on the maternity ward, Nurse Susan Anderson, oversaw caring for several of the 'pre-mies' within the neo-natal unit, including that deformed, premature infant.

Her maternity ward supervisor ordered her to contact the Chicago Archdiocese Catholic Family Services to begin the premature baby's paperwork and arrangements to be placed with a foster care family, starting the adoption process.

Susan Anderson was a middle-aged, over-weight maternity nurse. She had worked in the neonatal intensive care unit for the last eighteen years and had strong, definitive feelings regarding the hospital's new, pro-choice policies. The nurse was a liberal democrat who actively supported any pro-choice political candidates, including Illinois's newly elected governor. She was a strong supporter of the RHA law and the retraction of the state's partial-birth ban. Nurse Susan prided herself as a pro-choice advocate and was more than happy to embrace the new law allowing partial-birth abortions.

She had heard about Dr. David Fazio's 'heroic' efforts in trying to save that mother's life and allowing that deformed, physically damaged baby to be born.

"How selfish," she was overheard mentioning to one of the other maternity nurses.

"How can that doctor make a life or death call on an unwanted, grossly deformed baby, knowing the immense struggles that the family is going to incur in caring for that deformed child?" Nurse Susan loudly questioned.

Nurse Susan had been in the delivery room and experienced the birth of thousands and thousands of babies. And for reasons related directly to issues regarding the birth of babies like 'Baby Boy Hernandez,' Nurse Susan had experienced more than her share of deformed and contorted infants. Many of these deformed infants were never correctly diagnosed or imaged adequately during the first and second trimesters, only allowing these children to be born because it was too late to abort them. She felt that the partial-birth abortions performed on such births was an 'act of humanity,' in giving these children 'back to God', rather than allowing them to be a burden to their families.

Nurse Susan was very vocal about her pro-choice views and made no effort to quiet her voice when asked her opinion.

"These deformed children should have never been born," she would often say.

That early morning, she was attending to the care of one of the maternity ward patients who had a cesarean section birth the day before. Zoraida Hernandez of Room 7-821, Bed 2, was on pain medication as she was recovering from the unwanted birth of her deformed baby boy the day before. Nurse Susan had been assisting in her nursing care, administering pain medication, and supporting her needs.

"¿Cómo podría?" she continued to complain in Spanish loudly. "How could he?"

"Lo siento mucho," Nurse Susan continued to console her patient, letting her know how sorry she was for this unfortunate circumstance.

Nurse Susan continued to listen to her patient's loud protests, knowing that she had become another victim of Dr. Fazio's intense, pro-life standard. The more she heard Ms. Hernandez continually complain about how she was treated in the emergency room on that previous day, the angrier she became.

Nurse Susan Anderson was livid.

Dr. Fazio, in her opinion, was a self-centered, narcissistic bastard. She had seen firsthand the profound effects of the veteran baby doctor's pro-life decisions and watched so many mothers go home with their unwanted babies, many of them deformed. She had seen these adoption agencies' difficulties in getting these deformed babies into a foster home and eventually assisting them in being adopted. Most of them become wards of the state and are sent to disabled children's facilities, burdening the state and federal governments for their intense and sometimes constant interactive care.

Besides, she didn't care for David Fazio, MD. To be specific, she 'hated his guts' and couldn't stand the sight of him.

"What an asshole," she would often say about him behind his back and went to extremes to make sure that she wasn't in the same delivery room or the maternity ward as he was. According to Nurse Susan, Dr. Fazio had no conscience, no soul, and had no right to be pushing his pro-life viewpoints on anyone, let alone helpless patients like Zoraida Hernandez.

She also detested Dr. Fazio for being such a prolific womanizer. She had heard of some of his sexual conquests that the veteran baby doctor had with several of her young, fellow nurses. When it came to sleeping around, she thought to herself, and this self-righteous, pro-life asshole had absolutely no moral scruples at all whatsoever. In her opinion, Fazio didn't care who he hurt or how he destroyed other people's lives, both physically and emotionally.

She had recalled a friend and fellow nurse, Kelsey O'Connor, a pretty, 31-year-old, who had fallen head over heels in love with him a few years ago. David Fazio continued to 'wine and dine' her until after several dates, he professed his love for her and convinced her to sleep with him. He then proceeded to use her for several months, only spending time and sleeping with her when he was available while sleeping around with other women as well. The young, naïve maternity nurse finally caught Fazio with another woman and confronted him.

Dr. Fazio was unapologetic, acting as though he was proud of his infidelities.

"Boys will be boys," he coldly replied, as he callously discarded her, pushing her and her fragile broken heart aside. Kelsey was emotionally devastated for several months, having turned to binge drinking and excessive promiscuity before reaching out for help.

Nurse Susan finally took her young friend aside and referred her to a psychologist friend with a tremendous amount of trust. It took the young nurse a significant amount of time to mentally and emotionally get over her attachment to David Fazio.

On one recent occasion, Nurse Susan had the misfortune of working with the egotistical doctor during a C-section delivery while he was bragging to another male nurse.

"Girls are like buses. Jump on and off, but don't get too attached" she had overheard the baby doctor advising the male nurse in the delivery room that day. "There is one coming every ten minutes."

The thought of Dr. David Fazio made her violently sick to her stomach.

Nurse Susan continued to take care of the many premature infants in the neonatal intensive care unit that morning. As she approached the deformed 'Baby Boy Hernandez,' struggling to breathe and survive in that incubator, she became enraged and extremely emotional.

How could this asshole doctor do this?

Nurse Susan thought to herself repeatedly, gazing helplessly at that grossly deformed premature baby.

Nurse Susan then walked over to the nursing supervisor's empty desk. She then opened the top desk drawer and calmly grabbed the keys to the medication case located on the other side of the maternity ward.

She coolly opened the restricted medication cabinet and withdrew a vial of a drug used in open-heart surgery for adults. She didn't notice the small camera which had been recently installed above the medication dispensary unit.

This drug was commonly used to stop the heart from beating. She then returned the keys to the nursing supervisor's desk and casually walked over to 'Baby

Hernandez', who was still sleeping in the incubator. Grasping a needle, she filled it with ten cc's of the drug and injected it into the baby's buttocks while pretending to change the deformed baby's diaper. She was sure that no one else was noticing.

This poor baby needed to be taken out of its misery, she thought to herself. She needed to put an end to this abnormally deformed baby's suffering. She then turned the baby back over on its back and quickly walked away.

Within ten seconds, 'Baby Boy Hernandez' went into cardiac arrest and stopped breathing.

CHAPTER TEN
Doomed Relationship

It was a sunny, warm Saturday afternoon as I finished my shift on the seventh floor at Chicago-Western Medical Center. I had been on the maternity floor since six o'clock that morning, and I was grateful to see five o'clock come around. Even though I would be on call tomorrow, which was a Sunday, I was still looking forward to having the rest of the weekend off and whatever I could salvage from tomorrow for myself.

Rosa and I had planned to have dinner that Saturday evening at one of those fancy steakhouse restaurants on North Dearborn Street. She had made reservations for seven o'clock that evening, and I specifically requested to go somewhere casual for dinner that night. I was tired, and it had been a long day and a more exhausting week. The last thing I felt like doing was getting all dressed up in a suit and tie and going out for dinner that evening. Although I thoroughly enjoyed dressing up for work, wearing a nice button-down dress shirt, and one of my vast forays of fancy, upscale or silly ties, dressing up was off-limits on the weekends.

Just as I was wrapping things up at my office, returning a few phone calls, and answering a few emails, my cell phone rang:

"Honey.... what time will you be done?" It was from Rosa.

"I'm leaving here shortly. Where are we going tonight?"

"D 'Agostini's Steakhouse, on North Dearborn."

"Okay...am I meeting you there or picking you up?" I asked.

"I'll 'Uber' it. Our 'rezzy's' are at seven."

"Okay,...meet you there. I didn't eat today, so I'm hungry. Jeans and a button-down?"

"Perfect...see you there, David. Love you."

I quickly hung up the phone, as I didn't want to feel obligated to say 'love you' back. I guess I wanted Rosa to think that I didn't hear the last two words of our conversation. It wasn't because I didn't love or care for her, but I tried hard to control my emotions after almost a year. The last thing I needed in my life right now was the "L" word lingering around. My life was complicated enough.

I rode my bicycle back home to Lakeshore Drive, a twenty-minute bike ride from the hospital. Presuming that the traffic was light, and I didn't put myself at risk of being run over by overzealous weekend drivers, it was usually a relatively short bike ride home. Seeing that my bike rides are the only exercise I got during the week, I was grateful for the recent sunny, mild summer days in Chicago.

After taking a shower and getting dressed, I decided to take a taxicab to the D 'Agostini Steakhouse at 520 North Dearborn. I figured that was a good idea, just if I had too many of my favorite Makers Mark bourbons that evening.

"Hi honey," Rosa excitedly exclaimed as she greeted me with a wet, ten-second, 'take-no-prisoners' kiss at the table.

She was wearing a white pair of tight capri pants, which did a terrible job hiding her black satin thong underwear. She also had on a black, sequined short-sleeve blouse, which was half-buttoned, exposing just enough of her luscious cleavage to make me want to rush her home and rip her clothes off after dinner.

Rosa was a natural beauty. Her five-foot, four-inch frame carried her 36-24-34 measurements quite well, and it didn't take a genius to figure out that she worked very hard to keep up her sexy, traffic-stopping figure. Rosa was religious about getting her five-mile runs in every morning, and it always took some arm twisting to get her to try one of my many famously prepared, home-cooked Italian pasta dishes. She watched what she ate and consumed more than her share of salads, sushi, and fish.

But besides Rosa's gorgeous appearance, she was beautiful on the inside as well. She was brilliant, graduating magna cum laude from Valparaiso University with her nursing degree. She could have probably been accepted into medical school herself but didn't care for the additional years of education and sacrifice. She was culturally astute and could discuss anything from art to science to religion and politics. Rosa was patient, kind, generous, and very quick to forgive, no matter how many times I inconsiderately messed up.

She was also very religious. She carried a black-beaded rosary in her purse, which she often pulled out for Catholic mass at St. Benedict's Church every Sunday morning. She had a great sense of humor, although she could probably improve on some of her stupid, knock-knock jokes. Rosa was an avid movie-goer and knew every line from the movie 'Moonstruck.' She had probably watched every single mob-movie a dozen times or more. She could make a great impression of Marlon Brando from the 'Godfather.' Her 'Leave the Gun, Take the Cannoli's' impression never failed to crack me up every time we walked past an Italian bakery. Her mother was full-blooded Italian, so she was very understanding and tolerant of my family's traditions and quirky ways, especially my mother's requirement to attend Sunday dinners at her house when I wasn't on call.

Another thing that Rosa and I had in common was her views on abortion and pro-life. Because she was so religious, that term didn't exist in her vocabulary. Rosa was very active at St. Benedict's Pro-Life Council. She headed fundraisers to raise money for pamphlets, counselors, adoption agencies, and other pro-life materials distributed at the many abortion clinic vigils. She had intense feelings about terminating a pregnancy, especially a full-term one. I recall her being very emotional when that partial-birth abortion bill passed in Springfield. She was writing nasty letters and e-mails to state representatives for weeks.

For all the good things that Rosa had to offer in my life, there was only one small, minor little problem:

She wanted to get married—the 'Wedding Bell Blues,' big time. No ands, no ifs, and no buts.

I wish I could collect a quarter for every time she brought up the 'when are you going to put a ring on my finger' speech. I had explained to her several times that getting married wasn't high on my priority list and that I had an abysmal track record as a faithful husband. I advised her that she was probably better off not getting married at all, or at least not to me.

But Rosa wanted a family. At the age of 37 years old, her biological clock was ticking. She wanted the three thousand square foot house in Wilmette with the white picket fence and the three kids running to catch the school bus in the morning. She wanted a faithful husband, whom she could have his pipe and slippers ready for when he got home from work every evening. She wanted a lifetime partner that she believed only a stable marriage could give her, and she wasn't willing to concede. The living together arrangement wasn't going to work for her. Other than the occasional sleepovers was more than content to embrace our separate residential situations until that magic ring appeared on her finger.

But the more I thought about it, why should she compromise? She was gorgeous, both inside and out, and could get almost any man she wanted. She was probably on the 'Most Wanted' list of every male employee at Chicago-Western Medical Center, and I always noticed other doctors in the hospital flirting with her consistently. She was the total package and wouldn't have any problem replacing me if things didn't work out. But the marriage issue kept getting brought up more often during our dinner conversations, and they were becoming more and more contentious.

And lastly, she had a problem with my horrible sleeping habits. Rosa could almost always count on a terrible night's sleep whenever we spent the night together and pushed hard for me to get some sleep therapy regarding my horrific nightmares.

As I sat down at the table, I decided to greet her with some good news. "I had an appointment with a sleep doctor yesterday."

Rosa immediately smiled. "Really? With whom?"

"Dr. Jeanne Callahan. She's the director of the sleep center at Chicago-Western. Nice lady, seems to be very patient and understanding. She wants me to make a sleep study appointment."

"That's great, honey. Was this Dr. Worrell's referral?"

"Yes," I quickly responded, putting in my Maker's Mark drink order with the waiter.

"Dirty Martini, please," she ordered.

The two of us made small talk about our hectic days at the hospital, as our drink orders arrived, and the waiter took down our entrée orders. At that moment, I heard my name being called from the other table over.

"Dr. Fazio? Dr. Fazio?"

I looked over to my right behind my shoulder and noticed a familiar, gorgeous blonde trying to get my attention, having dinner with two of her beautiful girlfriends. She was a young maternity ward nurse who had just started at Chicago-Western Hospital a few months ago and didn't look much older than twenty-four or twenty-five years old.

I smiled and waved at her as she and her girlfriends made a toast to me from their table. They were all smiling at me and had this *'dump your date and come party with us'* look on their faces. Other than the fact that I was old enough to be their father, I was with Rosa and had no interest in walking over and talking to them.

Rosa had an angry look on her face, which leads to another one of her bad personality traits: she was extremely jealous and hot-tempered.

"Who are those girls?" she inquired.

"Oh, one of them is a maternity nurse in my ward. She just started a few months ago."

"Oh, I see," she mumbled.

The girls continued to look over at our table, and one of them kept whispering to the others, making it evident that they were gossiping about us. I looked in their direction a few times and continued to ignore them. But I could tell that their gossip and smiling at our path started to get on Rosa's nerves. This continued for about fifteen more minutes as I resumed to make a conversation with Rosa. I was trying to distract her while she continued to make eye-contact with the table where the younger girls were seated.

Finally, as they continued to stare at our table, Rosa got up and walked over to where they were seated to confront them.

Oh shit, I thought to myself. *Here it comes.*

"So, little girls," she began the confrontation. "Which one of you wants to screw my boyfriend?"

I looked over at them at their table and felt myself turning twelve colors of red. I was utterly embarrassed.

"He wishes," the off-duty blonde nurse said to Rosa. "Your boyfriend is old enough to be my sugar daddy," she sarcastically replied. At that moment, several other restaurant patrons were watching the whole restaurant drama unfold. I was trying very hard to look in the other direction, attempting to hide my embarrassment.

"No honey...you're the one who wishes. My 'sugar-daddy' has no use for anyone of you. You're the ones wishing you were getting it. Don't you all have some tattooed little boys that all of you can go off and bother?" Rosa replied.

At that moment, I rose from my chair and tried to pull my girlfriend away from the other table physically.

"Fuck you, you bitch," one of the other girls said.

"How much Viagra is he going to need tonight?" I overheard the other girl say.

"No, honey...fuck you!" Rosa loudly responded.

I then looked at our waiter, who was watching the restaurant drama unfold. I motioned him to come over. He began picking up our drinks from the table and moving us over to another section of the steakhouse, far away from the 'sorority' of pretty little blonde bitches sitting at the adjacent table.

We sat down again as Rosa tried to compose herself. The waiter then graciously brought over another round of drinks on the house.

"I'm sorry, Dr. Fazio," the waiter apologized.

"Don't worry about it, Pietro." I cheerfully smiled, reading the name of our waiter's name tag.

We sat there in silence for several long minutes as I waited for Rosa to cool down and compose herself.

"Was all that necessary?" I finally asked.

Rosa gave me the dirtiest of looks, as she then came back with a ridiculous response.

"Well, if I were your wife, they wouldn't have talked to me like that."

"Huh?" I responded. "What the hell are you talking about?"

"Other women never respect a man's girlfriend. That's why they said what they said. But if there were a ring on my finger, they would have realized that I was your wife or fiancée, and they would not have been flirting with you from the other table," she reasoned with a straight face.

I looked at her in shock, trying to comprehend the absurdity of her reasoning.

"Are you kidding me? How does an engagement ring have anything to do with this?"

"It has everything to do with this, David. If I were your wife, I would be treated publicly and at the hospital with more respect. I wouldn't have to deal with cackling little 'bimbos' flirting and making passes at you in public. I wouldn't have to overhear other nurses in my ICU ward, making short comments about how you're only using me for sex."

"Rosa, this is ridiculous. How can you reasonably make such a crazy assumption?"

Rosa only began to look at me with her eyes bulging out of her head, as she looked like she was ready to explode.

"You know I'm right, dammit."

I just looked at her. I was trying very hard to remain calm. I then took a long swallow of my scotch on the rocks. I was staring at her, trying very patiently to control my words, as I knew that I would not be able to take back whatever I said.

"Why don't you just say it, David?" as she was raising her voice.

"You have no intention of marrying me! Go ahead, David! Say it.... say it out loud and clear for everyone to hear."

By that moment, Rosa was furious. She had never started such a confrontation in public like this with me before. Before this, our marital discussions were discretely discussed in private or in a softer tone of voice.

"Rosa, please calm down…"

"No, David! I'm done calming down! I've been hinting to you for months about getting engaged, and you only continue to dodge the subject with me! Just say it so that I can stop wasting my time!"

"Rosa? Can we have this discussion somewhere else, please? This is not the time or place for this."

No, David, I'm tired of waiting. *This is the time and place*. Just say it, David. I'm just a good fuck for you!"

For some reason, she was getting even angrier. The more I tried to calm her down, the more she blew up, and the more upset she became. It was as though she was trying to work herself up over this minor incident purposely. I silently sat there in my stupidity, letting her berate me.

"FUCK YOU, DAVID!" she loudly yelled out in the middle of the restaurant as she got up again from our table and walked toward the exit door.

It seemed like everyone at D 'Agostini's Steakhouse was watching Rosa Hudson loudly walk out of that front entrance and hail a taxicab.

I only sat there, alone at the table, silently finishing my Makers Mark. I was mortified. I was desperately trying to absorb what had just happened mentally. The waiter, who watched my whole evening go down the toilet, came over with another drink. It was as though he was trying to console me.

"Would you still like me to bring your dinner?" he innocently asked.

"Oh yes," I cheerfully said. "Please wrap up her entrée." I was desperately trying to keep my composure, pretending that the last hour of my life didn't happen.

I continued to sit at the table alone, drinking my cocktail and eventually finishing my linguini and clam sauce. I thought about what had just happened and realized that perhaps, her marital mindset and her demanding wish to get married did not correspond with mine.

Was it our age difference? Should I have conceded and surrendered myself to her wishes? Was I wrong, acknowledging my scorned experiences with my ex-wives of the past as a reason to keep myself from getting married again? I felt conflicted and confused. I had always made it very clear to her that I was not interested in getting married again. Was she expecting me to change my mind? Was I wrong to have strong feelings for her and to want to spend time with her without the intention of marriage?

But for some strange reason, although I was furious, I wasn't emotionally devastated. In some odd sort of way, I almost felt relieved. The pressure of having to answer to her marital demands was no longer there, and I felt like a three-hundred-pound gorilla had been lifted from my shoulders.

I finished my dinner and settled the bill with my waiter. I then rose from my table and walked over to the bar at D 'Agostini's, making sure that I had walked past the three blondes who were flirting with me earlier.

"I'm very sorry about what happened earlier," I said to the young, blonde nurse still sitting there, eating her dinner with her friends.

"I will be at the bar. Why don't all of you come over and have a drink with me when you're done with dinner?" I suggested to the three 'sorority' girls.

"Sure, Dr. Fazio," the three of them almost said in unison. They all enthusiastically looked at me, as one of them winked her eye at me from behind her colossal large wine glass.

Within fifteen minutes, I was sitting at the bar, buying drinks for the three of them, laughing and flirting with each one of them for the rest of the evening.

It was well past midnight, and after sitting at the bar consuming several bourbons on the rocks, it was hard to decipher the several nasty texts and cell phone messages that I was getting. My phone was on vibrate, and it was going off every minute or so until I finally shut it off. They looked to be from Rosa, as she was angrily blowing up my cell phone. But I didn't respond or answer any of her texts or phone calls. I was so angry with her and the way she had embarrassed me in the middle of that restaurant. I didn't want to talk to her. And besides, I was having way too much fun.

My only other challenge on that evening was figuring out how the four of us would fit into a small taxicab and go back to my place on that Saturday night. We left the bar and called an Uber, and we were at my Gold Coast condominium by 12:30 am.

The three young blondes were thoroughly impressed with the flickering harbor lights and the lakefront view of Lake Michigan as they each continued taking turns kissing and making out with me on my sectional leather couch. One of them suggested that my condominium was too warm and needed to take her clothing off. They all stripped down to their bras and panties and took turns posing in front of my balcony window, yelling out at the Lake Shore Drive traffic down below. As I went into my liquor cabinet and pretended to be their bartender, they loudly turned up the music, dancing with each other half-naked around my high-rise balcony and onto my living room floor.

We were doing shots of cinnamon fireballs and Black Label whiskey all night until I could barely see straight. We were all stripped down to our underwear, and the four of us continued to party and make out with each other until almost five in the morning. Our little private party was turning into a big, alcoholic orgy without the sex. By then, my total exhaustion and inebriated state of mind had finally caught up with me, and I ultimately passed out on the couch.

It had never dawned on me that I had given Rosa the elevator code and the key to my condominium a few months back.

CHAPTER ELEVEN
Morning After

"DAVID? DAVID?" Rosa was screaming.

"WHAT THE FUCK IS GOING ON HERE?"

I woke up practically naked on the couch while Rosa was two inches away from my face, screaming at the top of her lungs. My head was throbbing. The three-party girls were still passed out, either on the couch or the chair, and were just waking up. Two of them were still in their bras and underwear, while the one was topless.

"How did you get in here?" I said, half groggy, still half asleep. It was painful to talk.

"You gave me the key, asshole...which, by the way, I've come back here to return."

I rubbed my eyes and looked around the room. There were clothes and garments strewn everywhere around the living room, as the girls were suddenly awakened by the screams Rosa was making. Two of them grabbed their clothes and started immediately running into the bedroom to get dressed, while the topless girl slowly got up, picked up her things, and casually walked into the bathroom.

"I'm sorry I interrupted your orgy," she thundered.

"No, Rosa. There was no orgy and no sex. These girls came over, and we drank and partied last night." I angrily replied. In all honesty, I didn't remember having sex with any of them.

"Yeah, I can see that."

"Besides, what the hell are you doing here anyway? You walked out and embarrassed me in the middle of the restaurant last night. Then you start blowing up my cell phone. For what? To make me feel even worse?"

I got up to put on my pants and shirt while the other girls were simultaneously walking out of my condominium. Rosa's intimidating presence was chasing them out one by one.

"I'm going to get my things," she rudely said as she walked into my bedroom and pulled out her clothes and belongings that she had left behind from nights past. Rosa had her clothes in one of my dresser drawers. I could hear her slamming doors and throwing things on the floor, making as much noise as possible.

I decided I was going to play it cool and not participate in her drama. With my shirt unbuttoned and wearing my jeans, I walked over to the kitchen and started the coffee pot, making myself a cup of coffee. I was not going to go into the bedroom and start a confrontation with her. That wasn't my style.

"Would you like some coffee?" I casually asked her while she was still busy slamming drawers and throwing more things around.

"Go to hell!" she yelled back.

I put some flavored hazelnut cream in my coffee cup and decided to walk back into the bedroom casually. I figured that maybe, she would possibly cool off, and we could talk things over.

Big mistake.

"Could we discuss this like adults? Or would you rather slam and throw things around, blow up my cell phone or walk out and make a scene in the middle of a public place?"

She glared at me, snapping back with her ferocious temper.

"You don't want to marry me, David. You would rather have your assortment of little bimbos to screw and play around with instead of settling down and making a life with me. You would rather go to the bar and screw your slutty little girlfriends instead of having a real, serious relationship with someone who truly loves you," she said in a loud, nasty voice.

She was looking around the bedroom for a bag to put her clothes and belongings in. I figured she was still hanging around for the drama. I could easily see several empty plastic bags in my closet that she could have used to pack her things and run out the door quickly.

"I thought that's what we had."

"Really? The minute we have a knock-down, drag-out fight, you run off and have a late-night orgy behind my back?"

"Well, I would have invited you, but..." I tried to joke.

"Fuck you, David."

She continued her rant about what a great girlfriend she had been to me and how she didn't deserve any of this. I stood there by the bedroom doorway, watching and listening to her tirade. Finally, I decided I had heard enough.

"Listen, Rosa," I loudly interrupted her ugly, abusive outburst.

"I never said I didn't want to spend my life with you. I only said, on many occasions, I might add, that I wasn't ready for marriage. I told you this many, many times. I had two horrible marriages under my belt, and I'm certainly not ready to jump into another one."

She stopped throwing things long enough to make a profound statement.

"And what does this have to do with me? Just because you married two psychotic bitches, why do I have to pay the price? I want to spend my life with you. I want children with you. I want us to grow old together. Am I so wrong to want you in my life forever?"

"I'm not ready for marriage again. I told you this on our very first date, Rosa. I have a lot of emotional issues to deal with, and jumping into another marriage is not the best decision for me right now."

"So, I'm supposed to suffer? I'm supposed to put my life on hold until you're ready?"

Rosa stood there for several seconds, silently glaring at me. I wanted to walk over to her and hug and kiss her, and possibly put this whole fiasco behind us. But I was afraid to approach her. I felt like I was staring at a cobra, ready to bite my head off at any moment.

She dropped whatever useless piece of clothing she was holding at that instant and walked closer to me.

"David, can I ask you a question?" I braced myself.

"Do you love me?"

A moment of silence.

I did not know what to say or how to say it correctly. I cared very deeply for her. I loved everything about her. I loved the way we interacted. I loved the way we made love. I loved the way we got along and communicated when she wasn't losing her mean, ferocious temper.

But could I say that I truly loved her? Her question took me by surprise, and at that moment, I was speechless.

Rosa stood there, glaring at me for several long, quiet seconds.

"I care for you, Rosa…"

"That's what I thought," she loudly blurted out.

She walked over to my closet and grabbed a plastic bag that was on the floor. She threw in her clothes and a few other personal belongings from the bathroom and started to walk towards the bedroom door. I tried the grab her arm, but she immediately pushed me away.

"Rosa, don't do this…let's talk like adults here."

"If you can't tell me how you feel about me, we have nothing else to talk about."

"Your question just surprised me, that's all."

"Go to hell, David. You shouldn't even have to hesitate. You should be yelling, 'I love you's' from the rooftop if you cared and truly loved me."

She then walked towards the doorway, ready to make her final exit.

"All the nurses are right about you. You're a narcissistic bastard. I feel sorry for you. With all your demons, all your sleepless nights, and all your nightmares, you're going to have a very miserable life."

I only stood there, still not believing she was seriously walking out.

"Even with all your young nurses and sex bimbos, David, you are going to die a very lonely, severely tormented old man," she loudly exclaimed.

"Do me a favor," she said in her final exit. "When you see me at the hospital, please look the other way. Goodbye, David."

I only stood there, holding my now cold cup of coffee, watching her walk out the door. I didn't know if I should run after her, tackle her onto the hallway floor and make love to her right, then, and there. Was that what she wanted? Did she want me to play that game? Did she want me to scream out, 'I love you; I love you...please, Rosa, don't go,'?

The front door slammed, and that was the end.

I stood there, barefoot in the kitchen, alone. It was only seven-thirty on that Sunday morning, and I had to be at the hospital in less than an hour. I was numb. I was speechless. I didn't know what to feel or how to react. I walked over to the veranda and opened the sliding door. I stepped onto the balcony and watched her climb into her blue Volkswagen Beetle and drive away on North Lakeshore Drive.

I felt empty. I felt abandoned. At that moment, I felt so damned alone. All I had to do was tell her that I loved her and maybe, all this drama wouldn't have ended so damned badly. She wanted my deep, unwavering love. She wanted my unquestioned loyalty. She wanted a dedicated, devoted, faithful husband. At that moment, I just couldn't give her any of that. I went into the bathroom and turned on the shower.

With the turn of the hot water knob and that one bar of soap, I simply washed all my pain away.

CHAPTER TWELVE
Consequences

The quietness of the intensive infant care unit was loudly broken when Nurse Mary Bernardo heard the loud alarms of the infant heart monitors of one of its patients. She quickly rose from her nurse's station and walked over to the incubator, where the failed heart monitor was beeping. It was the newly arrived 'Baby Hernandez,' the severely deformed premature infant that was delivered the day before, going into cardiac shock. Nurse Mary tried her best to revive the small infant, but by then, the pre-mies small little heart had flat-lined. The two other nurses, along with Nurse Susan Anderson, had immediately arrived to 'assist' Nurse Mary in trying to revive the baby. One of the attending physicians, Dr. Thomas Bates, who was one of the OBY-GYN residents on the floor, worked in vain to assist them in resuscitating the child.

"It's no use, Doctor," Nurse Anderson immediately said. "This poor baby was too premature and too deformed to survive."

Dr. Bates looked at Nurse Anderson, and along with Nurse Bernardo, agreed with the older nurse's assessment. Within twenty minutes, the deceased premature baby was covered with a blanket and, before taken to the morgue downstairs, was brought into the mother's hospital room. She had just been told that her premature, deformed, unwanted baby had just passed away.

"¿Quería ver a su hijo?" the Spanish speaking young nurse asked the patient, while the deceased infant was on a small gurney in the hallway, asking her if she wanted to view her child.

"No," she flatly said. "Quiero fingir que esta pesadilla nunca sucedió," stating that she wished that this nightmare had never happened.

Nurse Bernardo went ahead and filled out the necessary documents and paperwork, along with the premature infant's death certificate. Since the mother refused to have anything to do with the mortally deformed infant, the baby was without a first name for the birth and death certificates. She sat there for a moment, trying to think of a name for the poor unwanted child who had suddenly died without a first name. She then wrote down, 'Jesus.'

The rest of that day had gone by without incident, as Nurse Mary Bernardo was about to finish her shift at 5:00 pm. Before punching out, she was required to go into the medicine and prescriptions cabinet and take inventory. She took out the daily checklist and files used on her floor and went over to the drug cabinet to take stock of the drugs available for distribution. In comparing her computerized perpetual inventory list, she noticed that one heart medication, Procainamide, had been unaccounted for. She went back and asked several other nurses on the floor if that drug had been used during their shift, as Nurse Anderson had already left for the day. No one had any clue as to why that drug was missing from the secured drug cabinet. She noted the exception of her report and left it for her supervisor to investigate the discrepancy on her next shift.

When Head Nurse Talia Cesario arrived at her shift the next morning, she was made aware of the prescription drug discrepancy. She immediately decided to call security. Realizing that there was a newly installed camera behind the area near the drug cabinet, one of the security guards, along with an IT technician, viewed the tapes and recordings within the maternity and infant ICU floor over the last forty-eight hours. They matched each prescription withdrawal with the necessary documents signed off and requested by the corresponding doctors.

It didn't take long before they figured out who had withdrawn the prescribed medication.

Dr. Calvin Worrell was at his desk that morning when he had heard a loud knock on his office door.

"Come in," he loudly responded, knowing already who it was.

"Dr. Worrell, you wanted to see me?"

"Dr. Fazio, thank you for coming in right away; please sit down," the department head said to his senior physician as they both shook hands. Dr. Fazio immediately sat at one of two leather chairs facing Dr. Worrell's antique, wooden oak desk with carved out figures of Cowboys and Indians upon the neatly trimmed wood.

"May I get you anything?" he politely asked, making a gesture towards his liquor cabinet on the far wall of his office.

"No, thanks, Cal. It's still too early for me today. Besides, I have a delivery which I need to be at very soon."

"This won't take long, Doctor," Dr. Worrell behind his massive desk. "I understand there was an incident with one of your deliveries the other day."

"An incident?" Dr. Fazio replied, pretending not to know what Dr. Worrell was referring to.

"You delivered an unwanted, premature infant that was quite deformed in the emergency surgery. A Hispanic woman, by the name of Zoraida Hernandez, had requested that her baby be aborted."

"Her life was in danger, Cal..."

"Dammit, David!" as Dr. Worrell slammed his open hand on his desk. "This is the very goddam problem that both Dr. Caminiti and I warned you about."

98

He took a deep breath, trying to refrain himself from screaming.

"Do you realize the lawsuits that this hospital is exposing itself to when you perform such heroic acts as trying to save an unwanted, grossly deformed infant from being aborted late-term? You're not doing anyone any favors by saving the life of an unwanted, severely handicapped infant, who will end up being a ward of the state for the rest of its life."

"Cal, before the delivery, I had done the ultrasounds and all of the prenatal imaging, figuring that the baby's deformities could be surgically corrected after birth."

"Surgically corrected? How the hell did you figure that a child with such a deformed cranial abnormality could be surgically corrected, especially when the mother clearly stated that she did not want to deliver this baby?"

"I felt that delivering this baby through a Cesarean Section would increase the chances of both of them surviving."

"Well, I guess you figured wrong, David."

Fazio looked at the doctor, clearly confused.

"That deformed infant passed away this morning...thankfully."

"How so?"

"It suffered a massive cardiac arrest this morning."

There was a moment of silence.

"A massive cardiac arrest? That child was healthy with a strong beating heart. I remember the infant's vitals, and they were nowhere near any level that suggested that the infant had a failing heart or any kind of heart condition."

"Well, David," Dr. Worrell responded, "lucky for you and this hospital that the baby passed away this morning. If it had survived, this hospital and particularly, your decision to successfully deliver this baby would have put us in quite a hornet's nest."

Dr. Fazio sat there, silent.

"This Hernandez lady would have probably gotten all 'lawyered up' and had them file a malpractice lawsuit against you and this hospital. Somebody up there saved your ass."

Dr. Fazio shook his head.

"I don't understand how that baby didn't survive..."

"It's not for you to figure out, David. We all dodged a huge bullet, as far as I'm concerned. Had that baby survived and had the malpractice lawsuits started getting aimed at this hospital, we would have found ourselves in a precarious situation, and you without a job here at Chicago-Western," Worrell replied.

Fazio smiled at the head of his department.

"You're just looking for an excuse to do that, aren't you, Cal?"

"You keep fucking up and keep delivering unwanted babies, and I won't need one," he coldly replied.

The two of them sat there in a staring match for several seconds.

"Look, David, I like you. I want you to stay here at this hospital. You're a brilliant doctor. You proved it in delivering that deformed, premature infant the other day. But your days of playing Superman here at this hospital are over, David. You're going to have to start following the law. And right now, the law in the State of Illinois says that if a late-term expectant mother wishes to abort her child, you need to follow her directive."

Dr. Worrell was trying to stay calm in reprimanding his senior obstetrics physician.

Dr. Fazio continued to sit there for several minutes, trying to get his head around that pre-mies death and how that whole delivery situation was going

100

to affect his employment here at the hospital. The two of them sat there in silence.

"David?" Dr. Worrell addressed his physician. Fazio only glared back at him.

"Please give me your word that you're not going to let this happen again. If this situation should arise again, ask for the assistance of another physician, or just simply walk away. We all know your moral position at this hospital."

David Fazio only sat there for a moment, trying very hard not to say the articulated, Shakespearian words that were now coming into his head.

"I have to go back, Cal. I will talk to you later," as Fazio arose from his seat and headed out the door.

"David?" Worrell called out to him again as the two locked eyes, expecting his answer.

"I'll think about it," Fazio bluntly replied as he quickly exited Dr. Worrell's office.

Worrell sat there at his desk as he watched Dr. Fazio exit his office. He then began shuffling a few papers and files that were on his desk. On top of his document files was the drug inventory report from the infant ICU ward that was taken earlier and placed on his desk. In that file was a memorandum written by one of the IT technicians. That memo stated that the security tapes and surveillance records disclosed that the arrhythmia heart drug, Procainamide, had been withdrawn by Nurse Anderson that previous day, only moments before 'Baby Hernandez' going into cardiac arrest. Worrell had called the nurse's station earlier that morning and talked to Nurse Bernardo and Nurse Cesario about the validity of their drug inventory report. Dr. Worrell concluded that Nurse Anderson had probably administered the arrhythmia heart medication to the premature infant just before it went into cardiac arrest. Calvin Worrell wasn't surprised.

Nurse Anderson had done this sort of thing before, he recalled to himself.

Worrell took all the documents and prescription inventory reports, along with memorandums and applicable files, and casually walked over to his shredding machine.

CHAPTER THIRTEEN
Diamond Lil's

Diamond Lil's Bar & Grill was rather crowded on that muggy, humid Friday night, as Detective Dennis Romanowski was sitting at the bar, nursing his drink. The North Milwaukee Avenue establishment was one of the more popular watering holes in Wicker Park, as most of the off-duty coppers and firefighters went there after their shifts to tie one on before going home. The Chicago detective was on his second Tito's Vodka on the rocks (with a splash of lemon juice), eagerly waiting for his best friend to arrive. He had called Fire Chief Battalion Commander Terry Janko earlier before the end of his shift, and they arranged to meet at six o'clock.

It was just after six-thirty when Chief Terry finally walked in the door. He exchanged greetings with a few of the other off-duty coppers and firefighters playing pool and throwing darts before making his way over to the bar.

"I was afraid your old lady pulled your hall pass tonight," Denny smiled, ordering his best friend a Grey Goose on the rocks with a splash of water.

"She almost did. I got a stern warning about not coming home too late. The boys have baseball practice, and she wants me home at a decent hour. I feel like Cinderella with an early curfew," Terry replied. "I had some reports I needed to finish before leaving the firehouse."

"No worries, I get it."

They both raised their glasses with their usual TGIF toast.

"Don't you love being married? The over-weight wife, the entitled kids, and the white picket fence in

Portage Park? Gotta love the American Dream, don't you?" Denny joked.

"American Dream, my ass. After remortgaging my house, I figure it won't be paid off until I'm at least 75 years old. With the stress of this damn job, I don't think I'll live that long."

"I get it," Denny replied. "I've often wondered how our parents made less money, and yet they paid everything in cash, including their houses. They had no mortgages, put all of us through school, and had money left over to retire."

"That's not hard to figure out," Terry said, recalling their childhood growing up together. "Our parents never did anything, never went anywhere, and never spent any money. Our parents were cheap Polish immigrants who stashed their money under their mattresses and floorboards. They never had any credit cards, never bought new cars, or ever went on any vacations."

"Oh...so that's the trick. Work, go home, sleep, and get up and go to work again. I guess if you do that for forty years straight as our dads did, maybe you'll get ahead," Denny answered, finishing his second drink.

"We still have nothing put away for our kid's college," he observed. "Seems like we're living paycheck to paycheck. My wife suggested taking on a security guard job for a downtown jewelry store part-time. Living on a detective's salary just isn't easy anymore."

"I know, "Terry observed. "But living like our parents did, then retiring and dying on the couch watching TV is not the way I want to live," Terry said. He had sucked down his first cocktail and ordered another round.

"She probably just doesn't want you hanging out here after work anymore."

They both laughed and were enjoying their drinks while watching the Chicago Cubs play the Detroit Tigers in the fifth inning.

"Cubs are down, 6-2," Denny remarked.

"What else is new? I wish these damn guys would get some decent pitching," Terry observed.

"How's your head? You were a little spooked over that clinic fire last Sunday night," Denny asked.

"I still am," Terry replied. There was a pause of several seconds as the two of them locked eyes.

"What did the arson investigators say?"

"They're still scratching their heads. There was no forced entry from the back door, and the liquid oxygen tanks were not locked up where they normally are. It appears that someone had entered the building and started the fire from the back where the tanks exploded. It had to be inside a job, but none of the clinic's employees are viable suspects. They were all interviewed, had solid alibis, and everyone took lie-detector tests. They all passed with flying colors," Terry explained.

Denny shook his head. "That makes no sense. What outsiders would have access to the clinic and have a motive to torch the place?"

"That's what we can't figure out," the frustrated Fire Chief explained.

"Doesn't the fire department have emergency access to all facilities that have oxygen tanks?" Denny asked.

"A Chicago Firehouse has access to all buildings within their district in the case of a fire. That doesn't mean anyone within the department would go around setting buildings on fire, Dennis." The Chief quickly dismissed the detective's comment.

"SHIT!" One of the patrons playing pool loudly screamed as it caught the attention of all the bar customers.

They both sat there for a moment as Denny watched one of his fellow detectives' hands over a twenty-dollar bill to another copper over a lost billiards game. Someone had fed the jukebox a roll of quarters, and the 'Fleetwood Mac' songs were running back to back on that warm, steamy evening.

"How about your pro-life arsonist theory? Did you explain that to one of the investigators?"

"I did. The problem is there aren't any 'pyros' or 'perp's' who fit that 'm-o.' We haven't had any anti-abortion protestors set off any fires or cause any property damage until now. So, we have nothing to go on."

Denny shook his head. "No prints anywhere? No accelerants that could have been left behind?"

"Nothing that survived the fire. It's like someone got rid of the evidence before torching the place. Not a single clue."

"That's impossible," Denny replied. "There has got to be some evidence."

"Denny, I'm telling you. I even went there this week with a few of my men, and we scoured the place. When that liquid oxygen exploded, it burnt everything to a crisp."

"Do you know if there were any threatening phone calls to the clinic?"

"No," Terry replied. "We interviewed the staff, and since they lost one of the head doctors and two of their nurses, they didn't recall anyone threatening the medical staff before the fire."

"I would check the phone records. Perhaps get a list of the patients over the last twelve months. Something has got to turn up. An abortion clinic doesn't burn down by itself."

"Another round, boys?" asked the attractive, blonde bartender, who was sporting more than her share of tattoos across her arms and neck.

106

"Sure, thanks, honey," Denny replied.

At that moment, one of the nurses from Chicago-Western Medical had arrived with two of her girlfriends and took notice of the handsome fireman and detective sitting at the bar.

"Hey, Terry...how's it going?" The off-duty nurse walked over to give the chief fire battalion a long, wet kiss on the cheek.

"Hey, Linda...how are you?" Terry had known Nurse Linda Ciccone for many years since he started working at Chicago Fire Engine No. 1.

"You remember my friend, Denny Romanowski?"

"Of course. You're a detective from the Eighteenth," Linda replied.

"I'm impressed. I wish my memory was as good as yours," Denny noted.

"You've been at the hospital several times. We've met before."

"Can we buy you all a drink?" Terry offered.

"Sure. I'll have a vodka gimlet," Linda answered.

"I'll take a Blue Moon," said one of Linda's attractive girlfriends.

"Give me the same," the other brunette said.

Denny called over the bartender and took their drink orders, while Terry found a couple of vacant bar stools and tried to make the three girls comfortable.

The two other girlfriends of Linda's sat down while Terry and Denny chatted for several minutes. The other two were drinking their beers, and Denny was trying his best to make conversation with both of them while Terry and Linda had their dialog going. Somehow, the subject of the clinic fire Sunday night was brought up in their conversation. Linda had known one of the nurses, Terri Biela, whose funeral was earlier that day.

"Had a funeral to go to this morning. Terri was one of the casualties of that clinic fire on Randolph Street last Sunday night. Very sad."

"I'm sorry," Janko said. "We've been very involved in that fire investigation this past week."

"How's that going?"

"Not well," Terry replied. "Because the liquid oxygen tanks accelerated the fire in the building, everything was burned to a crisp."

"I'm sure it was. My girlfriend's funeral was a closed casket, and they said she died from third- and fourth-degree burns."

They both shook their heads as they continued to sip on their drinks slowly.

"It's kind of funny," Linda said as she was trying to talk over the loud Fleetwood Mac music.

"I treated one of our doctors earlier this week with some unusual burns on his hands," Linda mentioned.

"Really?"

"He had some burns on his hands on the same morning following that fire. He said that he had burned them making breakfast, but that just didn't make any sense to me. It's probably nothing."

Chief Terry Janko put his drink down on the bar and began to study his friend.

"Who is this doctor?"

"David Fazio. He's an obstetrician at the hospital. Excellent reputation, well respected."

Chief Terry Janko silently went into mild shock.

"I just thought it was weird. Here I was treating and putting gauze on this doctor's hands while that clinic was still smoking. I just couldn't figure out how he had burned his hands like that," Linda observed.

The expression on Chief Janko's face had suddenly changed, and they were both silent for a long moment. Janko had heard this name before, and a pale, white expression had come over him.

"Were there any doctors assisting at the fire?" she asked.

"Not that I'm aware of. There was no medical personnel there at the fire scene that I remember."

"That is weird," she replied.

"That is so unusual that he would have burns on his hands," the fire chief observed.

The five of them continued to drink and make conversation, as Janko realized that Diamond Lil's on a Friday night was neither the time nor the place to be discussing an arson fire investigation.

They all continued to make small take about the Chicago Cubs while the game was being broadcast on the overhead televisions. Janko looked at his watch and then threw a couple of twenties on the bar counter.

"I've got to get going. I've got an early curfew tonight," noticing that it was only 9:00 pm. He hugged his friends at the bar and said, 'good night' to a few more off-duty firemen before going out the front door. He walked down North Milwaukee Avenue until he found his parked Ford Escape.

Terry unlocked his car and was about to start it up. But then, his curiosity got the best of him. The name David Fazio was a distinctive name from his past, and that horrific name hadn't crossed his mind in many, many years. He pulled out his Apple iPhone and 'googled' that doctor's name. He scrolled down, noting that there was nothing unusual about him on the internet, except for one thing that caught his eye:

There was an article which he had written in one of the medical journals several years ago that was posted on a pro-life website. He pulled the material up from his phone and read several paragraphs of the published editorial. They were very religious, very conservative views posted by the doctor that had left no doubt regarding his pro-life position. In that article, Fazio accused all physicians who perform abortions as 'murderers,' having 'no respect for human life.' Terry Janko knew it was an unusual coincidence, but it was worth looking into.

Perhaps, he thought, he needed to visit this baby doctor.

CHAPTER FOURTEEN
Janko Pays a Visit

The maternity ward at Chicago-Western Medical Center was quite busy that early Monday morning, as several nurses were scrambling to attend to the several expecting mothers waiting to deliver their babies at any hour. Nurse Mary Bernardo was quite busy looking after several patients on her floor, as Nurse Susan Anderson was assisting Dr. Thomas Bates in delivering a healthy baby boy.

Dr. Fazio was finishing a routine Caesarian section delivery for breech birth, where the infant's umbilical cord was also wrapped tightly around its neck. He then successfully delivered a very healthy baby girl at seven pounds, eight ounces. He had just finished stitching up the young mother's womb when an assistant nurse informed him that he had two visitors to attend at his office after he ended his delivery.

David Fazio changed out of his scrubs, washed his hands, and calmly walked down the long hallway to his remote office located at the end of the maternity ward.

Seated within the waiting room of his office was Battalion Commander Terrence Janko, along with his assistant, Captain Stuart Durham, patiently reading some old People magazines, which had been stacked neatly on the coffee table. They had been there waiting for over thirty minutes.

"Dr. Fazio, you're a busy man," Commander Janko smiled as he extended his hand to the veteran obstetrician.

"The babies can't wait," grinning as he shook Janko's and Durham's hands.

"I'm Commander Janko, and this is my associate, Captain Durham. We're here from Chicago's Engine No. 1, and we'd like to ask you a few questions."

David Fazio stared at the Battalion Chief for several long seconds, trying to remember where he had heard his name before.

The doctor then calmly smiled. "Certainly," as they followed him into his office.

"I'm sorry if we caught you at a bad time," Janko apologized.

"No time is ever good, Commander. May I offer you anything?"

"No, thank you. We won't take up a lot of your time, Doctor."

The three of them sat down in Fazio's office, as the two firemen from Chicago Fire Engine No. 1 made themselves comfortable in the two black leather chairs in front of the doctor's desk.

"What can I help you with?"

"You are aware of the clinic fire explosion on Randolph Street last week, are you not?"

Dr. Fazio thought for a moment.

"The abortion clinic fire last week, where there were casualties? Yes, I am. I knew one of the physicians that perished in that fire, Dr. Michael Petrovitch. He was a good man," Fazio commented.

"Yes, well, Doctor...our department is starting to believe more and more that the abortion clinic fire was not a random event. It appears to be arson."

"Really?" Dr. Fazio observed.

"Yes...judging by the location of the liquid oxygen tanks and whoever had access to that building was able to throw an accelerant into the medical clinic and implode those tanks, which caused that intense, three-alarm fire," Janko said matter-of-factly.

"We've been investigating that clinic fire for the last week, and it was arson," Durham validated his commander's statement.

"I'm sorry to hear this," Fazio sincerely replied. "As I said, I knew one of the physicians who worked

112

there at the clinic. He was a senior physician and associate partner for that family planning clinic there."

Janko shook his head. "How did you get along with Dr. Petrovitch?"

"Me? Personally? I never had any issues with him." Fazio explained.

Janko glared at the maternity doctor for a long five seconds.

"Even though he was a doctor who performed abortions?" Janko asked in an accusatory tone of voice.

"To each his own," Fazio quickly smiled.

"We've heard that the two of you have had more than your share of disagreements," said Janko.

"Dr. Fazio, your refusal to perform abortions here at this hospital and your pro-life beliefs are a secret to no one," Durham stated.

"Nor should they be, gentlemen. I've gone to great lengths to make sure that everyone here at this hospital is aware of my pro-life beliefs."

"I understand you've had more than your share of misunderstandings with Petrovitch," Janko casually mentioned again.

Dr. Fazio looked surprised. "We had our share of moral debates."

"More than debates, Doctor. It was reported by several of your colleagues that you and Petrovitch got into some very loud, very heated discussions regarding your family planning differences. There seemed to be a lot of animosity between yourself and Dr. Petrovitch."

"Commander," Fazio quickly jumped in. "I don't have a problem with any physician who wishes to make a living performing abortions at either this hospital, another hospital, or any other family planning clinic that he chooses to perform them in," Fazio patiently explained.

"My issue with Dr. Petrovitch at our last medical symposium was that he was not only getting rich at his clinics performing abortions but was now looking forward to the watershed of new late-term abortions that are now legal in the State of Illinois."

A moment of silence as the two firemen studied the veteran maternity doctor.

"He always felt the need to brag about the number of abortions their clinic was doing and how much money they were all making on their bottom line."

Another silent moment.

"I bet you had a real problem with that, Doctor," Janko sarcastically mentioned.

Fazio locked eyes with the firehouse commander.

"Yes, unfortunately...yes, I did."

Durham kept focusing on Dr. Fazio's hands while he was explaining his personal beliefs.

"How are your hands, Doctor?" Durham asked.

"They're fine," Fazio responded, not immediately making the connection.

"I understand that you had some severe burns on your hands not too long ago," Durham stated.

Now Dr. Fazio was starting to get very suspicious of his two guests from Chicago Fire Engine No. 1.

"Gentlemen, where are you all going with this?"

A few seconds of silence.

"Dr. Fazio, it seems rather strange that you were treated with severe burns to your hands on the very morning after that clinic fire," Janko explained, trying to make a connection of his suspicions to the maternity physician.

"First of all, guys, my burns were not severe. I burned them while making breakfast that morning. They were fully healed within a few days, and I would not consider my hand burns to be 'severe.'"

Fazio held up both of his hands, proving that they were healthy and fully healed, without any apparent burn marks or scars whatsoever.

"Secondly, whatever connection you're trying to make here, I was in bed with my girlfriend that evening, and I can assure you that I was nowhere near that clinic. I have no desire to burn down abortion clinics, regardless of my beliefs."

"Can your girlfriend vouch for you that night?" Durham asked.

"Well, we just recently broke up but, I'm sure...she wouldn't have a problem."

"Doctor, there was some bad blood between you and Petrovitch," Janko observed.

"Not enough for me to burn down his clinic!" Fazio smiled.

Janko smiled and looked over to his associate. They were silent for several long seconds as if their arson interrogation with Fazio was now running out of steam.

"Well then, being that you're pro-life, hated Petrovitch and burned your hands the morning of that clinic fire, I guess our line of questions today are rather unfounded, Dr. Fazio," Janko cynically observed.

"I guess so, gentlemen. So, if you will both excuse me, I have some more babies here to deliver."

Dr. Fazio rose from his desk as if to bluntly suggest to both firemen that their informal interrogation, which they were so rudely conducting in his office, was now over. They slowly got up from their chairs and walked single file towards his office door.

"We're sorry to bother you, Doctor," Janko apologized.

"No, bother, gentlemen. If I can be of any service to the both of you, please let me know," Fazio politely said, not sincerely meaning a single word of that sentence.

"Thank you, Dr. Fazio," Durham politely said, as he was the first to leave his office.

Terry Janko lingered for a few seconds as he grasped the doorknob, hesitating for a moment to leave.

"Dr. Fazio? Could you do me a huge favor?"

"Certainly, Commander."

Battalion Chief Commander Terrance Janko of Chicago's Fire Engine No. 1 then went for Dr. Fazio's throat:

"Please be very careful where you sleepwalk," he casually suggested.

Captain Durham then interjected as they both quickly exited Fazio's office:

"*Don't close your eyes.*"

Dr. Fazio stood there, frozen, in front of his office door. How in the hell did those two firemen know about his hands being burned that morning? But more importantly, how in the hell did they know about his intense nightmares and his possible sleepwalking?

Fazio was suspicious. Who would have reported his hand injuries? How many people knew about his sleeping issues and especially his sleepwalking? He ran down a list of potential suspects in his mind. Would his old girlfriend Rosa have mentioned something? Would Linda Ciccone, the nurse who treated his hand injuries, have said something to someone? Fazio had dated and slept with enough nurses that his sleeping issues were common knowledge to everyone on staff within the hospital.

But even worse, his pro-life stand against performing abortions was now making him a viable arson suspect in this abortion clinic fire. And who would have mentioned his issues with Petrovitch? How did those verbal disagreements with that goddamn abortionist turn into public knowledge?

He thought long and hard when the distinct memory finally hit him like a ton of bricks. Fazio had

116

heard Terry Janko's name before, and he was now the Chief Battalion Commander at Chicago's Fire Engine No. 1.

He now suspected that somebody had it out for him. A colleague, a scorned girlfriend from the hospital, a disgruntled patient, perhaps? Someone was using this clinic fire as an excuse to tender revenge against him for whatever personal vendettas they may have. The veteran baby doctor had no idea that he had this many enemies within the hospital.

But he also knew that, no matter how bad his nightmares or his sleepwalking was, he certainly wasn't capable of setting a family planning clinic on fire, inhabited by nurses, physicians, and patients. He had enough moral issues with not performing abortions and committing murder on unborn infants. He certainly would never burn down a clinic and knowingly perpetrate a homicide as well.

But how did he burn his hands that morning? The breakfast explanation was only a temporary excuse that he told everyone that day, including Rosa and Nurse Linda Ciccone. But how did he burn his hands? Did he touch the stove while sleepwalking?

Or?

Fazio walked into the bathroom within his spacious office and splashed some cold water on his face. He looked at himself in the mirror and gazed into his own hazel brown eyes. They appeared to be almost green as they were tired, red, and slightly bloodshot from his usual lack of sleep.

This was all starting to take a toll on him, the nightmares, the lack of sleep, the pressures from the hospital, and now, suspicions from the authorities. David Fazio was on the edge of a severe, very intense mental breakdown.

He opened his medicine cabinet and took several valiums. Fazio then walked over to his water cooler and took a long swallow of cold water.

His hands were shaking as he was beginning to second guess himself.

Were his terrible nightmares and reckless sleepwalking now turning him into an arsonist?

CHAPTER FIFTEEN
A Sleep Doctor's Appointment

It was nine-thirty in the morning as I was stepping off the elevator onto the sixth floor when a familiar face wearing a long white coat immediately greeted me.

"Good morning, David," the lovely doctor addressed me, holding her Starbucks coffee. She was standing in front of the elevator door, waiting for me to arrive that morning.

"Good morning," I enthusiastically exclaimed, not immediately recognizing whom I was pleasantly greeting.

"Don't you owe me a follow-up visit?" she immediately asked, as I suddenly realized I was talking to my sleep doctor.

"I will, Jeanne. I've just been a little busy lately. A lot of babies being born these days.'"

"I'm sure," she said as she put her arm around mine and pulled me aside from the spilling crowds of people trying to exit and enter the sixth-floor elevator.

"How are you doing? Have you been sleeping well?" she innocently asked.

"Define 'sleeping well'?" I joked.

We continued to walk together towards the other side of the sixth floor. I had almost forgotten how pretty and pleasant she was to talk to. Jeanne had a personal effervesce that made her so extremely attractive, as her bubbly personality came across so sensually as if to pull at my heartstrings immediately. As she was fondly grasping my arm, I felt like I had a movie star flanked next to me as we were making light conversation about my horrible sleeping habits.

"Are those late-night demons still hanging around?"

"Depends if we're counting old girlfriends," I joked.

She smiled and took another sip of her just acquired cappuccino from the Starbucks kiosk downstairs.

"You know, Dr. Fazio...I have an opening this afternoon. Why don't you stop by, and we can continue our office appointment from the last time?"

"Jeanne, I'm pretty jammed until at least 5:30..."

"I'm available. I will pencil you in," Jeanne pleasantly but forcefully suggested. She locked her big brown eyes onto mine, and I was momentarily hypnotized for about three seconds.

"Don't be late, David...and bring your teddy bear."

Alrighty then.

I was standing alone in the middle of the sixth floor as I watched my beautiful sleep doctor walk down the hallway towards the elevator. As she was strolling away, I was mesmerized by her shapely figure. She could have been easily sauntering off in a Brazilian string bikini instead of a white lab coat. I was fixated with her voluptuous figure as she was entering the sixth-floor elevator.

I guess I had a sleep doctor's appointment after work, whether I wanted one or not.

I didn't know if I wanted to tell her about my sleep issues the night before. I woke up at four-thirty that morning, sitting outside of a 7-11 store five blocks away from my home. I must have walked there in my shorts and a tee-shirt, without any shoes, sitting on a bench adjacent to the parking lot of the store. My sleepwalking was becoming more prevalent, and I realized that I needed to do something about it.

I went through the remainder of my day, which included two Cesarean sections and three deliveries of all very healthy babies, including a set of twins. I had finished seeing patients in my office until almost 5:15 pm that afternoon. I quickly grabbed my backpack, and then suddenly, I got a cute idea.

I rushed downstairs into the gift shop and bought a brown, cute little teddy bear for $19.95. I had the gift shop attendant put a little bow on it, and I brought it with me upstairs to my sleep appointment.

"Dr. Callahan is expecting you," her secretary said as I quickly found my way to the hallway and walked to her back office.

"I didn't think you were going to make it," she earnestly confessed, as she got up from behind her desk and gave me an unconventional hug.

"Do you hug all of your patients?" I naively asked.

"Yes, I do," she quickly answered. "Especially the ones who sleep with their demons."

I smiled. "I brought along a teddy bear," as I presented it to her. She laughed and gave me another hug.

"I thought you were bringing one for yourself."

"My teddy-bears all wear Victoria's Secret."

Great answer.

She smiled and winked her eye. "I'm sure they sell those as well," she said.

She put my teddy bear gift on top of her desk and then shuffled some papers until pulling up my file.

"So, David...seriously, how are you sleeping?"

"I'm sleeping between three to four hours a night."

"Have you been sleepwalking?"

"To tell you the truth, I don't know," I lied.

"I've awakened on the couch many times, never remembering how I've gotten there from my bedroom to the living room," I fabricated. I didn't want to tell her the complete truth.

121

I neglected to mention my various surprise sleeping venues included the front of 7-11's, outdoor parks, adult theaters, and the front seat of my car on multiple occasions. I was ashamed of disclosing my chronic sleepwalking to her at that moment. For whatever reason, I was afraid that she would think I was some kind of goddamn psycho and prescribe to me another straight jacket.

"Have you been awakening with any marks or scars, like the burn marks you experienced a few weeks ago?"

"Not recently..." I

said although I wasn't positive. "I remember waking up the other day with a cut on my finger but can't remember how I injured it."

Another lie.

Dr. Jeanne was writing notes in her file while I was talking. She nodded her head patiently while I was talking, listening carefully as I described my sleeping habits.

"Any bad dreams, David?"

"All the time, but none that I can remember recently."

In all honesty, I do remember most of them, and they continue to haunt the shit out of me. Dr. Jeanne looked at me intently, wanting me to elaborate.

"Have you ever thought about keeping a journal or a notepad next to your bed? You could get into the habit of immediately writing down your dreams when you wake up every morning."

I thought about her suggestion.

"I'm not interested in doing that, Jeanne."

"Why not?"

I thought about my answer carefully.

"Some of my dreams are so vivid and so horrendous that if I try to remember them and write them down, they will only psychologically disturb me and throw me off-kilter."

I thought to myself that if I started to keep a journal of all my bad dreams, they would end up being new television scripts for the 'Twilight Zone.'

"But David, your vivid, even scary dreams are a key to why you're having so much difficulty sleeping. I can't help you if I don't know what it is you're dreaming about."

I looked at her intently, as I was starting to get defensive. "I'm not sure how visiting my demons is going to help my sleeping any better."

She calmly answered. "You have a lot of latent fears and obsessions that you need to address. I believe these demons are who you are deep inside, and you need to confront them."

I listened to her explanation and started to laugh. "Am I visiting a sleep doctor or a psychiatrist?" I jokingly asked.

"There are a lot of psychological issues that are tied to your sleep issues. You need to address those and why you have such vivid, terrifying dreams."

There was a silence of ten seconds or more when Dr. Jeanne Callahan asked another interesting question.

"Have you thought any more about how those burns you got on your hands the other morning?"

I didn't know how to answer her question.

"Not really," I replied.

She then looked at me intently. "David, anything you say here in this office is confidential, and we have a privileged communication relationship between a physician and patient," she explained.

I looked at her, wondering where she was going with this statement. She then dropped a bomb.

"You do realize that there was an arson fire less than a block away from your house on the very morning you had those burns on your hands?"

Although that statement did occur to me, I tried not to think about it, and I certainly wasn't going to admit to it. Not because I felt that I did or didn't do it, but because I genuinely didn't recall doing any such act, even if I was sleepwalking. I only remember the bizarre, vivid, horrendous dream of 'the babies burning.'

I looked at her intently. "So, you suspect that I'm an arsonist?"

"No, David, I didn't say that. I am only pointing out a mere fact that there was an arson fire with casualties going on very close to your home while you were experiencing your 'babies burning' dream."

We were both silent.

"Think about it, David. You're pro-life, you're a baby doctor, and your hands were burned on the same morning as that fire. A lot of coincidences going on there."

I thought about her statement. I didn't know if I should feel insulted and get upset with her for making that observation, or if I should just turn myself in to the police and admit to being an arsonist for starting a fire that I don't remember starting.

"So, you do think I started that fire?" I exclaimed.

"I didn't say that."

"Yes, you did, Jeanne. I came here looking for help with my sleep issues, and here you are accusing me of being a goddamn arsonist."

I was starting to get very upset with her. I don't know why I was getting so angry. Maybe it was a long day, or perhaps I had some guilt-ridden, pent-up hostility built up inside of me since that messy break-up with Rosa last weekend.

"David, I was only making an observation..."

"Screw your observations, Jeanne. I am not an arsonist, and I have no desire to start burning down abortion clinics," I declared as I was raising my voice.

"David, I'm sorry. I was only pointing out some obvious coincidences. And, I might add, if the authorities were to put these coincidences together, they could consider you a suspect."

Now I was getting pissed.

"Well then, Jeanne, why don't you just call up the coppers and let them know that the 'Abortion Arsonist' is now one of your patients."

"I would never do such a thing," she loudly replied.

"Why not, Jeanne? After all, you're a part-time sleep doctor, part-time psychiatrist, and a part-time detective too." I was starting to lay into her.

"Just because I'm pro-life doesn't mean I'm fanatical enough to start burning down abortion clinics." I loudly screamed.

"Really, Jeanne, you would make a great Detective Columbo."

Dr. Jeanne was only looking at me intently as if tears were starting to well up in her eyes. She must have realized how much her observations hurt me. She sat there in silence as if to wait for me to finish my emotional tirade.

I got up from my chair, realizing that this 'sleep doctor' session was an enormous big waste of my damn time.

"I don't know what the hell I was thinking," I said as I am starting to walk toward the door.

"David, please. Don't runoff. I didn't mean to insult you," she pleaded.

"Yes, you did, Jeanne. Just because I have bad, horrible dreams don't mean I go running around burning down abortion clinics."

I began to exit her office before angrily turning around. "This was a bad idea, Dr. Callahan. Send me your bill."

I then bolted out of her office. I didn't need some cracker-jack sleep doctor to tell me her simple little observations about what her theories were regarding my burned hands and her thoughts about that clinic fire.

The nerve of that bitch!

I walked out of the hospital and got into my car. I was too aggravated to go home and too upset to do anything other than going to a local watering hole and drown my anger in several cocktails.

I drove my Mercedes convertible over to River North to a little joint called Lincoln Tavern on North Halsted. Strangely enough, I happened to notice that the Chicagoland Family Planning Center had a storefront facility three doors away from the whiskey bar on North Halsted.

I could always count on finding some drinking buddies, usually sitting at the bar there. I parked my car down the street and walked into the tavern, ordering my first of several Maker's Mark beverages.

The next several hours that evening led to a nightmare that I thought could never happen.

CHAPTER SIXTEEN
A Man Walks into A Bar

I was still wearing my suit coat and tie when I walked into the Lincoln Tavern on North Halsted in Lincoln Park, and as usual, I felt a little overdressed for the place. It was a tiny, 'dive bar' located in a now very posh River North neighborhood that a few of my friends turned me on to because of their top shelve liquor drinks at reasonable prices.

The drab, ugly walls hadn't seen a coat of paint since the Beatles were together, and the long, oak bar still had unique graffiti carved into the oak wood counter-top from the 1950s. There is a standing joke that on one side of the bar countertop is an 'Adlai '56' engraving carved deeply into the wood, which gives the bar some character. No one knows if Adlai Stevenson did any actual drinking there, but occasionally, the bar patrons will do shots in his honor.

The bar has a lot of 'Chicago history,' which was probably why the owners were hesitant to splash some fresh paint on the walls. Rumor has it one of the more corrupt Chicago Alderman was shot and killed on the other side next to the jukebox by one of Sam Giancana's men back in 1961. There are some red spackles of blood on the wall that they say are remnants of the crime scene and a carved 'x' on the floor where the poor bastard fell and hit the ground. He was accused of sleeping with his girlfriend, Phyllis McGuire of the McGuire Sisters.

The Lincoln Tavern was one of those joints straight out of 'Cheers,' where everybody knows not only your name but also your kid's name, your dog's name, your wife's boyfriend's name, and your high-priced lawyer's name as well. All the bar patrons order drinks and hang out there for hours at a time as if they were homeless. It seems like everyone's life was up for discussion and displays there at that bar, and all the regulars talked about their problems as if they were continuing episodes from a television soap opera.

I ordered a Maker's Mark on the Rocks and sat next to one of my favorite pallies, who usually check into this watering hole before either going on air or a hot date.

"What's up, Chaz?"

"Hey David, what's going on?" We shook hands and did the customary man-hug.

Chaz Rizzo was a news reporter for the Channel Eight Eyewitness news team. We had gone to high school together at St. Ignatius over thirty-two years ago, and we managed to keep in touch for many years. I helped him once on a news story a few years ago about an abandoned baby that was found in the dumpster over in Englewood, and he interviewed me for one of his news broadcasts. He was a well-dressed, upscale guy that never left his house without his 'GQ' wardrobe, and he seemed to be well connected to everyone in the City of Chicago.

Channel Eight Eyewitness News usually had him doing most of the organized crime stories or Chicago Archdiocese pieces over the last several years. Rizzo spent a lot of time doing that 'Pedophile Priest Serial Murders' news story that was getting a lot of media attention last summer in Chicago. He did a news story last month on the recent passage of the 'Partial-Birth Abortion Bill' that had recently passed in Springfield, which I assisted him. There were several contacts that I had over at a few pro-life Catholic groups that we interviewed for the news piece, and I was also featured in the article. Rizzo talked about how many pro-life baby doctors, like me, were being 'strongly encouraged' by publicly state-funded hospitals to comply with the now current abortion laws.

We sat there and caught up on personal gossip as we gave each other the latest news on our professional and personal lives. He was single like me, having gone through a few nightmare divorces as well, and we both swore together that another marriage for either one of us just wasn't in the cards. I gave him the latest on my breakup with Rosa, whom he asked about, and we both agreed that my walking away from her marital demands was a good idea.

"So, David, I'm hearing some shit," he said after I popped for another round.

"About?"

"I heard Engine No. 1 is looking at you on that abortion clinic fire on Randolph Street?"

I was a little shocked at his comment, wondering where he had gotten his information.

"Where did you hear this?"

"Detective Dennis Romanowski from Chicago P.D. mentioned it to me when we were trying to get a story on it, and he said something about a 'pro-life baby doctor over at Chicago-Western,' so I knew it had to be you."

I was speechless for about five seconds.

"What else did he say?"

"Something about them trying to tie you into this because you were treated for some third-degree burn injuries on your hands on the same morning as that clinic fire," Chaz explained.

"They weren't third-degree burns. I burned them, making breakfast on the stove."

Chaz Rizzo laughed that girly giggle of his.

"Let me see your hands."

As I showed them, displaying how they had healed quite nicely, he laughed again.

"It's amazing where these rumors get started. Did they come over to talk to you yet?"

"The Battalion Chief and his associate come over to my office the other day," I mentioned.

"Did you get 'lawyered up'?"

I glared at him, as he was now starting to aggravate me. "Chaz, why should I 'lawyer up'? I've done nothing wrong. I don't go running around torching clinics," I loudly protested.

"I would if I were you. Romanowski mentioned something about this 'baby doctor' having sleepwalking issues and that he's been observed passing out in some strange places lately," Chaz explained.

"That's not true! What do they know about where I sleep and where I wake up?" I wasn't going to admit that to a news reporter, even if he was a close friend.

There were several moments of silence.

"They might be tailing you, David. I would be careful."

"I'm not worried, Chaz. I don't do anything wrong," I loudly defied in a very assertive voice.

Chaz looked at me after taking a slow sip of his martini.

"Look, David...we've been friends since high school. You're as clean as a whistle. You haven't gotten as much as a parking ticket in this city," Chaz began.

"But I'm telling you...no...I'm warning you...like a brother...these coppers and their arson squads, once they get a taste of blood, they're not going to let up," he warned.

"But I'm not doing anything wrong, Chaz."

"It doesn't matter. Sometimes detectives work backward. Sometimes, they make the suspect fit the crime, rather than the other way around. It's like trying to fit a wooden square peg into a round hole. If they keep shoving it hard enough, eventually, they will get it to fit."

Another silent moment.

"David, are you still having trouble sleeping?"

"Yes."

"Have you gotten treatment for it?"

"Eh…no…that didn't work out."

"Well," he insisted, "if you're not getting treatment and you're still sleepwalking, the arson investigators and the coppers are going to use that as an excuse to collar you in this crime. That's the way these guys operate, especially Chicago P.D."

I sat there, listening to Chaz's voice of reason.

"Take my advice, David. Do whatever you have to do to protect yourself and to try to stay clear of these investigators. They're under a lot of pressure from the Mayor's office to solve this arson investigation. The 'pro-choice' activists are putting a lot of political pressure as well, especially since there were casualties."

I ordered another round, and we discussed this arson investigation and how it was implicating me. I confessed to Chaz that I had some 'unusual episodes' but didn't believe that I was responsible for setting off any fires.

At that moment, two girls walked into the bar and greeted Chaz, who politely introduced me to both of them.

"Ladies, this is my friend from high school, Dr. David Fazio."

Both girls seemed to be on the younger side, which was Chaz Rizzo's preference. Even though we were the same age, he tended to date (and sometimes marry) much younger girls who seemed to be more attracted to his social status and his money rather than his stellar personality. Chaz Rizzo made a great sugar-daddy.

One of them was a stunning brunette named Lauren Skiba, who was in her late twenties and a court reporter for a Loop firm downtown. She was a single mother with a three-year-old daughter, and she made it quite apparent that she was looking for husband number two. She sat down next to me, and I got the pleasure of hearing her whole life story, which took all of about two hours.

The other woman, named Stephanie Stratton, must have known Chaz, as he continued to buy her drinks for the rest of the night. At about ten o'clock, they both excused themselves, and they went off together, leaving Lauren for my disposal. Since we had both already enjoyed six rounds or more, I knew that we both had more than our share to drink, and the possibility of driving that night wasn't an option.

I had left my Mercedes convertible parked at the Lincoln Tavern before, parked there along Halsted Street for the night. I made sure that my car was locked, and we took an 'Uber' to her place, which was somewhere on Wrightwood Avenue, although I wasn't exactly sure.

We spent the night together, having some exceptional sex for the rest of the evening. It wasn't my routine to run off and spend the night with some strange woman from a bar. But I had been 'over-served,' and running off into someone else's bed was a quick fix for the 'arson' accusations that I was possibly being suspected of.

I woke up at about 5:30 am that morning, sitting in my car with my suit on.

I didn't recall how I had gotten there, considering that we had taken an Uber to her house on Wrightwood Avenue the night before. I surmised that I must have gotten myself up from Lauren's bed, got dressed and somehow, ended up in my parked car not far from the Lincoln Tavern. I did not remember getting up and leaving.

I rubbed my eyes and looked around me, suddenly going into a state of shock. There were several fire trucks and an ambulance parked in front of the Chicagoland Family Planning Clinic.

There was a fire.

The clinic was still encompassed by smoke as my Mercedes was parked about fifteen hundred feet away from the smoldering building. I decided that I needed to start up my car and to get myself the hell out of there before any problems or questions started being asked.

As I was about to start my Mercedes, there was a loud knock on my window, from a strange voice that seemed to come out from nowhere.

"Good morning, Dr. Fazio."

CHAPTER SEVENTEEN
A Confrontation

Detective Romanowski and his associate seemed to appear out of nowhere as Dr. Fazio was trying to start his Mercedes convertible, which was parked on North Halsted Street.

"Where are you going, Doctor?"

The obstetrician didn't recognize the two detectives, even though one of them had known his name.

"Do I know you?"

"I'm Detective Romanowski, and this is Detective D'Aiello, my associate. We're with the Chicago P.D. Eighteenth District. We'd like to talk to you."

"You'll have to excuse me, but I have to go to work," he loudly replied.

"Not now, Doctor. We're giving you a hall pass today. You'll need to come into the precinct with us," Romanowski said.

"For what reason?"

"Look behind you, Doctor. There has just been another unexplained family planning clinic fire. And low and behold, your car happens to be parked fifteen hundred feet away," Detective Romanowski pointed out.

"Look, guys, I don't know what you're talking about. I was here with some friends last night, and I came back here to get my car this morning."

"And, of course, you can substantiate all of this, correct?" D'Aiello asked.

"Absolutely."

Both detectives looked at each other.

"Well, just for grins and giggles, let's take a ride in the police car," D'Aiello suggested.

Both detectives grabbed Fazio's arms while D'Aiello handcuffed his hands from behind. They both then escorted him over to the squad car, parked approximately a block north of the fire location. As they were escorting the baby doctor, they walked past several of the firemen who were still busy putting out the fire. Chicago Fire Engine No. 1 had been called to the scene, and Battalion Chief Terry Janko watched the two detectives escort Fazio over to the squad car. Both Terry and Dennis made eye contact, affirming that perhaps, they had apprehended their man.

After approximately forty-five minutes of transporting the potential arsonist and prisoner over from their squad car and into the holding room, Detective Romanowski opened up the locked door where Fazio was sitting, his hands handcuffed to the chair.

As the detective entered the room, Fazio began to protest loudly.

"Detective, is this necessary?" referring to his cuffed hands to the chair.

Romanowski smiled as he pulled out his keys and unlocked the handcuffs.

"I know you're a doctor and all, but sometimes we can't take any chances."

"Do I look like a hardened criminal to you?" Fazio asked, still wearing his dark suit and his undone necktie.

Romanowski looked at him, holding a styrofoam cup of black coffee.

"I'm not going anywhere, Detective. I'll be happy to answer your questions," Fazio asserted.

"Here, I brought you this," he said, handing the cup of black coffee over to the doctor.

"Thank you," the doctor said. He began to take loud slurps as he swallowed the hot, freshly brewed java while the detective started to make himself comfortable at the holding room table.

"Okay, Doc...let's talk. What were you doing on North Halsted Street?"

"Went there last night to have some drinks with a friend," Fazio replied.

"Which friend?"

"Chaz Rizzo...do you know him?" Fazio smiled.

A few moments of silence.

"Chaz Rizzo, from Channel Eight?"

"Yep...that's him."

A few more moments of silence as Romanowski was deep in thought.

"So then, where were you, and what exactly we're you doing from the time you left the bar last night until this morning?"

Dr. Fazio glared at the Detective.

"I got lucky," he managed to respond.

"Oh? With whom?"

Fazio began to think, hoping that he could remember her name.

"Some young broad, her name was Lauren, I think," the doctor hesitated, trying to think.

"Lauren Skiba...yeah...that's it. That's her name. We 'ubered' it over to her apartment on Wrightwood Avenue."

"Really? Okay, then what happened?"

Dr. Fazio smiled at the detective's stupid question.

"What do you think happened, Detective?"

"I don't know, Doctor. You tell me. Did you have more drinks? Did you watch TV? Did you guys play 'Scrabble'? Tell me exactly what you did after you both arrived at her house," the detective insisted on hearing all of the details.

The doctor thought for a moment.

"Let's see...I asked her to remove her clothing, and she then put on a patient gown. After thoroughly washing my hands, I put both of her legs on the examination table stirrups. Then I examined her for any obvious diseases like chlamydia, gonorrhea, or any other obvious STD diseases. Then I took a lab specimen and read her charts, getting an understanding of her medical history before I..."

"Cut the bullshit, Doc!"

"What the hell do you think we did?"

"I don't know. That's why I'm asking!"

Fazio continued to laugh to himself, shaking his head.

"Did you use a condom?" Romanowski asked.

"Who are you now, my mother?"

"Just answer the question, Doc."

"Yes!" the baby doctor loudly answered.

The two of them were silent for several moments as Romanowski grabbed a yellow pad of paper sitting on the gray steel table and started scribbling some notes. At that moment, Detective Mike D'Aiello walked into the holding room. D'Aiello looked at Romanowski as he showed him the yellow pad of paper.

"Seems our boy, here, makes house calls," Romanowski said.

"Really?" D'Aiello replied.

"Seems he spent the night with this woman, named Lauren Skiba, who lives somewhere on Wrightwood Avenue."

They both looked at each other.

"Did he use a condom?" D'Aiello asked.

"For fuck's sake, what the hell do you guys care whether or not I used a condom?" Fazio loudly protested.

"DNA evidence, Doc," D'Aiello replied.

"What did you do with the condom after you both had sex?"

"I put it back in my wallet," Fazio sarcastically replied.

Both detectives looked at each other. Fazio was now clearly aggravated with the direction of these stupid questions.

"Look, Doc...you play nice with us, and maybe, just maybe, you may get out of here in time to finish your shift over at the hospital. If you're going to talk smart, we'll keep you here all day and all night if we have to," Romanowski loudly replied.

"DNA evidence, guys? Really?"

Fazio started shaking his head, now realizing he should probably call a lawyer.

D'Aiello took another piece of yellow paper from the notepad and wrote the girl's name down.

"Did you happen to get her number?" D'Aiello asked.

"Well, considering that I wanted to sneak out of her bedroom and out of her apartment before she insisted on us getting married...no, Detective...I did not get her number."

The two detectives looked at each other and then glared at Fazio.

"We're going to call up this Ms. Skiba and see if she has any recollection of spending the night with you last night," Romanowski said.

The two detectives then left the holding room. Detective Mike D'Aiello walked back to his desk and began the process of trying to locate the 'one-night stand' that Fazio spent the night with. As he was continuing his search, his desk phone rang.

"Detective D'Aiello," he responded.

"Mike...we gotta problem." It was Romanowski on the other line.

"I just got a phone call from Chaz Rizzo from Channel Eight News. Fazio's story checks out."

"How did he know that we even picked him up?" D'Aiello asked.

"You know these goddamn reporters...God only knows where they get their information from. He says that unless we have some definite evidence, to cut him loose or he'll be doing a police harassment story on the six o'clock news, and what a bunch of bumbling idiots the Chicago P.D. detectives are," Detective Romanowski said.

D'Aiello seemed frustrated, as there were several moments of silence.

"Rizzo is an asshole," D'Aiello said.

"It doesn't matter. Rizzo is vouching for him. Says he spent the night with a friend of his girlfriend's that met him at the Lincoln Tavern last night."

"Fuck him!" D'Aiello protested.

"No, Mike...we gotta cut him loose," Dennis insisted.

"We'll keep a tail on him for a while and see if he does anything stupid. But for now, we don't have enough to hold him, and I don't need any problems or bullshit from Rizzo right now."

"Shit!" D'Aiello said, with intense frustration in his voice.

"Well, let's hold onto him for another hour or so and mess with his head a bit until we can nail tight his alibi."

After about another two hours, it was close to 11:00 am when both detectives returned to the holding room where Fazio was still patiently waiting.

"Today is your lucky day Doc. We found the condom that you used last night, along with your fat, ugly 'one-night stand' that you spent the night with," Romanowski jokingly lied.

"She says that you were a lousy fuck, even with the Viagra," D'Aiello played along.

Dr. Fazio smiled, knowing that they were both joking but trying to make a mockery of him at the same time. He then got up from the chair and went to walk over to the exit door.

"Hey, uh...Doc? Your pallie, Chaz Rizzo, saved your ass today," Detective Romanowski volunteered.

139

"I suggest you watch your back, Doc. Don't light up any fires anytime soon," said D'Aiello.

Fazio looked at them both and nodded. He knew he had to make a phone call to Chaz Rizzo as soon and he left the police station. He was very grateful to his friend and his unique connections to the Chicago P.D.

"Don't play with matches, Doc. You know what Smokey the Bear says," Romanowski said.

Then Detective Michael D'Aiello interjected his final parting words:

"*Don't close your eyes.*"

Dr. David Fazio smiled at both detectives as he bee-lined it to the exit door of the holding room. He stopped at the sergeant's desk and was given back his cell phone, his watch, and his wallet as he left the Eighteenth District. He then walked several blocks to a nearby McDonald's, where he ordered an Egg McMuffin and an orange juice.

He then picked up his cell phone and dialed a phone number.

"Thank you," David gratefully said immediately, as his high school friend answered the phone.

"You're welcome. It's always a pleasure to stick it to scum bag detectives like Romanowski. Those guys are under a lot of pressure to grab a collar on these arson fires, and right now, they don't have any suspects," Chaz Rizzo said.

"You saved my ass today, Chaz. I owe you."

"Well, you dodged a bullet this morning. The next time, you won't be so lucky."

A moment of silence as Fazio was consuming his breakfast. He was hungry, and his 'Mickey-D's' fast-food cuisine was temporarily distracting him from his severe problems.

"These guys are gonna be watching you, David."

"Yeah, I figure they will be."

"Remember what I told you last night, Doc. These guys are gunning for you. You're the only potential suspect that they have, and right now, they haven't got shit," Rizzo reiterated.

"Watch your back, pallie...please?"

He thanked his friend again and hung up the phone. As he sat there at McDonald's, finishing his breakfast, Fazio had finally come to a somber conclusion.

Dr. David Fazio would have to be very careful, every hour, every moment, and every minute of every day. He would have to watch his back and always be very aware of his immediate surroundings. He would have to be very careful of who he talks to at the hospital. He would have to be cautious and suspicious of all of his friends.

Someone knew that his car was going to be parked there, and someone must have set off that clinic fire.

Someone, but who? Who was trying to frame him?

Or an even scarier thought came to his head: What if he was the Abortion Arsonist? He was severely drunk last night and hardly remembered anything. What if he got up in the middle of the night and returned to his car, and subconsciously, set the abortion clinic on fire? He must have been sleepwalking last night as he didn't remember leaving that woman's apartment.

What if he did set those clinics on fire?

The baby doctor began to doubt himself, his actions, and his present state of mind. He would have to be mindful of his actions, his thoughts, and his psychological, mental state. But most of all, he would have to think two and three times...

Every night before he closed his eyes.

CHAPTER EIGHTEEN
A Visit Home

It was a sunny, quiet Sunday morning as I parked my Mercedes convertible in front of our family's grocery store on West Grand Avenue. It was just after ten o'clock, and my mother was expecting me over for our usual family Sunday dinner. I usually never showed up until after one o'clock in the afternoon. By then, I could smell my mother's 'Sunday sauce' aroma creeping out of the kitchen, breezing outside and flowing onto Grand Avenue.

I grew up the oldest of five children in a large, four-bedroom apartment upstairs above our family grocery store. Fazio's Italian Foods is a small grocery store at 1378 West Grand Avenue that was opened and started by my father, Antonio Fazio, in 1965. Our family grocery store was a staple of the Italian neighborhood on West Grand and Noble Streets and has been in operation by our family for almost sixty years. I grew up in that same large apartment above the store, and I fondly remember walking to school in the seventies to St. Rita Grade School on North Ada Street with my friends in the neighborhood every morning.

Back then, it was safe to walk back and forth to our Catholic school four blocks away, and I would often walk home for lunch with my friend Mauro. My mother would have either salami or mortadella sandwiches waiting for us when we got there, and we would often sit in front of the television in the family room, eating sandwiches, drinking milk, and watching cartoons.

That Sunday morning, I knew my mother was still in church, so I decided to walk into the grocery store to greet my father. Antonio Fazio, now 79 years old, was still working and overseeing the store as intently as the day he opened it back in 1965. My younger brothers, Carlo and Marco, both run the store now full time with my father, who is supposedly 'retired.'

I saw my dad, 'Papa Antonio,' as he was called around the neighborhood, behind the deli, cutting up some steaks and fillets for a customer.

"Hey Pop," as I walked over behind the deli counter to kiss him.

"Davide? What-ta you, on-a vacation?" My cranky old father was in a wonderful mood that morning, as the store was full of customers, and he didn't have enough help to take care of them, as usual. My parents both called me by my christened Italian name.

"I know you a bigga-shot doctor now, but we need-a some help. Grab an apron in da' back." My father still spoke English with a very thick Italian accent.

My father grew up in a small town near Cassino, Italy, called Casalvieri (about 168 kilometers south of Rome) and emigrated here from Italy at the age of fifteen years old. They first lived on Taylor Street, where he worked as a butcher at Lombardo's Grocery Store before going on his own on West Grand Avenue.

My mother, Costanza (everyone calls her 'Connie'), who is now 74 years old, married my father in 1964 at St. Rosalia Catholic Church on Lexington Avenue in the old neighborhood. She was born in Rome but was raised in a small town near my father's called Cervaro and came here to the United States on the USS Constitution when she was twelve years old.

The two of them raised a family of five children upstairs after opening the store here at Grand and Noble Streets. Besides my two younger brothers, Carlo and Marco, who now runs the grocery store, my sister Teresa went to school to become a nurse. After she got her MBA from Loyola University, she now works as a hospital administrator at North Shore Medical Center in Highland Park. My youngest brother, Giovanni (we call him Little Johnny), is a personal injury attorney and a partner with a large law firm in the Chicago Loop. He was the only one who was allowed to 'go-away' to college and graduated from Notre Dame University Law School after attending the University of Michigan.

I had worked for my father in the store at an early age and learned the meat cutting trade at fourteen years old. While most kids were either playing baseball or on the football team in high school, I usually had to rush home from St. Ignatius High School on West Roosevelt Road and work for my father at the grocery store after school. I often complained to my mother when I was a teenager that my father never paid me enough to sacrifice my teenage and high school years to work at the store.

But when it came time to go to college and medical school, I was on the 'Fazio Family Scholarship' plan. My father and mother paid for all eight years of my tuition, books, housing, and transportation at Northwestern University, no questions asked. They did the same for my youngest brother and sister as well. Their only request was that we all helped at the grocery store whenever we could. To this day, my father still makes me grab an apron and a butcher knife and go behind the deli counter to help customers whenever I'm over at the store visiting.

"Where's Mom?" I asked my brother Carlo, who had just unloaded some supply trucks in the back.

"David? It's Sunday morning. Where do you think she is?" That meant that she was still at mass over at St. Rita Church four blocks away.

"She started the Sunday sauce upstairs," he deviously smiled, as he was grabbing several boxes and loading them onto a dolly to help my brother Marco stock up the shelves.

I was famished that morning and was anxious to go upstairs with a loaf of fresh bread and dip it several times into the sauce while my mother was away at church. After all of these years, that was a Sunday ritual that all of my brothers shared since we were kids. But with my luck, she would probably walk in on me in the kitchen and hit me with one of her large, wooden spoons. My father had plans for me that morning anyway, and I was more than happy to help.

Honestly, with all the drama that was going on at the hospital and with these abortion clinics getting torched, the last thing I wanted to be that morning was a doctor. As I put my apron on and began slicing sides of beef, filleting steaks and short ribs for customers, I was happy to mentally 'check out' and do the very thing that I learned how to do since I was a young teenager working at the store for my father.

That morning, I was my father's oldest son. That morning, I was the son of poor, hardworking Italian immigrants who came to Chicago with only a fifth-grade education. That morning, I was a butcher, the son of a successful businessman, who sacrificed all his years and money to put his children through college, through medical school, through law school, and through graduate school. That morning, I was a first-generation Italian American who achieved the lifelong goal of being successful, thanks to the incredible sacrifices my father and mother made, making sure that we never fell short of accomplishing our dreams.

That morning, I was Papa Antonio's oldest boy, who made good and became a doctor.

As I was taking care of one of the customers, my father came over and started talking to an older lady over the counter.

"You know who that is?" I overheard him say as he pointed me out. "That-sa, my oldest boy, the baby doctor!"

I could hear him brag with pride as I was chuckling to myself, pretending that I wasn't listening.

"You must be David!" she said to me as she reached her hand out over the counter to grasp mine. "I've heard your father and mother brag so much about you. They are so proud."

I smiled as we made a pleasant conversation about where I worked and how much I enjoyed my profession.

"It's so nice of you to come here and help out your family at the store," she smiled.

"Not by choice," I laughed, although I was happy to do so.

About an hour later, my mother came back from mass and came downstairs to the store. She walked behind the counter and gave me one of her big, wet, garlic-flavored kisses on the cheek.

"I no see you in-a so long," my mother said. Her broken English wasn't any better than my father's.

"I was home a couple of weeks ago, Ma."

"Eh? You are supposed to come over for dinner every Sunday. Last-a Sunday, you no come. We wait, and we wait for you. You no show-up."

"Ma? I was on call last Sunday. I told you I had to work."

"You should-a come over for dinner anyway. You no that far, you know."

"I'm sorry, Ma." It was easier to apologize than to make her understand that I was on maternity call at the hospital last Sunday and couldn't leave. I ended up doing several emergency deliveries that day.

"We gonna have dinner in an hour. Your Zio Tony and Zia Angelina are coming over."

My mother was referring to her younger brother, Tony DiMatteo. He ran a tomato distribution business on South Ashland Avenue called DiMatteo Tomato

146

Distribution Company. Zio Tony and Zia Angelina doted on us as if they were our second set of parents.

My 'Zio Tony', who is also my godfather, is referred to by the media, the newspapers, mob watchers, and the FBI as 'Little Tony' DiMatteo, who is considered the 'Capo dei Capi' of all the crime families in Chicago. 'Zio Tony' always thought of me to be the favorite of all his nephews and would often walk into Chicago-Western Medical Hospital as if he owned the place.

"Do you know who my nephew is?" he would ask almost every doctor or nurse that he encountered.

"My nephew, Dr. David Fazio, is the best baby doctor in all Chicagoland," he would loudly brag to anyone at the hospital who would listen. He would often stop by the hospital once or twice a month, and I would take five or ten minutes out of my busy schedule to have coffee with him at the Starbucks kiosk downstairs.

I've often wondered if he had a financial hand in assisting my parents in putting all of us kids through college and especially my very costly medical education. When I graduated from Northwestern University Medical School, I graduated with no debt, thanks to the selfless sacrifices of my parents and probably (although he would never admit it) my Zio Tony.

Whenever we had coffee at the hospital, he would often ask me:

"Kid, you need anything?"

"No, Zio Tony... I'm doing fine, thank you."

I remember when I was at Northwestern University, I would be working at the store after school, and he would walk behind the counter and put four or five 'bennies' in my shirt pocket when my father wasn't looking.

"College is expensive," he would often say. "Don't go to the same college I went to."

Zio Tony was referring to the four years he did in Stateville for armed robbery and attempted murder. I remember on several occasions while we were growing up, Zio Tony asked my brothers and myself to 'go to work for him' and help him out at his tomato distribution company. My father adamantly refused to allow us to work for him, and out of respect to our father, none of us ever worked at the 'tomato factory.' Whenever we asked our dad that question, his response was always the same.

"I give-a you a clean name."

That was all we needed to know.

CHAPTER NINETEEN
Mary Bernardo

The glaring hot sun of that early summer morning in July was already at eighty degrees, as the parishioners were about to descend on Saint Michael's Catholic Church in Old Town. Their nine o'clock mass was usually well-filled every Sunday, but even more so on that humid day as early worshippers wished to avoid sitting in a hot, antiquated church any longer than they had to on that muggy morning.

It was a fair assumption to say that the forty-eight-year-old Mary Bernardo was a devout Catholic. She attended mass every Sunday morning, made her confession once a month on Saturday afternoons, and was involved in many of St. Michael's Church activities. Mary was part of a team of ladies who attended to all of the needs of the church, from ordering candles for holy mass to vacuuming and cleaning the sacristy every month. She was responsible for making sure that there were flowers at the altar every week and making phone calls to potential donors when there wasn't enough money available to buy them. Mary also ordered seasonal banners to hang from the rafters of the church, making sure that each colorful sign reflected the proper liturgy for that upcoming week.

Mary Bernardo was a single mother with two teenage girls, having been widowed five years ago by the death of her beloved husband of twenty-two years, Joseph. He died a quick death from glioblastoma (a brain tumor) after having worked as a machine operator for Union Local 150 for thirty years.

Since his death, her belief in her Christian Catholic values and the afterlife have become even more passionate. She now believed that the marital covenants she made when she married her husband went beyond their vows of 'til death do us part'. Mary felt that she needed to live a pure, chaste life to be reunited with her husband in the afterlife.

As Mary entered St. Michael's at ten minutes to nine, she found her place next to the fourth station of the cross in a pew near the front of the church. She kneeled, made the sign of the cross, and said some quick prayers to herself, grasping the beads of her rose-colored rosary.

She always prayed for the soul of her late husband and that he was resting in peace in heaven. She also prayed for her two teenage girls. They were both enrolled at Holy Trinity High School in their freshman and junior years there. As with all single moms, Mary was fast becoming acquainted with the problems of raising two beautiful teenage girls without a father. She was constantly challenged with the social issues associated with bringing them up righteously in a culture void of any moral ethics.

And lastly, of course, Mary prayed for her strength and sanity at work most of all. Mary Bernardo was a dedicated maternity nurse at Chicago-Western Medical Hospital. She had worked for the hospital for the last twenty-four years, spending most of those years attending to newborn babies being delivered within the hospital. She attended to the sick, premature babies that were born within the hospital, as well as the healthy, joyous arrivals that seemed to make her nursing career even more rewarding.

But like all current obstetrical and maternity nurses, participating in abortions was also a part of her job description.

And unlike some obstetricians (like Dr. David Fazio), Nurse Mary Bernardo had no choice. She was required to do her job in assisting the attending physicians in terminating those pregnancies when requested. She always said a quick prayer to herself and was emotional before injecting that needle into the mother's womb. Mary Bernardo would whisper several 'God Forgive Me" prayers before filling that vile with the potassium chloride solution needed to stop the beating heart of a healthy fetus. Handing the necessary tools like the forceps, the curettes, the syringes, and the required tenaculum to end the lives of those unborn babies abruptly was one of the more horrific realities of her nursing job.

But because of her financial responsibilities as a single mother and the exceptional nursing salary she earned with benefits there at Chicago-Western, she could not afford to leave her current job and transfer to another department or even another hospital. Mary Bernardo was financially strapped and morally conflicted. She always personally felt that her assistance in performing those abortion procedures would still be a black mark against her otherwise pristine soul, and she prayed every Sunday for the Lord's forgiveness.

As the nine o'clock mass began, Father Bertram O'Casey presided over the Sunday morning liturgy. He preached in his sermon about the 'horrors that face the unborn' in today's society and how a woman's choice to terminate such pregnancies was a 'selfish choice of convenience.' This particular homily had personally hit home for Nurse Mary Bernardo.

About a year ago, that previous summer, she was cleaning the church sacristy one Saturday morning, she was approached by Sister Magdalena Vitucci. She was conducting religious education classes there on that day at St. Michael's Church. She was an older nun in her late sixties who was with the Sisters of Mercy in Oak Park and was quite active within the community.

Sister Magdalena was a very vocal, very pro-life activist. She had been involved with pro-life protests and family planning clinic vigils since the early eighties and was very well known with all the political lobbyists in Springfield. The devoted nun from the Sisters of Mercy was a timid, meek, and mild, holy sister who was never outspoken about anything.

Unless the subject of abortions ever came into the conversation. Her eyes would then widen, and one could see the rage seeping out of the pores of her skin as she verbally cast her anger on all those abortionists who terminated the innocent lives of the unborn.

Sister Magdalena asked Mary Bernardo about her thoughts regarding the current abortion laws in Illinois and whether she was willing to attend a prayer group for those young mothers entering the local family planning clinics that they would keep vigil for.

Mary Bernardo was enthusiastic about doing so and praying their six-hour vigils at various family planning clinics in and around the city. They started with the small prayer group of about five or six ladies, consisting of Sister Magdalena, three other sisters from the convent, and herself last summer. They began at a family planning clinic in Ravenswood, and each week switched to another clinic every Thursday night in the city, from five o'clock until about midnight.

The Thursday night groups were small, and they usually read the gospel together, held lighted candles, and sang religious songs, handing out free rosaries and little religious pamphlets to all the women who tried to enter the family planning facility. Most women were receptive, but many others refused to be deterred by their vigils and continued to have their babies aborted.

Soon afterward, the Servants of Mary church councils from St. Michael's Church and several other parishes began to attend these Thursday evening vigils as well. Their small vigil group, which started with five ladies last summer, grew to almost forty to fifty people every Thursday night, like the Servants, along with their spouses and other religious supporters, began to assemble in front of these various family planning clinics.

About two months ago, Mary Bernardo remembered an incident that occurred at the Affiliated Abortion Clinic on Randolph Street in the Gold Coast neighborhood. One of the girls who tried to enter the clinic claimed that she was 'harassed' and was physically kept from entering inside. One of the doctors, who was the head of the clinic, came out of the facility and had a verbal confrontation with several of the Servants of Mary, who were attending the silent vigil. That verbal confrontation turned into a physical assault, and several of the Servants were arrested and hailed away from the clinic. The same situation occurred at the Chicagoland Family Planning Clinic on North Halsted Street, where some of the quiet vigils turned violent. They were admonished by Chicago's new mayor, sternly warning their prayer group of any more physical confrontations.

Sister Magdalena talked to Mary Bernardo last week about their prayer group being infiltrated by the Servants of Mary members and making them confrontational. Both agreed that if their quiet, silent prayer vigils for the souls of the unborn would turn violent and that the Servants of Mary members would not be welcome. Unfortunately, Sister Magdalena had neither the forcefulness nor the personal strength to verbally ban the Servants of Mary from attending their vigil services on Thursday nights. As of last week, there were over eighty-plus supporters holding candles, singing religious music, and passing out pamphlets to those women wishing to obtain abortions from a family planning clinic in the Lakeview neighborhood.

When the 'prayers of intentions' were announced during the mass, the lecturer asked for prayers for the medical personnel who had perished in the current arson fires within those clinics.

Mary went into mild shock. She immediately realized that the two abortion clinics that were recently burned down were the same two clinic locations where there were physical confrontations two months ago with several Servants of Mary members.

As the mass ended, Mary Bernardo stayed afterward to light a candle for her late husband in the back of the church. She noticed Sister Magdalena talking to Father O'Casey in the vestibule of St. Michael's.

"Good Morning Mary...are you ready for another hot one today?" Fr. O'Casey smiled.

"I have a bathtub filled with ice cubes when I get home," Mary jokingly replied.

"Well, Mary...that will certainly keep you virtuous!" he quickly responded, as they all shared a laugh near the entrance door of the church.

Sister Magdalena locked eyes with Mary and immediately knew what was concerning her.

"No," the nun quickly said to Mary.

"No, what?"

"No, there is no connection," Magdalena retorted.

"How can you be sure, Sister? We have done prayer vigils at almost fifty family planning clinics over the last year, yet the only two clinics where the police were called were both torched over the last two months," Bernardo explained.

"Torched by whom? One of the members from the Servants of Mary?"

Mary Bernardo was silent for several long seconds. She initially was surprised that the Chicago P.D. hadn't made the connection yet. She wondered if any of those Servants of Mary members attending the prayer vigils over these last several months were capable of torching an abortion clinic.

"Maybe," Mary slowly said.

She walked over to the table with the weekly Sunday newsletters and grabbed one for herself. She then walked over and hugged Sister Magdalena.

"Where are we meeting this Thursday?" she quietly asked.

"We have a clinic that we are gathering at over in the Pilsen neighborhood. I will email you the address," the Sister of Mercy replied.

"Thank you," she responded.

She shook hands with Father O'Casey and exited the church.

As she walked back to her car, she wondered how her Thursday evening prayer vigils were slowly turning into violent, anti-abortion protests. She sat in her car, turned on the ignition, and switched on the air conditioning. Still grasping her rosary, she said one more prayer.

She couldn't bear the thought of another abortion clinic fire.

CHAPTER TWENTY
Sunday Dinner

We were all taking our places at the long, oak table at my parent's house, which my mother had ornately set up in the dining room. It was Sunday afternoon at one o'clock, our usual time for our weekly family 'cenetta.' Everyone in my family, including my brothers, their wives, their children, my sister, her husband with their kids, and myself, of course, we're all required to be there at 1378 West Grand Avenue for Sunday dinner. Unless you had a doctor's note or a death certificate, there were no excuses. As far as my mother was concerned, your presence and participation in the Fazio Sunday family dinners were mandatory.

Growing up above the grocery store, our kitchen and dining room were essential rooms in our house. The old, antique wooden table was set up by Mama Connie for eighteen people. My mother made sure that each place setting, each china dish, each crystal glass, and every piece of silverware was adequately placed in its proper order. The cloth napkins were appropriately folded and inserted into the water glasses, similar to that of a white cloth restaurant. Looking at my mother's dining room table on Sundays, one would have thought that the Royal Family was coming over from Buckingham Palace for dinner.

Every Sunday, my mother, Costanza, got up at six o'clock in the morning to start making the 'Sunday sauce.' She would start with sautéing the meat and neck bones, which usually included a fair amount of short ribs as well. If, on occasion, she decided to make Bolognese sauce, then the ground up meat was adequately sautéed. And of course, sometimes she would be up early and start frying up meatballs for the sauce. Along with a generous helping of garlic and onions, my mother would then include her homemade tomato sauce from her stash of jars filled with squeezed tomatoes from the store cellar downstairs.

Mom usually replenished her homemade inventory every Labor Day weekend, an annual ritual that I was always required to attend and help out with every year since I was six years old. She would then turn the stove on 'low' and then go off to nine-thirty mass at St. Rita Catholic Church a few blocks away.

As kids, we usually had it timed perfectly. While growing up, my brothers and I would wait for her to leave for mass on Sundays. We would then grab a fresh loaf of Italian bread and take turns dipping it into my mother's homemade, fresh Italian tomato sauce, making a breakfast meal out of it before she came back home from mass. The covert ritual was a weekly tradition with my brothers and sister while growing up at our house.

I remember waking up early on Sundays, as the smell of my mother's Sunday sauce would be an overwhelming aroma within our household. Its romantic tomato scent would follow us down the stairwell, outside to the sidewalk onto Grand Avenue, and into my father's store. Customers would come in on Sundays and request a sample of my mother's famous Sunday sauce, which Papa Antonio only did a limited number of times while Mama Connie was away at church.

After a while, my mother eventually figured out where we were getting our Sunday morning breakfast from. She started marking an 'etched line' on the large cooking pot full of tomato sauce, and she knew when she got back home from church that the level of sauce in that pot had better not have changed. We tried using water and other ways and methods of fooling her, but it was no use.

She got wise to us. And when she figured it out, one of us got cracked with a wooden spoon when she got home. It was a standing joke with my brothers and me. We would take bets to see how long her new wooden spoons would last before eventually breaking one of them over our heads on Sunday mornings.

"No touch-a da' sauce until we eat at one o'clock," was her famous parting words to everyone at home before she left for mass on Sundays.

Her Sunday sauce was terrific, and it was always worth the trip home for Sunday afternoon dinners. I remember one of my ex-wives making the mistake of calling my mother's Sunday sauce 'gravy'. Mama Connie looked at her as though she was staring at an exotic working girl from the Admiral Theater on Lawrence Avenue. After some dirty looks from around the table and several uncomfortable moments of silence, my mother finally corrected her.

"Look-a honey. It-sa no called a-gravy. That-sa for da' turkey for Tanks-a-giving. Its-a Sunday sauce," my mother answered her in her thick, Italian accent.

We all took our places, with Papa Antonio sitting at the head of the table, of course, and my mother seated next to him. After a long passionate prayer of thanks from Mama Connie (which usually included her gratefulness for any of her children not ending up on the street or in jail), we often started eating dinner. Besides the Sunday sauce and neck bones, there was usually either tortellini or minestrone, a tossed Caesar salad, some boiled vegetables and potatoes, and of course, Mama Connie's famous homemade pasta, personally prepared by my mother. And, of course, several loaves of freshly baked bread were at the table as well.

Each week, the homemade pasta variated. Depending on the mood my mother was in, it was either homemade spaghetti, pappardelle, gnocchi, ziti, orecchiette, or linguini. She usually started making the homemade pasta the night before, using one egg and one cup of flour for every person. She then lovingly rolled and cut the pasta, using her pasta cutting machine, and always had more than enough for all of us on Sundays.

Our family Sunday dinners were a long-standing tradition that was the envy of every family in the neighborhood. Most sons or daughters from Grand Avenue grew up and moved away, only occasionally visiting their old parents who still lived there, once in a while and on holidays. For whatever reason, my strong-willed mother and hard-working father would never hear of it.

You either showed up for Sunday dinners, or you were utterly disowned by the family and cut out from the will. No exceptions.

I remember telling her years ago that I had to work a shift at the hospital, where I was on call and couldn't make it home for dinner one Sunday. Somehow, she managed to get on the telephone and to go through the chain of command with Chicago-Western Medical Hospital ranks until she was able to contact the head of my obstetrical and gynecological department, Dr. Calvin Worrell.

"Excuse-a me, Dr. Worrell," she said to him over the phone. "You gotta let-ta my son Davide come-a home for dinner on a Sunday at one o'clock. Me and-a my husband, we bot-ta very old, we very sick-a, and we don't-a know how long we gonna live. Capish?"

It became a long-standing joke within the department, as Dr. Worrell acquiesced and humorously made sure there was enough time on my schedule for me to break and run home for the Fazio family dinner on Sundays.

Papa Antonio always used the Sunday family dinners as an excuse to fill up another gallon of his homemade wine from his 'cantina' downstairs. Everyone usually had a glass, including the kids sitting

159

at the table. We all held up our glasses and made a toast, all saying 'salute" in unison, drinking to our good health, our family, and of course, the Republicans.

The family dinners usually lasted over four hours, including several courses, a plentiful amount of desserts, and many cups of espresso later. Each Sunday, we would all take turns picking up a cake or some biscotti for our Sunday dinners. The Fazio family dinner would never break up until my father brought out his homemade limoncello (after-dinner drink). At that point, our mother reluctantly allowed us to go home. It was unusual for our family dinners to break up before five o'clock on Sunday afternoons.

On that day, Zio Tony and Zia Angelina were invited over for dinner, so we had the pleasure of his company and his colorful, Shakespearian poetry at the dinner table. If my Zio Tony had to express himself without using the "F" word, he would be a silent, muted, Franciscan monk. I can't remember how many times my mother would verbally chastise her younger brother for the use of his eloquent 'French' at our family dinners.

"So kid, how's it going over there," he asked me at the dinner table, referring to my career at the hospital. Somehow, he must have heard of my issues within the hospital.

"It's going okay," I generalized, not wanting to discuss my career problems at the dinner table.

Zio Tony looked at me, knowing that there was more to discuss than what I was letting on.

"I hear they're putting some pressure on you," he revealed, now letting the 'cat out of the bag.'

"Pressure to do what?" my brother Carlo asked.

I then began to explain the situation to the family regarding the requirement of all the obstetricians at the hospital to perform partial-birth abortions for all those patients who requested one.

Because of the new governor and the legislation that was just passed, I explained the dilemma that I was confronted with and the pressure that was being put on everyone in my department. My parents gasped as Mama Connie made the sign of the cross while serving the homemade gnocchi's.

"So, what are you going to do," my sister Teresa asked.

"Nothing," I explained. "So far, I have refused to participate in performing any abortions, and the head of our department had stated that he respects my conscience decision."

"But," I also said, "there is no guarantee that when the occasion arises, and there is no one else around to perform an abortion, my refusal to terminate a pregnancy could be reason enough for my dismissal from the hospital."

"They can't do that," my attorney brother Giovanni said. "They can get sued up and down for forcing you to do something against your conscience and religious beliefs."

"Well, they seem to believe that they can, if they are in a situation where they are required to terminate a pregnancy, and no other doctor or midwife is around to perform it. I would be required to do so under the terms of my employment contract," I responded.

At that moment, I was enjoying the homemade gnocchi's so much I didn't even want to discuss the hospital situation anymore. But everyone at the dinner table wanted more answers.

"The hell with them," Zio Tony responded. "Get out of that hospital and set up your own joint. I'll finance you one hundred percent."

"Thanks, Zio, but I'm not sure I'm ready to do that right now."

"I told you, Bro," as my opinionated younger brother Little Johnny chimed in. "Get out of that hospital and that specialty. Times have changed, and you need to get out of there. You'd make a good pediatrician, and it wouldn't take you long to get set up."

"I agree. But I like my job right now, and I like the backing of the hospital and the hospital staff. Hanging out a shingle and starting on my own isn't easy at my age right now," I explained.

"It's never too late," Carlo said.

"Why can't you just move to a Catholic hospital? I'm sure Resurrection or Alexian Brothers would respect your position, and I know you wouldn't be pushed into performing abortions," my sister Teresa chimed in.

"Yes, but I would take a significant cut in salary, and I would have to start at the 'bottom of the food chain.' Right now, at Chicago-Western, I'm one of their senior physicians and at the top of their pay scale for obstetricians. I like my staff and everyone that I work with there."

My father and mother only looked at me attentively. Somehow, I could see the fear in my mother's eyes, as they were beginning to well up with tears. It was as if she was looking into a crystal ball into my future, and she didn't like what she was seeing.

I always wondered if my mother was a psychic or a gypsy of some sort. She seemed to know still what was ahead of me and my future. She predicted the demise of both of my marriages, long in advance before any of them were in trouble. She knew in advance when something was always wrong, without my ever having to say a single word. Mama Connie always knew when there was a difficult time in my life, and she always tried to encourage me to make the right decisions.

My mother was also well aware of my sleeping issues and the demons that came to visit me late at night. When all of my sleeping problems started as a young boy, she would wake up with me and lay next to me on my bed, comforting me until all of my bad dreams went away and I fell back asleep. Sometime later, she acquired a little plaque that was sent to her from Rome that she had hung in my bedroom. It still hangs there today on the far wall above my bed. I memorized it a long time ago and never forgot its meaning:

> Quando Dormo...
> Quando i mostri vengono a giocare,
> Quando gli occhi non possono mai chiudersi,
> Possiate che gli angeli uccidono i demoni,
> E mi abbracciano...quando dormo.

Translated:

> When I Sleep...
>
> When the monsters come to play,
> When one's eyes can never close,
> May the angels slay the demons,
> And embrace me...when I sleep.

There was now silence at the family dinner table, as everyone was trying to enjoy the remaining courses of our Sunday feast. The entrées were almost finished, and my mother was about to bring out the espresso coffee and desserts. As my sister and my sisters-in-law were sitting down again from clearing off the dishes from the table, my father filled up another glass of wine. Filling up everyone's glasses as well, I expected him to make another toast. But instead, he held up his glass and looked at me, saying only one Italian word:

"Attenzione."

CHAPTER TWENTY-ONE
Apology and Reconciliation

It was a little past 12:30 in the afternoon on that hot, summer day in July. I had a mildly busy morning, having done only one delivery and seeing several patients who were expecting over the next month. I had heard through Nurse Mary Bernardo that several patients had been admitted to the hospital maternity ward seeking late-term abortions. But Dr. Thomas Bates, the other obstetrician on duty this morning, performed the pregnancy terminations for both patients, each carrying healthy seven- and one-half month and eight-month-old fetuses. Dr. Worrell had instructed Dr. Bates and the other maternity staff that I would not be called or included in any late-term abortions performed by the hospital.

Although I was temporarily relieved that morning that I wasn't called or included in those procedures, I knew that all of this was only temporary. It was only a matter of time. I knew that the day would come when no other obstetrician, resident, intern, or mid-wife would be available to perform those pregnancy termination procedures. Then, of course, the responsibility would fall on my shoulders to perform them.

I was told by both Dr. Worrell and Dr. Caminiti that, when that occasion arises, I would be looked upon to perform those abortive procedures. My refusal to execute them would, in their view, because to suspension and possible termination from the hospital. They had both explained that, unofficially, that they would do whatever they could to make sure that my moral beliefs would not be compromised or put to the test anytime soon. But they could not guarantee that I would never be called upon to perform an abortion.

I said a prayer to myself, knowing that those healthy babies' lives were being unfairly and wrongly terminated. I wished I could radically do something to stop those abortions from ever happening at all. But I knew I was already on thin ice with the hospital administrators, and with these ongoing arson investigations going on, the less I said or did to make any waves, the better.

I had arrived at the hospital cafeteria to grab a chicken sandwich and a bowl of chili for lunch. As I was exiting the lunch line after paying the cashier, I noticed my old girlfriend, Rosa, having lunch with another physician, sitting at the table facing the window. I was sure she had seen me from the corner of her eye, but I decided to follow her final instructions and pretend that I didn't know who she was if I ever saw her at the hospital.

It didn't take her very long, I thought to myself.

I grabbed my lunch tray and decided to walk outside to the outdoor café garden, where several other doctors and nurses were having lunch. I found a table and decided to sit by myself. I was trying the put the events of those terminated pregnancies out of my mind and to enjoy the warm July sun. It was a Wednesday, also known as 'Hump Day,' and I realized that the weekend was only a few days away. I thought long and hard, realizing that I had nothing to look forward to. I wasn't currently dating anyone right now. There were no parties, picnics, or social events that I was invited to, and I had absolutely no tentative plans. For the first time in a very long time, I had a completely open schedule with nothing planned or going on for the weekend.

As I was eating my bowl of chili and enjoying my chicken sandwich, I noticed a familiar face sitting in the outdoor garden as well. She sat at the table facing me, and she immediately saw me and smiled before sitting down at the table to enjoy her Caesar salad.

I felt like a complete and total asshole.

Remembering how I had exited her office two weeks ago made me cringe to see her sitting at the table in the outdoor garden, smiling at me and casually enjoying her salad. I then decided to 'man-up' and admitted to my narcissistic, self-absorbed comments that I had so unfairly directed at her the last time I was at her office.

I grabbed my lunch tray and casually walked over to her table.

"Hey Jeanne, may I join you?"

She smiled. "Well, that depends if you want to be seen having lunch with Detective Columbo."

"Well, I guess I had that coming," as I sat down and settled my tray adjacent to hers, with my half-eaten sandwich and bowl of chili.

She gazed at me, knowing that she, at least, had a well-deserved apology coming.

"Look, Jeanne, I'm sorry about what I said to you the other day. I have been under some pressure, especially with the authorities lately regarding my sleeping issues. I just don't know who I can trust anymore. Again, I'm truly sorry for what I said."

She gazed at me with those hypnotic brown eyes of hers for five very, very long seconds. She then extended her hand.

"Apology accepted, Dr. Fazio."

Feeling a little resolved, I tried to make myself comfortable and finish my lunch without putting my foot back into my mouth for another time. We sat there in silence for a few minutes more.

"How are you sleeping?"

"Like shit."

"I'm not surprised. What do your nocturnal demons look like this time? Or are they only abstract females wearing Victoria's Secret underwear?"

"Okay, I guess I deserve that shot too. Let me know when this beating is over."

"Which color do you prefer? Black, red, or pink?"

"Black, please."

She giggled to herself, knowing that she had way too much fun.

"You know, David; maybe you don't need a sleep doctor. Maybe what you need is a clinical psychiatrist who will make house calls and bring along a phlebotomist who can draw your blood and test you for STD's."

I almost choked on that one.

"Those are the services you REALLY require," she said, as I could tell she was thoroughly enjoying herself.

"Okay, Jeanne. I get it. I'm an asshole. I will stand up against that wall while you call up the firing squad from the French Foreign Legion," I said, pointing over to the red brick wall along with the hospital's outdoor garden.

"I was thinking more al-Qaeda," she said, still smiling.

"Wow, you don't make it easy for a guy to apologize at all, do you?"

She was smiling with glee, knowing that she was successfully giving me enough verbal abuse to make the digestion of my lunch even more difficult. There were a few more moments of silence as I realized that perhaps, sitting with her during lunch may not have been such a good idea.

"Okay, well, the first part of your penance has been completed," she finally said.

"Oh?" I curiously asked, "What's the second part?"

She looked at me with those hypnotic, sensual, brown eyes of hers.

"I've been invited to an outdoor garden wedding in Winnetka this weekend. My best friend's daughter is getting married on Saturday," she mentioned while studying my face, waiting for me to react.

"I put down 'two people' when I responded to the invitation last month, figuring that one of my sons would possibly escort me. But both have their social plans, and neither one of them wants to be seen dancing with their mother at a wedding. So as of right now, it looks like I will be going alone..."

Another moment of silence.

"I know this is short notice, but would you be available?" she asked.

"For?"

"To escort me to a wedding this Saturday?"

Now it was my turn. I smiled to myself, realizing that moments ago, I was mentally complaining about the fact that I had no social plans for the weekend.

"Is this the other part of my penance?"

"For now, yes."

"Isn't there a doctor-patient rule here? Aren't doctors supposed to be discouraged from dating their patients?" I innocently asked.

"You fired me, David. Remember?"

I nodded my head.

"This means I now have the option to call up the authorities and let them know that the 'Abortion Arsonist' is no longer my patient," Jeanne replied, as she was smiling from ear-to-ear.

"You're not funny," I earnestly protested.

"I'm joking!" she said, trying to get me to laugh.

"Oh, come on, David. Lighten up! Come with me this Saturday. We'll have fun!"

I smiled, knowing that she probably had me with that 'Detective Columbo' comment.

"Okay, but I'll have to check my schedule," I calmly replied.

She smiled and gazed into my eyes with that hypnotic stare of hers. Somehow, she already knew that I was interested in going and that I was full of shit.

"Cocktails are at 6:30. I will text you my address," she said as she picked up her lunch tray and began to walk back into the hospital.

"Wait a minute! I haven't checked my schedule yet!" I loudly protested.

She looked at me and laughed. "I will see you Saturday."

It was a little after five-thirty on that warm, bright Saturday afternoon, as I was making a left hand turn off Sheridan Road onto Forest Avenue. I had decided that it would be safe to put down the top of my Mercedes convertible since the Weather Channel didn't call for any rain for the next few days in Chicago. I was enjoying the harbor views of Gillson Park Beach and the Baha'i Temple in Wilmette, with all the sailboats gracefully floating off the expansive waterfronts, their docks, and nearby wharfs filled with people enjoying that beautiful Saturday afternoon.

The bride and her groom couldn't have picked a more beautiful summer day to get married. It was a calm, breezy 78 degrees without a cloud in the sky, which would make any prospective outdoor garden party and especially a wedding, an even more glorious event.

I don't usually get too excited about many things, but for some reason, I was excited to escort Jeanne to this garden party wedding. I had gone over to the Hugo Boss men's store on Michigan Avenue and picked up a new, slim-fit, three-piece blue suit on sale for $836 last Wednesday night. I had to slip an extra hundred bucks to the salesman for the tailoring fees, with the caveat that they have this suit ready for my pickup this afternoon. I was wearing a crisp, white shirt with my gold, diamond cufflinks, my gold Rolex watch (a graduation gift from Zio Tony that I seldom wear), and a thin, new Valentino black tie.

That morning, I had awakened early in my bed without an incident. I then got up to see Angelo, my barber on Taylor Street, who has been cutting my hair since I was twelve years old. We had a pleasant visit as he washed and cut my hair while I perused his latest copies of Men's Health and Playboy magazines.

"You're getting more and more gray hair, Dr. David. In another year, you're going to be completely white," Angelo said, as he was cutting my salt and pepper hair short the way like it.

Angelo was in his eighties but still enjoyed cutting hair in his small, one-chair barbershop on Taylor Street. He had been cutting my hair for so long that I can't remember getting a haircut from anyone else. Going to his barbershop once a month was like visiting family.

"Your Daddy's got white hair too," Angelo said.

"I have some men's hair color for you," he added. "You know, the younger girls don't like men with too much gray hair."

"As long as I still have my hair, Angelo, I don't care what color it is."

"You know Angelo," I passionately explained, "I think I'm through with chasing these young 'puttana's.'"

"They're all looking for money...a sugar-daddy with a fat checkbook and a diamond ring. I'm through with all that shit. Maybe a woman closer to my age, educated and more seasoned, would make a lot more

170

sense for me at this stage of my life," I said while he was trimming my sideburns.

He stopped for a moment and looked right at me.

"That's the smartest thing I've heard you say in a long time," Angelo said, making sure that both of my sideburns were evenly cut.

When he finished my haircut, he brought me to the back of his shop, where he has a small kitchenette, complete with a stove and a large refrigerator. He offered me a dish of some of his homemade mostaccioli with fresh ricotta cheese at ten o'clock in the morning, which I couldn't refuse. We then enjoyed a glass of his homemade red wine.

"Viva Mussolini," as we always toasted to his favorite, war-time Italian patriot.

"Thank you, Angelo...see you next month," as I slipped him a one-hundred-dollar bill.

I kissed him on the cheek and left his shop to finish my morning errands.

I then went to Nordstrom's downtown to pick out a new pair of black Ferragamo shoes before picking up my tailored new suit. For some reason, I was putting a lot of effort into impressing Jeanne for this wedding, and I wanted to look my best. I didn't want her to think that I was this heartless, self-absorbed, narcissistic bastard who cared very little about anyone except myself. I wanted to show her that I was truly honored to escort her to her girlfriend's daughter's wedding, and I wanted her to be proud to dance with me in front of her friends. At the last minute, I decided to stop by the flower shop and picked up a white rose and gardenia wrist corsage.

As I slowly drove down Forest Avenue, I looked at my GPS directions in my car until I approached the large, red-bricked, clay-shingled house at 715 Forest Avenue. It seemed to be over one hundred years old, with antiquated gray stonework around its stained-

171

glass windows on an expansive city lot, with its enlarged, Chicago bungalow design. The house looked old school in a North Shore sort of way, with Lake Michigan and Gillson Beach less than two blocks down the street.

I pulled up the brick paved driveway and noticed the curtains in the front window being shuffled around as I got out of my car. I approached the front door and rang the doorbell, hoping that anyone but Lurch from the Addams Family would answer.

Well, I was close.

A young man, probably over six feet, five inches tall, with broad square shoulders and a massive chest, opened the front door. He looked like he could pass for a college linebacker, with his large muscular arms and his Olympic-Vee chest. He was wearing a white, sleeveless sweatshirt with some red, Greek fraternity letters printed on the front.

"May I help you?" the young man asked.

He answered the front door the same way my brothers and I used to when our sister was getting picked up to go on one of her dates almost thirty years ago, minus the baseball bat.

"I'm Dr. Fazio…I'm here to pick up Jeanne."

"You're here for my Mom?"

"Eh…yes."

I felt like a total idiot. There I was standing, holding a corsage, looking like a young high school preppie picking up his date for the senior prom.

"It's okay, Michael, let him in, please," I overheard Jeanne say in a loud voice, coming from the upstairs.

"Won't you come in?" he said, in a low, Addams Family tone of voice. I thought for sure he was going to pick me up by my suit coat and throw me on the couch, as my lean, five-foot, ten-inch frame wouldn't have stood a chance.

I gingerly entered the house and found my way over to the red, antiquated velvet coach. I immediately noticed the stuffed animal teddy-bear that I had purchased for her a few weeks ago, sitting on a small coffee table near the door's entrance. There I sat, holding her corsage in a plastic box, my legs together, patiently waiting for my date to come downstairs and greet me. Her over-sized son, Michael, was sitting in the other chair, giggling and smirking to himself while he was texting someone on his iPhone. I figured he was probably texting one of his fraternity brothers, letting him know how ridiculous I probably looked sitting there on that couch waiting for his mother to come downstairs.

The décor of the living room was very old-fashioned, with antique coffee tables and large wooden chairs. There was a large, antique walnut table with twelve chairs in the adjacent dining room, with very old valuable paintings surrounding a black, Steinway grand piano. On the other side was a massive fireplace with white, travertine marble and assorted small, family pictures placed upon its mantle. I had the urge to get up and look at some of the photos, but 'Junior-The-Family-Bouncer' had his eyes fixated on me.

After a few moments of silence, I foolishly decided to try and make conversation.

"So, what school do you go to?"

"State," he grunted.

"State what?"

"Michigan State," he grunted louder. I could tell he was forcing himself to answer my simple questions.

"Oh...I see."

Another moment of silence.

"Do you play football?"

"Yes." Junior was forcing himself to answer another simple question. He never took his eyes off his cell phone.

"What position?"

"Linebacker, second string."

How did I guess? I thought to myself? Another silent moment.

"So, what are you studying?" I asked.

"Not sure…maybe accounting."

"Oh," I answered.

More moments of silence.

"How are your grades?" I asked.

"What are you, a damn cop?" he looked up and barked out in a loud voice.

"Oh, no…just asking." I apologized. I could immediately tell that his grades were a sore subject. He glared at me for a few long seconds.

"They're okay, I guess. I should be off academic probation this fall."

"Oh, that good, huh?"

He snarled at me just as I could hear Jeanne coming down the stairs. I got up while holding the corsage in my hand and walked over and presented it to her.

Jeanne smiled. "Wow, I haven't gotten one of these since my senior prom in high school."

I could see 'Junior' in the background, sitting on the chair with his iPhone, smirking and rolling his eyes.

Jeanne was wearing a black Halston satin tiered gown with spaghetti-string straps and was open in the back. She had her glamorous hair styled up, wearing light red lipstick and rose-colored makeup around her cheeks. She looked gorgeous.

I helped her put on the wrist corsage, and she kissed me on the cheek, thanking me for the flowers.

"Did you guys want to go outside in front of the rose garden so we can take some prom pictures?" Junior asked in a sarcastic tone of voice.

Jeanne looked at her son with an angry sneer on her face. He was too big and too large to receive a backhand from his mother.

"There are some frozen pizzas in the fridge. Don't even think about having a party tonight."

"Oh, come on, Mom... it's Saturday night."

"Well, okay, just a few friends, but keep it on the down-low. I don't want another phone call from the Wilmette Police Department."

I could see the 'Okay-Mom-Whatever-You-Say' look on his face as we were leaving the front door. I opened the car door for her and then got in from the driver's side. As I pulled out of her driveway, we both smiled at each other. At that moment, 'Ain't Too Proud' by the Temptations started blaring from the Sirius XM Radio of my car.

We were both now ready for the time of our lives.

CHAPTER TWENTY-TWO

A Grand Wedding

It was just after 6:45 pm that evening, as I pulled my car onto the private graveled road on Indian Trail and Hill Streets. There was a long line of expensive cars and sport car convertibles parked along the side of the upscale road as a valet directed me where to park. The large gray stoned mansion served as an incredible backdrop for the expansive pitched tent, with waiters in white tuxedos serving its guests. All of the white wooden chairs were lined up in front of a decorative rose garden, with a beautifully decorated flower arched pergola in white gardenias adorning the front of the makeshift garden chapel.

I visually counted over three hundred guests at this garden wedding, most of whom were dressed in formal gowns and tuxedos, holding champagne flutes and mingling with each other across the expansive green, manicured lawn.

"You didn't mention anything about this being a black-tie event," I commented to Jeanne.

"Black-tie was optional, or so it said on the invitation. Besides, you look like you stepped out of a page from GQ magazine," she complimented.

I have to say, my newly tailored, blue Hugo Boss suit felt and looked great that night, and I didn't feel intimidated at all by any of these Winnetka, hoity-toidy snobs. We held hands and walked together across the front lawn, where we were approached by several waiters offering drinks, appetizers, shrimp cocktails, and expensive caviar.

"What do your girlfriend and her husband do?" I curiously asked.

"Her husband is an attorney and a senior partner of a patent law firm downtown. As you can see, he does very well," Jeanne commented.

"My girlfriend, Adrianna, is a trophy wife. She pretty much spends her days at the North Shore Country Club playing golf and making high teas at the Drake Hotel. I know she does some volunteer work for some politically connected PAC firms."

"Sounds like a blessed life," I observed.

By that point, we had found a high-top table inside the tent and began consuming our cocktails and appetizers. It wasn't very long before we were picked up on the radar by her girlfriend.

"Jeanne!" she loudly exclaimed, as they gave each other one of those 'class-reunion-hugs' that girls give when they've gone longer than a week without seeing each other.

They hugged and complimented each other as the mother of the bride locked eyes with mine.

The look on her face immediately changed. I think we both had the same reaction at the same time, as the jovial expression on her face had quickly subsided for a moment.

"Who is this handsome man who is escorting you tonight?" she innocently asked.

Nice acting, I thought to myself. She knew damn well who I was.

"This is Dr. David Fazio. We both work together at Chicago-Western," she mentioned. Her girlfriend extended her hand, and we both graciously extended 'How do you do's.'

It took me all of about three seconds to figure out who "Jeanne's girlfriend' really was.

Her name was Adrianna Hunter, and I had a run-in with this North Shore dominatrix before. Ms. Hunter was a very active, well-connected, pro-choice political activist. She was very politically connected, and both she and her husband had bought a lot of 'pro-choice' politicians down in Springfield and here in Chicago. They also had some significant investments in several healthcare, medical facilities, and family planning clinics in and around the city.

I was asked to speak at a family planning seminar a few years ago at the Four Seasons Hotel, which was sponsored by a political activist coalition group downtown. As Ms. Hunter took the podium, she went on to berate any politician, doctor, clergy, or anyone else who didn't believe that abortion was the absolute right choice for any woman with an unwanted child. There were about ten of us sitting as a panel of 'activists,' and I was asked to speak because of my very verbal 'pro-life' views. I remember after making my pro-life speech that she came back on the podium and publicly berated me in front of a room full of Illinois politicians, accusing me of being 'heartless' and 'egotistical.' She was quite adamant regarding her pro-choice views, especially in cases of saving the lives of physically disabled and deformed newborns. Our respectable panel of experts turned into a loud, verbal, political debate.

I contested her publicly on the open microphone, and I think I verbally beat her up a bit. I pretty much held my own during that discussion, which impressed a lot of the Illinois pro-life politicians and several clergy members from the Chicago Archdiocese that were there. We all knew at that seminar that as long as we had a Republican governor in Springfield, no matter how worthless anyone thought he was, that he would never allow a 'partial-birth abortion' bill to become law in Illinois.

But the minute a Democratic governor was elected last November (supported by strong PAC's financially funded by North Shore couples like the Hunters), we knew that our pro-life views and bans of such horrific abortion procedures would be flushed down the toilet.

It was like it happened overnight. The minute the new Illinois House of Representatives convened, a state representative representing the North Shore district proposed the 'partial-birth abortion bill' to become law. It was done very discretely, with no fanfare or publicity from the media. My theory is the media, newspapers, and television news channels were paid off to 'look the other way' by PAC groups financially supported by people like the Hunters.

Anyways, long story short, this woman is a charter member of the 'C-U-Next Tuesday' Club. A card-carrying, dues-paying, office-holding member in good standing. Period.

She had a lot of money and a lot of time on her hands, which made her a very dangerous political activist indeed. She was the type of woman who could make or break any Democratic politician's career with the wave of her magic wand, and she didn't take very kindly to anyone who didn't cower to her liberal, political views. She had no use for Republicans, and she didn't have any purpose for 'pro-life' obstetricians like me. She was the last person that I ever thought I would run into again and especially, as a close friend of Jeanne's at a garden party wedding.

We went on to exchange pleasantries about how nice the back yard looked and how gorgeous the summer weather was for this party. Adrianna promised Jeanne that they would catch up with us later after the wedding ceremony.

The ceremony for the bride and groom went smoothly without a hitch, as everyone was silent when the Episcopalian minister asked if anyone was against the two of them getting married. Jeanne was whispering to me some background information on the groom during the ceremony. The young man, Thomas Suffolk, was from a prominent North Shore family whose father was an attorney and on the board of

179

trustees for several banks in the Chicago suburbs. He was a new graduate from the Vanderbilt University Law School, and by the size of his family's balance sheet, was probably hand-picked by his future mother-in-law.

There were long, decorated tables set up on the backyard lawn of the Hunter mansion, as a twenty-piece orchestra began playing some soft dinner music after all the endless toasts and nuptial congratulations were made.

Our dinner consisted of New England clam chowder, Caesar salad with chicken, chateaubriand, and stuffed salmon, with baked, breaded artichokes, asparagus wrapped with bacon, and escargot as a portion of the appetizers. The wine was plentiful, as the 'exclusive reserve' chardonnay and pinot noir kept getting poured into our glasses by the many waiters that were serving our table. The dinner guests that we sat with were a few of Jeanne's girlfriends that she had known for years, and some through her girlfriend Adrianna. The dinner conversation was, of course, enjoyable, void of any religious or political subjects or discussions. The bride and groom had their first dance, while the 'political activist' queen and her submissive husband were keeping a close eye on all the waiters and the dinner guests that they were serving.

We started dancing after the chocolate mousse desserts were served and finished. An old song that I hadn't heard in years was being played by the twenty-piece orchestra, which got everyone in a slow-dancing mood. "All Day Music" by War was just one of those songs from the 1970s that could get you in a romantic mindset very quickly, and Jeanne was holding me very close while we slowly danced to the music.

"Thank you for coming with me to this wedding. I appreciate it," she gratefully said as we were slow dancing cheek to cheek.

"The pleasure is mine," I replied. "I'm having a great time."

She smiled and kissed me on the cheek as we continued twirling on the dance floor for several more songs.

After about a half-hour or so, Adrianna Hunter and her unassuming husband were dancing close to us. She then asked Jeanne if she could cut in.

"I'd like to dance with this handsome man of yours...do you mind, Jeanne?" she demanded.

"Of course not."

We both switched dancing partners, and Adrianna started holding me very close to her, pushing us further and further away from her husband and Jeanne, who were dancing together.

"So, Doctor, do you think we could put our differences aside, seeing that you're now dating my best friend?" she outright asked.

"Depends if you can sleep at night, Ms. Hunter. You pulled quite a political upset last fall in Springfield, getting your liberal boy into the Governor's mansion."

She smiled at me, trying very hard to cover up those bright, sharpened fangs that were sticking out of her mouth.

"I sleep just fine, Dr. Fazio," she smiled.

A silent moment passed as I continued to dance with the devil.

"I hear you're not sleeping very well," she smiled. I was completely surprised by her remark.

"How would you know that?" I innocently asked.

"Honey, the whole City of Chicago knows about your bad sleeping habits! I hear the Chicago Fire and the Chicago P.D. are giving you a hard time over those family planning clinic fires," she casually mentioned.

"Wow, you're pretty much everywhere, aren't you?" I politely said, trying very hard not to grit my teeth while responding.

We danced for a few more silent moments, as I was desperately struggling to keep myself from choking this goddamn bitch, right there on the dance floor.

"Who is that good-looking actor that you remind me of?" she started flirting.

"That guy who plays in that movie 'Goodfellas'?"

"Ray Liotta?"

"Yeah...that's him. I'll bet you get a lot of endearing compliments about looking like him all the time."

"Uh-huh."

At five feet, ten inches tall, and 170 pounds, it was nice to know that my modest frame and good looks were being compared to a famous movie star. By now, her tightly wrapped hand was slowly moving from my waist towards my buttocks.

"What is that amazing cologne you're wearing?" she then asked.

"Creed Aventus."

She nestled her nose next to my neck.

"You smell so yummy."

We danced to another slow song.

"You know, I could make all of these little problems of yours go away," she quietly said.

"Really? And who are you? The 'Fairy Godmother'?" I stupidly asked.

I had momentarily forgotten who I was talking to. This North Shore temptress was probably more powerful than the Cook County State's Attorney's office, and her political power stretched far and wide. Her partisan connections and liberal tentacles reached out and extended everywhere.

"Of course, I am, Doctor. You already know that. I am very used to getting my way with everyone, especially in Chicago."

She then looked at me. "I never take 'No' for an answer."

By that moment, I was visually searching for Jeanne as she was dancing on the other side of the dance floor. Adrianna's fingers were twirling the hair on the back of my head while her hand was grabbing my butt cheeks even harder.

"Why don't we meet up for lunch next week? I'm sure Jeanne wouldn't mind."

I was suddenly shocked at her proposal, as she whispered into my ear.

"I can be your 'Fairy Godmother,'" she sexually exclaimed in a very soft voice while planting several warm, wet kisses on my right cheek and earlobe.

"With the wave of my magic wand, I can make all of your dreams come true."

At that moment, I had suddenly realized that I was dancing with the female version of Lucifer, the stricken angel that was sent to Hell in the Old Testament. She was the complete, total definition of an evil seductress or a malevolent femme fatale. I was physically getting nauseous at the prospect of Jeanne's 'best friend' not only making a pass at me but wanting to 'control' and 'conquer' me as well.

As the next song started, Jeanne immediately walked back from dancing with the quiet, unsuspecting Mr. Jefferson Hunter, and we both danced several more songs together. By then, it was almost eleven o'clock, and I had to be at the hospital at 6:00 am for early rounds the next morning.

We said our good-byes to everyone, including the bride and groom, and began to approach the valet for my car keys. Jeanne started talking to another wedding guest, and at that moment, and we were momentarily separated. Adrianna suddenly approached me from behind. She grabbed my butt and handed me her business card, disclosing her PAC affiliation and, of course, her handwritten, very personal phone number.

"Can I expect a call from you next week," she softly asked, strategically placing her hand on my ass while no one was looking.

"Of course," I dutifully said, "after I insert a serrated knife into both of my eyeballs."

Adrianna looked shocked, as that wasn't the answer that she was expecting.

I had my share of married women from the North Shore before, and they were pretty much all the same. They all played the 'Ozzie and Harriet' act in public with their rich, affluent husbands while going downtown and 'whoring around' with any man or 'boy-toy' that would give them the sexual attention they craved.

These married, North Shore ladies were all 'man-eating' cougars. They usually filed their divorce papers with the Cook County Clerk's Office after several years of a problematic marriage but then handsomely retained their lawyers to keep their litigation tied up in the family court system for a very long time. Most of these divorce cases stay tied up in court for several years to keep their rich, philandering husbands under control. It was a silly, foolish game that all the North Shore whores played, and I vowed a long time ago that I was not interested in playing that game ever again.

Besides, Adrianna was supposed to be Jeanne's best friend. Go figure.

I left Adrianna Hunter standing there, giving me a dirty look while I grasped Jeanne's arm, and we climbed into my Mercedes convertible. As we drove away, Jeanne started saying what a wonderful time she had, and after several glasses of wine, she probably had too much to drink. She was holding my right arm with her left hand while periodically kissing my fingers.

"Is Adrianna *really* your best friend?" I innocently asked.

"Why? Did she make a pass at you?"

I laughed and gave her the business card she had given me.

"I expected her to," Jeanne said. "She has absolutely no scruples. I try to keep her at arm's length."

"I've met your 'friend' before," I said, as I calmly explained the situation and the circumstances where we had encountered each other a few years back during our drive home.

As we pulled up to her house on Forest Avenue in Wilmette, there were several cars parked on her driveway and the street surrounding her home. The loud music was blaring, as the young kids dancing and drinking in the living room could be seen from the road.

Jeanne immediately looked distraught as I opened the car door for her. She quickly kissed me and excused herself.

"I will talk to you later," she coldly said, as she walked into the front door to deal with her son and the twenty or more of his drunk friends.

I laughed to myself and thought nothing of it. I was just thankful at that moment that I didn't have any teenage children of my own to deal with.

I drove back to my condo on Lakeshore Drive, dutifully untying my Windsor knotted tie and taking the elevator up to my place. It was almost midnight as I was in my pajama bottoms when the door buzzer rang. It was the security doorman downstairs.

"Dr. Fazio, you have a visitor," he said.

Within two minutes, my front doorbell rang.

"I didn't give you a proper good-bye kiss, so I came to ask for a do-over," Jeanne said as I opened the door. She was dressed in a tight pair of jeans and a loosely fitted white tee-shirt. Even dressed in casual clothes, she still managed to look incredible.

"Well, you were busy dealing with your son's party. I understand."

Jeanne didn't respond. She only came in and put her arms around my neck and began feverishly kissing me for what seemed like several long minutes. We continued kissing and all the mashing and grabbing that went with it, as I had managed to pull off her tee-shirt and bra while she grabbed my pajama bottoms and threw them to the side. It didn't take long for the two of us to end up naked on my couch, with the veranda door wide open and television on, airing late-night reruns of "Bluebloods."

I stopped kissing her just long enough to admire her incredibly gorgeous body, complete with her sensuous 36-DD breasts and large nipples. She had a tight, six-pack core that would have made any female tri-athlete envious.

I knew that I would have to depend on my power naps to get me through work at the hospital the next day. After intensely making love for several hours, we both rested and smiled at one another. We both drifted in and out of romantic conscientiousness, getting several stolen moments of sleep while our naked bodies were intertwined. As the warm summer breezes of Lake Michigan were swirling around my bedroom, my only wish was that the rest of that evening and early morning would never end.

It was an incredible night that I would never forget.

CHAPTER TWENTY-THREE
Dominatrix

The most dominating sound of that early Monday morning was the loud noises of all the police desk phones ringing loudly. The Chicago Police Station District Eighteen was unusually busy for a Monday morning, as Detective Dennis Romanowski was preoccupied with trying to put some cream cheese on his bagel without using a utensil.

All the usual suspects off the streets of Chicago were checking in that morning, as Romanowski was getting confused as to which gangbangers were. It has been a busy weekend, more than usual, for the end of July, with several drive-by shootings in which one of them critically injured a nine-year-old little boy. He was shot in the head and killed while walking home with his friends at four o'clock on a Saturday afternoon.

It was only eleven o'clock in the morning, but Detective Romanowski was already tired of this crazy, busy Monday. His desk phone had been ringing non-stop, and the only thing he had a chance to accomplish was to walk into the district kitchen and grab a stale, sesame seed bagel. He was shuffling papers and finishing up some police reports from the prior week. It had been a busy summer so far, and the increasing numbers of homicides and drug busts in his district were becoming overwhelming.

His commander had asked him to get involved in that arson fire that occurred on Randolph Street a few weeks ago, which he only agreed to do so to help out his pallie, Battalion Chief Terry Janko.

The case was already over three weeks old, and the arson investigators, along with Janko and his team, were not able to tie in a viable suspect to that fire.

The Mayor's office was now getting involved. Mayor Janice Kollar had just been elected last April.

She was a former prosecutor with the Cook County District Attorney's office, and besides being African American and openly gay, ran on a platform of reforming the significant rising crime rates in the city. As the homicides and drive-by shootings from these gangbangers in the neighborhood were increasing, Mayor Kollar had every district commander on her speed dial list, putting pressure on them every day to try to capture and apprehend these perpetrators. Because of the three casualties that occurred in that abortion clinic arson fire, Mayor Kollar now had a new thing to bitch about. She was leaning on the detective's district commander to capture a suspect, whoever that arsonist may be.

As he was about to get up and walk over to the cafeteria to refill his cup of black coffee, his desk phone loudly rang.

"Detective Romanowski," he eagerly answered.

"I'm on my way," the voice on the other end of the line declared. "I've just picked up a dozen fresh bagels from Dunkin' Donuts. I don't want you guys to starve."

Detective Romanowski's initial response was 'who the hell is this' until he recognized the pushy, female voice on the other end. She had left him an email earlier, demanding an appointment with him at 11:00 that morning. Despite his objections and protests, he knew that he had no choice but to be gracious and polite and to allow her to walk into the Chicago Police Eighteenth District like she goddamn owned the place.

Adrianna Hunter was a very powerful, very rich, and very dominant political activist within the City of Chicago. Although she lived in a spaciously large mansion in Winnetka, she was in the city almost every day pursuing whatever political, social, or religious causes Adrianna felt she needed to get involved with. Many politicians within the city's inner circle sarcastically referred to her as 'Wonder Woman,' as she perceived herself as a comic book, crime-fighting hero doing whatever it takes to make this crime-infested city a better place. Most everyone within the Chicago P.D. called her the 'Queen of Spades' or, more recently, "Cruella deVil."

But Romanowski appropriately referred to her as a 'very expensive prostitute,' who had enough money and power to emasculate any of her male victims that didn't satisfy her animalistic needs.

Adrianna was one of those physically attractive ladies that guys like to classify as 'twenty-footers.' She looked great from twenty feet away. Adrianna was somewhere in her sixties, but all of the Botox injections and facelifts could fool any unassuming victim into believing that she was in her late thirties. She wore upscale, custom-designed, Christian Dior dresses to her high teas at the Drake Hotel and only shopped on Michigan Avenue. She spent millions of dollars every year to keep up her expensive, downtown socialite image, from her specially designed Paris wardrobe to her brand-new black Ferrari sports car.

Adrianna Hunter made the antagonist character 'Cruella de Vil' from Disney's 'One Hundred One Dalmatians' look like June Fucking Cleaver.

She was rich. She was powerful. She had nothing else better to do with her time. And the popular consensus was, you didn't fuck with her.

"Good morning, darling," as she came strolling into Detective Romanowski's office, with a large box of a dozen bagels. She bent down and kissed Dennis on the lips, which he didn't appreciate. Adrianna was very well dressed, of course, wearing a blue blouse unbuttoned halfway, disclosing her Victoria's Secret black lace bra and its 36-C contents. She had on a black leather skirt that was a little on the short side, and her Creed Aqua Fiorentina perfume was immediately overbearing.

"There's some cream cheese and some utensils, so you don't have to use your finger," she mentioned, and she placed the Dunkin' Donuts box in the middle of his desk.

"Good morning, Adrianna," Romanowski said. He didn't waste any time attacking her box of goodies, as she made herself comfortable in front of his desk.

"So, are we catching any bad guys today?"

"Absolutely, Adrianna. We have them all roped up, and we're sending them out of Gotham City," the detective declared, slapping a generous amount of cream cheese on his fresh, sesame seed bagel.

She looked at him and smiled. "I didn't realize you were Batman."

"I didn't realize you were Commissioner Gordon," Dennis responded. By now, the detective was thoroughly enjoying his freshly baked sesame seed bagel.

"Catwoman, my dear. You're already confused, and it's only Monday morning."

"It's been a busy morning, Adrianna. My telephone hasn't stopped ringing this morning, and I've been dealing with all of this weekend, gang-banger bullshit. We've got a dead nine-year little boy that was shot in the head by some gang-bangers last Saturday afternoon that we're trying to deal with."

"I know…it's all over the news," Mrs. Hunter replied.

A moment of silence, as the detective's mouth was still full.

"I don't know where to start. We have so many 'bangers' out there that we don't know which one to choose from, as they have this area-turf war going," the detective exclaimed.

"Now, we have the Mayor up our asses."

Taking another bite and talking with his mouth full, he continued, "None of these bangers are 'ratting' each other out right now. I've got a phone call into Detective Dorian over at the Sixteenth to give me a hand on these homicides."

"Detective Dorian? Now there's a piece of work," Adrianna Hunter exclaimed.

She had several encounters with the veteran police detective and has made her feelings well known about him. From what Dennis remembered, Philip Dorian was probably the only detective within the Chicago Police Department that had told Adrianna to 'go fuck herself' when she tried to interfere with one of his investigations.

"How is the 'Abortion Arsonist' investigation going?"

"Slow, Adrianna. I've been working with Chief Janko over at Fire Engine No. 1 along with a few other arson investigators. But we haven't come up with any solid leads."

"What are you talking about? You have that Dr. Fazio that Janko talked to last week. The baby doctor with the burnt hands, remember?"

"Adrianna, he's got a solid alibi. We interviewed his former girlfriend, some nurses in the ICU named Rosa Hudson. She vouched that they were asleep together at his condo on that morning."

"She's protecting him. How do you explain the burnt hands?"

"They were minor burns that he says happened while making breakfast," the detective replied.

"Burning his hands making what? Goddamn toast?"

'Adrianna, we don't have enough evidence even to pick him up, let alone arrest him on an arson charge. This guy is squeaky clean. Just because he has some minor burns on his hands doesn't conclusively say that he's an arsonist. We need more evidence."

Adrianna was now starting to get aggravated.

"Dennis, we go back a long time. I helped you get off the streets, saving your ass from writing parking tickets in Logan Square. You're a detective now, thanks to me. You owe me, Dennis. I want this 'pro-life' baby doctor picked up and arrested. He has caused a tremendous amount of damage to our pro-choice cause," Adrianna explained.

"What are you talking about? You've pushed through that 'partial-birth abortion law' in Springfield. You shouldn't have anyone standing in your way."

"Are you kidding? All the lawmakers have been getting inundated with emails from every Catholic Church and every Catholic Diocese in the State of Illinois threatening to excommunicate any lawmaker who supported that bill. Now, these pro-life groups and the Servants of Mary church councils are doing all night, twenty-four-hour vigils in front of all these family planning clinics, intimidating every woman who tries to enter them," Hunter was loudly complaining.

"What did you expect, Adrianna?"

"I want these pro-life bastards far away from our clinics," she loudly stated.

The Hunters were significant investors in several of these family planning medical centers throughout the Chicagoland area, as she has financially supported the buildouts and the setup of many of these medical facilities. These clinics are now beginning to reap a profitable reward to her and her husband, and she didn't need the bad press of any vocal baby doctor from Chicago-Western, putting a detriment on those profits.

Chaz Rizzo from Channel Eight Eyewitness News did a cover story on the 'covert passage' of this partial abortion bill in Springfield a few months ago. In his feature story, he had interviewed Dr. Fazio regarding his pro-life views and how the passage of this law was going to turn Chicago into the 'Abortion

Capital of the Midwest.' Some political PAC groups and several influential Chicago individuals were mentioned in his news piece, which included Mr. and Mrs. Jefferson Hunter.

Adrianna sat there for a moment, watching Dennis Romanowski continue to feed his face with bagels while he tried to work on his computer in her presence.

"Adrianna, if you will excuse me," he finally said, realizing that there was nothing else to talk about, "I need to get back to work here. I've got a busy day ahead of me."

She started to display her famous Italian temper as she began to throw a tantrum in front of his desk.

"Look, Dennis...I put you where you are now, and you owe me. I can easily pull those same strings and send you back to eating goddamn bagels at the Dunkin' Donuts where I found you," she said, as Romanowski sat there at his desk, speechless.

"I want this Fazio guy picked up. I can't have him torching anymore of our clinics."

"Adrianna...I just can't..."

"You heard me, Dennis. I want this baby doctor off the damn streets. I'm already pressuring Chicago-Western Hospital to fire him the minute he refuses to perform a patient who requested an abortion. I need you on board."

"Adrianna, why the hard-on for this guy? Did you grab his cock one night, and he turned you down?" Romanowski didn't appreciate being intimidated by this man-eating cougar.

Adrianna Hunter started to turn red in the face, embarrassed by the detective's rude comment.

"Don't fuck with me, Dennis. I want this doctor picked up!"

Adrianna then abruptly got up and stormed out of the detective's office.

Romanowski, feeling pressured, knew that he had to do whatever was needed to keep his current job and to not make enemies with influential, upstanding citizens like the Hunters. He didn't want any problems, and he didn't need her going over his head and making him look bad in front of his commander and the rest of his district.

But he also knew that they didn't have enough evidence to pick up Dr. Fazio and blindly charge him with arson. He needed some hard, investigative evidence. He needed something at the crime scene that would directly tie him to those arson fires. A witness, a security camera tape, a personal item, a piece of physical evidence, something.

He then picked up the phone.

"Hello, Terry? We have a problem here..."

CHAPTER TWENTY-FOUR
Ravinia

The noise of the bustling cars and motorcycles was whisking by Sheridan Road on that early Saturday afternoon as I was on my way to pick-up Jeanne. It was a beautiful summer day, and I was grateful that I had taken that Saturday off to get a few things done around the house. I had the top down on my Mercedes convertible, and the sunny, summer weather couldn't have been more beautiful.

Jeanne had called me that morning, suggesting that we go on a picnic that afternoon, and I was more than happy to spend the day with her. We had been dating for over a month now, and in all honesty, we were having a blast.

Jeanne was beautiful, educated, patient, and kind. Although she was one hundred percent, Irish, she seemed to mesh very well with my very Italian family, especially last Sunday at dinner. My parents and siblings seemed to enjoy her company and her sense of humor. Jeanne and I had been spending a lot of time together, between lunches at the hospital and dining out together two or three times a week.

The more I had gotten to know Jeanne, the more those emotional barriers of mine were starting to crumble and come down. We spent a tremendous amount of time talking about our families, our backgrounds, our past marriages, our old loves, and our lives. Jeanne was so easy to talk to, and she made me feel as though we had known each other for years.

We were spending a lot of time together, and her absence at home didn't seem to be getting noticed by her sons. Her boys appeared to be enjoying their summer schedule and didn't miss their mother in the least. Except for a few summer bashes here and there, her college-age sons seemed to be glad that their mother was preoccupied with someone else.

"Bring a blanket and some wine," were my only instructions, as she was eager to pack the rest of the food and goodies for our afternoon spread.

I drove down Forest Avenue in Wilmette to pick her up that afternoon. Jeanne came out of her house and gave me one of her famous, wet, and wild strawberry kisses, giving me a tight hug before instructing me to help her load up the car. She was wearing a dark pair of shorts with a casual white midriff blouse, which exposed her belly button and summer sandals. Her hair was up in a ponytail, and she was wearing a dark pair of Ray-Ban sunglasses. She appeared to be dressed as though she were going to a summer beach party and looked amazing.

She had a huge wicker basket that we loaded into the back seat of my car, and I suddenly felt like Yogi Bear stealing a picnic basket from Jellystone Park. She also had me load up two folding chairs and a small folding table, along with a little cooler.

"Are we traveling out of state?" I joked as I closed my car trunk.

She smiled but didn't say anything. I opened the door for her, and after we were both seated, I started driving onto Sheridan Road, going north.

"Change of plans," she suddenly said.

"A change of plans? What?"

She then held up two tickets for Ravinia in Highland Park for that Saturday night. She passed them over to me while I was driving so that I could read who the headlining act was.

They were two lawn seats to the Earth, Wind, and Fire concert at Ravinia.

I smiled as she kissed me on the cheek. She knew how much I enjoyed Rhythm & Blues music, and she wanted to surprise me.

"I got them from my girlfriend Adrianna, who we both know is your favorite 'Wicked Witch from the North.' She gave them to me the other day, but I wanted to surprise you," Jeanne explained.

"Very cool," as I was smiling from ear to ear.

She held my hand as we were driving north on Sheridan Road, with the warm wind was blowing through our hair. Driving on the north shore and looking out towards the water, Lake Michigan was picturesque that afternoon as the variant sailboats looked like they were floating on glass.

Jeanne kissed me a few more times while I was driving, trying her best to distract me while rubbing her left hand on my leg.

"I always want to make you happy," she smiled, teasing me with more kisses on my earlobe.

"Jeanne," I reprimanded her. "If you keep this up, we'll have to pull over!" as she continued to place warm kisses on my cheek and neck.

I did my best to concentrate on my driving, going north up to Lake Cook Road and then eastbound to Ravinia in Highland Park. She had parking passes, so we were able to park close by and enter the concert park on the lawn. Since it was early in the afternoon, we were able to lay out our blankets reasonably close to the pavilion as others were just starting to file into the concert park.

"What a perfect night for a concert," I said, as we set up our table and chairs.

I was wearing a pair of white Bermuda shorts and one of my blue Hawaiian shirts. If I had a straw hat, I could have probably passed for a Parrot Head going to a Jimmy Buffet concert. We started munching on an antipasto tray, some chips, and some other treats. We then began making ourselves comfortable as I opened a bottle of Belle Glos Pinot Noir.

Jeanne and I exchanged pleasantries and caught up on each other's lives over the past few days, talking about her sons and all of their summer adventures. She had packed up some large submarine sandwiches that were cut up into small appetizers with toothpicks, along with some olives and a spinach artichoke dip with some variant kinds of crackers.

"How are you sleeping?" she asked me.

Being that she was a sleep therapist and that I was one of her patients for a very brief time, that question was always brought up whenever we were together. I didn't want to tell her that I had been sleepwalking more than usual these last several nights, having awakened that morning in a hallway chair in the atrium of my condominium complex downstairs.

"Ok, I guess." I tried to lie, as I didn't want her to worry.

"David, you're sleepwalking again, aren't you?"

I looked at her, somewhat perplexed.

"How do you know?" I asked her in a defensive voice.

She laughed. "Darling...it's what I do for a living. I can see how bloodshot your eyes are, and I noticed a few new bruises on your forearms and your legs. I can tell you're not sleeping very well."

In the last month that we had been dating, we had spent the whole night together only a handful of times, as she was always eager to get back home to her incessant party-animal sons.

"I guess I need you to conduct a personal sleep study for one of your favorite patients," I replied, winking my eye at her at the same time. "I know you make house calls."

"You can't afford me, schmuck-boy," she laughed.

"Seriously, David...we need to have a serious conversation about your sleep issues."

"Jeanne? It's not like I haven't tried to get help. The pressures they're putting on me at the hospital to perform abortions, and with these coppers looking at me funny with all of these arson fires going on, I'm under a lot of pressure," I tried to explain.

She smiled and held my right hand with both of hers, caressing my fingers and trying to calm my nerves. She could tell that I was a little on edge.

"David...have you ever considered changing specialties? Like maybe pediatrics or internal medicine? You wouldn't have the pregnancy termination issues that you currently have right now."

"Yeah, but at what cost, Jeanne? I would be at the bottom of the totem pole, and I would probably take a huge pay cut. Not to mention the board exams that I would have to sit for. At my age, honey, it just isn't worth it."

Jeanne looked at me, still caressing my hands.

"But look at what all of this is doing to your health. All of this shit is beating you up, big time. You need to make some changes. Either change specialties or change over to a Catholic hospital, somewhere that won't be making these abortion demands."

I nodded my head, knowing that she was right. But I also knew that, because I was still recovering financially from my last divorce and understood the financial impact making such a drastic change would have on my income, that such a difference for me was totally out of the question.

"I just can't right now, Jeanne. I can't afford to."

She looked at me with those hypnotic brown eyes of hers, almost staring me into a trance.

"Your health is worth it. You can't keep doing all of this, David. The pressures will kill you."

I looked at her and nodded my head, acknowledging her observation. I knew that she was one hundred percent right. But it was frustrating, both emotionally and physically, and I knew that all of this crap was starting to take a toll on me. I laid back on the blanket and closed my eyes as the warm summer wind that evening seemed to massage and relax my over-stressed body with each gust of fresh air.

She laid down on the blanket next to me, and we poured ourselves another glass of wine. She began stroking my shoulders and my neck as if to try to relax me and to make all of my pressures and problems magically disappear. Most of the concert-goers had already entered the concert park, and our small piece of real estate was starting to get smaller and more congested.

Jeanne then took my half-empty glass of Pinot Noir, placed it on the grass next to the blanket, and then she started repeatedly kissing me, on my cheeks, my face, and my neck. I was beginning to get extremely excited as we laid on the blanket while I held her beneath me and returned the favor. Her fully clothed body next to mine felt terrific as I continued to kiss her across her neck, placing kisses on wherever her skin was exposed. I started kissing her around her stomach, placing kisses over her blouse.

"David? We're in public!" she laughed as my head was promptly buried in her chest.

"Not to worry," I explained in between kisses. "Most everyone on the lawn in Ravinia is practically doing the same thing."

"No, David. They're all eating and drinking and waiting for the concert to start. If we keep this up, security will probably kick us out and tell us to get a room!" she smiled.

"Would that be so bad?"

"Come on, David!" as she kissed me back on my face and neck. "Don't you want to see this concert? You like R&B and Funk music!"

"Of course. But fortunately, you're a wonderful distraction."

We continued to kiss and embrace each other until the concert started.

Earth, Wind & Fire put on a great concert, performing for almost two hours, doing their hit songs like "September," "Let's Groove," "Shining Star," and the Beatles hit "Got to Get You into My Life." We both enjoyed listening to music under the darkened sky. The stars were bright and abundant as they moved and danced across the urban, Midwestern heavens. We were holding and kissing each other throughout the concert, as she was gently slapping my hand whenever it found its way under her blouse.

It was just past ten o'clock went the concert finally ended, and we came to an agreement that we would continue our 'mash and grab' session at another location, somewhere other than in a public place like Ravinia.

We rolled up the blanket and picked up our basket, cooler, table, and chairs. Jeanne and I then proceeded to walk back to our car, singing the concert tunes to each other like two little children in grade school. By the time we got into our car and started to leave the Ravinia parking lot, we were laughing and singing practically every stupid, corny song that came into our heads.

We had both enjoyed the summer concert, and we were having a great time, enjoying that warm summer evening and each other.

"David? You realize that you can't sing. You know this, right?" she mentioned.

"We can't all sing Motown," I laughed, kissing her on the cheek while trying to keep my car on the road.

It was almost an hour, just after eleven o'clock, before we arrived at my condominium on Lakeshore

Drive. We couldn't have been in my bedroom more than five seconds before she assaulted me, unbuttoning my shirt as I eagerly undid her blouse and black bra. We were wildly undressing each other like two high school teenagers. She stood there naked, showing off her unbelievably well-shaped body. Her abdomen looked like an athlete's chiseled six-pack as if she spent all of her spare time doing sit-ups and core exercises.

"How do you stay in such great shape?" I ignorantly asked her as we both laid there horizontally in my bed. I only asked because I knew she spent very little time working out.

"It's my Irish DNA, fueled by whiskey, rye, and green beer!" she joked, as she continued to kiss me on my stomach and my chest.

Her breasts were perfectly shaped, as her rosy nipples seemed to protrude with every kiss that I implanted on her chest. She was sun-tanned and very well-toned, as I placed wet, long kisses along every inch of her curvaceous body.

We continued our lovemaking for what seemed like hours. The curtains and windows of my bedroom remained wide open the whole time, overlooking the River North shoreline and all the fantastic skyscrapers lined up and down the Lake Michigan coastline. It felt wonderful to make love to Jeanne, and I felt myself falling deeper and deeper into that emotional abyss that was covered with the scary, intimating "L" word. We fell asleep in each other's arms that night, hoping that the sunrise would never come.

As I closed my eyes, I felt utterly uninhabited. I felt completely fearless, unashamed to admit my deep, real feelings that were overwhelming me on that steamy summer evening.

I was no longer afraid to say the "L" word.

CHAPTER TWENTY-FIVE
Nurse Anderson

The maternity ward of Chicago-Western Medical Center was quiet that Thursday evening, as Nurse Anderson was finishing her patient charts. It had been a hectic weekday, with sixteen newborn babies born during her shift alone. The veteran nurse had been on the maternity floor since six o'clock that morning. She was looking forward to completing her twelve-hour shift and going home after six o'clock. It had been a long day.

It was almost 5:45 pm as Dr. David Fazio was still making the rounds on the maternity floor. He stopped by the nurse's station to drop off and pick up some new charts, updating medication dosages and making sure the newborn children he had delivered that day were still healthy. Nurse Anderson saw Dr. Fazio walking towards the nurse's station on the seventh floor and went on the other side to avoid him. There was no love lost between the two of them, and she always made sure that she avoided him at all costs.

Fazio noticed Nurse Anderson walking over to the other side of the seventh-floor nurse's station away from the patient charts, and he smirked to himself. He had not had a chance to discuss the 'Baby Hernandez" incident a few days ago, and he wanted to talk to her about it.

Fazio was suspicious. This was not the first time a severely deformed infant did not survive the first forty-eight hours of life and recalled another incident where, on Nurse Anderson's watch, a severely deformed infant had mysteriously passed away.

Fazio grabbed the new charts that he needed and decided to approach Nurse Susan Anderson calmly.

"Good evening, Nurse Anderson," Fazio tried to warmly greet her as she was standing in the corner of the nurse's station, fumbling with some papers, her back facing him.

"Good evening," she coldly replied.

A moment of silence, as Fazio stood there with his charts, facing her back.

"Nurse Anderson, could I have a word with you?"

"Not now, Doctor. I'm busy finishing some charts, then I have to take drug inventory before the end of my shift, which will hopefully be in fifteen minutes," Susan Anderson replied in a very curt, assertive voice.

Fazio walked over to the other side of the station, where he could make eye contact with her. Her head was still looking down, trying not to look at him.

"What happened to that Hernandez baby that mysteriously passed away the other day?"

"Doctor, I have no time to talk to you right now. I told you that I am trying to get out of here."

"You can spare five minutes for me, Susan."

"No, Dr. Fazio," she replied in a loud voice. "I do not have five minutes for you. Not now, not ever."

"What's your problem, Susan?"

"You know damn well what my problem is, Doctor. You were instructed by the patient to abort that baby. You decided to 'Play God' and deliver that deformed infant against that mother's wishes."

"The mother would not have survived that abortive procedure."

"Oh, cut the bullshit, David. You decided to deliver that baby because aborting it was against your moral scruples," she loudly answered. "Which is a fucking joke, because other than trying to 'Play God' in the delivery room, you have no moral scruples."

Fazio stood there smiling, listening to this middle-aged, over-weight maternity nurse lay into him. He was well aware of her firm, definitive feelings regarding the hospital's new, pro-choice policies. He had known about her liberal beliefs, and she made no qualms about supporting any political candidate who was pro-choice, including Illinois's newly elected governor. Nurse Anderson was more than elated when the RHA law was passed in Springfield and the retraction of the state's partial-birth ban. Anderson was a pro-choice maternity nurse who prided herself as a pro-choice advocate supporting the partial-birth abortion mandate.

"Oh, I see, Susan...so this is personal, isn't it?"

Susan Anderson glared at him, ready to leap at the doctor, and put her hands around his throat. She wanted to squeeze that cocky smirk off his face.

"Well, Susan, my congratulations," Fazio said.

"For what?"

"Well, apparently, you seem to be much better at 'Playing God' than I am."

A moment of silence.

"The rumor is that you were the last one in that prescription and drug cabinet before that baby's heart mysteriously stopped beating. My guess is you injected the potassium sulfide into that newborn while no one was looking," Dr. Fazio said in an accusatory voice.

"I did no such thing."

"Oh, I know you won't admit it. And as long as Dr. Worrell is covering up for you, you won't be seeing any murder charges anytime soon."

Nurse Anderson placed her charts on the desk and then walked over towards the baby doctor, within inches of his face. She was over five feet, eight inches tall, and with her weight and body mass, could probably work the door of any 'dive-bar' as a scary, vicious bouncer.

"Don't insult me, Fazio. I was nowhere around that infant when it passed away. It was a lucky thing that that poor baby died. You and this hospital were in line for a nice little lawsuit," she growled.

"As I said, Susan. You're better at 'Playing God' than I am."

As Dr. Fazio was confronting the maternity nurse, he was starting to feel warm and took off his white lab coat. He placed it on top of one of the chairs within the nursing station.

"Go to hell, Fazio. You're an egotistical bastard," she loudly replied.

By this point, she was starting to get bored with this confrontational conversation. She grasped her charts and tried to walk over to the other side of the station, away from Fazio.

"You're still pissed about your girlfriend, aren't you...what was her name again? Kelly?"

"Her name was Kelsey, you asshole."

"Yeah, that's it. You still have a hard-on for me since I dumped your little girlfriend."

She stopped to glare at him once again.

"Listen, you jag-off. You did a great job of messing up that little girl's head, and it was a miracle that she survived. She was practically suicidal, no thanks to you."

"And this is my problem, how?"

Nurse Anderson walked back over to invade Fazio's personal space once again.

"Yes, you, asshole. That is your problem. Show some compassion and empathy for all the little nurses you screw and discard around here on a monthly basis," Anderson loudly confronted him, her voice getting louder. Two of the nurses from the other side of the seventh floor were now taking notice of the embattled confrontation.

"You're the most hated doctor in this hospital, if you haven't noticed, because you can't keep your goddamn penis in your pants."

By now, Dr. Fazio was laughing. "And I hear that you're my biggest fan, Susan!"

"Fuck you!"

Nurse Anderson was starting to turn her back on him again, but Fazio grabbed her arm to stop her from walking away.

"Susan, consider this a fair warning. Regardless of how you feel about me, you don't have any right to terminate the life of a deformed infant. In my book, that is not a mercy killing. That is called murder."

She quickly pulled her arm away.

"Don't touch me, you asshole!"

"Susan...I mean it. If another incident like this ever happens again, I will go to the authorities. And I don't give one damn about my job here at this hospital, about you or Dr. Worrell."

A moment of silence as she continued to glare at him.

"I'm serious, Susan. Not even Cal will be able to protect or cover up for you."

Nurse Anderson only stood there as Dr. Fazio put his charts back at the nurse's station and walked away, leaving the maternity nurse standing there, holding her patient records.

'This goddamn son-of-a-bitch,' she mumbled silently to herself.

How dare he question her morals, her beliefs, and her values in terminating that infant baby's life? How dare he classify that as 'murder' when what he does in delivering an unwanted, deformed newborn infant as 'righteously correct'? Dr. Fazio was an egotistical, self-centered, narcissistic bastard.

That son-of-a-bitch never had the experience of watching the profound effects of his heroic decisions in the delivery room. He had no idea of the difficulties he caused, never having to watch so many mothers go home with their unwanted babies. Dr. Fazio had never experienced the hardships that these families go through, eventually placing these infants into adoption agencies or trying to get these deformed babies into a foster home. Fazio had never thought of the burdens his heroic efforts were causing these deformed children and the hospital, clueless to the procedures of trying to assist these deformed, unwanted babies into being adopted. These poor infants almost always become wards of the state, sent to disabled children's facilities, and further burdening the state and federal governments for their intense, constant twenty-four-hour care.

She was tired of Dr. David Fazio's heroic, selfish, pro-life efforts. Dr. Fazio physically repelled her, and the very thought of this conceited bastard made her nauseous. In her mind, Dr. Fazio needed to go away.

Far away. Away from this maternity ward. Away from this hospital. Dr. David Fazio needed to go far, far away.

At that moment, she noticed Fazio's lab coat lying on the desk chair, which he had forgotten to take with him. She picked it up and looked at it as sinister thoughts starting occupying her head.

She thought about defecating all over it with her bodily wastes and returning it to his office. She thought about tearing it up into shreds and using it to mop her kitchen floor with it at home. Maybe, she thought to herself, she could have a cross-burning ceremony, with Dr. Fazio's lab coat cloaked over a mannequin while setting it on fire for all his ex-girlfriends to see. She smiled to herself, thinking of all the different ways she could express her intense anger and hatred for this self-centered bastard.

She then thought of an incredibly ruthless idea.

At that moment, she grabbed his misplaced lab coat and hid it in the bottom drawer of her locked desk.

CHAPTER TWENTY-SIX
Linda Ciccone

Nurse Linda Ciccone had just gotten out of work on that warm Thursday evening from Chicago-Western Medical Center. Her mother was babysitting her daughter, and her husband was working late that evening. Although she was tired, she didn't want to go home immediately and made plans to meet up with her girlfriend, Monica. Linda had more than a few good excuses to go out and tie one on with her girlfriend, as it had been a stressful week so far. She had several friends that she went out with once or twice a week for cocktails after work. Her husband worked the night shift at a tool and die shop in Melrose Park and didn't arrive home from his stint until six o'clock in the morning.

Linda was a pretty, shapely brunette in her middle forties who had just recently remarried for the third time. Her husband, Tony, who was several years younger than she was, was more than willing to get married and assist her in raising her ten-year-old daughter, Olivia. Linda was happy to be married and settled again, eager to enjoy the personal and financial benefits of having a husband and being in a full-time relationship.

Her husband was a first-generation Polish American who worked very hard for a living and was very frugal with his money. Other than enjoying a drink of Johnny Walker Black on the rocks in the morning when his night shift at work was over, he had very few vices or bad habits.

Linda cared for Tony as he doted on her whenever he could. Her husband sent her flowers on special occasions and holidays and bought her lavish gifts on her birthday, at Christmas, and on their anniversary. It was apparent to everyone who knew them that Tony was ecstatic to be a part of Linda's life. He adored his new wife and her little girl and would do anything to please his new family.

Linda Ciccone (who chose to keep her maiden name) loved her new husband. But she wasn't *in love* with him if one can understand the difference. Linda emotionally settled on her third marriage, figuring that at her age and with her working schedule, it was going to be difficult for her to find another man who would be willing to marry her and assume all of her baggage. And in Linda's case, her baggage was her excessive credit card debts and her ten-year-old little girl. When Tony Rozanski asked Linda to marry him, she wasted no time planning the wedding, booking the flight to Las Vegas, and getting married at the Bellagio Casino and Resort in front of several guests and close friends.

The third time was a charm, she thought to herself, and was willing to spend the rest of her life being with a man whom she moderately liked and made love to on occasion. But her true love, the man who had swept her off of her feet and had all the qualifications of being the perfect husband, made himself unavailable to her eighteen months ago.

Linda was jilted. Linda felt emotionally abandoned. She never got over that terminated relationship.

Linda Ciccone first started dating David Fazio three years ago when they first met each other at the hospital Christmas party. They went to see the play 'Dirty Dancing' together after a fantastic dinner at the Il Porcino Restaurant and drinks at Redheads afterward. It didn't take very long for the two of them to become smitten with one another, and they both started a scorching relationship.

Linda had brought David home to meet her mother and her very impressionable young daughter.

David then invited Linda to be a guest at one of their Fazio Family Sunday 'cenetta' s' and got along well with David's parents and his family. During the summer that they were together, they traveled to Mackinac Island and drove along the coast of Lake Michigan, stopping at every beach town along the way to have a picnic or visit a lighthouse.

David and Linda had a lot of personal qualities in common. Besides, both of them being first-generation Italian Americans, they had a lot of personal qualities in common. They were both highly educated medical professionals, and their families were essential to them. They both got along famously, very seldom disagreeing on anything. They spent most of their time laughing and kidding around with each other over stupid jokes that only they understood.

They had joined a hospital bowling league on Wednesday nights and played on a hospital softball league together that summer. David convinced Linda that he had loved her unconditionally and wanted to spend his life with her. After nine months, she was expecting David to propose to her and was planning to spend the rest of her life with him.

But the engagement ring never came. After a whirlwind, nine-month, hot and heavy relationship, it was over. David suddenly broke it off, admitting that he had become bored with the liaison. He point-blank told Linda that he didn't want anything to do with getting married again and preferred to start dating other girls.

Linda Ciccone was crushed and devastated. She was angry and extremely bitter. The breakup took a terrible toll on her emotionally, experiencing a tense, internal pain that she had never felt before losing Dr. David Fazio, MD. It took a whole year for her to get past her emotional pain and abandonment issues that Fazio had caused her. She felt used. She felt deserted.

She felt like she had been tossed aside like 'yesterday's pizza box.'

It was during that period that she met her current husband, Tony Rozanski, at a Chicago bar in the city. He immediately fell in love with her, sending her a dozen roses every Friday before each one of their dates. Tony would also send a box of chocolates to her ten-year-old daughter. Rozanski saw in Linda the love of his life and was willing to do anything to please her and keep her happy.

After their intense, two-month relationship, Tony asked Linda to marry him. Her mother warned her about jumping into a marriage with a man whom she was dating on the rebound, but Linda didn't care. The nurse wanted the security and tranquility that came with being married to a man who was willing to do anything for her. She desperately wanted to settle down. Linda Ciccone wanted to put her past relationship with David Fazio in the 'rear-view mirror.'

After returning from her Las Vegas wedding, she settled down with Tony, and they bought a condominium together in Logan Square. Tony paid for her daughter to go to a private Catholic school nearby. Rozanski continued to send his new wife flowers at work, took her out for lavish dinners downtown on Saturday nights, and continued to spoil her whenever he had the opportunity.

"You're a lucky girl, Linda, to have an honest, hard-working husband like Tony," said her girlfriend, Monica. "This man kisses the ground you walk on!"

Linda felt lucky, indeed. But she wasn't emotionally fulfilled. She had only settled, and she knew it. Linda had hoped that by getting married again and settling down with another man, that she would finally put David Fazio out of her head.

But that didn't happen. She would still get butterflies in her stomach every time she saw Dr. Fazio in the hallways of the hospital on many occasions after their breakup. At first, she avoided making eye contact with him altogether. Then, they slowly started to acknowledge and greet one another. In time, Dr. Fazio and Linda Ciccone became friends, as he offered her his congratulations on her new husband and her marriage. They started talking, kidding, and laughing with one another again, both of them realizing that all of this had probably worked out for the best.

"Now that we're friends, we can be in each other's lives forever, right?" David said to Linda casually one day.

She smiled.

Linda Ciccone wanted so hard to believe that. But deep down inside, she would always feel a small feeling of bitterness whenever she heard of another nurse or staff member in the hospital currently dating Dr. Fazio. She wanted to publicly warn them to create a website titled 'FAZIOLADIESBEWARE.COM' and start an anti-Doctor Fazio fan club within the hospital.

Who the hell does he think he is? Linda would often say to herself whenever his name was brought up. How did she allow herself to fall in love with such a narcissistic bastard, who treated every single woman who worked in that hospital as if they were all a part of his harem?

David Fazio was a charming, successful, ambitious, good-looking physician with movie-star qualities and carried himself like the Greek god 'Adonis.' Fazio's attitude toward females communicated to everyone that he was God's gift to the opposite sex. And every single, eligible female in that hospital helplessly swooned over him. At Chicago-Western Medical Center, David Fazio was 'Dr. McDreamy' from 'Grey's Anatomy.'

Worst of all, she realized that after eighteen months and another marriage later, she still was deeply in love with Dr. David Fazio, despite his shortcomings and his prior cruel behavior. Although she couldn't deny it any longer, she would never admit it to anyone other than to her conscience. Whenever she made love to her new husband (when she felt obligated to do so), Linda would close her eyes and pretend she was still making love to David. She even bought her new husband the same bottle of cologne that David wore, Creed Aventus, at $379 a bottle, and would always ask him to wear it in bed before they made love. Linda would still feel her heartbeat rising whenever she saw him and would struggle to keep from blushing whenever he spoke to her. Fazio always made her heart flutter whenever he greeted her, even if they were only 'just friends.'

Linda Ciccone met up with her friend at Diamond Lil's on North Milwaukee Avenue. She parked her car and met up with Monica, who was having a Vodka and Cranberry, seated at the bar alone.

"Hey Linda," Monica Atkinson greeted her close friend as she ordered a drink from the bar.

Monica was a police dispatcher over at the Eighteenth District at the Chicago Police Department and was well aware of the 'goings-on' happening in her district.

"I'll have a Stella," she said to the bartender. "I've got a taste for a beer."

"On a hot evening like tonight, I don't blame you," Monica replied.

They exchanged pleasantries, as Linda lied about how happy she was and how beautiful her new life was with her relatively new husband.

Monica looked at her best friend suspiciously, knowing that she was giving her a line of shit. She knew better.

"No regrets?"

"None," Linda insisted.

"Well, good, so you won't have any problems when we pick up your old boyfriend."

Linda looked at Monica at first, not knowing who she was talking about.

"Who?"

"You know who. David Fazio, your favorite doctor."

Linda looked at Monica, bewildered at first, not understanding why the police would be interested in arresting Dr. Fazio.

"We all have a hunch that he's the Abortion Arsonist."

There were several moments of silence as Linda silently took the first swig of her cold, Stella Artois beer. Linda suddenly began to experience a full array of emotions, from excitement and jubilation to concern and anxiety. Linda was encouraged that perhaps, the 'karma train' had finally caught up with Fazio, and he would eventually be punished for all the selfish emotional acts and broken hearts he had left behind along the way.

But there was another part of Linda's emotions that were concerned and anxious for him, knowing the seriousness of these potential charges could quite possibly, put Dr. Fazio away for the rest of his life.

Monica looked at Linda, expecting her to start doing the 'happy dance' right there in the middle of the bar. Monica Atkinson had met David Fazio several times and personally thought he was an egotistical, self-centered asshole. She was well aware of Linda's pain when Fazio discarded and abandoned her almost two years ago. Monica was very fearful of Linda Ciccone's state of mind after that toxic relationship, sometimes worrying if her close friend was on the brink of committing suicide.

She was happy for Linda when she found another man in her life and quickly married and settled down with him. Monica had met Linda's husband several times and thought that he was a catch.' She knew that Tony had entered Linda's life at the right time in her life. Even though theirs was a 'rebound relationship,' Monica was happy that her friend had gotten married and finally put her relationship with 'Dr. McDreamy' behind her. She knew that Tony had come into Linda's life for the right reason. In her mind, Monica knew that Tony Rozanski had saved Linda from herself.

"I expected you to be jumping for joy, considering the way he dumped you."

Linda gazed at her friend. "I'm so conflicted about him. There's a part of me that wishes he would burn in the deepest depths of hell," she said as she took several more sips of her cold beer.

"And then there's another part of me that's worried for him."

Monica finished her cocktail and ordered another round.

"After the way he dumped you, I wouldn't feel any concern if I were you," she said. "Whatever happens to that bastard, he deserves it."

Monica squeezed the lime in her vodka and cranberry cocktail as she elaborated.

"Fazio was picked up on that second arson fire on North Halsted a few days ago. Our Detectives Romanowski and D'Aiello had to cut him loose because they couldn't pin anything on him, and he had a tight alibi," Monica elaborated.

"Really?"

"Yeah...I guess he had spent the night with some young bimbo who vouched for him, along with his TV reporter buddy."

"Who? Chaz Rizzo?"

"Yeah, that's him. They were drinking together the night before, and he was able to vouch for him."

Linda looked at her friend and was momentarily speechless.

"Your old boyfriend has a nasty habit of sleepwalking."

Linda was well aware of Fazio's sleeping issues. During their relationship, she had found him waking up and sleeping in other parts of the house several times when they were together. She even found him sleeping in his car a few times when she didn't see him in bed.

She was suspicious that morning when Fazio asked her to bandage his burned hands on the same morning as that clinic fire on Randolph Street a few weeks ago. And it was for that reason that she mentioned it to her fireman friend, Commander Terry Janko. Linda had just gone to the funeral of her nursing friend, Terri Biela, and was still distraught over the way she and two other victims had perished in that fire.

"Fazio has some pretty strong pro-life viewpoints too, I understand," Monica mentioned.

"Yes," Linda said. "He won't perform abortions, and he's been reprimanded a few times about it by the hospital. He's always been very vocal about it."

Monica smiled. "Our detectives are keeping an eye on him. All we gotta do is catch him playing with matches, and he's our boy," she coldly said.

Monica looked at her friend and raised her glass to make a toast.

"Here's to the 'karma train.'"

They both raised their glasses as Linda slowly smiled. Perhaps, she thought to herself, it was time to let David Fazio receive what he so justly deserved. After the way he had 'broadsided her' and discarded her out of his life, maybe it was time that David Fazio finally got what was coming to him. Her heart wasn't the first he had broken, and she certainly wasn't the last one to be humiliated by him. Maybe, after all the ways he had mistreated and used so many nurses in that hospital, that something terrible enough had finally happened to shake him to his core.

A strange sort of resolve began to settle in with Linda at that moment, mentally. She was now starting to realize that, even if he was innocent of starting any clinic fires, that he was responsible for the burning of so many other souls that he emotionally devastated at that hospital.

Maybe, she thought to herself, David Fazio was getting what he deserved. There was now the possibility of his being picked up, arraigned, and eventually convicted for arson and involuntary manslaughter, and she shouldn't feel sorry for him.

To her, it doesn't matter whether he had set those abortion clinic fires or not. He had hurt her and many other girls as well. Now, perhaps, Dr. Fazio was finally getting what he had coming.

Linda Ciccone took a drink of her cold beer and smiled. "Yes," she said to her best friend.

"Karma is a bitch."

CHAPTER TWENTY-SEVEN
A Summer Picnic

The St. Peregrine's Annual Church Picnic was assembling at the Forest Preserve on Cumberland and Irving Park Roads, as Dennis Romanowski and his wife were just arriving on that hot Sunday afternoon. They had brought along their twelve and ten-year-old children, Adam and Samantha, to help them unload the food and other goodies under the picnic pavilion where most of the church members were gathering. Diane Romanowski, the police detective's beautiful but somewhat overweight wife of fifteen years, was excited to spend that August afternoon with her family and friends from church. She began to unload the pasta salads, hamburgers, steaks, and Polish sausages from their Subaru Outback.

"Have you heard from Terry and Gina?" Diane asked her husband as she was getting the food plates out of the car.

"They should be here shortly. Terry texted me a half-hour ago."

There were already over seventy people gathered under the large, wooden covered pavilion covering several picnic tables where most everyone usually gathered for their family picnics at the Forest Preserve.

Being that Terry was Denny's best friend since childhood, the two couples had a lot in common and were together often, especially on the weekends. They didn't live far from each other in Chicago's Portage Park neighborhood and did many activities along with their two children and the Janko boys.

As Terry and Gina pulled up to the parking lot of the Forest Preserve in their Jeep Cherokee, little Adam Romanowski held up his brand new, power-blaster water gun, which he intended on immediately using once the Janko boys armed themselves. Terry and Gina

219

looked like they were having a heated discussion in the car, as they waited several long minutes before shutting off the ignition and unloading the kids.

Michael and Tommy Janko, eleven and nine years old, were both busy playing baseball in their respective little league teams and hadn't spent a lot of time with the Romanowski's. The kids were now looking forward to their intense water battles that afternoon during the picnic.

The squirt gun water fights had become such a long-standing tradition at the yearly church picnic that many of the adults participated in the water gun fights as well. Most everyone usually arrived in their bathing suits and tee-shirts, and all the families at the picnic were looking forward to a carefree, enjoyable summer afternoon.

Terry and Gina began unpacking their car and brought their food goodies to the picnic table. The kids started immediately commiserating with each other on who had the largest or the best power-blaster water gun. The four of them sat down as Denny opened up several cold Corona beers for the adults to consume. It was barely one o'clock, and it was already 95 degrees in the shade. It was perfect weather for a hot, summer, take-no-prisoners water-gun fight.

"So…how's it going with our arsonist friend? Have we caught him playing with any more matches?" Terry asked his best friend.

Gina annoyingly looked at her husband.

"Boys? Do we have to start talking shop already? You guys haven't been sitting longer than five minutes," Gina reprimanded her husband and his best friend.

"Could we have a nice, relaxing afternoon without talking about cops and robbers?"

Gina personally did not want to hear any more about the 'Abortion Arsonist,' as the subject of catching this fire starter seemed to be consuming her husband.

"Cops and robbers? Boy, are you dating yourself!" Dennis joked.

"She watched a lot of 'Dick Tracy' when she was a kid!" Terry sarcastically commented.

The four of them laughed as Terry and Dennis walked over towards the barbeque pit, where the others were starting to barbeque all of the steaks, hot dogs, hamburgers, and chicken legs that were available for everyone to eat and share on that day.

Gina and Diane were good friends and were very close. They hadn't talked in a while, and the two of them went off into a corner, speaking in a low voice. They had a lot of catching up to do.

Gina confided in Diane that she and her husband had been fighting regularly lately. It seemed that Terry was more interested in being a good fire chief and a great friend to his fellow firemen, even if it meant his drinking and partying with them after work. Terry seemed to believe that being a 'good buddy' to his fellow firemen was more important than being a full-time husband and father to his family. To make matters worse, Gina shared with Diane that her husband was an abusive, very mean alcoholic.

Terry and Denny were standing together on the other side of the picnic area, preparing the meats and other food goodies to begin grilling.

"We've got some detectives tailing Fazio around, but so far, other than crashing at other women's houses now and again, he seems to be keeping his nose clean," the detective explained.

"You saw that we picked him up after that North Halsted fire last week, but we didn't have enough on him and had to cut him loose," as Denny was inserting a freshly cut lime into his cold beer.

"Yes, I saw that," Terry said.

Terry started to bring all of the hamburgers, hot dogs, and sausages over to the large barbeque pit set up alongside the picnic area to begin cooking. The wives were setting up the salads, pasta dishes, and other food goodies on the large picnic table for everyone to start sharing. Denny followed him over to the BBQ pit and, while still holding his beer, began putting down all of the meats onto the grilling grate.

"You know," Denny continued, "none of this is making any sense to me."

"Why?" Terry responded, holding up the spatula to begin turning over the hamburgers.

"This Fazio guy is no dummy. He's a smart, well-educated doctor out of Chicago-Western Medical Hospital who has no problem what-so-ever getting laid every night," the police detective observed.

"I mean, Terry...really? Does this guy have nothing else better to do than to be torching abortion clinics? For what reason? Why would he want to do such a thing? What's in it for him?"

Terry looked at his best friend, absorbing the beads of sweat starting to trickle from his forehead from standing too close to the barbeque.

"He's a fanatical, pro-life baby doctor," Terry declared.

Denny shook his head. "I don't think so, Terry...the only thing this guy is fanatical about is girls and chasing pussy. He don't go to any of them pro-life abortion clinic protests or none of them vigils that you see these pro-life groups doing." Detective Romanowski stated, as his Chicago accent was now more prevalent.

"When we picked him up last week, he was coming back to the bar to pick up his car from some broad's house. His car was parked about fifteen hundred feet away from that torched clinic on Halsted. He didn't smell like smoke or accelerant and didn't have any evidence that he had physically been burning anything."

Terry stopped turning over the hamburgers just long enough to make his point to the Chicago detective.

"He fits the arsonist profile, Denny. We just gotta catch him in the act or find the evidence that we need to make these arson charges stick."

"Catch him in the act? Of doing what?" Dennis argued. "The only thing we're gonna catch this guy is doing is either playing with himself or getting laid!"

Terry was silent for several minutes, trying to concentrate on cooking all of the hamburgers, hotdogs, and sausages on the grill.

"How many girlfriends can this guy have?" the fire chief asked.

Denny started laughing as he was finishing his cold beer.

"A lot, Terry. We went to the hospital and talked to a few of his staff and some of his fellow employees there at the hospital," Denny explained. "This doctor has a bad habit of shitting where he sleeps."

"What do you mean?"

"I mean, he's probably slept with seventy-five percent of the nurses there at that hospital," the detective smiled.

Terry started smiling while shaking his head. "That doesn't make him very smart."

"No," Denny said slowly, "It certainly doesn't. He's got more nurses at that hospital that hate his guts; he's scorned an awful lot of women there."

"So, what are you saying?"

"I don't know, Terry. All I know is if you start pissing off enough ladies in one place, especially at a hospital, they're going to do whatever it takes to destroy you."

Janko was listening while barbequing the steaks.

"If you're a doctor at a hospital, especially if you're doing a lot of surgeries, that doctor better has

223

those nurses assisting him and making sure that they're all working together to save lives," the Chicago detective commented.

"This Fazio guy has a lot of goddamn enemies. And all of them are angry women, mostly nurses," Denny observed.

Terry Janko was silent, continuing to shake his head.

"With all the nurses in that hospital that hate his guts, this guy ain't got no time to be torching clinics."

"How do you explain his bad sleeping habits and his sleepwalking?" Terry mentioned.

Denny started to laugh while opening up another ice-cold bottle of Corona.

"If you had that many nurses gunning after you, would you be able to sleep?"

Terry smirked as he began placing slices of cheese on the now well-done burgers.

"Maybe we should be looking elsewhere for our suspect, Terry. I'm starting to think this baby doctor isn't the Abortion Arsonist."

"He's going to make a mistake somewhere," Terry loudly insisted. "He's probably waiting for all the media hype and the publicity to die down before torching another clinic."

The two of them sat down as Terry started to serve up the cheeseburgers and hotdogs to all of the kids. They had been complaining of being hungry before starting their afternoon, water-gun fights.

"So? What do you want to do?" Terry asked his best friend.

"We can tail him for another week or so. But sooner or later, we gotta back off. This guy isn't giving us any reason to tail him around. Just because his hands were burned on the same morning as that clinic fire on Randolph doesn't mean this guy plays with matches."

Terry looked at him silently for several minutes. By then, the wives had fixed their husbands a plate of food and brought it over with some beer refills to keep them quiet and out of trouble for an hour or so. Gina and Diane then went off with some of the other parishioners at the picnic, watching several of them play 'baggo' about one hundred yards away. Some other people were picking out teams to start playing 'bocce ball' on the large green lawns nearby while the kids were filling up their gun-blasters with water.

"Who else could be responsible for setting those fires?" Terry asked.

"Could be anyone. Maybe some of his old girlfriends? I have no clue. When you listen to some of these nurses talk about him at the hospital, the way they all foam at the mouth, you would think they were all talking about Harvey Weinstein," Romanowski said.

Terry Janko started to smile while sucking down his second Corona.

"This guy ain't no arsonist, Terry. I'll put money on it." Denny proclaimed. "David Fazio is a pro-life baby doctor who has nothing to gain by torching abortion clinics. Why would a well-trained, highly respected obstetrician go around lighting up family planning clinics? It makes no sense," the detective reasoned.

A moment of silence as the two friends stared at each other. Janko was listening intently to his best friend.

"A pussy hound? Definitely. This baby doctor has a hard time thinking with anything other than his dick," Dennis said in a softer voice, taking another sip of his cold Corona. He was careful to make sure the girls weren't listening.

"But playing with matches? I'm telling you, Terry. This guy ain't our boy."

They both took another sip of their beers as Terry grabbed a hot dog for himself, now applying the condiments.

"Fazio is a womanizer," Denny declared. "But he ain't no arsonist."

Terry Janko looked at Denny while shoving the hotdog with mustard and onions into his mouth.

"I don't agree, Dennis. I think we need to be patient and put in some more police work," the Battalion Chief calmly insisted while talking with his mouth full.

It was as if the Battalion Chief was fixated on arresting and charging David Fazio for those random acts of arson. It was as though he was trying to take a wooden square peg and continue to keep shoving it forcefully into a round hole. He had no other suspects and no other leads. He only had his interview with Fazio and a statement from his friend, Linda Ciccone, verifying that his hands were severely burned on the morning of the Randolph clinic fire. Janko was under a tremendous amount of pressure from the Chicago Fire Department Superintendent to find this arsonist, at any cost. And at this stage of the game, Chief Janko didn't care how or where Fazio was arrested.

"Terry?" Dennis asked his best friend, again in a softer voice while no one else was listening.

"Can I ask you something?"

Janko and Romanowski locked eyes with each other.

"Why do you have such a hard-on for this Fazio-guy? I keep telling you, I don't think he's our boy."

Terry Janko now looked at his best friend, his eyes widening and his voice and his insistence being more assertive.

"Fazio is a goddamn fanatic, Denny. Whether he's torching these clinics while sleepwalking or lighting them outright, he's still a fanatic. We need to get whatever evidence we can to get this nut-job off the streets."

Terry looked at his best friend, knowing that his resolve to solve this case and to put the blame squarely on Fazio was apparent. Chief Janko firmly believed that Dr. David Fazio had torched those abortion clinics, and it didn't matter to him whether they had the evidence verifying that or not.

"Okay, Terry. Whatever you say. But I'm leveling with you..." the police detective said while fixing a hotdog for himself.

"Don't be surprised if this baby doctor turns out to be anything but an arsonist."

CHAPTER TWENTY-EIGHT
A Meeting at Starbucks

It was a little past 7:30 in the morning as I was looking at my watch, trying to make sure that I didn't miss her. I had heard from several other nurses at the hospital that she came into this Starbucks on Madison and Aberdeen Streets every morning. This woman used to be a maternity ward nurse before going to work for a private medical group in the West Loop that she has now been working for over the last thirteen years.

I knew I couldn't reach out to her by text or email, as she probably would not take very kindly to me suddenly contacting her. I thought about calling her at work, but I knew that she would probably hang up the phone on me and know of my intentions to speak with her. Even though we had some 'bad history' over thirteen years ago when she was a nurse at Chicago-Western Medical Center, and I desperately needed to talk to her.

I had already ordered my grande cappuccino with the extra shot of espresso and was sitting at the corner of the coffee shop. I knew that my guerilla warfare assault in surprising, and meeting up with her was rather ballsy, but I was becoming desperate. I knew that there was someone out there trying to frame me, and contacting her was my first clue.

At about 7:40, she walked into the Starbucks and immediately got into line, reaching inside of her purse for her credit card. She was still as beautiful as I remembered her, with her bright blue eyes and wavy brown and blonde streaked hair. Her figure was as ravishing as I recalled, and from where I was sitting, she looked as though she hadn't changed a single bit. She seemed to be more beautiful now more than ever in her middle age.

I decided to wait until she placed her beverage order before approaching her. She stood in line and gave them her request, which was probably a venti flat white. I guessed that this was still the same drink she used to order from Starbucks that I would always pick up for her and bring to the hospital. I smiled to myself as my heart started rapidly beating out of my chest.

I got up from the table in the corner, abandoning my coffee, and bravely approached her while she was waiting for her drink.

"Hey, Gina."

She immediately looked in my direction, as a slight smile came over her face. She then seemed to go into mild shock.

"David," she slowly said. "So strange seeing you here. What a coincidence!"

I carefully approached her, and we put our arms around each other, giving each other an intense hug. I hadn't held her in so many, many years. For a few seconds, I pretended that she was still mine again.

"What are you doing here?" she quickly asked me.

"I was in the area and needed to take care of my caffeine fix. I have a medical seminar to go to not very far away on Wacker Drive," I lied, hoping that my bullshit excuse sounded believable.

"Oh," she said, guessing that I was telling her the truth.

We hadn't talked for over thirteen years, and at the time of our breakup, we had a very messy separation that took us both a considerable amount of time to recover.

Nurse Gina Janko was a maternity nurse on the seventh floor of Chicago-Western Medical Center for several years before we caught each other's attention. She was a newlywed at the time and had just married Terrance Janko, a fireman out of Chicago's Firehouse

Engine No. 1. We had worked together and had become terrific friends during her employment in our maternity department.

Our intense, romantic relationship didn't start until one night at the bar. It was a little place called Dos Amigos Bar and Grill on Ashland Avenue, and most of the doctors and nurses were going there every night after work. It was a 'dive bar' but became our nightly drinking establishment and watering hole. I remember it was Cinco de Mayo, and Gina was there with several of her girlfriends from the hospital when I walked over to her, and we started talking.

Gina had been married for several months to Janko, and they were already encountering a very rough patch in their marriage. It seemed that Janko was spending more and more time drinking and partying with his firehouse buddies and spending less and less time with her at home, and she was feeling extraordinarily neglected and alone.

In any case, we both drank more than our share of margaritas that night until we found ourselves making out, mashing, and grabbing in the back seat of my car in the parking lot. I probably had most of her clothes off before we decided to go to the Marriott on Michigan Avenue, not very far away, and spent a great night of lovemaking together in bed. Her husband was working one of his 72-hour shifts at the firehouse, and she was in no hurry to go home that night.

At first, our relationship consisted of only very casual sex. Gina was a 'friend-with-benefits,' and we seemed to be there at each other's beck and call whenever the urge to go off and fornicate somewhere came over either one of us. She was in her late twenties and was newly married at the time, and although she had no desire to divorce her fireman husband, she was getting more and more attached to our intense relationship. I was married to my second wife during that period as well, and although my marital problems were becoming insurmountable, I had hoped at the time that I could avoid getting divorced again.

In any case, we were both consenting adults experiencing problems in our marriages, and we both looked to each other in a hotel bedroom for our intense therapy and counseling sessions. She would cry to me about problems with her drinking, partying husband, while I cried to her about my narcissistic, controlling wife. Neither one of us seemed to have any desire to break off our marriages at the time. Our frequent marital counseling sessions at the Marriott also appeared to be a convenient place for the two of us to get together and vent about our emotional relationship problems.

Of course, our therapy and sex sessions weren't just exclusive to the Marriott. We found time and space to make out on the couch in my office, my bathroom, the hospital supply closet, in the parking lot, outdoors under the rafters during a baseball game, and several times in an empty patient room on the seventh floor. We once even had sex on a spare bed in a patient room with the curtains closed while a patient was sleeping and in an induced coma on the other bed. This hot and heavy affair went on for several months, extending through that summer many years ago.

Like everything else, all good things come to an end. Fireman Janko found one of my texts on his wife's cell phone and immediately confronted her. It didn't take long for him to figure out where his young bride was going at night after work at the hospital, while he was at the firehouse, drinking and partying with his buddies after his shift.

Unfortunately, I was caught as well, as one of the Marriott hotel charges ended up on one of my credit card statements that I didn't recall using. In any case, my now ex-wife had gotten my American Express bill in the mail and found the hotel room charge on my credit card, which I could no longer deny.

Things ended very messy and very ugly for our once very intense romantic relationship. As my marriage was going towards the direction of the Domestic and Family Division of the Cook County Courthouse, I had assumed that Gina's marriage to the fireman would dissolve as well. But at the last minute, while they were both shopping for divorce lawyers, they decided to give their marriage another chance, and I was suddenly shut out in the cold.

I became the 'fall guy' after her husband caught Gina. She had her husband believing that she was all but 'forced' into having sex with me and that I coerced her into meeting me at the Marriott twice a week. They both ended up doing intense marital counseling, and as part of her penance, resigned from Chicago-Western to work for a group of dermatologists in the West Loop.

We never said much to each other after her husband busted us, although I'm sure she knew about my costly, very messy divorce years later. It had been over thirteen years, and we both hadn't seen and talked to each other since she abruptly left the hospital without even saying good-bye.

Several of the nurses on our floor still kept in contact with Gina Janko. I had kept mental tabs over where she was living, where she was working, and how she was doing. The last I had heard, she was married and living in a brick bungalow in Portage Park with her Fire Chief husband and their two little boys.

Gina got her drink beverage and followed me over to the corner of Starbucks as we sat down. I immediately assumed that she was in a hurry, but she seemed to want to take the time for us to sit down and visit again after all these years.

"You haven't changed, Gina. Time has been good to you."

She smiled. "You look great too, David. Every time I see that 'Goodfellas' movie, I think about you. You're aging very well, even with the gray hair."

"Thanks," I blushed. Gina was referring to the Ray Liotta resemblance. We exchanged pleasantries about her boys, their baseball leagues, and her husband's promotion as the Battalion Chief of Fire Engine No. 1. That took all of fifteen minutes.

"Sounds like you're doing well....I'm divorced now," I casually mentioned.

"Yes...I heard this. I'm sorry. No chance of another Mrs. Fazio?"

"Not in this lifetime. I've more than learned my lesson," I said while taking another sip of my cappuccino.

She then looked at me straight in the eyes.

"Okay, David. Let's cut the bullshit. Why are you here stalking me?"

"Really?" I exclaimed. "My oh my! Our oversized egos haven't changed one bit, have they?"

Gina laughed. "David, I know about the arson fires, and I know about my husband pursuing you."

I looked at her intently for several silent moments.

"Does he know that you know?"

"No...not yet. I've been playing it cool, watching all of this unravel."

We sat there for a few long seconds, staring at each other. I just couldn't believe how beautiful Gina had gotten over the years. There were some very slight wrinkles around her eyes that she covered very well with her make-up. But Gina looked like she was still in her twenties instead of being middle-aged.

"Terry knows I'll eventually accuse him of drudging up some old bad feelings when he realizes how much I know. I've been trying to avoid the subject and pretending to look the other way when the issue of the 'Abortion Arsonist' comes up."

"You've always been a smart lady."

"Thank you," she replied.

"So, what do you want from me?"

I looked at her, deciding to come clean with my stealth intentions.

"I need to know what's going on, Gina. All of a sudden, I have the coppers and the arson investigators up my ass, thinking that I now go around torching abortion clinics."

She looked at me, trying to feel empathetic.

"I heard that you burned your hands while you were sleepwalking on the same morning as arson fire on Randolph Street. Now they're all trying to pin these arson fires on you."

"But why, Gina? Why would everyone suddenly start trying to nail me with all of this arson bullshit?"

Gina looked at David, now shaking her head.

"David? Seriously?" I looked at her, waiting for her profound statement.

"You've made a lot of enemies at that hospital, thanks to your movie-star good looks and your penis."

I shook my head, not wanting to believe what she had to say.

"Maybe you should go to a dog obedience school."

"Why?

"A dog never shits where he sleeps. But unfortunately, you've never learned that valuable lesson."

She took a long sip of her flat-white coffee.

"You've arrogantly burned a lot of bridges at that hospital, and now people, and especially nurses, are looking for ways to crucify you and get you out of the way at Chicago-Western. Your verbal, pro-life viewpoints haven't helped you either. So now you have plenty of enemies coming out of the woodwork, including my husband."

She paused, taking another drink from her coffee.

"What better way to 'burn you' than to tag you as the Abortion Arsonist?"

"But who would be setting these clinics on fire? No matter how badly I may be sleepwalking, I don't go around torching clinics or buildings where there are people inside." I proclaimed.

"Are you sure?" Gina asked. "Sleepwalkers don't usually remember what they do while they're sleepwalking. And the problem now is, all the authorities are now well aware of your bad sleeping habits."

"But why is your husband chasing me now, after all of these years? It's been over thirteen years now. Everyone should have gotten past all of this."

"Not Terry. He doesn't mention it to me anymore, but I can tell all of this shit still bothers him. And since your name has resurfaced again, he's been having trouble sleeping at night. He sometimes goes out for long drives in the evening, never telling me where he's been or where's he's going. He's become quite tormented over all of this. His resolve and hatred towards you are as bad, if not worse, than when all of this happened between us thirteen years ago."

I looked at her intently, knowing that none of this was good news.

"He's still pissed off at the fact that someone was screwing his wife while he was out screwing around," Gina said.

"So, what do you suggest?" I asked my very beautiful but now happily married ex-girlfriend.

She only got up from the table, grasped her coffee, and then kissed me on the cheek. It was as though she was trying to avoid answering my very simple question.

"Goodbye, David. If I see you stalking me again, I'm going to sic my ferocious Battalion Chief Commander-Husband on you," she smiled as she winked her eye.

I couldn't tell if that was a warning for me to stay away from her or giving me another invitation to meet her at the Marriott on Michigan Avenue.

As she was walking away, she turned and loudly warned me: "David...please watch your back," then she inserted, *"and don't close your eyes."*

I watched her leave Starbucks and get into her Jeep Cherokee parked across the street. Then I, too, decided I needed to go back to work at the hospital. As I was leaving, I noticed a familiar, unmarked black Ford Escape SUV parked across the street on Madison. A man was sitting inside, making eye contact with me, staring and watching me while holding a white styrofoam cup of coffee. He looked so damn familiar.

It took me a minute until I got into my car to figure out who it was that was in that car following me back to Chicago-Western Medical Center.

It was Detective Romanowski.

CHAPTER TWENTY-NINE
Meeting at Chicago-Western

The parking lot of the Chicago-Western Medical Hospital on West Harrison Street was packed with cars, as Battalion Chief Terry Janko pulled up in his bright red Crown Victoria sedan, looking for a parking space near the entrance door.

He noticed Detective Romanowski's Chicago P.D. squad car parked illegally up in front, taking up two handicapped spaces close by. The summer rain had let up that afternoon, as there were large puddles of water scattered everywhere around the parking lot. There was still a very light drizzle as Chief Janko parked on the far side of the parking lot and walked through the rain, slightly sprinkling up to the front door entrance, where the Eighteenth district detective was patiently waiting.

"Must be nice to be a high-class detective from the Eighteenth. I see you get a handicapped, double-parking spot." Janko casually mentioned to the detective as he walked in from the damp parking area.

"It was raining harder before you got here. I didn't want to get my brand new, J.C. Penny's $49.95 corduroy jacket all wet," Detective Romanowski sarcastically replied.

"I get it. Probably because it's so cheap, you're afraid it's going to shrink while you're wearing it?"

"Yeah," Dennis laughed, "that's it."

The two of them entered the hospital through the front door and into the large reception area, which was filled with patients, doctors, nurses, and other hospital staff. The aroma of the Starbucks kiosk was mesmerizing, as the coffee smell dominated the hospital atrium as there was a long line of medical staff lined up to get their caffeine fix that afternoon. The two of them casually walked over the elevator after asking for directions to the maternity floor from a senior citizen operating the information desk.

When the two of them arrived on the seventh floor, they asked a nurse working at their desk at the nurse's floor station for Dr. Calvin Worrell, head of the maternity ward, and whether or not he was available to speak with them. When the nurse realized after paging him that he wasn't accessible, she paged Nurse Susan Anderson, who was the senior head maternity nurse on duty on that Tuesday afternoon.

"Good afternoon, may I help you?" Nurse Anderson politely extended her hand to both the chief battalion fireman and the detective.

"Hi...I'm Detective Romanowski from Chicago Police District Eighteen, and this is Chief Janko from the Fire Engine No. 1," as they both shook her hand.

"We would like to ask you some questions regarding Dr. David Fazio, who works in this department."

Nurse Anderson smirked to herself as she stood there silently for a second, wondering why a firefighter and a Chicago P.D. detective would be here at the hospital, asking questions about Dr. Fazio.

"Certainly," she eagerly answered as she let the two to a private patient waiting room at the end of the seventh-floor hallway. There was no one in there, and she asked them both to take a seat while she closed and locked the door.

"What can I do for you, gentlemen?"

"We're here to find out some information on one of your doctors' that works here in your maternity ward, and we were hoping that we could talk to Dr. Worrell," Romanowski said to the head nurse.

"Dr. Worrell isn't always available here at the hospital, but I'm glad to answer whatever questions you may have," she politely volunteered.

The detective took out his notebook while Chief Janko sat at the adjacent chair, studying the middle-aged nurse.

"How long have you known Dr. Fazio?" the detective asked.

"For as long as I've been here, over eighteen years," the nurse answered.

"Have you worked with him in all those years?" the detective questioned.

"Yes."

A moment of silence.

"We understand that he is a pro-life obstetrician here at this hospital. How have his personal beliefs affected your job duties and the other medical staff here at the hospital?"

Nurse Anderson thought for a moment.

"Well, his pro-life beliefs and actions have created some conflict amongst the other doctors and nurses who are forced to abide by the new state abortion laws. Dr. Fazio seems to have exempted himself from performing these procedures, leaving the responsibility of aborting these pregnancies on others within the department," the nurse replied.

"Has he made any statements regarding his contempt for those doctors who perform these procedures," Janko asked.

"Oh yes...all the time," Anderson lied.

In reality, Fazio had seldom ever mentioned or passed judgment on any of his colleagues who performed those abortive procedures. He only excused himself, based on his personal religious beliefs, that he would not execute any abortions and, more specifically, partial-birth abortions within the hospital.

"How so?" Romanowski asked.

239

"He has been very condescending to the other medical staff here in the maternity ward for terminating those pregnancies. Because of his seniority and maybe perhaps, the administration not wanting to cause any stir, he has left him alone and not hassled him. However, he's been told that if there was no one else on the ward available to terminate a pregnancy and he was the only one on call or on duty that he would be required to do so," Nurse Anderson answered.

"Has that ever happened?" Janko asked.

"Not that I'm aware."

The detective and the fire chief looked at each other.

"Has he ever mentioned any contempt for Dr. Petrovitch from the Affiliated Family Planning Center?"

Nurse Anderson thought for a moment.

"I heard that he had some very loud, verbal exchanges with him in front of our medical staff at one of the medical symposiums that we had outside of the hospital. I overheard him mentioning his name many times, calling him a 'baby killer.'"

Nurse Anderson was doing her best to 'color the truth.'

"Really?" Janko remarked.

"Yes. Dr. Fazio's contempt for Dr. Petrovitch was no secret," Nurse Anderson exaggerated.

Detective Romanowski took down several notes while Chief Janko continued to ask a few more questions.

"Did Dr. Fazio threaten Petrovitch?"

"Well, no, I never heard him threaten him. But I did recall him once mentioning several times how he'd wish someone would 'blow up that abortion clinic on Randolph Street' so that they wouldn't kill any more innocent babies."

Janko and Romanowski looked at each other again.

"Really? You heard him say this?" the detective asked.

"Yes. It was common knowledge that Fazio had no love for 'those abortionists on Randolph Street.'"

In reality, Dr. Fazio never said any such thing.

The detective continued to take down notes. They both asked the head nurse some particular questions as to Fazio's behavior around the hospital and especially on the seventh floor, and what else he may have mentioned regarding the other medical staff who performed those abortive procedures.

It was fair to say that, because of Anderson's animosity towards Dr. Fazio, that she exaggerated many of the personal facts and observations that the two were asking her regarding the pro-life obstetrician. Many of her answers were contemptuous, exaggerated to make Fazio look like some sort of pro-life monster.

In the way she was answering their questions, Anderson made Dr. David Fazio look as though he was out to obliterate and ruin any medical professional who disagreed with his pro-life religious ethics.

At one point, Chief Terry Janko started to feel sympathetic towards Nurse Anderson, as she described how Fazio had ruthlessly, so many times at the protest of the mother, deliver severely deformed babies and leaving them to become wards of the state, despite the mother's wishes.

"I agree with you, Nurse Anderson," the fire chief said. "No doctor should play God in that delivery room."

At that moment, Romanowski gave a dirty look to his best friend for voicing his personal opinion.

After they continued to question the head nurse for thirty minutes or so, they took down more notes until ending their intense interview. Chief Janko handed Nurse Anderson his business card, containing his firehouse address and personal cell number.

Everyone shook hands, and the two left the ward on the seventh floor.

"What the hell is wrong with you?" Romanowski chastised his friend. "Since when did you start voicing your opinion during an interview?"

"I don't know, Denny. When I realized how Fazio was going against the will of these mothers and delivering these unwanted babies, I got angry," Terry replied.

"You know better, Terry. You need to start holding your cards a little tighter to your chest. You've been letting these clinic arson fires make you a little goofy lately."

"I know. I don't know what's wrong with me."

The two of them exited the elevator onto the lobby of Chicago-Western Medical Center. They continued to walk together as they exited the hospital's front entrance together and started to walk over to their cars.

"Hey Terry," Dennis mentioned, "I've still got that electric hedge trimmer that you loaned me a month ago. I've been lugging it in my car for a while. Can I give it back to you?"

"Sure," the Fire Chief replied.

Dennis pulled his black Ford Escape SUV squad car next to Terry Janko's red fire battalion vehicle. He had already started his automobile and pushed the trunk button from his glove box while he sat inside, waiting for Dennis to load the hedge trimmer into his trunk.

As Dennis grabbed the trimmer from his vehicle and began to put it inside, he was a little startled at what was in the car trunk. There was a large gasoline tank, partially filled with gasoline, torn-up rags, and a box of fireworks. He placed the trimmer inside and examined the fireworks. They were M-80's with extra-long wicks.

Dennis shook his head and quickly closed the trunk.

"What are you, fucking nuts?" Dennis asked his best friend as he approached him while he sat in the car.

"What?"

"What the fuck do you mean, 'What'? What the hell are you doing driving around with an almost full tank of gasoline and some firecrackers? What do you have, a goddamn death wish?"

Terry looked at Denny and turned several shades of white.

"What the hell are you talking about?"

Terry quickly shut off the car and opened his trunk. Inside was a large tank of gasoline and the fireworks, along with some torn up rags, just as Dennis said.

"I swear on my kids, Denny...I don't know how this shit got here?"

"What the hell do you mean, Terry? Who else drives this car?"

Terry thought for a second.

"Just me. But I swear to God, I had no idea I was driving around with a large tank of gas and a box of fireworks."

They both looked at each other, speechless for several long moments.

"You better call the firehouse and let them know you're driving around a Molotov cocktail. You can't continue to drive this vehicle. What if someone hits you or something ignites those firecrackers?"

Terry was speechless.

"I'm only a half a mile away from the firehouse. I will drive slow with the flashers on and unload this shit out of my trunk when I get there."

"Terry, it's not safe..." Denny loudly protested.

"I'll be fine, Dennis. I've got to put my head around this and figure out how all of this shit got in here."

Dennis looked at his best friend. "Be aware of your surroundings, Terry," was all he managed to say.

The two of them hugged, and they both got into their squad cars and went back to their prospective stations.

When Terry got back to the Engine One Firehouse, he immediately parked his car and inquired to the other firemen on shift if anyone knew how a tank of gas and some fireworks ended up in his car's trunk.

Everyone shook their heads, and no one knew anything about it. Chief Terry then removed the contents from his trunk, leaving the electric hedge trimmer in the back seat for him to take home.

Terry didn't think anything more about the incident over the next few days, although he couldn't figure out who had put those fire accelerants into his car trunk. He was the only one who had the keys to the car, and as far as he was aware, he was the only person who drove that vehicle.

Two days later, Captain Stuart Durham was at his desk working on some reports when the UPS driver come into the firehouse with a package to deliver.

"How are you, Captain," the UPS driver greeted Stuart as he signed for the small, ten by twelve cardboard box, gift-wrapped with brown wrapping paper and tightly taped together. The box was addressed to "Chicago Firehouse, Engine No. 1." He shook the box, as it felt incredibly light. Before opening it, he looked at the return address on the upper left-hand corner of the box.

It just simply said: "Chicago-Western Medical Center."

244

CHAPTER THIRTY
Arrested

It was a wet, rainy September morning, as I woke up outside of my condominium complex on North Lakeshore Drive. I must have gotten up for some fresh air in the middle of the night or was having trouble sleeping, and I fell asleep sitting at the bench in front of the lakefront.

I was sleepwalking again.

Sometimes, the cooler air of Lake Michigan in the middle of the night helps me to rest. I have an easier time sleeping in a sitting position than I do laying horizontally, I told myself.

I had experienced another one of my violent, horrific dreams, and I must have awakened myself in the middle of the night. I looked at my watch. It was almost five o'clock in the morning, and the sun hadn't quite risen yet. I noticed that I was wearing a white pair of shorts that I had on from yesterday, and I was wearing my tee-shirt inside out and backward. I must have been exhausted when I got up in the middle of the night...

Or?

I quickly got up from the park bench and walked over to my condo building across the street. The night guard greeted me as I got into the elevator, and I tried to enter my apartment. It was locked.

I must have locked myself out in the middle of the night again, as this had happened before. I went downstairs and bothered the night watchman to do me another favor and help me get back into my condo.

"Locked out again, huh, Dr. Fazio?"

Even the night watchman was familiar with my sleepwalking.

"I'm sorry to bother you again, Javier."

The nightwatchman went into his drawer and grabbed a master key. He then called the maintenance man with his radio, and within several minutes, they were able to let me back into my condo.

I turned on the coffee pot and the shower, knowing that I had to be at the hospital at six o'clock that morning. For background noise, I usually turn the television on while I clean up and get ready. As I was pouring coffee into my mug, I overheard the news broadcast on Channel Eight:

'We have a breaking story this morning, as another family planning clinic has burned down on West Division Street. There appears to be a casualty in the blaze...'

I almost dropped my hot, scorching coffee on the floor as I listened to the news broadcast blaring out of the television in my living room. At that moment, I went into shock. I didn't know what to do. I looked at my hands and smelled my clothes. There were no burns on my hands. There was no smell of gasoline, no smell of smoke on any of the clothing that I had on last night.

I suddenly knew that I would be suspected of starting this. I wanted to run into my room and start packing some clothes into a suitcase and run. I had to leave Chicago. I had to get the hell out of here. But where would I go? How could I escape?

I didn't know what to do.

I took a valium to calm my nerves and went into my liquor cabinet. I poured myself two fingers of Johnny Walker Black and gulped it down quickly. I had to settle myself down, and I knew I couldn't panic. I wanted to run. But I had nowhere to go.

I grabbed my cell phone and called Jeanne.

"Good Morning Loverboy..."

"Jeanne? There's been another fire..."

She automatically detected the panic in my voice. "Oh my God," she abruptly said. "Has something happened?"

"Not yet," I replied. "But I've got a feeling they're gonna try to tag me hard for this."

"Where did you wake up this morning?" Jeanne asked.

"I was in bed," I lied. I didn't want to involve her in any of this.

"Jeanne...if anything happens to me, call up my brother Carlo at the store. He will know who to contact and what to do."

"Okay," she said obediently as I was ready to hang up my cell phone.

"I love you, David," Jeanne loudly said before hanging up the phone. She had never said that to me before.

"I love you too," I blurted out as I ended the call.

I grabbed my tie and my suitcoat, my cell phone, and my car keys. Before leaving, I paused for a moment and took a good look around my Gold Coast condominium. For some odd reason, a feeling of finality came over me.

I wondered if I would ever be inside of my own house again.

The office of Dr. David Fazio MD was crowded with several police officers, reporters from the media, and several firemen from Chicago's Fire Department. They had all been anticipating the arrival of Dr. Fazio, as Detective Dennis Romanowski had a warrant for his arrest.

It was almost seven-thirty in the morning when Dr. Fazio arrived at his office after waiting and procrastinating downstairs in the lobby. Fazio was told by some of his staff via cell phone that there was a large party waiting for his arrival at his office on the seventh floor.

Dr. Fazio, at that moment, had still not acquired a lawyer and had not consulted with anyone regarding the pending arson charges that were about to be launched against him. Dr. Fazio knew deep down in his heart that he was not an arsonist. Even if he was a sleepwalker, there was no way that he would have initiated an arson fire on any building without his waking up and realizing what he was maliciously doing.

Fazio tried to be confident that all of this would work out for the best. He had to have his faith in himself and God, knowing that the truth would eventually come out.

As Fazio opened his office door, he was bombarded with media reporters shoving microphones in his face.

"Are you the Abortion Arsonist?" one reporter bluntly asked.

"No, I am not!" Fazio quickly said as a barrage of additional questions from other reporters came flying at him as he tried to make his way into his office. As he entered, Detective Romanowski and Fire Chief Janko approached the obstetrician, holding up a warrant for his arrest.

"Dr. David Fazio, you are under arrest for the arson fires that have resulted in the homicides of four people and the fire destruction of three family planning clinics in the City of Chicago," Romanowski said.

Another nurse named Sophia Camerata, 29 years old, had perished in the clinic fire that morning.

Two other officers grabbed Fazio's arms and pulled them behind his back, and immediately handcuffed him. Romanowski then continued to read him his Miranda warning:

"You have the right to remain silent. Anything you say can and will be used against you in a court of law. You have the right to speak to an attorney and to have an attorney present during any questioning. If you cannot afford a lawyer, one will be provided for you at government expense."

"What am I being arrested for? I am NOT an arsonist," Fazio continued to protest.

The policemen and detectives present did not answer him. They only hurriedly escorted him out of his office at Chicago-Western Medical Hospital. A parade of reporters and others followed the arson suspect as he was about to be driven to the Eighteenth District for processing. As the patrolmen and police officers were bringing their arson suspect into the parking lot and a police patrol car, Detective Romanowski looked at Battalion Chief Janko as they both made eye contact. The fire chief was smiling from ear to ear.

Chief Terry Janko now knew that they finally captured the Abortion Arsonist.

CHAPTER THIRTY-ONE
A Visit from Zio Tony

The drab, gray walls of the ten by twelve-foot prison cell were dreary and dilapidated, as Dr. David Fazio sat on the single mattress, situated within the middle of the room. He had been at 2700 South California for twenty-four hours now and knew very little about why he was being held in jail. He only knew that he was being accused of being an arsonist and knew nothing else. Which fire was he being accused of? What evidence did they have? Were there other casualties? He had not even planned to hire a defense attorney and had no idea who to call. He only knew that, with the privilege of only one phone call to make, that there was only one person in the whole world that he should immediately contact.

'If you ever need anything at all, kid, you know who to call,' was the phrase that he had always said to him, and those words were ringing in his head. He asked the correctional officer to give him a cell phone to dial that significant number.

Within two hours, Fazio was escorted in handcuffs and ankle chains out of his jail cell and into a conference room with only three filthy, high ceiling windows. The walls bore a drab, green paint color that was so old and dirty; it was starting to turn yellow. As he sat down on that cold, steel chair, he overheard the familiar voice that he hoped would make this incredible nightmare go away, coming down the hallway towards the conference room.

"Hey kid," as his uncle and beloved godfather came into the room, demanding a presence as he entered that only could be compared to kings, royalty, or, more realistically, a Chicago capo mob boss.

"Your brother Carlo called me too. I came as soon as I could."

250

He kissed him on both cheeks as he sat down on the wooden chair across the table. A prison guard stood at attention next to the door, as if he was planning to stick around.

"Why don't you get the hell out of here so I can talk to my nephew...in private," he demanded, as the tall, African American prison guard quickly left the room.

Anthony "Little Tony" DiMatteo, or 'Zio Tony, was only five feet, five inches tall but was a monumental giant in the organized crime world. Everyone in Chicagoland knew that he famously expressed his volatile, violent actions first and asked questions later. Little Tony had a quick, uncontrollably violent temper, and his reputation for insanely random acts of violence had always preceded him.

Rumor has it that he recently shot a man from under the table at the Pagliacci Restaurant directly in his testicles several times. The poor bastard had just finished his linguini and clam sauce and angered the Mafioso for shorting him a hundred bucks on 'the vig.' Two waiters, upon the orders of the owner-chef and Tony's friend, dragged the dead body from the empty dining room into the kitchen, disposing of it later. His now gray-haired, slim, and trim figure still made him an intimidating figure to any formidable enemy or foe from both sides of the street.

As he sat down, there were several moments of silence, as David Fazio was initially speechless. He did not know what to say or how to explain his present situation to his beloved uncle and godfather, knowing that he had somehow managed to get himself locked up and jailed. Before that day, Dr. Fazio had never spent a single minute of his life in a jail cell.

"I heard what happened," Little Tony managed to say. "We're going to try to get you out of here. I called the best attorney in Chicago for these kinds of problems, and he should be here to talk to you soon."

Little Tony mentioned the name of an attorney that he had never heard before.

"If anyone can get you out of here, it will be him."

"Zio Tony, I have no idea what's going on."

"Well, I do. I talked to the detective, and according to him, you're the Abortion Arsonist."

He paused for a moment.

"According to this goddamn detective, you've been running around in your sleep setting these abortion clinics on fire. They also found a lab coat with your name on it that was partially destroyed in this last fire on West Division Street."

"That's not true, Zio Tony," he protested.

"Yeah, well, David...the problem is, you don't remember. You're a known sleepwalker with very shitty sleeping habits, and the truth is, you don't goddamn remember."

David Fazio was silent.

"According to these assholes, you and Mrs. O'Leary's fucking cow started the Chicago Fire in your sleep. Because you're a baby doctor who doesn't believe in abortions, you've been their prime suspect for a long time."

Dr. Fazio was speechless as Little Tony took a deep breath.

"One of the nurses at the hospital told one of the detectives about your getting treatment for your hands being burned the day after one of those fires."

"That was probably Linda," he immediately said.

"I must have burned them in the middle of the night."

"Seriously?"

A moment of silence.

"You don't remember how you burned them, and nobody is buying your bullshit story about you burning your hands while making breakfast."

David sat there completely distraught.

"This is so unbelievable. I've never burned anything in my life. I can't even start a fire in my fireplace or my barbeque without a gas starter. I have never said anything to anyone or done anything to make someone believe that I would want to burn down a family planning clinic," David said.

"I'm not a pyromaniac, and I'm certainly not an arsonist." The baby doctor loudly declared.

"Well, they got you on some deep shit, David. You're gonna need a good lawyer."

Fazio was perplexed. He had no memory of performing any crime and knew that these charges of arson, along with the casualties of those people who were killed in the fire, would probably cause him to spend the rest of his life in prison.

His life was ruined, he thought to himself. He could no longer be a doctor and deliver babies. His name and reputation were now destroyed, and he no longer would be a respected member of the Chicago community. He would stand to lose it all, his luxury condo, his car, his savings, and investments.

Everything.

At the ripe old age of fifty years old, his life and everything he had ever worked for would be gone.

He looked at his uncle with tears in his eyes. How did his sleeping issues and the culmination of these disastrous events lead him to this?

At that moment, the door of the prison conference room had opened, and the guard let the gentleman inside.

He was wearing a black, pin-striped suit and a crisp white shirt. He was tie-less, as though he had just removed his tie before entering the prison building.

"Michael, this is my nephew, Dr. David Fazio."

He was still grasping his briefcase while extending his hand out to his new client.

"Michael Prescott," he introduced himself as Dr. Fazio stood up to shake his hand.

Michael Prescott was a prominent criminal attorney with a downtown Chicago Loop law firm. He had defended several high publicity criminal cases, and along with his knowledge of criminal and international law, had successfully defended several high-profile clients. Many of his clients were organized crime figures or allegedly corrupt politicians who had gotten caught with their hands in the 'cookie jar.' He was also an international law expert and had defended several international law and murder cases in Europe and around the world.

He sat down at the table with the other two and opened his briefcase, withdrawing a yellow writing pad and a pen.

"First things first...may I call you, Dave?"

"David will do."

Prescott smiled. "Okay, you may call me Michael. Are they treating you okay?"

"I'm fine. They have served me food a few times, but I haven't been very hungry," Fazio stated.

Prescott settled himself down and began taking a few notes while Little Tony sat there observing his nephew.

"Well...can you tell me what you know about these arson fires that you supposedly started?"

Fazio sat there, perplexed.

"Well, that's just it, Michael. I don't remember starting any of these fires."

Prescott looked at his new client and glanced over at Little Tony, who was shaking his head.

"Well, I just finished talking to Detective Romanowski and the prosecutor, Assistant District

Attorney Douglas Janes. They are accusing you of three family clinic arson fires, two of which there were fatal casualties. At the last one on West Division Street, they have DNA evidence and a destroyed lab coat with your name on it. According to the Eighteenth District detective, that puts you at the crime scene. They also have several witnesses who are going to testify that your hands were burned and bandaged that day after one of the arson fires last June," his attorney explained.

Fazio was speechless.

"Besides the destruction of property, they're charging you with four first-degree murders," said Prescott.

Little Tony was looking at his nephew, patiently waiting for his reaction.

Dr. Fazio only sat there, still reiterating his only defense.

"I did not start any fires. I am not an arsonist. Do I have trouble sleeping? Yes, since I was a little kid in grade school. Do I sleepwalk? Yes. Sometimes, I wake up in strange places that I don't remember how I got there or ended up passing out there. But I would remember starting a fire and being an arsonist, especially while sleepwalking."

Prescott looked at Little Tony DiMatteo, and they both made eye contact.

"Well, if your only defense is not remembering setting any of these fires, we're going to have a difficult time getting you out of these first-degree murder charges. Unless we can come up with a valid defense and a stronger alibi as to where you were and where you were sleeping on the night of these fires, any judge or jury is going to throw the book at you. Someone needs to attest on your behalf. Unfortunately, you live alone, and other than a few girlfriends who have occasionally spent the night with you, no one is stepping up. Not to mention all of the media publicity that this case is now bringing."

Little Tony interrupted the attorney.

"Wait, let me get this straight. They found my nephew's lab coat with his DNA on it at the last fire. How can that be? He doesn't sleep with his lab coat on. And why would he be wearing his lab coat with his name on it if he was an arsonist, setting a building on fire?"

Michael Prescott looked at the veteran Mafioso and nodded his head.

"I know, Mr. DiMatteo. It doesn't make any sense."

"What? Are you goddamn kidding me?" Little Tony loudly replied.

"It's like me going to rob a goddamn liquor store, leaving my driver's license with the store clerk before I steal his goddamn money and leave."

"I know. But the prosecutor, Doug Janes, is insisting that they have a solid case against Dr. Fazio."

"Solid case, my fucking ass!" DiMatteo loudly replied.

"Somebody is framing my nephew. I would bet a million dollars on it. My nephew, even if he were a sleepwalker, would not set an abortion clinic on fire wearing his lab coat in the middle of the damn night. There is no goddamn way!"

"I know. It doesn't make any sense," Prescott replied.

Little Tony stared at the attorney.

"Look...you hire an investigator, a detective...I don't care if you gotta hire Detective Fucking Colombo, you do whatever you gotta do. My nephew, my godchild, is innocent of these charges. And I'll pay you a million dollars to prove that in court," Little Tony demanded.

"This kid can't even light a match from a matchbox, let alone start a fire."

There were several moments of silence, as David Fazio only sat there, shaking his head.

"My life is ruined," he only managed to say. He had tears streaming down his face.

Little Tony and Michael Prescott sat there, initially looking at each other in disbelief. The attorney made some more notes in his notepad, then returned it to his briefcase.

"Okay, David, I will be back here tomorrow and let you know our progress with all of this. You have a bond and an arraignment hearing tomorrow. I will be here with you."

"How does it look, Michael," Little Tony asked.

He sat there and paused for several moments.

"Well, Prosecutor Janes seems to believe that you're a flight risk and is refusing to request the judge to let you 'bond out.' We will just have to wait and see what happens tomorrow."

They all looked at each other for several long, silent moments.

"In all honesty, it doesn't look good."

At that moment, the attorney got up and shook his client's hands.

"I will be back here tomorrow," he said as he knocked on the door for the prison guard to let him out of the prison conference room.

As Prescott left, Little Tony stayed behind to sit with his nephew. Fazio had tears streaming down his face, and he continued to rub his eyes and bury his face in his hands for an extended period.

"Your parents are worried, sick. My sister hasn't stopped crying since they picked you up at the hospital yesterday," said Zio Tony.

Fazio started to openly weep as his loud, whimpering noises began to echo off the drab, ugly green walls. Little Tony got up to hug his nephew.

David Fazio was inconsolable. At that moment, Fazio knew that he would do anything, even if he had to start his life over, to escape the grim prospect of having to spend the rest of his life in prison. It was unfair for him to spend his life incarcerated for crimes that he was confident that he never committed.

"David...how badly do you want to get out of this goddamn shithole?"

"Zio Tony...are you kidding?"

Little Tony looked at his nephew, his eyes locked with his.

A long moment of silence.

"I will call your mother and father to help you get your affairs in order," he said, as he began to get up and rise from the table. He then kissed his nephew on both cheeks before leaving. As much confidence as he had in his formidable uncle, he was sure that there was nothing that he could do.

At that moment, David Fazio knew that his life was over.

CHAPTER THIRTY-TWO
An Unjust Conviction

"Congratulations," a female voice could be heard on the line.

Detective Romanowski had just picked up his ringing desk phone, and at first, had no idea who was calling him.

"Thanks," he sheepishly replied, still trying to figure out who was calling him.

"It's all over the news. You guys did some excellent investigative work in capturing the 'Abortion Arsonist.' I knew you and Janko would catch this bastard."

At that moment, Terry recognized the voice on the other end. She never started any phone conversation with the usual greeting like ordinary people.

"Good morning, Adrianna," as he took a sip of his black coffee.

It was only ten o'clock in the morning, and his desk phone had been ringing off the hook. Every reporter in the City of Chicago wanted to interview him and get a statement on the arrest of the Abortion Arsonist.

"We booked him yesterday and put him in lock-up. His lawyer and his 'mobbed-up' uncle just showed up this morning."

"Who is his uncle?"

"Little Tony DiMatteo," Terry replied.

"Are you kidding?" Adrianna replied.

There was a very long silence on the phone as she pondered the effects that this could have on Fazio's possible conviction. Adrianna Hunter was well aware of who Little Tony DiMatteo was and the power and influence he wielded on the City of Chicago.

As the 'Capo dei Capi' of all the Chicago crime families, she knew that Little Tony was the most powerful and definitely the most ruthless of all of the city's organized crime figures. He had connections everywhere, and it seemed as though everyone from City Hall to Cook County to the Illinois District Attorney's office was somehow connected to DiMatteo and his 'merry band of men.' The Mafioso seemed to have 'favors' and political markers scattered everywhere, and he wasn't afraid to call up any of them. Adrianna had crossed paths with Little Tony's influence within the city many times before, and she knew that he was a very powerful nemesis.

"Who is his lawyer?"

"Michael Prescott."

"Oh fuck!" she loudly exclaimed.

Adrianna was more than aware of the moderately famous criminal attorney within the City of Chicago. Prescott had been in the news for several high-profile criminal cases over the last several years. His law firm partners, on behalf of their clients, filed several motions against Adrianna and her political 'PAC' group. Those legal maneuvers were based on some zoning issues against a family planning clinic she was trying to finance for a group of doctors a few years ago. Prescott's firm had some 'pro-life' clients that were trying to stop Adrianna from opening up another family planning clinic.

Hunter knew that when the 'partial-birth' abortion laws finally passed, that the family planning clinics that she had heavily invested in would become financial goldmines. She knew that the City of Chicago would become the Midwest's primary hub for abortions and that women from around the country would be flocking to Chicago to terminate their pregnancies. She and her family would stand to make a handsome profit' on the financing of those family planning clinics.

"These bastards will probably stop at nothing to get Fazio off the hook. What hard evidence were you able to acquire connecting Fazio to these arson fires?"

"He left his lab coat at the last one, with his DNA all over it."

More silent moments on the phone.

"What does the prosecutor say?" she eagerly asked.

"With four victims and three arson fires by a perpetrator who openly threatened one of those abortion doctors recently, he's figuring it will be a slam dunk."

More silence.

"I'm going to call the prosecutor's office right now. I'm going to tell Mr. Janes that I want their sharpest, the most experienced attorney prosecuting this case," Adrianna exclaimed.

"I know Michael Prescott and Little Tony. They don't screw around. They will do anything, legal or illegal, right or wrong, to get this baby doctor exonerated," she observed.

"You guys better have your goddamn 'A' game ready. Getting a conviction on this guy won't be easy."

At that moment, Romanowski started to show his impatience with her.

"Adrianna, don't you have anything else better to do than to call up and intimidate coppers?" the detective tried to say to her in a joking way.

The Northshore dominatrix laughed loudly over the phone.

"Checking the testicle size of all of you Chicago coppers is what I do best," as she abruptly hung up the phone.

David Fazio had been sitting in his prison cell at Cook County Jail for over three weeks, staring at the

261

drab, gray walls of his ten by a twelve-foot prison cell. He had many visitors during that period, including his parents and family, several visits by Michael Prescott, his attorney, and Little Tony DiMatteo.

Cook County Jail was a miserable place to be incarcerated. It was full of gangbangers, drug dealers, rapists, murderers, and life-long hardened criminals who only knew how to live from the wrong side of the law. The single mattress situated within the middle of the room was his only piece of furniture, next to an old, dilapidated toilet and a dirty sink stained with dirt that hadn't been cleaned or scrubbed in years.

Fazio was trying his best to survive mentally. His girlfriend, Jeanne Callahan, had come to visit him several times and brought him some books and magazines for him to read. He wasn't allowed to have a laptop, and his only writing utensils were a black pen and a yellow notepad. To pass the time, David began keeping a journal, writing down his thoughts and emotions during this very unpleasant experience of incarceration.

But Fazio was breaking down. He knew that he wasn't an arsonist. But he also realized that his bad sleeping habits and especially, his sleepwalking, was a black mark against him.

Truthfully, David couldn't honestly say whether or not he was or wasn't the perpetrator who set those clinics on fire. He didn't remember anything that he did while he sleepwalked. Fazio didn't remember how or why or where he woke up on many occasions and never had any idea how he got there. He only knew in his heart that, although he was a sleepwalker, he wasn't an arsonist.

It was almost three o'clock in the afternoon when the corrections officers came over to open his jail cell.

"You have some visitors," the African American prison guard said.

Fazio followed the guard over to the large room, bearing an old wooden table and some very worn-out wooden chairs. As he entered, he noticed his Zio Tony and his attorney Michael Prescott sitting at the table waiting for him. He sat down after greeting both, shaking hands with Prescott while kissing his uncle on the cheek.

"How you doing, kid?" Tony asked.

"I'm trying to survive."

David was noticeably thinner and paler in color than the last time he had seen his uncle. He looked at the two of them as if they had some important news to break to him.

"I've been in conference with the prosecutor, Doug Janes," Prescott started the conversation.

"Because they found your lab coat at the last arson fire on West Division Street, the D.A.'s office feels they have a strong case against you. With those three arson fires and four deaths as a result of them, they are pushing for four consecutive life sentences in jail."

David looked at his uncle as he continued to shake his head.

"They feel that they can get a jury to convict you, and with your sleeping issues and your conflicts concerning abortions, the prosecutors think they can convince a jury."

"Fuck that shit," Little Tony immediately said. "This kid has never done anything wrong in his life. Just because they find his lab coat at the fire scene and he can't sleep at night isn't enough to convict him, Michael," Tony loudly reasoned.

"Come on...this is bullshit," declared the Mafioso.

"Tony...let me finish."

The attorney looked at David as if he was trying to break some bad news gently.

"The D.A.'s office is willing to make you a deal."

"What kind of deal?" David asked.

Prescott hesitated for a moment, expecting Tony's wrath.

"They want you to change your plea to 'guilty' on all counts. They're willing to give you twenty years on four charges of involuntary manslaughter, which I think is an exceptional deal," Prescott stated.

"WHAT?" Little Tony screamed. "FUCK THEM!" as Little Tony got up and threw his chair onto the other side of the room.

"How the hell can they convict this kid, with a clean record, who never got as much as a goddamn parking ticket, on involuntary manslaughter? This is total bullshit, Michael."

Little Tony began ranting loudly while the prison guards were standing outside, peering into the window, making sure that everything was okay.

"The problem is the lab coat, Tony. Nobody seems to know how it got there, and with the evidence of his sleepwalking and his burned hands on the morning of that first fire on Randolph, they feel they have the evidence to convict. They now have witnesses that will testify to his intense sleep issues and his sleepwalking. And what's worse, my client here can't honestly remember what the hell he does when he sleepwalks."

"Somebody planted that goddamn thing," Tony screamed. "My nephew doesn't go to sleep with his lab coat on!"

"They wouldn't be making this deal if the prosecutors knew they had a slam-dunk case, which we both know that they don't," DiMatteo observed.

"Maybe," Prescott said. "But it is unusual for them to offer such a generous deal at the beginning before collaborating more evidence against the defendant."

"The D.A.'s office is jammed with cases, and they don't have the people to try this case properly. They would rather plead out than bust their ass to keep a defendant in jail."

"It may be a tough case to prove," Prescott reasoned. "But it will be a tougher case to defend."

Michael then looked directly at David.

"Do you always know what clothes you put on before you sleepwalk?"

"No," Fazio responded.

"Do you have any hospital lab coats at home?"

David thought for several moments, then nodded his head.

"Yes."

"Then, you could have quite possibly, put on your lab coat while you were mentally not conscience and walked out of your condominium with your lab coat on that night...correct?" Michael asked David.

"Now, why would he put on his lab coat before sleepwalking?"

"Why would he sleepwalk at all? What control does he have over his conscience mind when he suddenly sleepwalks?" Prescott asked.

"Maybe he was cold that night, and his lab coat was the only thing available for him to put it on before he left the house," the attorney hypothesized.

David looked at his uncle and his attorney. He knew that he couldn't remember anything and couldn't truthfully testify one way or the other what he did or what he was wearing on any night that he was sleepwalking.

"These are all questions the prosecutor is going to ask you during a trial. Unless you have some solid proof, or we have any testimony from someone that can positively testify that you were not at those clinic fires when they were started, this will be a tough defense. Even security cameras proving that you weren't there would help us," he said.

"What about surveillance cameras in the condo complex of Michael's lobby?" Tony asked.

"The homeowners' board of your condominium complex has been pushing for surveillance cameras to be installed, but because of the exorbitant costs, the homeowners have always voted it down," the attorney responded.

"I interviewed the security guard, Javier, at your condo. Although he doesn't remember your ever walking out in the middle of the night wearing your lab coat, he remembers your leaving the building in the middle of the night several times."

A moment of silence.

"If he's subpoenaed, which I'm sure he will be, he'll probably affirm to your sleepwalking under oath."

Michael paused. "It is going to be very difficult to prove your innocence, David."

David Fazio only sat there in that old wooden chair, totally mesmerized and in shock. He was utterly speechless.

"With twenty years, there is a good possibility that you could get paroled after five or seven years."

"NO!" David suddenly stood up and screamed.

"I can't do twenty years! I can't do five years! I don't want to stay here for one more goddamn night! I need to get out of here! I want to go home!"

David was starting to have a nervous breakdown as he got up from his chair and began pacing the room like a caged animal. He then sat down on the floor in the corner of the room and started crying uncontrollably.

"My life is over," I kept saying over and over again.

"I just want to fucking die!" he loudly said.

Prescott and Little Tony looked at each other, watching David have his emotional breakdown there in the corner of the room. They were all silent for about ten minutes or more, watching and listening to David Fazio rant and rave about how innocent he was and how he no longer wanted to live.

At that moment, Little Tony turned to Prescott.

"If he pleads guilty and takes the twenty years, what are the odds of his parole?"

"If he's a model prisoner...maybe five years. He would be eligible after seven years for sure."

Tony looked at Prescott more intently.

"Can he do his time in Stateville?"

Prescott thought about it for several moments.

"I can request that. I'm sure that wouldn't be a problem. But Stateville Prison in Joliet is a shithole. Why would you want him to go to Stateville?"

"I have some friends there that could keep an eye on him. At least I know he'll be safe."

Little Tony looked at his nephew, crunched in the corner in the fetal position on the floor, still sobbing uncontrollably. Fazio was now wholly oblivious to the conversation that Tony was having with his attorney. The Mafioso knew that his nephew was becoming very unbalanced and completely unhinged mentally. Tony was deathly afraid his nephew would find a way to harm himself while in prison severely.

Michael Prescott was also fearful. The chance of clearing David Fazio of these arson charges and the four homicides that were associated with these fires was slim. Even with his best defense, he did not have the evidence that would prove that Fazio *didn't* start those fires. He knew that he would be doing his client a terrible injustice by trying to win this case in front of a jury. And if they were to lose and Fazio was convicted, he knew that the baby doctor would probably receive the maximum sentence. David Fazio will never see the light of day. And to try this case, Attorney Michael Prescott knew it would be almost impossible to win.

Like walking into a gunfight with a green, plastic water pistol.

But Prescott also realized that, unlike his tough, mobbed-up Uncle Tony, that David Fazio didn't have the mental toughness or the emotional wherewithal to do time in federal prison. Because there were victims involved, the possibility of getting him sent to a 'Club Fed' minimum security campus, like in Wisconsin or West Virginia, was totally out of the question. He knew Fazio would have to mentally 'toughen up' and get ready to do some time.

Michael Prescott looked at Little Tony.

"What do you want to do? He needs an answer by tomorrow."

Little Tony looked at Prescott and decided for his incoherent nephew.

"Tell him we'll take the deal."

CHAPTER THIRTY-THREE

Jailhouse Favor

The sun was beginning to set across the cloudless sky, as loud, chirping birds flying overhead were the only noises heard within the prison parking lot. The area around Stateville prison was desolate, except for the corrections officers, employees, and prisoners entering and exiting the area.

Little Tony was quietly sitting alone in his black Maserati parked across the street from the parking lot. He was waiting for an old friend to emerge from the prison gates and exit over to his car, ready to return home from his shift that Thursday evening. It had been a long time since Tony had visited with his friend, and he knew there would be some apprehension when the two of them met once again.

Prison Warden Thomas McCafferty was a long-time warden in charge of the prison, over thirty-five years. He had seen his share of convicts enter and exit his jailhouse, including the likes of hardened criminals who were convicted of homicides, drug charges and trafficking, rapists, gangbangers, mobbed-up gangsters, and violent, serial murderers. McCafferty was a hardened man who had seen more than his share of bad guys. He wasn't scared or intimidated by the likes of anyone, both inside and outside of those prison walls.

McCafferty and Little Tony had some history. Many years ago, Little Tony was convicted of armed robbery and attempted murder back when he was a teenager. McCafferty, at the time, was a prison guard on Tony's prison cell floor. Because of Tony's charming personality, both he and McCafferty fast became friends, allowing him to have some conjugal visits with many of his girlfriends at the time. McCafferty also looked the other way when large packages of food and personal items (including a serrated knife) were smuggled into his jail cell. Tony took care of the particular services and favors of his corrections officer, including sharing some of his personal stash that he received regularly. When Little Tony was released after spending four years in Stateville, he continued to stay in touch with his former jail cell prison guard. In time, McCafferty was promoted to assistant prison warden and then eventually, the head prison warden there in Stateville.

Almost ten years ago, McCafferty needed a personal favor. His wife of twenty-six years was actively cheating on him. McCafferty had intercepted several salacious texts from his wife's lover on her cellular phone and wanted a divorce. But the prison warden knew that, with the divorce laws of Illinois and with its mandatory lifetime alimony mandates, the warden would be working for his ex-wife for the rest of his life. McCafferty, of course, didn't like that option and looked to his friend Little Tony DiMatteo for assistance.

At first, Little Tony didn't want to get involved. He figured that nobody's ex-wife or her lover needed to be on his hit list, no matter how close Little Tony was to McCafferty. The risks and the extensive publicity weren't worth it, DiMatteo reasoned. But after meeting with McCafferty several times, they had come to an agreement for the personal hit:

Fifty thousand dollars in cash and a "Get Out of Jail Free" card.

DiMatteo figured that he could always use the favor if someone in his family were ever convicted for a crime and got sent into Stateville Prison. He met McCafferty on a hot summer night at the Forest Preserve off Irving Park and Cumberland. The prison warden handed him a large black handbag with fifty thousand dollars in large, unmarked bills.

Within two weeks, Mrs. Maria McCafferty was seen going into the Justice Arms Motor Lodge on the corner of Harlem and Ogden Avenues. One of DiMatteo's 'associates,' Frank Calogero, waited for Mrs. McCafferty to enter the hotel room on the second floor. Within twenty minutes, her lover arrived and knocked on the hotel room door. But Frank Calogero's surveillance had uncovered another interesting fact: The man who was sleeping with Mrs. McCafferty was also a 'made man' with the Marchese Family.

The DiMatteo associate made a phone call to the boss.

"Boss...you're not gonna believe this," Frank Calogero said. "The guy who is nailing this married broad is 'Pretty Joe' Ippolito with the Marchese's."

'Pretty Joe' was his nickname for obvious reasons. The man spent more time looking into the mirror, combing his perfectly coiffed hair than he spent taking care of Marchese Family business. Ippolito was a well-known womanizer, married of course, who had absolutely no scruples when it came to whomever he was sleeping with. He was a family captain with the Marchese Family and ran the numbers and illegal betting parlors for his boss.

When DiMatteo had gotten word that the intended target was Pretty Joe and his 'cumare,' Little Tony knew he had a huge problem. He couldn't just whack a 'made man' from another family without getting the family's capo's permission first. And if the only justification was because he was screwing another man's wife, the possibility of his getting another Capo's approval for his murder was remote at best.

"What do you wanna do, boss?"

"Sit tight, Frank. I've gotta make some phone calls."

At that moment, DiMatteo tried to make a phone call to Don Carlo Marchese, who didn't even bother answering the phone. He knew he would have to arrange another meeting, so he figured that making the hit that night was definitely off.

After several minutes, DiMatteo called back his associate.

"Forget this hit, Frank. This will all have to wait for another time."

Frank Calogero was about to pull out of the parking lot when Pretty Joe Ippolito and his girlfriend stormed out of the hotel room. Calogero watched as the two of them loudly argued in front of Ippolito's black Cadillac.

"You mother-fucker," she kept yelling at Ippolito, continuing to berate him in public while he stood there in his car, trying to take control of his out-of-control, married girlfriend. She was irate, apparently finding out that Pretty Joe Ippolito was sleeping with an innumerate number of other girls.

As the two of them were arguing in front of his car, Ippolito noticed Frank Calogero sitting in his Cadillac a short distance away. Figuring that he was probably there to put a hit on him, he immediately withdrew his revolver and shot at Calogero, barely missing him while hitting his windshield.

With Calogero now under fire, he got out of the car and pulled out his weapon, shooting back at Ippolito, hitting him right square in the forehead. It was a clean shot, and 'Pretty Joe' Ippolito was dead before he hit the ground.

Mrs. Maria McCafferty began screaming, attracting attention to the violent crime scene. Figuring that Calogero had come to that hotel to take out the woman and her lover anyways, he walked over to the hysterical lady. Calogero put a .38 caliber bullet point-blank directly into her head. He then casually drove away, as his Illinois license plates were immediately covered with tapped newspaper.

Little Tony recalled the incident almost ten years ago, as the 'hired hit' gone wrong had caused DiMatteo a considerable amount of embarrassment with the Marchese Family. Don Carlo was extremely angry with DiMatteo at first and threatened to incite an all-out family war on the DiMatteo's. 'Pretty Joe' Ippolito was a valuable captain within the Marchese Family. It was only after the two men sat down and had dinner together at a discrete restaurant on the Northside that two men made amends. After that incident, Little Tony swore he would never get in the middle of a marital divorce ever again, even if it were for a valuable favor.

Three months later, Frank Calogero was found dead on his driveway, sitting in his Cadillac with a .38 bullet in his head. His murder was a revenge killing by the Marchese Family that Little Tony had regretfully approved of. It was an exchange of chess pieces that, unfortunately, cost the DiMatteo family one of his captains.

Thomas McCafferty finally emerged from the jailhouse exit door and was ready to enter the gated parking lot when Little Tony pulled his black Maserati in front of his path.

"How ya' doing, Tommy?" DiMatteo greeted the jailhouse warden as he rolled down his window.

At first, the warden didn't recognize the man in the black car until he took a hard look at him. Even though DiMatteo now had white hair, he had not changed much, and his voice was still recognizable.

"Hey, Tony...is that you?"

"Yeah, Tommy...it's me. Get in. We need to talk."

At first, the prison warden hesitated, peering closely into his almost brand-new Maserati. When he noticed that no one else was in the car with Tony, the warden was less intimidated.

"Tony, I have to get home. My daughter is expecting me over for dinner."

DiMatteo suddenly got angry. "Get in Tommy, or I'll shoot you right here in front of this goddamn shithole you call a prison," he immediately demanded.

McCafferty slowly walked around the front of the car and got in the passenger's side of DiMatteo's black, luxury sports car.

The two of them left Crest Hill and immediately drove to Joliet with Little Tony DiMatteo initially, not saying a single word.

"So, Tony...what's up?"

"You remember that little favor we did for you many years ago, right?"

McCafferty hesitated. He had not thought about that messy 'murder for hire' favor that he had paid DiMatteo for ten years ago when his wife and her lover were both killed in front of that hotel on Ogden and Harlem Avenues.

The prison warden nodded his head, as he knew that the 'Get Out of Jail Free' card was about to be cashed in.

"You do realize, Tommy, that your wife's murder almost started a family war between us and the Marchese's. If I had any idea that your goddamn whore wife was doing a 'made man' from another family, I would have never taken the job."

"I know, Tony."

Little Tony DiMatteo looked at the prison warden while he was driving.

"Do you remember the kind of heat we were under? I even had that Chaz Rizzo from Channel Eight up my ass, along with the District Sixteen coppers hanging around my shop like lost little puppies. Do you remember that, Tommy?"

DiMatteo started to enter the freeway exit onto I-355, slowly accelerating his Maserati on the expressway.

"Yes, Tony, I remember."

Tony accelerated the car even faster, now hitting ninety miles an hour.

"Do you remember what happened to one of my men, a 'made man' by the way, who had to get whacked because of your stupid, 'zoccola di puttana' bitch wife?"

McCafferty was speechless.

"Do you know how hard I had to suck off Carlo Marchese? Do you realize how hard I had to suck his dick just to keep our families from getting into an all-out street war, thanks to you?"

Little Tony continued to berate the warden.

"I don't suck nobody's dick, Tommy. You know this, right? But I had to suck off Carlo Marchese's cock goddamn dry just because I had to do you a goddamn favor, you mother-fucker!"

"Do you have any concept what I had to do, who I had to sacrifice, just because you were too goddamn cheap to get a divorce and pay alimony to your bitch whore wife, who probably liked it in the ass?"

"Yes, Tony, I do remember, and I appreciate everything that you did for me," the warden said.

Little Tony accelerated his car even faster, now going over one-hundred miles an hour.

"You know, Tommy, these Maserati's come with a factory defect. The passenger door accidentally opens up at very high speeds," Little Tony smiled, driving his car down the empty highway down I-355.

At that moment, Little Tony pulled out his switchblade and cut the passenger seatbelt.

"Slow down, Tony," Tommy insisted, as Tony kept driving the car faster and faster.

After several minutes of speed racing down I-355, his Maserati was fast approaching a tractor-trailer truck up ahead.

"Tommy...do you remember our 'Get Out of Jail Free' card?"

"Tony...that was a long time ago. I paid you cash for that hit, Tony. I can't do that kind of shit anymore. This is a different time," McCafferty exclaimed in a scared voice, as Tony's car was now starting to tailgate the tractor-trailer at high-speed.

"That wasn't our deal, Tommy. I don't give a damn how long ago it was. A 'Get Out of Jail Free' card never expires, you asshole!"

Now Tony's car was within inches of the truck's bumper, going over one hundred and ten miles an hour. With one hand on the steering wheel, he reached into his glove box and pulled out his revolver.

"Now Tommy...tell me again about this card," as Tony pointed the gun at the prison warden's testicles.

"Tell me again, Tommy...what is it again that you can't fucking do?"

Thomas McCafferty was now scared to death, as he was beginning to sweat. The front of his trousers is now soaked with his urine.

"Okay, Tony...please slow down! Please, Tony! I will do whatever you want," he began to cry with fear.

Little Tony DiMatteo smiled as he pulled over to the right, into the slow lane, and slowed down his vehicle.

As his car decelerated to fifty-five miles an hour, Tony balanced the gun on his lap while he continued to drive around the upcoming traffic.

"I need a big favor, Tommy. My nephew got pinched on a bullshit arson and homicide charge. He is getting transferred from Cook County to your joint next week. I need you to keep an eye on him."

Little Tony continued to carefully negotiate the upcoming traffic, handling his Maserati like one of the Andretti's.

"I need you to come up with a good plan to get him out. He's a highly educated doctor, and he won't mentally be able to do time."

Little Tony tried to make eye contact with the warden while still driving.

"He won't survive in there. He won't make it."

McCafferty looked at Little Tony in silence as he turned his car around. Within several minutes, he had driven back to the Stateville Prison and dropped off the warden.

"Come up with a plan, Tommy. A good one. I need him out before Christmas."

Little Tony practically pushed the prison warden out of the car as he closed the passenger door and sped off. Tommy McCafferty only stood there, on that one-lane highway, as he watched the black Maserati speed off.

At that moment, McCafferty wished he had never given a mobster like Little Tony DiMatteo a "Get Out of Jail Free" card.

CHAPTER THIRTY-FOUR
Stateville Prison

David Fazio was laying down on the hard, uncomfortable cot of his solitary prison cell. He was trying hard to read a book amid all of the loud, echoing noise, the dysfunctional annoying sounds of the other prison inmates along his floor. The small, drab room was only six feet by eight feet, with heavy-duty double door locks that could only be opened from the outside by the correctional officers. The cell was recently painted with a white-wash colored paint, which couldn't cover the dark pen and marker graffiti that was scattered everywhere around the walls. The prisoners were required to wash and paint the walls of their jail cells once a year, but the graffiti was so old and antiquated that it couldn't be removed or painted over. There was a dirty sink and a toilet located in the corner, which very often didn't flush because of the old, antiqued plumbing system within the ninety-year-old prison.

The Stateville Correctional Center is located in Crest Hill, near Joliet, Illinois. It is an older, maximum-security prison facility known for housing such as infamous inmates as John Wayne Gacy, Richard Speck, Nathan Leopold, and Richard Loeb. Most inmates within the prison were high-profile prisoners who were convicted of murders and various degrees of homicide. Because of the nature of Fazio's crimes, he was transferred and placed into that correctional facility. The infrastructure of the prison had deteriorated quite severely over the years, with its crumbling walls where daylight could be seen through the cracks. It is a facility that is always filled beyond capacity, with many of the solitary prison cells filled with more than one prisoner.

Fazio's state of mind had become equivalent to that of a compliant, quiet, vegetative state. He tried to keep to himself over the last three months since arriving there from Cook County on 27th and California, and he learned to become very anti-social. He had only received a hand full of visitors, only seeing his mother and father once during that whole period he had been there.

His Zio Tony came to visit him, probably the most out of his whole family. He explained to his nephew that the intense visits his parents would make to the prison had been taking a psychological toll on them. Because of their ages, his siblings would not allow them to come to prison any longer to visit him. Fazio felt entirely abandoned by his family.

Jeanne Callahan had come to visit him a few times but was quite busy with her medical practice and was finding it harder and harder to break away. They had been corresponding through written letters (as he was not allowed access to a computer or emails).

Still, they realized that his arson and involuntary manslaughter convictions were too hard for her to bear. Since Fazio had no idea if he would ever be granted probation and ever leave prison, he felt that it was best for her to move on and abandon their relationship. Jeanne had written a couple more letters, which David had so far not answered.

"Forget about me and move on with your life," were the last words that David Fazio wrote to Jeanne Callahan, his loving girlfriend.

Because of Fazio's pro-life beliefs and his convictions for arson and homicide, he has not been a very popular prisoner amongst the other inmates. There are still many rival gang members that were incarcerated there in Stateville and have threatened to 'crack him around' whenever he was left unguarded. He had come close to being beaten and molested a few times but had thus far managed to escape any physical or sexual altercations safely.

The correctional facilities were supposed to be rehabilitative prison. It attempted to reform its prisoners with activities such as bible studies, educational classes, gyms and workout facilities for physical fitness, and other social events to assist them in enhancing their minds and their mental state. But in the case of David Fazio, his psychological state of mind was declining. Other than working out, lifting weights, and what little cardio he could do in the prison yard, Fazio spent most of his time reading. He went to the prison library twice a week and would read through several books and novels each week. He was asked by the prison warden a few times if he was interested in teaching some GED high school classes since Fazio had a medical degree, but he refused.

David Fazio, mentally, was in a lonely, psychologically darkened catacomb that he saw no physical or emotional escape. He often thought about suicide by either manufacturing a sharp object from one of the kitchen utensils or possibly instigating a dangerous encounter with one of the rival gang inmates located in the more heavily guarded prison floors. It was not uncommon for the whole prison to go on lockdown, as many fights between inmate rival gang members and correctional officers erupted regularly. Stateville was a dark, savage environment, where human beings are entirely forgotten and written off by society due to their crimes.

It was safe to say that David Fazio no longer wished to live.

One afternoon, two prison guards entered his jail cell while he was napping. Fazio had been sleeping up to twelve to fourteen hours a day, which was another symptom of his deep depression. The guard handcuffed his hands and placed ankle chains on his legs while he was escorted downstairs to the visiting area. There waiting for him was Zio Tony.

His godfather rose from his chair and kissed and hugged his nephew several times before they both sat down at the table.

"How ya doin', kid?" Little Tony asked.

David Fazio only sat there and shrugged.

"I'm still alive," he only managed to say after some hesitation.

Little Tony looked at his nephew and became extremely concerned. It had been over a month since he had been at Stateville to see his nephew, and he was visibly shaken by what he saw. Fazio had lost an extreme amount of weight and looked to be 160 pounds or less. His hair was completely white, and his face looked drawn and haggard as if he had aged twenty years. His eyes were sunken with dark circles, and despite the considerable amount of sleep he was getting, he still looked extraordinarily worn and tired.

"Are you eating?"

"If you call what they serve here as food, sometimes," Fazio replied.

Little Tony grasped his nephew's hands together while he began to talk.

"You don't look very good, kid. You gotta put in your time here. Within five years, you'll be eligible for a parole hearing."

"I don't think I can survive here for five more years. I can't imagine the gates of hell being this bad," the prisoner said.

"Look, David...you gotta keep busy. You're not gonna be able to do time here if you physically deteriorate."

"I don't care," the former baby doctor said. His eyes were drawn, and he kept staring at the floor. It was as if he was too ashamed to look at his uncle in the face.

"You gotta trust me, kid. We're trying all we can to convince the parole board to grant you an early hearing."

"Come on, Zio Tony...stop bullshitting me. There isn't any chance that they'll ever let me out of this goddamn shithole. I'm the Abortion Arsonist, remember?"

Tony looked at David, completely startled. He had never seen his nephew so depressed and so mentally defeated.

There were several long moments of silence, and the two of them sat there, having little else to say. He only asked about his parents and his family, hoping that they were surviving despite his being incarcerated. The television within the visiting room was loudly blaring CNN in the background, as the other prisoners were trying to talk over the loud background noise.

Finally, Tony began to break the news that he had arrived to tell him.

"David, your condo on Lakeshore Drive has been sold. We managed to get $1.3 million for it. After all of your legal expenses and closing costs, you still netted over a million bucks. With this cash and your other investments, you've got a little over two million dollars sitting in a Cayman Islands trust account under my consigliere's name."

David looked at his uncle with little reaction.

"So...what good will all that money do me in here?"

"Sit tight, David. I'm still trying to work the parole board angle. I've still got some friends here who are watching out for you."

"If the parole board is my only hope, I have a 'zero chance' of ever getting out of this shithole."

At that moment, Little Tony squeezed his nephew's hands, making him look deeply into his eyes.

"What?" David asked.

Little Tony didn't say a word. He only gazed at his nephew's dark, encircled brown eyes, making sure that he had his nephew's undivided attention. Knowing that there were jail guards and other inmates within close range, Little Tony couldn't say everything he needed to say. He couldn't tell him what was really on his mind or what he wanted to communicate. He only stared into David Fazio's eyes, confidently communicating a single, solitary message.

Everything was going to work out, his eyes seemed to say. David Fazio gazed back at his uncle, knowing that he couldn't talk. They both sat there for what appeared to be hours, as Little Tony looked into his eyes as if to scare away all of the demons out of his nephews' deep, dark psyche.

The corrections officer then came over to get Fazio, letting him know that their thirty-minute visit was over. They both got up from their chairs as Little Tony whispered a proverbial Italian phrase that his mother would always tell him in his ear:

"Non preoccuparti, figlio mio... gli angeli stanno vegliando su di te."

Zio Tony kissed his nephew on both cheeks, and two prison guards escorted Fazio back to his jail cell.

For several hours, David kept thinking about what his uncle was trying to communicate to him there in that visiting room. He knew the translation of his mother's proverb, but she would always say this to him whenever he woke up in the middle of the night from a bad dream. She would console him as a little boy, telling him that proverb over and over again, until he would stop crying and fall back asleep. The Italian proverb was a famous phrase that all Italian mothers from their small little town used to say to their children whenever they were awakened from a bad dream.

He laid back down on his prison cot, saying that proverb over and over. He could hear his mother's voice in his head until he, too, finally fell back asleep.

"Do not worry, my young child...the angels are watching over you."

CHAPTER THIRTY-FIVE
Prison Fire

It was a little after five o'clock in the afternoon in Stateville when the inmates were buzzed out of their jail cells and line up, single file, before going downstairs into the mess hall for their supper. David Fazio obediently walked along with the others until he approached the dining room. He grabbed a clean tray, a styrofoam plate, plastic fork, and knife and proceeded to the food counter, where they were serving grilled chicken, spinach, and roasted potatoes. He walked over to an empty table near the window and began to eat his dinner by himself.

He gazed outside the window, as it was now the month of November. It was starting to get colder outside, as the leaves were beginning to turn colors. He was out earlier in the prison courtyard, trying to enjoy some fresh air for an hour before going back inside.

He had been reading a novel, 'Catch-22' by Joseph Heller, about the complicated character of Captain John Yossarian in his exploits as a bombardier in the U.S. Air Force during World War II. It seemed that Fazio, at that moment, had a lot in common with the main character of that book, as Yossarian's one wish was to survive the madness of war. It reminded him momentarily of how he wished to escape the personal miseries of his incarceration as he visually fantasized about being the main character of his new novel.

After dinner, David Fazio walked upstairs back to his jail cell. He laid his head down on his pillow, noticing that his cot had a funny, Lysol-like smell to it.

For some strange reason, he thought for a moment that his cot and jail cell had the strong odor of an accelerant. He then realized that the correctional officers had washed and mopped the floors of the jail cells on his seventh prison floor and realized that the strong smell was that of a cleaning solution.

Fazio laid on his cot, reading his 'Catch-22' novel until after 9:00 when finally, the prison lights went out, and he soon fell asleep.

Around 11:30 pm, one of the guards was walking along the seventh floor when he immediately saw smoke coming out of Fazio's jail cell. Before he could approach the smoked filled cell, there was a loud explosion. Screams were coming from the jail cell as the other prisoners began yelling "FIRE" as loudly as they could from their cells.

Several of the corrections officers ran up towards the intense fire within Fazio's jail cell. At the same time, some of the other prisoners were awakened by the loud, screaming sound of ringing fire alarms and sirens. The prisoners all grabbed their coats and were able to escape outside. In contrast, the guards grabbed several fire extinguishers and tried to frantically put out the intense fire and exit down the stairwells exiting outside to the prison courtyard. At that moment, several other prisoner administrators came upstairs with the warden, as some of them assisted the guards in trying to put out the fire.

Within thirty minutes, the black, ashen contents of the jail cell had been extinguished from the intense fire. But unfortunately, there was a fatality. Underneath the collapsed cot and falling materials off of the prison walls was an entirely burned, charred body of a prisoner who had fried in the intense fire, burned totally beyond recognition. The prison medical staff had been summoned and approached the body of the prisoner, realizing that he was dead at the scene.

Dr. David Fazio, at age 51, the formerly esteemed obstetrician from Chicago-Western Medical Hospital, was now dead. The former baby doctor's intense, pro-life beliefs, his narcissistic behavior, and his lousy sleeping habits had gotten him a wrongful conviction of three counts of arson and four counts of involuntary manslaughter. He had now unjustly perished in a jailhouse fire in Stateville, his body now burned beyond recognition.

There was a small paragraph the next day in the Chicago Sun-Times, hidden on page four, disclosing the doctor's accidental death in a prison fire at the Stateville Correctional Center. It later went on to say the 'no foul play was suspected.'

As he was promised, David Fazio was finally sleeping in peace with the angels.

CHAPTER THIRTY-SIX
David's Funeral

Crowds of people were beginning to gather inside of St. Rita Church in the Near West Loop neighborhood, as Antonio and Costanza Fazio arrived early on that cold Saturday morning in November for their son's funeral. There was a closed, oak wooden casket with the charred remains of their once very successful physician-son, sitting on a bier in the vestibule of the church. David's brothers, Carlo, Marco, and Giovanni, were following close behind their parents, as their wives, children, and significant others gathered with them around David's casket to say goodbye. His sister Teresa arrived at the church very early and was there to meet the family as they arrived.

While making the funeral arrangements, the Fazio Family decided that there would be no wake or a long receiving line of people at the Belmont Funeral Home. They wanted to get this over with. They wanted to give their brother and son a Catholic, Christian burial. They wanted to offer the repose of his soul to the kingdom of heaven, knowing that he was wrongly convicted of the arson and murder charges that he was completely innocent of. They decided to receive family and friends that Saturday morning at nine o'clock, and the funeral mass would promptly begin at ten. Why prolong the pain and agony of explaining to all the hundreds of family and friends what had happened to David? How he went from being a successful baby doctor and physician to a jail inmate at Stateville, convicted of arson and murder?

Jeanne Callahan arrived soon after at the church. She was extraordinarily demonstrative and was breaking up emotionally as she knelt next to David's casket and said a long prayer. At times, she was almost inconsolable as she intensely hugged the family as they stood alongside the casket, greeting all of the friends and family going through the reception line. It was almost a quarter to ten when Zio Tony and his wife arrived at the church. Tony and his wife did not even bother kneeling in front of the casket to pay their respects and immediately approached the funeral reception line.

For as close as Little Tony was to his godchild and favorite nephew, Jeanne immediately noticed how little emotion and grief David's uncle was displaying. Little Tony seemed almost to be happy, somewhat jovial, as he was laughing and joking with Marco and Carlo as he went through the reception line and expressed his condolences to the immediate family. Jeanne almost felt offended, witnessing his uncle's nonchalant behavior throughout David's funeral. Different people express their grief and emotions differently, she thought to herself.

As everyone filed past the closed casket, all of David's friends and family were still in shock as to why the 51-year-old physician, who had such a successful and promising career, could end up wrongly convicted and dying tragically in a prison cell fire. It was such an irony that someone whose life was so devoted to helping others and curing the sick could be maltreated by the legal system and end up incarcerated for defending the rights of the unborn. Jeanne overheard many of David's family and friends, rightfully condoning the random acts of arson that he was accused of performing.

"Those family planning clinics had no right to be terminating the life of those unborn infants," she overheard one family member exclaim.

"Such a tragedy," everyone was whispering on how David's successful life was so unfairly cut short.

As Jeanne Callahan's relationship with David grew more romantically involved and emotionally closer as the months went on, she became very familiar with

Fazio's enduring, horrific demons and the terrible sleeping habits that embattled him his whole life. She was fearful that a tragedy of this magnitude could happen.

David was a pro-life physician, and he was extremely vocal and opinionated in a state public hospital where abortions and unwanted pregnancies were the norm. He should have switched to pediatrics, she said to him many times. He should have jumped over to the pediatrics department and taken the appropriate board exams to become a fully licensed pediatrician. He loved children, and he loved bringing life into the world. He could have finished his medical career over the next twenty years caring for the little children he loved so much, rather than taking on the hopeless battle of trying to defend the unborn.

As she sat there in the third pew, behind the Fazio family, Jeanne was bitter. She was angry, she was hurt, but most of all, she was emotionally devastated. She should have done a better job treating him for his sleep disorders, she kept saying to herself. Jeanne had survivor's remorse for not doing a better job of personally taking care of him. They had only enjoyed a three-month relationship together before he was incarcerated, but it didn't take her long to realize that she was head over heels in love with him. David Fazio was her soulmate; she soon realized too late. David was her world. She should have done a better job of protecting him from the elements of a pro-choice society that had it out for obstetricians who didn't believe in performing abortions.

David's criminal attorney, Michael Prescott, arrived at the church to pay his respects. Jeanne had met him before, along with his fiancé, Sienna DiVito. They greeted and hugged Little Tony and his wife, as they were loudly jovial about something completely unimportant. They both expressed their condolences to

David's parents and siblings before kneeling at the casket and saying a quick prayer for David.

As the family and guests began to take their seats at the church, Jeanne noticed something unusual. Three members of the Chicago Fire Department had taken their seats at the last pew of the church, along with several members of the Chicago P.D. What were they doing here, she asked herself? It was bad enough that they had investigated and accused David of being an arsonist and putting him in jail. Why were they at his funeral? Did they need verification of the 'Abortion Arsonist's' death? She almost wanted to approach them and inform them that they weren't welcome at her significant other's funeral. But she let the classy, gracious side of her take over, and she only gave them a quick, cold smile when then looked over at her direction in the church.

As the funeral mass began, David's casket was escorted to the front of the church. The hymn "How Great Thou Art" reverberated across the magnificent, grand stone walls of the old Catholic Church, with its intricate stained-glass windows and antiquated carved woodwork. She tried to control herself as the eulogy about David was given by his brother Carlo, whom he said, 'everyone in the neighborhood looked up to.'

"David never forgot where he came from and was never afraid to throw on an apron and help his family at the grocery store," Carlo said at the funeral mass.

"He was the admiration of our Grand and Noble neighborhood," he eulogized. "All the little children who grew up in our neighborhood, the generations that came after us, wanted to go to school, study hard, and become successful like David Fazio. He was the pride of West Grand Avenue."

Antonio and Costanza Fazio were utterly beside themselves, as Marco assisted his mother and father from almost completely collapsing from grief. Carlo had broken down a few times while giving the eulogy, while David's sister, Teresa, stood there completely motionless. Jeanne looked over to Zio Tony a few times during the funeral mass, as he stood there without emotion, looking stoic with his wife, trying to look respectful. During moments of the eulogy, there were times that Little Tony had a smirk on his face.

At that moment, Jeanne became suspicious.

David's nephews and a few of his friends put on the white gloves and stood next to the casket as the pallbearers at the end of the funeral mass. They dutifully followed his remains toward the outside of the church, while the cantor sang an operatic rendition of the "Ave Maria" at the end of the funeral requiem. The traditional song seemed to reverberate from the magnificent walls of St. Rita Church, with its ornate statues of Jesus and his twelve apostles. The emotional Italian lyrics transcended its sacred sounds for all those who came to witness the ascension of David Fazio's tormented soul. As the crowds of people exited the Italian neighborhood church, everyone stood at the front of its ornate wooden doors, where the Fazio family attended and baptized all of their children, seemingly wiping their eyes as they were overtaken with emotion.

Everyone except Little Tony.

As the funeral mass concluded, everyone watched the pallbearers load the casket onto the black Cadillac hearse and climbed back into their cars. Jeanne Callahan followed the long procession down West Grand Avenue, past Grand and Noble, where the black Cadillac hearse momentarily stopped in front of the Fazio Grocery Store. It then proceeded down Grand Avenue, past all of the red lights and the several patrol cars escorting the procession to Queen of Heaven Cemetery on West Roosevelt Road. Jeanne was driving her car in that very long procession, grieving all alone as the parade of vehicles finally arrived at the cemetery. The funeral hearse pulled up in front of the many aisles of neatly arranged marble crypts towards the newly developed section of the cemetery, each row named after an obscure saint.

Jeanne stood there, outside of the mausoleum, as the pallbearers carried the coffin to David's final resting place. There was an open marble crypt at the third row from the bottom, whose stone slab had already been removed, awaiting the arrival of her soul mate's body. The priest mumbled a few more prayers as each of the gatherers placed a red rose on top of the oak, wooden casket. All the mourners, including David's family, stood silent as the special forklift lifted the coffin, with two undertakers alongside it, and slowly pushed David Fazio's body into the empty marble crypt, eye level in the third row.

As Jeanne Callahan watched her significant other and best friend become forever entombed, she said the Lord's Prayer to herself, wishing eternal rest for his soul. With her face soaked with tears, she silently waited for the rest of the mourners to leave until she was the very last one facing David's gravesite, alone.

She solemnly stood there, with one hand in her coat pocket facing the November cold, and holding the last red rose with the other. She placed it on the ground beneath David's crypt, then loudly said goodbye to the tomb of her beloved boyfriend.

"I will always love you," she said out loud, hoping that David's silent remains would somehow hear her. Then she looked over to the parade of cars, slowly driving away from the cemetery and to the location of the family luncheon.

Mamma Maria's Ristorante was a favorite eating place of David's. It was a favorite of his when he was alive, and the family had decided to have the funeral luncheon there on North York Road in Bensenville.

As Jeanne arrived, she noticed that most of the tables were already filled with funeral guests and attendants who had expressed their sympathies towards the family that day. Zio Tony, she also noticed, was standing at the bar with Michael Prescott, as they were both drinking glasses of scotch whiskey and saying an afterlife toast to his nephew. She gazed at him, standing at the bar, and decided to approach him and pay her respects.

"Hello, Zio Tony...I hope you remember me," she said to the Capo dei Capi.

"Oh, hey...Jeanne, right? You're that doctor broad that David was going out with," he said in a wise-guy tone of voice. They had met once at one of the Fazio family dinners. He greeted and kissed her on the cheek, his breath already smelling of alcohol.

"This is just too bad, isn't it?" he said loudly, as everyone at the bar could hear Zio Tony drinking a toast to his late nephew.

"Yes..." she cowardly replied, "It is."

She stood there silent, waiting for the other funeral guests to walk away from Little Tony DiMatteo as she wanted to make sure that no one else would hear their conversation.

"Zio Tony, do you mind if I ask you a question?"

"Sure thing, Missy," he loudly said, smiling. "Ask away!"

A moment of hesitation, making sure no one was close by.

"Where is David?" she asked in a meek, soft voice.

Zio Tony looked at her as an alarmed look overcame his face. His face color turned several shades of red as his typically dark complexion turned to that of embarrassment.

"Huh? What do you mean 'Where's David?'" he then laughed, shaking his head.

"You heard me, Zio Tony. Where is he?" she asked again in a soft voice. Only this time, she was more assertive.

Little Tony DiMatteo looked at her silently for several long seconds, momentarily speechless.

"You're a sharp doctor broad!" Little Tony laughed. "Now I know why David was so fond of you!" he started smirking as if to ridicule her absurd question.

"He's in a marble condominium at Queen of Heaven Cemetery, where we just left him," he loudly replied with a smile, amused at the question.

"That's where we're all gonna end up!" he laughed, as several others around him were smiling at his response.

Jeanne Callahan's voice then became louder and more insistent as she asked him for the third time.

"Cut the bullshit, Tony! Where is he?"

This time, several bystanders overheard her question and began to stare at the two of them, as if to be in some kind of loud confrontation.

Little Tony gazed at her silently for several seconds. The 'nerve of this broad,' he thought to himself, approaching him after his nephew's funeral and mention that his nephew's body could be someplace other than in that casket.

"Look, lady...I don't know where you get off, but we are all here at a funeral luncheon, showing our respects to my beloved nephew and godchild. So, if you'll excuse me, I suggest you direct your disrespectful questions outside of this family gathering." he curtly replied.

Little Tony then turned his back on her and walked away, while still holding his glass of scotch, mingling with the other guests at the luncheon.

Judging by Little Tony's reaction, Jeanne knew that something was amiss. His initial shock at her asking that question immediately convinced her that her suspicions could quite possibly be warranted. She became sick to her stomach, knowing that the body of David Fazio may not be in that mausoleum. Judging by the way Little Tony was expressing his lack of grief over the death of his beloved nephew, she knew that there were several reasons for her to be apprehensive.

She wasn't going nuts, she thought to herself. She didn't imagine all of this out of her own intense, personal grief. She knew that Little Tony's underworld reputation proceeded him and that he was quite capable of accomplishing anything.

Jeanne Callahan was beginning to wonder if David's body was *really* in that crypt at Queen of Heaven Cemetery.

CHAPTER THIRTY-SEVEN
Coroner's Report

It was the Friday after Thanksgiving, and Dr. Jeanne Callahan was sitting at her desk, in between appointments. She had seen several patients most of the day and hoped that she could cut out early. 'Black Friday' seemed to be a traditional holiday for everyone after Thanksgiving, who didn't have the burden of being physicians. Taking the day off from work, spending the day at the malls, shopping, and buying early Christmas gifts were activities enjoyed by most everyone. But being a neurologist and a sleep specialist, Jeanne didn't have those luxuries available to her.

It was almost three o'clock, and Jeanne had been depressed since David's tragic death and funeral. She didn't give herself the time to grieve. She didn't want to. Jeanne didn't want to accept the death of the very person who seemed to bring her the joy and happiness that she hadn't ever experienced throughout her life. Jeanne was devastated by David's tragic death, with the bizarre means by which he was incarcerated and then suddenly died. She couldn't accept it. And there was a part of her that didn't want to.

Her three o'clock patient had canceled their appointment, and Jeanne was physically exhausted. She called her administrative assistant on the phone.

"Vanessa? Call and cancel the rest of my appointments today."

"But Dr. Callahan, your four o'clock patient, scheduled this appointment with you several weeks ago."

"I don't care, Vanessa. Reschedule him for next week sometime. I'm just too tired today."

Dr. Callahan was visibly depressed, and she knew it. It appeared that she could not get her mind off of David. She walked over to her office door and abruptly closed it. Jeanne then went over to her leather couch in her office, laid down, and cried. It was almost an hour later when her desk phone rang.

"Dr. Callahan, the assistant coroner, is on the telephone for you," Vanessa said.

Jeanne had asked her associate to contact the assistant coroner from the Cook County Coroner's office earlier in the week. She wondered if she could get a hold of David's autopsy reports and examine them herself. In some strange, quirky way, she needed to find some closure. She needed to see David's body physically.

They say that grief is one of the strangest of all human emotions and probably the least understood by society. People react and behave differently in approaching and dealing with this complicated sentiment. Some people use alcohol, drugs, promiscuous sex, or even their death to help them deal with their intense grief. Some people, like Little Tony, refuse to acknowledge the emotion entirely and try to use laughter and humor to disguise their severe emotional pain. Then, of course, most turn appropriately to counseling or grief support groups to help them cope and understand their intense feelings and the insurmountable pain that goes with them.

Unfortunately, David's body was charred and burned beyond recognition. With his casket being closed and with Little Tony DiMatteo reacting so strangely throughout his funeral, Jeanne needed closure. She obviously, could not get a court order requiring the body to be exhumed. And Jeanne felt embarrassed interrogating the funeral director who prepared his body for burial. Therefore, acquiring the autopsy report was probably the only thing available to her to give her the closure that she needed. Because of her medical profession, she knew that she could do whatever she could to acquire the relevant reports regarding his death.

"Thanks, Vanessa," as she wiped her eyes and picked up the phone.

"Dr. Callahan? This is Dr. Jack Myette from the Cook County Coroner's Office returning your call."

"Thank you for calling me back, Dr. Myette. I was wondering if I could get a copy of my patient's autopsy report. His name is David Fazio."

There was a moment of silence.

"Doctor, I would need you to come in fill out some paperwork."

"Yes, I understand. But I need some verification to include in my patient's reports before I can close out my patient files, and coming in would not be convenient for me right now." Jeanne lied.

"For your reports? Really?" Myette questioned.

"Yes. I am a sleep specialist and a neurologist, and I need to verify that his untimely death was not related to any sleep issues or any neurological symptoms that may have contributed to his ultimately being killed in a fire. I need to indicate in my reports that this accidental death was indeed not a suicide."

Another moment of silence.

"Okay," Dr. Myette replied. "Could you send me an email with the name and date of death of the deceased?"

"Of course," Jeanne replied.

She thanked the assistant coroner and immediately sent him an email requesting a copy of the coroner's report for David Fazio, along with his date of death.

Within an hour of her request, she had received an email from Dr. Myette. That email included David's death certificate and attachment of the actual coroner's reports, along with the forensic reports and schedules regarding the deceased's body at the time of the examination.

Jeanne spent an hour reviewing the documents before noticing something peculiar. Next to David's name and birthdate, he listed his blood type, body weight, and height. The report stated his blood type 'O Positive,' bodyweight '120 pounds', and height at '5 feet, 6 inches tall.' When she reviewed the part of the report requesting examination of the deceased's dental records, the word 'unavailable' was typed in the space.

Red flags started going off in her head. Were these errors in the autopsy report? She knew for a fact that David was five feet, ten inches tall, and at least 170 pounds. She knew this because she was only five feet, four inches tall, and even with two-inch heels, David was still four inches taller. She didn't know his blood type but knew that she could dig up the necessary records to verify that information.

She also knew that he had lost a significant amount of weight, but fifty pounds in less than three months was unusual. Did David shrink in jail? Did he lose that much weight while he was incarcerated?

Jeanne happened to know David's dentist, who was also a very good friend. She called Dr. John Scott Aiello at his Westchester office, who initially expressed his condolences regarding David's death.

"Dr. Aiello?" she asked, "Did the Cook County Coroner's office request any dental records from your office regarding David?

"You know," he replied, "It's funny that you ask me that. I knew about his death and the prison fire, so I expected someone to call me from their office to request those dental records. I presumed that his body was burned beyond recognition. I had his dental records out and ready to send to them. But they never called," Dr. Aiello explained.

"No one from the Coroner's office ever called you?"

"Nope. I never heard from anyone."

"Interesting," Jeanne said. "You wouldn't happen to know his blood type, would you?"

Dr. Aiello laughed. "I would only know that because he listed that on our original patient information sheet several years ago."

Dr. Aiello put her on hold and acquired Fazio's dental records. After a few moments of shuffling through his file, he answered, "Here it is...Type A negative."

She thanked him and hung up the telephone.

Wrong height, wrong weight, wrong blood type, and the dental records are unavailable.

What the fuck?

Now Jeanne was suspicious. She reviewed the rest of the coroner reports, turning each page of the acquired reports back and forth repeatedly, pondering her next move.

What should she do now? Should she approach the State's Attorney's office and request that they open a homicide investigation and suspicious death based on the errors she found on the autopsy reports? Should she request the body to be exhumed after acquiring a court order? This would only bring more grief and pain to David's family, not to mention what Little Tony DiMatteo's ultimate reaction might be.

She then decided to pay someone a visit.

The DiMatteo Tomato Distribution Company was quite busy that Saturday morning, as Jeanne had difficulty finding a parking space for the white BMW X5 that she was driving. Since it was the holiday weekend, she did not expect the food distribution company on South Ashland Avenue to be so busy. She parked her car on the far end of the parking lot and walked quickly in the damp cold to the primary office entrance. She was carrying a leather briefcase along with her as she approached the receptionist, who was sitting behind a separation wall with a sliding glass window.

"Mr. DiMatteo, please."

"Is he expecting you?"

"No, I'm a friend of the family."

"Your name?"

"Dr. Jeanne Callahan."

The receptionist picked up the phone and called his office.

"Someone will be right with you."

Jeanne sat down in the lavish reception area, complete with expensive leather couches and a 'do-it-yourself' espresso bar, where there were Lavazza espresso pods and styrofoam cups, ready to consume.

After about twenty minutes or so, someone came downstairs to the reception area to greet her. He was a tall, large burly man, looked to be in his seventies, with 'over-dyed' black hair and a mustache.

"Dr. Callahan? I'm Sal Marrocco, Tony's associate."

"How do you do?" she replied.

Jeanne stood up and extended her petite, gentle hand to the six-foot, four-inch, 275-pound giant. His overly large hands practically consumed and made her hand disappear into his, as he politely tried his best to give her a gentle handshake.

"What can I help you with?"

"Well, if you don't mind, I would like to speak with Zio Tony...in private."

Marrocco smiled.

"Well, Doctor, I can assure you that as his financial advisor, anything important that you have to say to him can be said to me, and I promise that I will relay the information," Marrocco said politely.

Jeanne started to get angry.

"Look, I know Tony sent you down here to find out whatever it was that I wanted and to get rid of me. But I must talk with him."

"Dr. Callahan? Mr. DiMatteo is very busy this morning. You don't have an appointment to see him, and he won't be available for the rest of the day," Sal Marrocco politely but sternly insisted.

A moment of silence, as Dr. Callahan stood there in front of the six-foot, four-inch wall that probably stood between the perception of David's death and, perhaps, the real truth.

"Okay," Jeanne began, "I have some certified documents here from the Cook County Coroner's office that tell me that his nephew's body was completely charred and burned. He shrunk four inches and weighed fifty pounds less than his nephew's typical height and body weight. Not to mention a different blood type and dental records that, according to the coroner's office, were 'unavailable,'" the gutsy neurologist stated, right there in the middle of the reception room.

"Now, if Mr. DiMatteo still insists on not seeing me, I have an appointment with the Cook County District Attorney's office Monday morning. I'm sure that they can help me." Jeanne was bluffing, but she got her point across.

Sal Marrocco glared at her, knowing that Dr. Callahan's only intention on that cold Saturday morning was to make a lot of trouble for Little Tony and his 'merry band of men.'

"So look, Friar Tuck...either you bring me upstairs to see Tony, or I will keep my appointment on Monday at the State of Illinois building."

A moment of silence, and the two of them stood toe to toe, right there in the middle of that reception room.

"Come with me," Marrocco finally said as he used his card key to open the door.

She followed Marrocco upstairs, walking up two flights until she reached another door. As the consigliere opened the door for her, a lavish conference room with a long, mahogany wooden table and two dozen leather, high top chairs awaited her.

"Please be seated, Doctor. Can I offer you some coffee?"

"No, thank you."

Several minutes passed by as she patiently waited for Little Tony. She could overhear him screaming at Marrocco, demanding to know why he wasn't able to get rid of her.

Finally, the door opened, as 'Little Caesar' and his hired hood entered the room.

DiMatteo came out swinging. "I told Sal here, to goddamn get rid of you, but you're still here."

"I don't think you want me to go anywhere, Zio Tony."

"Don't fucking 'Zio Tony' me, you little bitch. You come in here, into my office, to my place of business, trying to fucking extort me," Little Tony screamed.

"That's not true!"

"Fuck you, Doctor Whore! You threaten me with some State's Attorney bullshit and a fucked-up coroner's report..."

"I need some answers, Tony!" she screamed

"Answers to what?" Tony screamed back. "David is dead. Do you fucking understand? My nephew is dead. He is at his final resting place in a marble crypt in the Saint Thomas Aquinas section of Queen of Heaven Cemetery in Hillside, Illinois. Now, which part of that don't you fucking understand?"

"FUCKING UNDERSTAND?" she screamed even louder.

"How about these autopsy report discrepancies? Should I fucking understand these? Should I fucking understand that he was only five feet, six inches tall, at 120 pounds, with a different blood type and no dental records, even though they were clearly available from his fucking dentist? Which fucking part of the fact should I fucking understand that the fucking coroner never requested the dental records to positively identify the fucking body?" Jeanne loudly screamed, her voice reverberating off the conference room walls.

A moment of silence.

"So...the coroner fucked up. So what?"

Jeanne started to laugh. "Are you kidding me? This is a blatant cover-up, and you goddamn know it, Tony."

Jeanne then started to cry. "David's body is not in that crypt! I know it. And I will do whatever I have to do to prove it! I will find out if I have to hire the best attorney and petition the State's Attorney myself to exhume that marble crypt."

Jeanne's face was now drenched with tears, as Sal Marrocco and Little Tony sat there at the other end of the conference table, totally speechless.

"I have lots of money and lots of time, Tony. I'm not going away. I will not stop until I get some answers. But sooner or later, I will get them."

Another few silent moments, as she looked at David's uncle.

"Why won't you help me?" she loudly cried.

At that moment, Little Tony got up from the other side of the conference table and walked closer to Jeanne, who was sitting on the other end. He pulled up the chair next to hers while Sal Marrocco continued to sit there on the other side of the conference table.

"Sal, give us a minute," as the consigliere dutifully left the room.

"Look, Missy...you gotta forget all this," Tony tried to talk to Jeanne sympathetically.

"David is gone. You need to move on. We all need to move on. It's terrible what happened to him, and I wish every day that I could have done more for him and not allowed any of this to happen. It's a terrible situation. But you gotta move on, Jeanne. Otherwise, this shit is going to eat you alive."

Jeanne stared at Tony DiMatteo silently for several long minutes, wiping her eyes with a tissue that he handed her from the Kleenex box.

"It's time to let go, Jeanne," he said. "Besides, David had demons."

Jeanne got up from the conference table and stared at the old, veteran Mafioso.

"I need to find out the truth, with or without your help. I'm not going to be able to move on with my life until I know the truth," Jeanne cried.

"I loved David. I loved him with all my heart, and I won't ever be able to make peace with that until I know the truth. I'm sorry, Tony," she emotionally sobbed, tears streaming down her face.

She grabbed her briefcase and headed for the exit door. Her expression suddenly changed as she glared at DiMatteo for a moment, as if venom were coming out of her pores.

"Tony...do not let me find out that you're hiding something. If I ever find out that you know more than what you're telling me..." she paused.

Tony sat there with a smirk on his face, waiting for her to complete her open threat.

"Yes?"

She grabbed the doorknob and pulled the door open before pausing.

"There's a special place in hell for monsters like you," she boldly said as she left.

She found her way out of the building and into the parking lot, opening the car door of her BMW. She sat there for a moment in deep thought before pressing the ignition button to auto-start her car. She was pensive, but now, more determined than ever to find out the truth regarding the death of Dr. David Fazio.

Jeanne Callahan now knew what she had to do.

CHAPTER THIRTY-EIGHT
Valentine's Day – Over a Year Later

Terry and Gina Janko were driving up towards North Milwaukee Avenue to their favorite Italian restaurant as the freezing rain annoyingly solidified into ice on the windshield. It was Valentine's Day, and it was Gina's idea to have a 'date night' with just the two of them that evening. They were both silent as they took turns changing the stations of the radio of their Jeep Cherokee every time one of them heard a song that they didn't like. Terry especially made it a point to change the radio station every time an Elvis tune came on, knowing that his wife's favorite singer of all-time was Elvis Presley.

The two of them decided to go out together alone for the first time in many, many months, as Mrs. Janko had trouble finding a babysitter for their two boys. Because they hadn't needed one in such a long time, Gina had difficulty finding someone who would watch their kids for the evening, promising that they would be home at an early hour.

It had been a little over a year since the prison death of the 'Abortion Arsonist,' and the Chicago Fire Department had formally thanked Detective Romanowski and Chief Janko for their excellent investigative efforts in capturing the perpetrator of those abortion clinic arson fires. Last summer, they both had received certificates of appreciation from the Mayor of Chicago, thanking them in an elaborate City Hall ceremony covered by the media for saving the city from an arsonist that was obviously out of control.

This Valentine's Day dinner at Pasta D 'Arte was not only a date but was a peace offering of sorts for the two of them. The Janko's were continuing to have extensive problems in their marriage. They had gone through long periods of silence recently, not talking to one another for days at a time for various reasons. Terry's continuous partying and drinking with his fellow firemen was a constant problem throughout their marriage. In contrast, Gina's spending habits and nagging regarding the boys' school and sports schedules were a consistent problem. Terry was never home, and he was never around to participate in their children's lives. Their kid's misbehavior and her husband's violent temper towards his family were persistent marital problems that the two of them couldn't resolve. Terry, on various occasions, had also come home after drinking and beat her up several times. But out of shame and embarrassment to his best friend, Gina never called the police or filed charges.

Gina was at a breaking point and was psychologically, just inches away from a nervous breakdown. She felt as though she was the mother and father to both of her boys. It was apparent that Terry refused to participate in being a father and husband to his wife and kids. She was trying in vain to fix their marriage and their lives. Gina had suggested marital counseling to Terry several times. She even asked the parish priest at St. Peregrine's Parish to come over to the house and help them with their relationship issues.

But Terry Janko wouldn't have any of it. It was as though he had given up on their marriage years ago and only stayed in the marriage because he didn't want to be involved in a messy, long-term divorce.

The subject of divorce had come up several times in the couple's many verbal and violent disputes. It was as though one was waiting for the other to pull the trigger, yet neither one dared to make the first move.

Terry pulled their Jeep Cherokee in front of Pasta D 'Arte Ristorante on North Milwaukee Avenue and handed the keys over to the valet. They had 6:30

reservations, and it looked like there would still be a waiting time for them to get a table. Chef Mark Giannini, who was the owner and a friend of the Battalion Chief, had seen them walking through the front door and immediately left the kitchen, wishing them both a Happy Valentine's Day.

"Thank you, Mark," Gina immediately kissed the chef.

"So nice to see you both. We should have a table ready for you soon. I'm so sorry for the wait."

"It's Valentine's Day, Chef Mark. We get it," the Battalion Chief smiled.

Chef Mark excused himself and went back into the kitchen, as the couple waited for several more minutes until the hostess had a table for them. The restaurant had been newly remodeled, with a mixture of an old school renaissance design with its hardwood floor and oversized wooden rafters. The restaurant was romantic and quaint, with a warm atmosphere that both Gina and Terry truly enjoyed during their many dinners there. As they both sat down, a friend from the firehouse noticed the couple and approached their table.

"Happy Valentine's Day, Gina," the firehouse captain immediately kissed Mrs. Janko, postponing his warm handshake to the Battalion Chief until greeting his wife first.

Stuart Durham was seated at the bar with a few of his friends when he noticed the two of them enter the restaurant and were eventually seated. Gina seemed to be nervous when she made eye contact with Durham, as they exchanged pleasantries regarding their firehouse activities and the late winter freezing rain. The captain wished them an enjoyable dinner and walked back to the bar with his friends, still making eye contact with Gina periodically throughout the evening.

The Janko's put in their drink order, with Terry ordering vodka on the rocks with a splash of lime, while

Gina ordered an Old-Fashioned. They tried to make small talk, observing several other couples who were sitting adjacent to their table that looked familiar.

Terry ordered the special, the pan-seared branzino con pomodoro, while Gina got the chicken cacciatore. They were both silent during their dinner, speaking only briefly about the boys in school, their grades, and their recent parent-teacher conferences that the Battalion Chief couldn't attend.

They had difficulty conducting a civil conversation. They were having problems in their marriage, and it was getting to the point where neither one of them couldn't hide it any longer.

As the expressos and desserts arrived, Terry finally broke the ice.

"So, Gina…tell me what you want."

"Tell you what?"

"Tell me what it is that you want. We need to divorce. We need to separate. We both know that we can't fake this anymore, and all of the 'date nights' in the world aren't going to fix us. We both need to go our separate ways."

Gina was silent for a moment.

"Well, for starters, Terry, you could come home after your shift and be a better father to your boys. They ask for you all the time, and they're starting to get used to your not being around anymore. Obviously, you don't want to be home with them," Gina observed.

"Honey, it's not my fault that I have a firehouse to run."

"Well, what about your family? You have neglected your family for so long your kids don't even know if they have a father anymore. And God forbid you should miss a night out at Diamond Lil's with your friends and firehouse buddies, especially on Friday nights."

Terry coldly glared at his wife as she lectured him.

"You're an alcoholic, Terry, and you need to get help. You need to stop drinking. It's not going to make your problems go away."

"An alcoholic? What the hell are you talking about? Just because I have an occasional drink once in a while?"

"Once in a while? Are you kidding? Your breath constantly smells like either a gin mill or of Scope mouthwash, which you conveniently keep in the glove box of the car. You won't stop drinking."

Terry glared at his wife again before responding with a hurtful answer.

"At least I'm not a cheater," he hit below the belt, reminding his wife of her illicit affair with David Fazio many years ago.

"How many times are you going to bring that up? How many times do I have to suffer for a mistake that I made thirteen years ago before the kids were born? And by the way, how many firehouse bimbos have you had over the years that I supposedly don't know about?"

"We don't have any firehouse bimbos," Terry loudly insisted.

"Bullshit, Terry! I have eyes and ears everywhere, and I've heard about all of the firehouse visitors you've had spending the night there. I'm not stupid!"

The two of them continued to loudly banter back and forth as the other couples sitting close to their table were starting to take notice of the two of them arguing. As Gina was trying to calm herself down, she looked over at the bar, where Stuart was sitting. He continued to make eye contact with them, nodding his head at her on several occasions. He then raised his drink at her behind her husband's back, as if to make a silent toast to Terry Janko's wife.

After the bill came, the two of them immediately put their coats on and began to exit the restaurant, waiving 'good-bye' to Chef Mark from the kitchen. Durham continued to sit at the bar, watching the couple exit the front entrance, pushing open the heavy, wooden oak doors.

Janko gave his parking receipt to the valet when Gina immediately excused herself.

"Terry, I need to go to the bathroom. I will be right out," she said while she immediately went back inside of the restaurant.

Stuart Durham noticed Gina coming back inside, walking past the bar towards the ladies' room. The two of them made eye contact as the firehouse captain nodded his head at her while he continued drinking his martini at the bar. She smiled back at him and quickly entered the restroom.

Suddenly, a long black Cadillac Escalade pulled up in front of the restaurant, and two large men got out and approached Chief Janko.

"You need to come with us," one of them said. There was no one else outside waiting for their cars as if the valets had planned not to be a witness to the fire chief's abduction.

"Who are you guys?" as Janko tried to pull his arms away. The two larger men, both over six and a half feet in stature and over 350 pounds, looked like professional football linebackers as they quickly forced Janko into the backseat of the car. The back doors were immediately slammed closed as Janko sat in the backseat of the oversized, luxury Cadillac Escalade between two very large men. The whole abduction took less than ten seconds, as no one bore witness to the fire chief's disappearance. There were no outside cameras, no parking valets around, and there were no witnesses.

When Gina came back outside, she was expecting her husband to be waiting for her in their Jeep Cherokee. Instead, the valet had just pulled their car up in front of the restaurant and opened the door, expecting the two of them to get inside and drive away.

But her husband wasn't there. Gina looked around, walking around the restaurant building, looking for her husband, and loudly calling his name. She asked the valet to assist her in looking for her husband, and after twenty minutes or more, she asked Stuart Durham to leave the bar and help her in looking for Terry.

An hour had passed before the police were called, and several patrol cars arrived in front of the restaurant. Gina, now in a panic, called Diane Romanowski, crying loudly over the phone, frightfully stating that her husband was nowhere to be found.

"Denny, please get here…quickly," as Diane passed her cell phone over to him. "I can't find Terry!" she loudly cried, barely keeping her composure over the phone.

Detective Romanowski, wearing only a white tee shirt and blue jeans, showed up in his squad car several minutes later. He had also heard the police blotter over the radio after receiving the frantic phone call from Gina.

They all started combing the neighborhood, with several police officers going door to door around the surrounding houses and buildings, asking if anyone had seen anything. There were no security cameras in the front of the building and no surveillance at the hot-dog drive-in establishment next door. It was as if Janko had disappeared in plain sight that night, while the drizzling frozen rain continued to pour down that evening. Before the end of the evening, Romanowski assisted Gina in filing a missing person's report.

On the night of Valentine's Day, Battalion Fire Chief Commander Terrance F. Janko, of the City of Chicago Fire Department Engine No.1...was never seen again.

At least not alive.

CHAPTER THIRTY-NINE
Final Ride

"Do you know who I am?" came a voice from the front seat of the Cadillac Escalade.

Chief Janko tried to peer over to the front seat but couldn't get a glimpse of who was talking to him.

"How can I recognize you if I can't see you?" Terry Janko replied.

By that time, he had been in the back seat of that car for over twenty minutes. He had been elbowed and punched several times by the giant gorillas sitting on either side of him for trying to escape and could now taste the blood that was pouring profusely out of his nose.

The voice from the front seat adjusted the rearview mirror so that he could make eye contact with his abducted prisoner while his chauffer continued to drive the car southbound down the Kennedy Expressway.

Janko studied the image in the mirror, quickly realizing who he was. He suddenly felt his heart drop down to his stomach.

"Do you have any idea who I am?" he asked again to his backseat detainee. Janko was speechless.

"Do you realize who you goddamn framed? Do you realize who you inadvertently goddamn killed in prison?" the man continued to talk in the mirror.

"Do you realize who you destroyed, whose life you goddamn ruined, and who you managed to fucking frame as the 'Abortion Arsonist, you cock-sucker?"

Janko, again, was silent, as he began to fear that any answer would earn him another punch in the face.

The man in the front seat turned around, now looking at Janko square in the eyes.

"Answer me, you mother-fucker! Do you know who I am?"

Janko answered, "You're Little Tony."

"No," Tony answered in a loud voice. "I'm Tony-Your-Worst-Goddamn-Nightmare-DiMatteo, you fuckball. I'm the godfather to my nephew, the baby-doctor whom you goddamn framed and got thrown into jail for aggravated arson and four counts of involuntary manslaughter, crimes which my nephew never committed, you rotten bastard."

"I didn't frame your nephew," Janko loudly replied.

At that moment, both men elbowed Janko so hard in his face that he felt his two front teeth break off in a gushing flow of blood coming out of his mouth.

"You're a lying mother-fucker, you rotten bastard. Someone from Chicago-Western sent you my nephew's lab coat, and you planted it at the scene of the crime before you set that last clinic on fire. One of your goddamn men at the firehouse ratted you. He saw a package that you guys received from the hospital with my nephew's lab coat in it, which suddenly appeared at the scene of that fire," Little Tony ranted.

"One of your firemen saw you driving around with a gasoline tank and a box of heavy fireworks in the trunk of your car too, you asshole."

Janko was now silent, knowing that he was currently being judged by a one-person jury in the front seat of the car. And this one-person jury was probably the most powerful, most evil, most ruthless bastard in all of Chicagoland.

"You framed my nephew, you arsonist, son of a bitch! You're the one who set those clinics on fire because you had a hard-on for my godchild, who used to fuck your wife's brains out!"

"That's not true!" Janko protested.

Another volley of punches in his face, directly aimed at both of his eyes. They were now starting to swell, and Janko was beginning to lose consciousness.

317

At that moment, Little Tony handed his Beretta to his men in the back seat. They then continued to pistol-whip Janko, taking turns beating his face to a pulp while he tried to cover his face with his hands.

After over an hour and half of driving away from Chicago, going over the Chicago Skyway, and onto I-94, they went south down I-80 and exited off the Valparaiso exit. The black Escalade eventually drove down a desolate, dark gravel road. Along the side of that road was an abandoned warehouse, set back within a large field of thickened weeds and large brush with overgrown oak and maple trees.

The Cadillac Escalade pulled up in front of the empty warehouse. By this time, Janko was barely conscious, as the two men grabbed him by his hair and his coat and pulled him out of the car. Little Tony pulled out some duct tape from the glove box and tightly wrapped the tape around his mouth several times.

As he struggled to walk, they brought him into the warehouse. Tony's chauffeur pulled out some thick rope from the back of the car and securely tied up Janko's hands and feet. At that moment, Little Tony grabbed a gasoline tank from the back of the Cadillac and splashed the contents onto the fire chief.

One of the men threw the rope over one of the steel rafters and pulled Janko by his feet upside down until he was hanging by his feet ten feet up in the air.

"You're going to die the same goddamn way my nephew did, you rat-bastard!"

One of Tony's henchmen pulled out a box of matches. With all of them standing back, he threw the match at Janko as he struggled, hanging upside down from the rafters of that empty warehouse.

Janko lit up like a fireball, his body wiggling and struggling to break free from the upside-down noose. He was a blazing inferno, looking like a ball of fire until the rope burned off, and Janko's body fell and laid on the ground, his body still wiggling and on fire.

Little Tony just looked at Janko's body, still squirming and wiggling on the ground, still on fire. He shook his head.

"This mother-fucker just don't wanna goddamn die," he said, as he asked for his gun back from one of his henchmen.

He then grabbed the firearm and pointed it towards the head of the burning corpse. Turning off the safety, he pulled back the gun's chamber. Little Tony DiMatteo then emptied the gun clip directly into the fire chief's head, firing off several rounds until Terrance Janko's burning body was a charred, motionless corpse.

"That's from Dr. David."

CHAPTER FORTY
The Queen of Spades

The newsroom at the Chicago Sun-Times was especially loud that late afternoon, as everyone was trying to make their news article deadlines for the following morning. It had been a slow news month for February, as everyone in the newsroom was looking for newsworthy articles for their morning addition. The newspaper reporter who usually covers the downtown newsbeat and City Hall stories was busy, finishing up a story on the effects of the new retail marijuana sales and its impact on the City of Chicago's current budget deficit.

Suddenly, his desk phone loudly rang.

"Crawford here."

"Paulie...are you sleeping at your desk again?"

It was Mike Daudelin, the assistant editor, who had nothing else better to do than to spy on his reporters when he wasn't on Facebook.

"Yeah, right, Chief. You probably could hear me snoring from your office,"

The assistant news editor had just enough time to laugh at his stupid joke before giving his star, downtown reporter a directive.

"Delete your solitaire game and come into my office."

Paul Crawford, who had been employed by the Chicago Sun-Times for over thirty years, had a great rapport with his assistant editor. He commonly referred to him as 'Chief' as he loved to equate himself with Perry White from the Metropolis Daily Planet. Crawford usually covered any newsworthy stories coming out of City Hall and any downtown news articles. The assistant editor liked to give the veteran reporter his pick of the 'hot' news items coming across his desk.

Mike Daudelin was a no-nonsense, pull-no-punches kind of guy who always went to bat for all of his reporters, no matter how busy he was working hard on Facebook or Instagram. He was a six-foot, five-inch, 310-pound former Michigan State linebacker, and he was more than happy to go to bat for any of his reporters if they were jammed up on a story. Crawford and Daudelin had been working together since the 9-11 terrorist attack story broke in 2001, and they enjoyed a mutually respectful relationship over the many years of working together.

Crawford walked into his office and noticed a Burger King sandwich bag sitting on the far corner of his desk as he asked the reporter to come in and shut the door.

"Let me guess...two whoppers for three bucks? That fast food shit is gonna kill you, Chief."

Daudelin looked at Crawford, almost annoyed.

"Do I tell you what you can goddamn eat for lunch?"

"How was the burger? I didn't have lunch, so I hope you saved me one."

"Get your own!" Daudelin barked as Crawford laughed and sat down in front of his messy, cluttered desk.

Daudelin's desk could undoubtedly be declared a federal disaster area, with old lunch bags, strewn garbage, old papers, and stained coffee cups and that haven't seen a dishwasher in years. The newsroom's standard joke was that Daudelin kept his desk messy to make the other editors think he was overworked, preoccupied, and busy doing his job.

The assistant editor was still picking at some of his now stale French fries at three-thirty in the afternoon, wiping his dirty, greasy hands on his already dirty white shirt before taking a drink from his extra-large Diet Coke.

"What are you working on?" he asked.

"That marijuana sales and tax collections story regarding City Hall. You said this story was on fire and that you needed it finished tonight."

"I'm pulling you off. Something bigger just popped from the police blotter."

"Oh, goody. I was falling asleep in front of my computer."

"Yeah, I noticed. How many Solitaire games did you win?"

They both laughed together before the reporter finally got sober.

"What's up?" Crawford finally asked.

"There's a homicide at the Chicago Sheridan on Wacker Drive. They found a woman's body in one of the hotel rooms."

"Really?" Paul asked. "Any idea who?"

"There are some rumblings. Someone important. That's why I'm sending you over. They still haven't officially identified the body yet."

Paul Crawford sat in his chair for a moment, trying to take a mental inventory of which female Chicago socialite or essential person would have been found murdered in a local hotel room.

"What time did this happen?" Crawford eagerly asked.

"The coppers were called about a half-hour ago, but she's probably been dead for a while. Go over there and check it out."

"I don't have a photographer, so you're on your own. Run over there as soon as you can."

"Got it, Chief," as Crawford quickly got up from his chair, still trying to figure out who the victim was that he was going to investigate.

"And Crawford...be careful out there. Every time I send you out in the street, I worry."

"No worries, Chief," as Perry White from the Daily Planet smiled from behind his desk.

The reporter grabbed his suit coat and his backpack, which usually included a portable laptop and a couple of small writing tablets. Grabbing his Minolta camera from the bottom drawer of his desk, he ran downstairs to the lobby and caught a cab from the Sun-Times building over to the Chicago Sheridan Hotel.

The whole block of Wacker Drive was blocked off by several police cars around the adjacent perimeter of the multi-floored hotel facility. Crawford was trying his best to penetrate through the squad car blockade and get into the Sheridan. As he walked toward the entrance, his good buddy from the Sixteenth District was outside talking with another patrolman.

"We gotta stop meeting like this," Crawford joked, recalling that he had seen him several months ago on another news story, where a Mafioso was found hanging from the window of the Blackstone Hotel.

"When are they going to get rid of you, Crawford? Aren't you getting a little old for chasing down these news stories?"

Tommy Morton was a detective out of the Sixteenth District and had seen more of his share of dead bodies, killings, and gruesome homicides.

"Don't I wish? I keep blowing my money on lottery tickets, but my number never comes up."

Detective Morton smiled, his eyes still focused on his notepad.

"What do we have, Tommy?"

"Got a dead body upstairs. Some old broad from the Northshore."

Crawford looked at the detective, waiting for more information.

"Okay...I give. Who?"

"Talk to Dorian. He's on the Eighteenth floor."

Paul Crawford cut through some twenty or more patrolmen gathered in the Sheridan Hotel's lobby, showing his press badge to a couple of coppers guarding the elevator. When he arrived at the eighteenth floor, he followed the long hallway where several other media and camera people were assembled, trying to get a good shot of the victim located in Room 1821. As he got there, his good friend from Channel Eight news was already getting ready to do a live newsfeed when Crawford interrupted him.

"Chaz...what's up? Fancy seeing you here." Paul Crawford and Chaz Rizzo from Channel Eight news had known each other for years. They shook hands and gave each other the usual 'man-hug' before giving him the scoop.

"Just got here, Paulie, waiting for a confirmation on the victim's identity. Overheard it over the radio from Detective Dorian but waiting to confirm."

"What did you hear?"

"We think it's 'Cruella deVil,'" Rizzo said, smiling.

Crawford started to laugh as he listened to Rizzo suddenly begin to sing the Disney tune as if he were auditioning for a part in the Broadway play:

"Cruella deVil, Cruella deVil,
If she doesn't get you, no other spook will..."

Smiling, Paul Crawford shook his head at the lack of homage and reverence Chaz Rizzo was remunerating at the crime scene.

Based on the name moniker, Crawford immediately knew who he was talking about. It was Adrianna Hunter, age 61, from Winnetka, Illinois. The Chicago socialite and downtown empress found dead at the Chicago Sheridan Hotel by a room service maid early that afternoon. Based on the unconfirmed information from Rizzo, the Chicago socialite had checked in under her name around 11:00 that evening. It wasn't clear whether she had arrived by herself or another companion. Still, based on the concierge, Ms. Hunter regularly checked into the hotel whenever she was 'overserved' at a local bar downtown and didn't want to make the thirty-minute drive to her opulent mansion in Winnetka.

Before getting the full story, Crawford approached Detective Philip Dorian from the Eighteenth District, who was standing outside in the hallway, interviewing one of the hotel maids.

"Hey, Philly, how we doing?" Crawford greeted the usually grumpy detective.

"Just fine before you showed up, Crawford," he smiled and shook the news reporter's hand.

"Have we 'I-dee'd' the victim yet? I hear its Cruella."

"How did you guess that, Crawford? Maybe it was the overbearing expensive perfume coming from down the hallway?" the detective replied.

The reporter continued to ask the detective questions, as the Cook County Coroner had just arrived at the crime scene. There were several other detectives taking pictures and assessing the victim in the hotel room.

"So, what was the cause of death?" Crawford asked.

"Right now, it looks like a drug overdose."

"Really? Was Adrianna a drug user?"

Dorian scratched his head, looking a little perplexed.

"That's what has us all confused, Crawford. No one has ever known her to be a drug user, as there are no needle marks on her arms or any drugs, pills, or paraphernalia within the room."

"Okay," the reporter asked. "How do you think she ingested the drugs?"

Detective Dorian motioned the reporter over into the hotel room, where the other detectives were assessing the victim's naked body on the bed.

'Based on the position of the body, it looks like whoever she was with had sex with her first. Then quite possibly, while she was sleeping, injected a lethal dose of heroin into her body using a suppository into her anus," the detective explained.

"Wow," the reporter reacted.

By then, Chaz Rizzo was writing down a few more notes and then confirming with another officer at the scene, positively confirming her identity. It was indeed Adrianna.

Crawford pulled out his camera from his backpack and took a few pictures of the hotel room and the scene of the crime, along with a photo of the coroner covering up the body before putting it into the black body bag. He interviewed several other detectives at the crime scene. It didn't take long for himself and Chaz Rizzo to figure the scenario and how Adrianna Hunter had met her end.

Other information regarding Adrianna's last night alive was starting to become apparent.

She was out partying with a friend at the Sale e Pepe Ristorante on North Rush Street, near the area called the "Viagra Triangle'. There is a lively bar there that caters to the upscale 'rich and famous' patrons from the 'Gold Coast,' where most of the customers are 'Q-Tip' seniors with seven-figure incomes. This was Adrianna's usual Thursday night watering hole, and she was well known to hang out at the bar. She was out that night, staking out a new victim for one of her sexual conquests for the evening.

To say that Adrianna Hunter was a Northshore 'cougar' with an enormous sexual appetite was an understatement. Her discrete, innumerate sexual conquests would rival any college sorority girl or even an upscale Las Vegas prostitute. It is well known that she would go downtown to several local expensive bars and nightclubs to look for an unassuming male victim with a large wade of cash. She always found it easy to find another man, or a young 'boy-toy,' who was 'horny' enough to go to bed with a sixty-one-year-old lady who, as a twenty-footer, could pass for a thirty-something.

"This old broad found a very dangerous lover last night. She probably took him upstairs, thinking that she was going to have her way with him. When he was done with her, he probably rolled her over while she was sleeping and jammed it up her ass with a suppository full of heroin," Rizzo hypothesized.

Crawford walked back to Detective Dorian, who was still standing in the hotel hallway of the eighteenth floor, talking with one of the other coppers.

"So, Detective...any ideas who did this?"

"Really, Crawford? This broad had more enemies than Donald Trump. Everyone in town hated this goddamn bitch. They didn't call her 'Cruella deVil' for nothing."

He looked at the Sun-Times reporter rather coldly, not feeling sure about whether he should be volunteering any information to the media. When it came to acquiring any newsworthy facts from the detective, he was definitely on the stingy side with the way he treated media reporters.

"Right now, until we review the hotel surveillance cameras, all we have is a dead socialite who overdosed on heroin."

"Well, seeing that the drugs were injected by suppository, it has to be a homicide, right Detective?" Paul Crawford observed.

"I wouldn't be so quick to call this a homicide. Not just yet."

Paul Crawford went downstairs and hung out with Rizzo and the Channel Eight news truck, writing various pieces of information before returning to the newsroom. Chaz Rizzo went on air shortly after, breaking the story on the six o'clock news that evening.

The next day's headlines for the Chicago Sun-Times were:

Socialite Found Dead in Chicago Hotel

Sal Marrocco was in the gym early that morning, finishing up his spin class. He had forgotten to bring along his cellular phone into the gym, and several texts and messages were waiting for him when he got back to his locker.

Because Little Tony only carried a burner phone, which he exchanged out every few months, he seldom received messages or texts. His primary contact was usually through his consigliere, Sal Marrocco. When something urgent had to be communicated to Little Tony, it often went through Marrocco.

As the consigliere opened his locker and grasped his phone, he read the text to himself. It was from an unknown sender, using a burner phone:

The Queen of Spades is sleeping.

Marrocco smiled to himself. Several days before, a young, aspiring associate of the DiMatteo Family, Gianni DeLuca, was assigned his first real 'hit.' He was told to tail Adrianna Hunter for several days until he was able to get her alone and befriend her at the nightclub, where she usually goes on Thursday nights. Knowing that she would probably try to pick him up

328

and bring him somewhere where she could have sex with him, she lured him to the Chicago Sheridan that late Thursday night.

After DeLuca had his way with her, he waited for her to fall asleep before injecting her with a suppository filled with a heroin speedball, more than enough to kill her.

Marrocco saved the text and, after getting cleaned up and dressed in the locker room, went into Little Tony's office.

The Capo dei Capi was extremely pleased.

"Thank God this goddamn bitch is dead," Little Tony exclaimed. "She won't be up to anybody's ass anymore."

Marrocco laughed. "I think this time, she got it exactly where she truly deserved it."

They both started laughing, knowing that they now had a young, new, ambitious hitman that they could reliably count on.

The 'Godfather' had taken revenge on all those who destroyed the life of his beloved nephew and godchild.

Convinced that Adrianna Hunter was responsible for pushing the Chicago P.D. and the Chicago Fire to arrest and convict his nephew, DiMatteo was also pleased about one more reality:

That he had now efficiently imposed revenge on another one of his nephew's mortal enemies.

CHAPTER FORTY-ONE
Eighteen Months after Fazio's Death

The bright, South American sun was unrelenting that Sunday afternoon, as the local grocery store was quite busy with patrons. The Super Mercado de San Carlos was a popular grocery store within the large city of San Carlos, Uruguay, with a population of a little over 25,000 people. Many of the patrons lived locally within several blocks of the super mercado, and the popular grocery store was always regularly serving its customers. The 'carne y carnicero,' which had a large butcher department, employed several full-time butchers that cut and prepared meat, pork, and chicken as a popular requested staple to its customers.

A butcher named Paolo DiGiorgio had been working for the super mercado for a little over a year now and was familiar with his employer's business, the store, and its local environment. His language skills had greatly improved over the last year, and he was becoming more efficient in speaking the standard Spanish dialect of Rioplatense, which is a combination dialect of both the Spanish and Italian languages. He was well-liked by his employer and his fellow employees and seemed to be very skilled with a butcher's knife. Paolo made over six hundred pesos per week and managed to live in a one-bedroom, eight hundred square foot studio apartment just above the jewelry store in downtown San Carlos.

"Paolo, por favor corta más filetes por favor, luego pon los aires en el suelo," the manager said, requesting that the new butcher put out the freshly cut steaks and fillets onto the grocery display case.

Paolo was an older gentleman, with long white hair and a salt and pepper beard, probably in his middle fifties. His horn-rimmed glasses were now a necessity in treating his acute stigmatism. He was grateful and more than happy to have a job being employed at the popular grocery store in San Carlos. The experienced butcher was a rather shy man but was always very friendly to all the store's customers and his fellow employees.

Paolo DiGiorgio was a loner and pretty much kept to himself. When others used to ask him about his past, he only mentioned that he used to be employed as a butcher for a small grocery store in Chicago. He made it a point never to say much about his past life or his family.

On many occasions, he went out with his fellow employees to a local bar after work in downtown San Carlos and mingled well with his workplace friends. Being a rather handsome older gentleman, he was asked out by many older ladies that he encountered at the local bar. Even though he flirted with everyone, he seemed never to be interested in going out and starting any kind of close relationship. Paolo would usually finish his one or two Dos Equis beers after work and return home alone. It was fair to say that Paolo, for whatever reason, was a loner and didn't wish to intermingle with anyone socially. He didn't have any close friends and kept everyone around him pretty much at arm's length. At the super mercado, Paolo was a man with a very mysterious past and never said much to anyone.

One Sunday afternoon, a young pregnant woman was shopping at the super mercado, pushing her grocery cart down one of the aisles adjacent to the meat and butcher shop. She pushed her grocery cart up to the display case where Paolo was working, helping another customer. When Paolo was available, the young lady got Paolo's attention.

"Buenos Dias," she said to Paolo.

"Buenos Días."

"Podría tener dos grandes asados de loño de cerdo, recién cortados por favor. Los necesitaré para cenar esta noche," she said, requesting a large, freshly cut pork roast for dinner.

Paolo acknowledged her request and went into the back room behind the display cases to cut the pork loins for the roast she requested. Several large butchered pigs were hanging in the back, and the butcher quickly fulfilled her order. He promptly wrapped them up in white paper and marked the weight on both loins, passing them across to her over the display cases.

"Gracias."

"De nada," he acknowledged, as the young pregnant woman put them into her cart and pushed it down the aisle where the canned and packaged goods were stacked and shelved.

The stock boy had just wiped down and washed the floor from a broken tomato sauce jar that another customer had dropped onto the floor. The grocery aisle had just been mopped and cleaned and was still damp and slippery. The young, pregnant woman pushed her cart along the corridor, not noticing that it was still wet.

At the front of the grocery store, a young, well-dressed American woman entered the front door of the super mercado and requested the location of the butcher shop.

"Donde estas...your butcher department?" she asked the store manager, in her limited Spanish and combination in English.

"En la parte de atrás, hacia la esquina más lejana de la tienda," the store manager said, pointing to the back of the supermercado.

Although the well-dressed woman, who appeared to be American, didn't understand, she followed the direction of where the store manager had pointed.

Suddenly, there was a loud crash towards the back of the store. Broken glass and toppled cans and jars had spilled off the store shelves. Several employees rushed into the direction of the store aisle accident. There on the floor, the young pregnant woman was unconscious, lying in the middle of the aisle, blood spilling from under her dress and her head.

Paolo, standing behind the butcher display, watched the whole incident happen. He rushed from behind the meat counter and quickly began to attend to the injured, unconscious female.

He yelled out to another employee, "Consigue un poco de agua caliente y algunas mantas frescas. También necesitaré algunas vendas".

He requested some hot water, some bandages, and some blankets to attend to the injured pregnant customer. Upon immediately examining her, he knew that she had suddenly broken her water bag and was going into intense labor. He placed the blankets under her head and attended to her head wounds while she was now gaining consciousness and groaning loudly with labor pains. He washed and sterilized the area with hot water while he positioned her legs to allow her to deliver her baby.

"Empuje por favor," he kept yelling at the woman as she continued to scream, trying hard to push out the baby. At the same time, another employee assisted Paolo in helping the young lady deliver. They both continued to support the young lady for about twenty minutes until finally, a healthy baby boy was abruptly delivered into the world.

Paolo smiled as several employees, customers, and the store manager continued to witness the butcher skillfully deliver and attend to the injured pregnant woman. As the baby was successfully delivered, everyone in the store began applauding. At that moment, someone had called the fire department, and several 'bomberos' and 'policías,' firemen and policemen were arriving at the store. All had stood there and joyfully clapped for the shy, soft-spoken butcher who delivered that healthy baby boy.

As everyone was busy applauding and congratulating Paolo, the well-dressed American female who had entered the store earlier had witnessed the whole impromptu delivery. While the crowds of people began to depart and the fire department put the woman on a stretcher, the two policemen covered up the newborn child in a blanket, and both were taken into an ambulance and transported to the San Carlos Hospital.

As everyone was clearing the grocery aisle area, the American only stood there, alone, staring at Paolo.

Paolo looked up and suddenly noticed the well-dressed female. He smiled, shaking his head as he immediately recognized her while tears began to stream down his cheeks.

An important person from Paolo's past, from his other life, had unexpectedly arrived. She had suddenly come to rescue him from all the nightmares, all the monsters, and all the lonely, sleepless nights that have continued to haunt him for the last eighteen months. At that moment, the butcher could feel all his demons escape him, as the hypnotic, tender gaze of those sensuous, big brown eyes pierced through his body. It was as though he had been abruptly and unexpectedly impaled by lightning, and it felt wonderful.

She walked over to him and placed her soft left hand on his right cheek before gently greeting him.

"Hello, David," she said in a soft, alluring voice.

It was Jeanne.

CHAPTER FORTY-TWO
One Month Later

It was five-thirty on a Tuesday morning, as Salvatore Marrocco pulled into the parking lot of the DiMatteo Tomato Distribution Company on South Ashland Avenue. It was his usual time to show up at work, as he made himself available to work out at the company gym every morning. This was his daily routine, as his boss, Little Tony DiMatteo, usually went into the shop early every morning to get his early morning workout in. It was a casual time every day for the family consigliere to catch up with the Capo dei Capi regarding the family business and daily activities from the previous day.

Marrocco went into the locker room and changed into his workout clothes, then walked into the company workout gym, where there were several employees already working out on elliptical machines and spinning bikes. There was a cute, female spinning instructor conducting a spin class there as Little Tony was already on his spinning bike doing cardio.

"Your late, Sal."

"I know...I overslept."

"You need to stop drinking that homemade vino every night. It's knocking you out," as Tony was furiously spinning his bike to the music and instructions of the trainer.

"I know," Sal replied.

They continued to spin their cycles, adjusting the speed and tension according to the instructions of the trainer. Sal Marrocco was already breaking a sweat as he had a white towel wrapped around his neck while wearing a black and red sweatsuit.

Sal Marrocco tried to start a conversation with his boss, but he didn't seem to be in the mood. Little

Tony didn't have a lot to talk about that morning, as he appeared to be in a very reflective state of mind.

DiMatteo was deep in thought that morning. He was thinking about his nephew David, the fire chief who framed him, and the way the medical community had so harshly treated his beloved nephew. Because of David's strict Catholic upbringing, he refused to perform abortions, but he wanted to deliver babies. The way the medical profession was set up for him, he was not allowed to do one without the other, and that was his nephew's demise.

Had David Fazio left obstetrics and gone into another specialty, he would have still been alive and well and living in Chicago. Little Tony could have helped his nephew get set up in a medical building, opening up his practice and professionally assisting those in need without the pressures of performing abortions. His nephew could have had it made, and he would have done very well. Tony DiMatteo kept beating himself up, knowing that there were a thousand different ways that he could have helped his beloved nephew.

Tony was grateful to the Stateville warden and his 'Get Out of Jail Free' card. Thomas McCafferty had cleverly set up the jailhouse fire and switched the bodies. He had found a homeless man who had died in the middle of the night in downtown Joliet and quickly planned with the Kendall County Coroner to have the body sent over and put into Fazio's jail cell while he was at dinner. In the middle of the night, the homeless man's body, which was hidden under Fazio's bed, was switched just before setting the cot on fire. By that point, Fazio had already left his jail cell. Dressed in a prison guard uniform, Fazio was quickly able to leave the Stateville prison, where he then boarded a four-passenger Beechcraft King Air 350 airplane at the Joliet Regional Airport.

David Fazio arrived at Miami International Airport several hours later. With a fake passport and using a new alias, David was able to get through security. Flying on standby, he boarded a United Boeing 737 flight to Argentina, where Little Tony had some friends living in Buenos Aires. David stayed at the villa of his dear friend, Signor Carlos Estevez, a well-known South American drug trafficker, for two months until he was able to set him up. He eventually found him a job and a place to live where no one would ever suspect finding him. He found him a job as a butcher in a little grocery store and a small apartment in the tiny town of San Carlos, Uruguay.

His nephew, although he was no longer in Chicago, was alive and well, far away from his medical community enemies. David was now able to start a new life away from the people in Chicago who tried so desperately to destroy him.

"Tony, are you okay?"

"Yeah, Sal...just a lot on my mind."

They started to discuss some business regarding collections and outstanding business receivables, as Marrocco had overseen the delivery of some gambling slot machines to a restaurant on the Northside. They continued to discuss the details of their delivery and some other miscellaneous business matters.

They finished their workout, and after showering and getting dressed, Marrocco went upstairs to his office in the upper corner of the tomato distribution facility. The consigliere poured himself some coffee from his Keurig coffee machine and sat at his desk, logging into his computer. As the first thing he did was to check his emails, he read through the two dozen or so emails until he found an unfamiliar correspondence from an unknown addressee.

It was from a jcallahan1973@gmail.com with the subject area "Lost & Found."

Dear Mr. Marrocco,

'Who was once lost has now been found.'
Luke 15:34

I am writing this email to inform you that, after an intense investigation by several private detectives which I had hired, that I have finally found who I have been passionately looking for over these last eighteen months.

It seems that a grocery store company Christmas card was unknowingly posted on the internet from a very remote part of the world. Thanks to the facial recognition programs that were available to one of my detectives, he was able to find the person whom I've been seeking.

We have been living together for the last five weeks here in this most remote part of the world, and we have indeed found our paradise. We now plan on being married next month and are currently in the process of setting up a medical clinic here in town. I was able to get a license to practice medicine here, while my future husband, because of his extensive training and medical background, will be able to assist me as a physician's assistant, despite his alias.

This is a lovely part of the world, and the two of us are more than happy to spend our eternity here in this beautiful country. I am now in the process of selling my home in Wilmette.

I am sure you know the arrangements and process of forwarding my future husband's liquid assets from the foreign bank account that has been entrusted in your name. We will need our money to open up our new clinic and settle down here in our new world.

We send our regards to you and the family, along with a message that we are all *sleeping much better now. Let Zio Tony know that there are 'no demons in paradise.'*

Fondly,

Dr. Jeanne.

The Consigliere smiled as he read the e-mail. He immediately deleted it from his computer after printing up a single copy for his boss to see. He then walked over to Tony's office to show him the correspondence.

When Tony read it, he was in shock at first, not understanding how his nephew was able to be found.

"How the hell did this little bitch find him?" Tony initially asked.

"Apparently, your nephew posed for a company store Christmas card, which was posted somewhere on the internet," the Consigliere answered.

Tony DiMatteo smiled. "Doesn't my goddamn nephew know better? If you're trying to get away and hide from the world, you don't post a picture on the damn internet."

Marrocco laughed. "I'm sure it was the store where he was working that posted the picture. Besides, David Fazio is certifiably dead, buried in a crypt at Queen of Heaven Cemetery, remember?"

"Well, if this bitch can find him, I'm sure someone else can find him too."

Tony paused for several long minutes, his eyes welling up with tears while holding the email.

"It just breaks my heart that his mother and his family still go to that cemetery once a week and bring flowers to a grave where my nephew isn't buried," Tony confessed, shaking his head.

"But I just can't tell them the truth. There is just no way…"

"I know Tony…it's heartbreaking. His mother and father will have to realize someday that this was the only way you could save him. He would have never survived in prison, spending the rest of his life in that jail cell in Stateville. He would have been dead in a year."

Tony was silent, wiping the tears away from his eyes.

"Well, I only hope he's happy. It's not every day that someone gets a second chance in life."

Tony then got out his lighter and burned the email, letting the burned ashes fall into his empty garbage container.

"I learned that passage in catechism many years ago when I was a kid. For some strange reason, I've never forgotten it."

He then looked at his consigliere and quoted the Bible passage:

"For this son of mine was dead, but now he's alive again! For he was lost, but now he has been found!"

Sal Marrocco winked and smiled at his boss before walking out of Tony's office.

Sitting alone at his desk, Little Tony smiled contently to himself, knowing now that his nephew had finally found peace.

Far, far away from his nocturnal demons.

CHAPTER FORTY-THREE
Six Months after Janko's Death

McCarren International Airport was unusually busy on that summer day in August, as Gina Janko arrived from Chicago's Midway Airport. She had purchased a Southwest Airlines round trip ticket to Las Vegas two weeks ago and was now meeting her new fiancé at the airport.

It had been over six months since the untimely death of her husband Terry and almost two years since the tragic, unfortunate prison death of David Fazio. Gina didn't want to waste any more precious time and desperately wanted to move on with her new life. Gina wanted to forget the tragedy and the constant physical abuse of her marriage. She tried to ignore the terrible, untimely death of her late husband. And most of all, Gina wanted to push aside the last several miserable years of her old life in the past, as she was now ready to embrace a new beginning and a new future.

Mrs. Janko had taken off of work on that Thursday and was planning to spend a long, romantic weekend with her significant other at the Wynn Hotel and Resort on the north end of Las Vegas Boulevard.

She disembarked from Gate E-14 and picked up several of her suitcases, which she had checked onboard, then went outside to find her ride. It didn't take long for her to see the black Lexus SUV that she was instructed to look for.

"Welcome to Vegas, baby!" he said, as Gina kissed and embraced her fiancé in the middle of the arrivals area of the airport. He helped her load up her luggage and drove away from the airport. Her fiancé was now about to surprise her with a special gift.

"I've got a surprise for you, honey. We have an appointment at three o'clock."

Fireman Captain Stuart Durham, who was once formally with Chicago Engine No.1, had just transferred to Fire Department Engine Company No. 70 on North Clark Street. He had requested a transfer after the death of his colleague, his battalion chief, and close friend, Terrance Janko.

Captain Durham was finding it extremely difficult to move on with his career at the Chicago Fire Department, with the death of his close Battalion Chief friend and now with his recent engagement to Janko's widowed wife, Gina.

Durham had arrived in Las Vegas the night before to get things ready for his fiancé for that weekend. It seems that they had an extraordinary ceremony and occasion planned, which required the extensive use of Durham's checkbook and personal credit cards.

That Saturday evening, Gina Janko and Stuart Durham were planning a wedding ceremony at the Chapel of Love.

Gina had always wanted an "Elvis Style' wedding on the Vegas Strip, complete with Elvis impersonators and his famous rock and roll music. Durham had arranged for the costumes and impersonators to be on hand when the two of them excitedly tied the knot that weekend and didn't want to let one small detail of this happy occasion be left unattended.

They were expecting the arrival of their closest friends and family to be on hand for their wedding, a second marriage for both of them. Her parents, Mr. and Mrs. Salvatore Taglia, were expected to arrive late Thursday evening, and both Gina and Stuart wanted to make sure everything at the Wynn Hotel would be ready for their arrival.

Her husband's best friend and his wife, Denny and Diane Romanowski, were both invited to this joyous occasion but declined to attend. Detective Romanowski was still mourning the violent death of his best friend and wasn't emotionally ready to embrace Gina's new life with Captain Stuart Durham.

Truth be told, Detective Dennis Romanowski wasn't okay with any of this.

Not even fucking close.

Denny was very bitter and suspicious of Gina and Stuart, as there were a lot of unanswered questions as to how her husband Terry ended up getting killed by the DiMatteo Family. He also questioned the legitimacy of their relationship, as the two of them seemed to be in a hurry to now get married, less than six months after his best friend's violent death.

Detective Romanowski had done some snooping around. As he began the investigation into the passing of his best friend, he found out some interesting facts related to his death.

It was long rumored that Gina's father, Salvatore Taglia, was a retired 'made man' with the DiMatteo Family. It probably set up his son-in-law that evening when they both went out for Valentine's dinner at the restaurant on North Milwaukee Avenue.

Gina had been complaining about her husband's physical and emotional abuse to her father for many, many years and had more than a sufficient motive to 'set him up.'

Gina had been seen several times with Durham as early as two years ago, well before Terry's untimely death. Denny was extremely suspicious that Gina and the firehouse captain had planned the violent death of his best friend for a long, long time. It was no coincidence that Durham was at the restaurant on the night that Janko had disappeared, as he was probably overseeing the fire chief's abduction.

Someone from Fire Engine No.1 had acquired Fazio's lab coat that was sent in a package from an 'anonymous' sender from Chicago-Western Hospital. Dennis later found out that it was from none other than Nurse Susan Anderson. She had supplied and mailed that lab coat to the firehouse. It then somehow magically appeared at the last clinic fire on West Division Street. Nurse Anderson, regardless of who the actual arsonist was, wanted someone from the firehouse to discretely plant Fazio's lab coat at the scene of the crime during the next clinic fire investigation.

And it was probably Gina who informed her father, who in turn told Little Tony DiMatteo, of Terry Janko's probable involvement in the framing and eventual indictment of his beloved nephew.

Terry Janko indeed wanted Fazio to be the arsonist, regardless of who the actual perpetrator was. His lab coat at the crime scene, along with his chronic sleepwalking and pro-life principles, facilitated his arrest and conviction.

It was Gina who probably sent the text to her father from the restaurant bathroom, alerting the DiMatteo Family of when they would be finished with dinner that evening. It was very gracious of Mrs. Janko in allowing her husband to enjoy his 'last supper' at his favorite restaurant before being picked up by the DiMatteo Family last Valentine's Day.

Detective Dennis Romanowski finally figured out that Dr. Fazio wasn't the 'Abortion Arsonist' after all.

Someone else had torched those clinics. Someone else had incinerated and killed those abortion clinic victims. And someone else had the blood of his best friend Terry Janko completely drenched in their hands. The detective had his suspicions, and he now realized who the real perpetrators were.

But he couldn't prove any of this. No one witnessed Janko's abduction, even though he suspected it was the dirty work of the DiMatteo Family. He couldn't show who had planted Fazio's lab coat at the last fire, even though Nurse Anderson was seen by another nurse personally acquiring his lab coat from the nurse's station.

And he couldn't prove that Nurse Anderson wanted to make sure that the next arson fire had direct evidence of Dr. Fazio being there and looked to Chicago Fire Engine No. 1 to make sure that it happened. Nurse Anderson still maintained a close, on-going relationship with Gina Janko since she was an employee on the seventh-floor maternity ward at Chicago-Western Medical Center. Romanowski was sure that the two of them hatched this elaborate scheme to eliminate the arrogant, womanizing Dr. Fazio from Chicago-Western Medical Center and free Gina Janko from her abusive, alcoholic husband. These were all suspicions that he couldn't prove.

With Janko's wife having mob ties to the DiMatteo Family through her father and her now convenient marriage to one of the firemen at Engine No. 1, loud alarms were going off in Dennis Romanowski's head. This whole scenario puts the two of them right in the middle of it all as prime suspects. It was quite apparent that the two of them probably engineered the whole thing.

There was also the recent settlement of Chief Janko's one-million-dollar life insurance policy, for which his beloved and bereaved wife was the sole beneficiary. This financial windfall would make for a smooth, comfortable transition for Gina and her new husband as they embraced their new life together.

But all of these presumptions were just innuendos and hearsay. Even though Denny Romanowski had figured out who the actual 'Abortion Arsonist' really was, he couldn't prove any of this beyond a reasonable doubt.

And there wasn't a goddamn thing he could do about it.

Adding insult to injury, Mrs. Gina Janko had the nerve to send the Romanowski's a wedding invitation to her elegant, lavish nuptials in Las Vegas. The last thing that Denny wanted to see was his best friend's wife, the woman who assisted in the execution of his best friend, to now bear witness to her getting remarried.

But not just to anyone. But to his firehouse captain, his supposed close friend, who was having an affair with his wife and who probably helped plan Terry Janko's violent abduction that evening.

All of this gave Mrs. Gina Janko and Captain Stuart Durham the green light to enjoy their extravagant Las Vegas nuptials on that August summer weekend. The thought of the two of them together made Denny sick to his stomach.

The planned nuptials that weekend included an elaborate, 'Elvis-Style' wedding at the Chapel of Love on the Vegas Strip, with a ride in a white 1959 Cadillac Eldorado down Las Vegas Boulevard to the Wynn Hotel and Resort, where an elegant, ten-course wedding reception awaited them.

The only thing that Dennis Romanowski mentally wished for the two of them was nothing less than a thousand burning, violent deaths...deaths of the same caliper that they indirectly inflicted on his best friend.

That Saturday evening at six o'clock, Gina Janko, wearing a white, low cut dress and a black, Pricilla Presley style hairdo, was escorted down the wedding aisle by her father, Salvatore Taglia, to the music of Elvis Presley's 'Love Me Tender.'

Both Stuart and Gina stood in front of the Elvis impersonator, Parson William Reynolds, as he officiated over their joyous wedding in the chapel filled with approximately thirty-five or more friends and witnesses. Stuart and his best man were, of course, dressed in white, sparkling Elvis-style jumpsuits, black wigs, and very dark, aviator sunglasses.

When the officiant, who was dressed in black, with black hair and long black sideburns, asked them to exchange their wedding vows, the two of them held up their hands together for everyone at the ceremony to see.

On the day she arrived at the airport, Gina and Stuart had an appointment at a tattoo parlor on the Las Vegas strip. They chose as their wedding gifts to each other a universal symbol that they would both have colorfully etched and tattooed on the inside of their forearms.

They both smiled, knowing that as they exchanged their wedding vows, they now forever shared an image that would endlessly serve as a reminder to the two of them...an emblem of their timeless, perpetual love.

It was a tattoo of a lighted match.

Made in the USA
Columbia, SC
22 March 2021